CHILE DEATH

A CHINA BAYLES MYSTERY

Susan Wittig Albert

Thorndike Press • Waterville, Maine

Published in 2001 by arrangement with The Berkley
Publishing Group, a member of Penguin Putnam Inc.

Thorndike Press Large Print Mystery Series.

The tree indicium is a trademark of Thorndike Press.

The text of this Large Print edition is unabridged.
Other aspects of the book may vary from the original edition.

Set in 16 pt. Plantin by Minnie B. Raven.

Printed in the United States on permanent paper.

Library of Congress Cataloging-in-Publication Data

Albert, Susan Wittig.
 Chile death : a China Bayles mystery /
Susan Wittig Albert.
  p. cm.
 ISBN 0-7862-3161-0 (lg. print : hc : alk. paper)
1. Bayles, China (Fictitious character) — Fiction.
2. Women detectives — Texas — Fiction. 3. Herbalists —
Fiction. 4. Texas — Fiction. 5. Large type books.
I. Title.
PS3551.L2637 C47 2001
 813′.54—dc21   00-065771

Acknowledgments

Grateful thanks go to Diana Finlay, first, last, and only editor of the regrettably defunct *Chili Monthly*, who generously shared her well-seasoned chili fancies with me. Thanks also to Susan Hanson, fearless reporter, who led me to Diana, proving once again that this world is entirely within the compass of the Old Girls' Network, and to Ann and Judy and Mary at the Bertram Free Library, who graciously renew my library books over the telephone.

And as always, thanks to my husband, Bill, who is the real chilehead in the family. He was also the first person in my life (although not the last) to point out to me that most people spell chili with only one *l*. (I grew up near Springfield, Illinois, which long ago christened itself the "Chilli Capital of the World.") He willingly eats everything I cook, except for the kidney-bean-hamburger-and-tomato stew that I personally consider to be the world's tastiest chilli.

CHILE DEATH

*Also by Susan Wittig Albert
in Large Print:*

Hangman's Root
Lavender Lies
Mistletoe Man

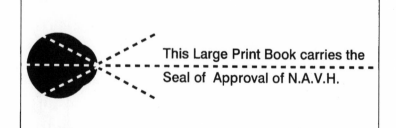

Author's Note

The Texas Hill Country is home to many picturesque small towns, but Pecan Springs is not among them. It is an imaginary place filled with (mostly) imaginary people to whom I have given make-believe lives. To the extent that you come to believe in them, I have succeeded in a writer's most agreeable task: seducing her readers into the virtual reality of fiction. I plead guilty, however, to slipping a few genuine people, places, and events into this invented world, just to see whether you're still awake.

Another thing: Occasional mention is made in these pages to the healing properties of herbs. These references are based on my research into the documented (and often scientifically verified) uses of medicinal plants, but are *not* intended to substitute for advice from a qualified health care practitioner.

And finally: I am asked from time to time whether humor might not distract readers from the underlying serious themes of the China Bayles mysteries, which involve violated trusts, broken dreams, and murder. For your consideration, I offer George Bernard Shaw's celebrated answer to a similar question: "Life does not cease to be funny when people die any more than it ceases to be serious when people laugh."

If You Know Beans About Chili
*You Know that Chili Has No Beans**

You burn some mesquite
And when the coals get hot
You hunk up some meat and
   you throw it in a pot
With some chile* pods and garlic
And comino and stuff
Then you add a little salt
Till there's just enough
You can throw in some onions
To make it smell good
You can even add tomatoes
If you feel like you should
But if you know beans about chili
You know that chili has no beans.

If you know beans about chili
You know it didn't come from Mexico.
Chili was God's gift to Texas
(Or maybe it came from down below)
And chili doesn't go with macaroni
And damned Yankees don't go with
   chili queens;
And if you know beans about chili
You know that chili has no beans.

Kent Finlay
© 1976 Paper Napkin Music, BMI
used with permission.

*Culinary note: To cook chili, you have to know how to spell. *Chiles* are peppers, ranging in temperature from mild to incendiary. *Chili* is a thick stew made with meat, peppers, herbs, sometimes tomatoes, and (if you live north of the Red River) beans. If you live in Springfield, Illinois, or other northern or eastern locations, you might spell chili with two *l*'s: chilli. Texans *never* make chili with beans, unless they're looking for a fight.

Chapter One

The recorded history of the genus Capsicum *begins with Columbus, who undertook his voyage of discovery in search of (among other things) black pepper, the most valuable of Eastern spices. Columbus did not find what he was looking for, but in the opinion of many people, he bit into something much better. He became the first European to blister his tongue on a hot pepper.*

China Bayles
"Hot Pods and Fired-up Fare"
Pecan Springs *Enterprise*

Most times, it isn't easy to know where to start a story, or what to include in the telling. The threads of any present moment are spliced into the weave of the past in a complex and often inexplicable way, and just when you think you've got the pattern figured out, another seems to emerge and the meaning unravels. Or to use a different metaphor, the present and the past swirl together like different colors of paint you're mixing in a bucket, one color marrying with

11

the other in swirls that eventually belong to neither. Exactly when the two become something different than either are alone, it's impossible to say.

I know where this story begins, although I don't yet know how it ends, or what other stories may become woven into it. My life got derailed when Mike McQuaid, on temporary assignment with the Texas Rangers, was gunned down on a lonely road west of San Antonio. Until that rainy February night, I was moving along with confidence into the future, dividing my time between my business (my herb shop, Thyme and Seasons), my family (McQuaid and his twelve-year-old son, Brian, with whom I live), and a few good friends. On that night, the sky fell, and for a long time I wondered whether the darkness would ever end. But one morning, to my surprise, the sun came up, and opened a new chapter.

I also know what this story, this chapter of my life, is about. It's about partners and friends, partnership and alliance. It's about deception and death and the various ways we fail in our obligations to one another. But it's also about trust and teamwork and accepting our mutual interdependence.

But enough introduction. As Fannie Couch says, "Ain't no point messin' around. Tell the good part first and then the bad, and the rest will follow along on its own."

Fannie is widely venerated as the oracle of Pecan Springs, Texas. I guess I'd better follow her advice.

The good part is that McQuaid is not going to die. The bullet that was lodged against his spine has done the worst of its damage, and unless some unforeseen complications occur during his long recovery, he'll make it. He's a strong, tough man who has been beaten, knifed, and shot before, during the years he was a Houston cop. He is a survivor. He's surviving.

The bad part is, well . . .

"He *is* going to walk again," Brian says fiercely. He looks up at me with his dad's eyes, steel-gray and angry at the unfair hand that fate has dealt out to his father. He pushes back the dark hair that has fallen across his forehead and says it again, to convince himself and me. "He *is*, China. I'm going to help him."

"Sure," I say, in as bright a tone as I can manage. Brian appears confident, but I know where his demons are corralled, and it's not fair to add mine to the herd. I give him a hard quick hug, a rare thing between

13

us, because he is after all a boy and I am not quite his mother. "How about taking a pizza when we go see him tonight?"

"Yeah." Brian is determinedly, heart-breakingly cheerful. "With anchovies and jalapeños. And chocolate ice cream. No, Double Chocolate Fudge. He has to keep his strength up." The fierce look is back. "He's going to walk again, China. I *know* he is."

McQuaid's parents aren't so sure. When we meet at the hospital, Mother McQuaid is red-eyed and tearful and her smile sags under its own weight. Like Brian, she is intent on keeping McQuaid's strength up, delivering enough cookies, cakes, and hand-knitted argyle bed socks to supply every patient in the hospital.

But Dad McQuaid is angrily bluff, in turn raging at the nurses and ranting at the doctors. "Them guys're s'posed to be so smart, how come Mike ain't walkin' yet?" he demands. "What'd they learn in medical school? What're they doin' for all that money they get paid?" Then the anger empties out, and he's limp and despairing and numb. "He ain't never gonna walk agin," he says to me outside the room, wiping his eyes. I murmur disagreement but pat his shoulder, mimicking Brian's

14

comforting gesture. I feel as if we've all been flung into deep water, and Brian and I are the only ones who can swim.

No, that's not true. There's my mother, who not only knows how to swim but is sure that she is strong enough to tow the raft, with all of us aboard.

My relationship with Leatha has been an unhappy one, even after she sobered up a couple of years ago, married Sam, and moved from her luxurious Houston home to his rather primitive ranch near Kerrville. It's hard to forgive her for not being the mother I wanted so desperately when I was growing up, hard to forget coming home from school and finding her already embarked on her own private happy hour, which invariably ended when I put her to bed, drunk as a skunk, and cooked a frozen dinner for myself. I know, I know — it's all in the past and I should bury all those toxic memories and live with what she is now, a recovering alcoholic who desperately wants to be a part of her daughter's life. But it's been a stubborn hurt. The only time we've held one another in years was the night McQuaid was shot, when we wept with our arms wrapped around each other.

Which Leatha took as an invitation. A week after the shooting, I opened the door one afternoon and saw her lugging three suitcases, two cosmetic cases, and a carton of self-help books up the porch steps. In my surprise, I didn't protest hard enough, and the next thing I knew she had installed herself in one of the guest bedrooms of the large Victorian house that McQuaid and I leased last year. Having resprayed her silver bouffant and renewed her mauve lipstick, she came into the office where I was on the phone and the computer at the same time, checking the ad copy that was due at the Pecan Springs *Enterprise* office that afternoon. Brian was there, regaling me with details of the lunchtime fight he had with his friend Arnold and demonstrating the actual kung-fu punches and kicks they had traded, punctuated with *pow*s and *blam*s. And Howard Cosell, McQuaid's elderly and ill-tempered bassett hound, was parked under my chair, licking a sore paw and complaining in his gravelly voice that the boy was interrupting his nap.

Leatha raised her voice above these cacophonies. "You'll be spending a lot of time with Mike and you can't neglect your business," she announced briskly, "so I've come to stay for a while. As long as you need me."

I put down the phone. "I don't need —" I started to say, but Brian preempted me.

"That's cool," he said, stopping his martial arts demonstration and getting straight to the heart of the matter. "Can you make waffles for breakfast? China used to, but she's too busy right now."

"You're old enough to make your own waffles, Brian." I spoke more shortly than I intended, but I was annoyed that he'd gone over to the enemy so quickly. To my mother, I said, "Brian and I can manage for ourselves, Leatha. Anyway, Sam will get lonely — and what will happen to all your projects?"

The energy that Leatha once poured into the bottle now goes into worthwhile causes. She has taken on Kerrville's Friends of the Library, the Courthouse Restoration Project, and the Hospital Auxiliary. To judge from the newspaper clippings she sends, she is a one-woman volunteer army, always anxious to help whoever seems to need it. To be honest, I find this pungently ironic. Where was she when *I* needed her, forty or so years ago?

"Sam won't be lonely long," Leatha said with equanimity. "His oldest daughter by

17

his first wife left her husband and is moving back home with the baby. And his youngest son has dropped out of college and is living in the bunkhouse." I don't try to keep up with the comings and goings of Sam's family, which seems to ebb and flow like some sort of mysterious tide. "And the projects will just have to take care of themselves for a while. I'm taking care of *you*, China." She smiled at Brian. "You, too, Brian. And maybe, some of these weekends, you can go to the ranch with me. That river is full of fish just dying to be caught, and Sam hung a rope swing in the cypress tree, over the swimming hole. He also bought a big brown horse named Rambo. He's got four white socks and a white blaze on his forehead — and he's the perfect size for a big guy like you."

I gritted my teeth. Flattery, flattery.

"Rambo!" Brian squealed excitedly. "Oh, wow." He turned to me. "When can I go, China? When, huh?" Then he stopped and pulled his dark brows together, looking serious. "But maybe I better not. I better stay and cheer Dad up. He gets kinda down sometimes."

I made another effort. "Leatha," I said, "Brian and I really don't need —"

"Yes, you do," she said, very firmly. "You

18

certainly do. *Both* of you."

Brian looked from one to the other of us, figuring the angles. The ranch might not be in the cards, but there were always waffles. "Blueberry is my favorite," he said.

"Mine too," she said with a bright smile that showed all her teeth. "I absolutely *adore* making blueberry waffles. Meanwhile, maybe you can tell me where the laundry soap lives. There's a pile of very muddy jeans in the bathroom." She wrinkled her nose. "With a monstrous creature on top. It is *green*."

I was bemused by the thought of my elegant mother (who for years had a maid to rinse out her stockings) actually washing Brian's grubby jeans and making blueberry waffles for him. But Brian (who is supposed to put his own jeans in the washer) was enthusiastic.

"I'll show you the soap," he offered helpfully. "The monster is Einstein. He's an iguana, and he's very smart. But he won't bite unless he's sitting in the sun."

Leatha looked startled. "In the sun?"

"Yeah. Sunshine makes him frisky. It triggers his aggressive genes." He prodded Howard Cosell with his toe. "Hey, Howard, you dumb old dog. Wake up. We're going to do the laundry." Howard

Cosell raised his head and bared snaggly yellow teeth, promising that *he* would bite, if certain people didn't go away and let him finish his nap.

Leatha had recovered her poise. "Well, come along, then," she commanded, rattling her silver bangle bracelets. "And while I'm here, it might be better to keep Einstein in the dark." She narrowed her eyes. "What about those other creatures of yours, Brian? That . . . tarantula?"

"Ivan the Hairible? Oh, I still have him," he said eagerly. "Would you like to see?"

Leatha shuddered. "I think not." She turned around, surveyed me, and said, briskly, "Really, China, don't you think you ought to get your hair cut? I'm sure Mike would appreciate a less straggly you when he's able to be up and around."

Howard Cosell gave a resigned sigh and covered his eyes with his paws. I suppressed a snarl and went back to the computer. I didn't need a crystal ball to know that this arrangement was not going to work.

Through the long, anxious weeks that followed, I wasn't sure which hurt most: being with McQuaid or not being with him. Like most people, I hate hospitals —

the chill white sterility of the hallways and rooms, the antiseptic smell, the curt, crisp efficiency of the nurses. I wonder if they're taught not to care in nursing school or whether those frozen faces come with the uniform — or whether they really *do* care and have to pretend they don't or fall apart.

But the hospital was only a backdrop to the real pain. Before the shooting, McQuaid was a big man with a big man's powerful presence, a former football quarterback and ex-cop who'd kept his strong muscles and his flat belly and — most notably — his cheerful attitude. He could be commanding and authoritative, especially when he was lecturing in one of his classes at Central Texas State University, where he's on the Criminal Justice faculty. But most of the time, he was confident and optimistic, your basic nice guy.

McQuaid was still big and still strong — it would take more than a couple of weeks on his back to change that — but the attitude was gone. Trussed up with plastic tubes, wired to machines, and able to move only his hands (even that little bit was an enormous improvement over the first few days, when he couldn't move at all), he would close his eyes and go inside himself, away from me, silent, remote, utterly despairing. I understood what took him away, but my understanding didn't ease his pain or calm his fear or bring him back from the dark place he had gone.

The suffering wasn't just his, either. For five years, McQuaid had wanted us to get married. Out of pride in my independence and self-sufficiency, I had always refused — until just before the shooting, when I woke up to the way I really felt about him and was ready to agree. But by that time, he'd gotten involved with somebody else. With Margaret Graham, a woman fifteen years younger than me, his partner in an investigation into corruption high up in the Texas Rangers' chain of command.

But although their brief affair was over and Margaret and I had become friends, the shooting changed McQuaid's view of the future — and his desire to get married. "Let's let it ride for a while" was all he'd say when I brought it up. He didn't have to tell me why. I knew that he feared he'd never be whole and healthy again, and he didn't want to burden me with his care, with half a husband.

But as I sat beside his bed, reading provocative snippets from Constance Letterman's gossip column in the *Enterprise* or reporting on my recent consultation with Brian's math teacher or just watching Mike sleep, I would think of the numbing moment when I feared I had lost him, and feel grateful. Whole or half, healthy or disabled, it didn't matter. McQuaid was here, he was alive, and that was enough.

Beneath the gratitude, though, I was heavy with sadness and loss. Why had I been so afraid of intimacy, of caring, of marriage? Why had I built such a wall against his love? If only I had been able to give more, we might have shared more. If only I hadn't been afraid to be vulnerable, we might have been more open with each other. If only . . . if only . . .

At those moments, I had to turn away to keep him from seeing the tears. I didn't want him to think I was weeping for him — for what he had been and might not ever be again. I was weeping for myself, and regretting what *I* had been.

Chapter Two

There are about twenty species and hundreds of varieties in the genus Capsicum, *indigenous to tropical America. In their native habitat, they are perennial and woody, growing to seven feet tall, though in American gardens they are grown as annuals, reaching a height of three feet. Two highly variable species of the genus provide New World peppers — the red peppers. Bell peppers, pimento, paprika, chile, and cayenne peppers all belong to the species* Capsicum annuum. *The Tabasco peppers come from* Capsicum frutescens, *grown commercially in the Gulf states and New Mexico.*

Steven Foster, *Herbal Renaissance*

If you've had an accident or major illness in your family, you know that there's the crisis stage, then there's what comes after. In some ways, it's easier to cope during the crisis, because you're so numbed by the pain that the main thing is just to stumble through it, trying not to think. When that part is over and the new realities begin to emerge, you have to plan and organize and think again. You have to alter your life to fit the changed circumstances. You have to do more than just muddle through, you have to carry on.

In many way, carrying on is easier in a small town like Pecan Springs, where people care about you. They go out of their way to let you know that they're thinking about you and hope it all turns out for the best — conventional small-town sentiments, maybe, but the kindness helps. There were lots of calls and best wishes during the crisis weeks McQuaid spent in the hospital in San Antonio, and after we brought him back to Pecan Springs, the concern continued.

"Ain't seen you much lately," Lila Jennings said one morning in mid-April, when I stopped at the Old Nueces Street Diner. "Figger you've been purty busy, with Mike out there at the Manor an' your shop an' all." The Manor is the convalescent center and nursing home where McQuaid was now a resident, so he could do daily therapy.

Lila is fiftyish, with bleached blond hair, as thin as a stalk of Johnson grass. Three or four years ago, she and her husband, Ralph, bought the Old Nueces Street Diner — a converted Missouri and Pacific

Railroad dining car, rescued from oblivion and refurbished — and renamed it the Doughnut Queen in honor of Lila's famous homemade doughnuts, which have been written up in every magazine and newspaper from Houston to El Paso. Ralph's two-pack-a-day habit caught up with him last winter, but Lila's daughter Docia moved down from Dallas to take over the kitchen duties. Docia suggested that they expand the menu and serve lunches and light suppers, so they put back the original sign and the Doughnut Queen is the Diner again. What goes around comes around, or something like that.

Lila filled my cup with steaming coffee and added, "How's that ol' Mike-boy doin' since he moved in out there at the Manor? Chasin' the nurses up'n down the hall, I bet."

I grinned. "Not yet. But he will if his therapist has anything to say about it. She's built like the Dallas front line, and about as mean." Nobody was promising full recovery, but McQuaid had progressed from moving his hands to moving his arms, and the doctors were beginning to be optimistic about his chances for a substantial recovery.

Lila swiped the red Formica counter

with a damp rag. "So what're you havin' this mornin'?"

I didn't have to hesitate. "Raspberry doughnut and coffee." I'd already eaten breakfast — cereal and orange juice with Brian, while he ate Leatha's blueberry waffles. "Make that three doughnuts," I amended. "I'll take a couple out to the Manor for McQuaid."

"Yeah, well, if I was you, I'd keep an eye on things out there," Lila said, plumping one doughnut on a plate and dropping two into a brown paper bag. "We put Ralph's mama in that place, first thing happened was somebody stole her teeth."

With a grunt, Harkness Hibler shifted on the stool next to me. "Lila, I am so damn tired of hearin' you tell that old tale. Ralph's mama's been dead ten years, and things've changed out there. Didn't you read that investigative piece we did last year? The Manor is the best rehabilitation center in the state, bar none."

Harkness is the managing editor at the *Enterprise*. The newspaper, which used to be a weekly, is now published by Arlene Seidensticker. Not too long ago, she took it over from her father and made it a daily. Arlene said she was ashamed that New Braunfels and San Marcos both have dailies, while Pecan Springs (which has more tourist traffic, not to mention the university) had to make do with a weekly. Hark prefers the lazier rhythms of the weekly and was ready to hand in his notice, but Arlene gave him a raise and promised not to interfere in his editorial decisions, and he agreed to stay on. The work has tolled on him, though. He used to be about forty pounds overweight, but that's mostly gone. He's leaner and maybe a little meaner, and wears the world-weary look of somebody who knows that today's story is tomorrow's history.

"Well, for yer information, Mr. Skinny Smarty-pants," Lila retorted frostily, "the Manor ain't changed all *that* much. And I don't give two hoots about your fancy invest-y-ga-shun. You want to know what's really goin' on out there, you talk to Edna Lund. Her dad died out there. Ask her what *she* knows about the Manor. Ralph's mama's teeth ain't nothin' to what goes on out there ever' day."

She picked up the coffeepot and flounced down the counter to fill a cup for Bubba Harris, the police chief, who was sitting at the end, chewing on his unlit cigar while he consulted with Darryl Perkins about the state of the weather, the price of oil, and yesterday's injury list from the Cowboys spring training camp.

Bubba has had more perplexing matters on his mind lately, however, and his habitual scowl has recently deepened. For years, Bubba has run the Pecan Springs police department more or less out of his back pocket. But the last City Council election produced some new members, and this Council is playing an activist role in law enforcement. According to the newspaper, they have instructed Bubba to invest in two women officers, an updated dispatch system, and mandated sensitivity training for the entire staff — including Bubba himself, who is not what you would call a highly sensitive person. The newly imposed limits to departmental home rule add up to a steep learning curve and a bad headache for a chief who has had things his way for the last quarter century. No wonder he scowls.

Darryl Perkins, on the other hand, has plenty to smile about. He owns the Do-Right Used Car dealership and part interest in the radio station and is married to Pauline Perkins, the Fighting Mayor of Pecan Springs. (Pauline is now in her fourth term and laying battle plans for her fifth campaign.) Darryl is a big man in this little town, but that's only in public. In private, at least in my opinion, Pauline is the bigger man.

I pondered Lila's remark as I ate my jelly doughnut and drank my coffee. "Maybe Lila is right, Hark," I said finally. "I think I'll talk to Edna Lund. Just to hear what people are saying about the Manor."

There are a couple of nursing homes in Pecan Springs, and I had heard the usual horror stories when I first began looking for a place for McQuaid to convalesce. There'd apparently been some trouble at the Manor a few years ago, but things seemed to have straightened out, and the new rehab unit was every bit as good as Hark claimed. I also liked the nursing supervisor, a woman named Joyce Sanders, whom I had met when I'd made the arrangements for McQuaid's move. She had seemed honest with me about the home's problems in attracting and keeping good staff. The arrangement wasn't forever, of course. McQuaid had been there several weeks already, and the doctor said he could move back home in another three or four. In fact, he could probably do that right now, although he didn't show much enthusiasm for the idea. But he wasn't enthusiastic about much of anything these days, which was part of the problem.

Hark gave me a comforting grin. "Lila's just blowin' smoke. They'll take good care of McQuaid out there." He spooned salsa from a red-topped jar onto his scrambled eggs, smothering them. Lila puts her hottest salsa, made with habaneros, tomatoes, and onions, into jars with red lids; the milder stuff, made with jalapeños, goes into jars with green lids. You can't trust the lids, though. Some of the local jokers think it's funny to switch and watch their buddies hop up and down, spouting flames. "But if you're curious," he added, "you might want to talk to Fannie Couch. She told me she's doing a piece on the Manor for her radio program sometime this spring."

"Good idea," I said. "I'll do that."

Hark split his attention between me and the eggs. "By the way, the Honchos met last night. JuneFest's not too far off, and we're lining up chili cookoff judges. McQuaid's done it for the past five or six years — think he'll be up to doing it again?"

"He's certainly up to it," I said cautiously. The Honchos are the local pod (yes, that's right) of the Chili Appreciation Society International, and McQuaid is an active member. "Actually, he's getting around just fine in his wheelchair." I paused. "Whether he'll do it or not is another matter."

Hark gave me a sympathetic look. "Like that, huh?"

"Well, you've got to see it from his point of view," I said, being loyal. I finished my jelly doughnut and fished a paper napkin out of the chrome holder to wipe the sugar off my mouth. I don't know where Ralph and Lila rounded up these forties and fifties restaurant fixtures, but they're all here — red-and-chrome tables and chairs, vintage napkin holders, old Dr Pepper signs, and framed newspaper clippings commemorating such events as Lyndon Johnson's first election to the Senate, the Texas City fire, and Hurricane Carla, which roared inland at Port O'Conner with 175 mph winds in September of 1961. There is even an ancient Wurlitzer jukebox outlined with tubes of bubbling yellow neon, although it doesn't play.

"Oh, sure, I understand," Hark said. "If it was me, I don't know whether I'd want folks to gawk at —" He dove for his cup, swigged coffee, coughed, swigged some more, and wiped his streaming eyes. Lila's salsa is fierce. "But Mike's got friends," he said, when he could talk again. "They'd like to see him out and about again. Anyway, it'd be good for him. Take his mind off his legs." He blew his nose in his napkin.

"Right. But it's not me you've got to convince. Ask him."

Hark went back to his eggs. "That's Jerry Jeff Cody's job. He's president of the Honchos this year. I'll tell him to give Mike a call. But there *is* something I need to talk to you about." He gave me a speculative look. "I fired Wanda Rathbottom yesterday."

Wanda Rathbottom is the owner of Wanda's Wonderful Acres Nursery, president of the Pecan Springs Garden Club, and the wife of a county judge. What she *isn't* is a writer, a fact which is sadly apparent in the garden column she has written for the *Enterprise* over the past few years. And since her manager, Grady Stice, is the real brains behind the nursery, it's fair to say that she isn't much of a gardener, either, which is also apparent in her column.

"Congratulations," I said dryly. "What took you so long?"

He looked sheepish. "I know, I know. But Wanda's a friend of Arlene's, and the

33

nursery drops a bundle into advertising. I had to wait until Wanda's stuff got so bad that even Arlene noticed." He forked up a fat, stubby sausage link, dipped it in salsa, and bit one end off. Lila serves authentic East Texas hot links, imported from Pittsburg, Texas. She says nothing else tastes right with her hot sauce, and most people agree. "I read that piece on hot peppers you wrote for the Austin *American-Statesman*, and I wondered if maybe you'd do some columns for us," Hark went on. "Not just gardening stuff, though. Cooking, gardening, crafts. The works."

I didn't have to think twice. "You've got yourself a columnist," I said.

He was severe. "Don't do it for the money. What we pay will buy you a plate of chicken fried and a pitcher of beer every couple of weeks. Not even a piece of pecan pie to top off."

"I think I can handle that." It wasn't money I coveted, of course, it was exposure. The *Enterprise* is the only newspaper in town and it has a wide local readership, not to mention the tourists who buy subscriptions just so they can have a taste of the Hill Country after it's started to snow in Minnesota or North Dakota or wherever they've gone home to. A regular column would not only encourage walk-in shoppers, but new mail-order business as well.

Hark speared another hot link and it squirted juice onto the counter. "Guess we got us a deal, then. When can I have your first two-three columns? I'd kinda like to have some in the can, so if you miss a deadline we got something to fall back on."

I calculated swiftly. "Two weeks?" The sooner I got started, the sooner those new customers would start coming.

"Yeah, that'd be great. Thanks, China." He raised his voice. "Hey, Lila, goldurn it, you gonna let a guy thirst t' death in front of your eyes while you're makin' out with the chief of po-lice? Bring me some more of that lousy coffee." He banged his empty cup on the counter. "On the double."

"What's your hurry, Hark?" Lila inquired sweetly. "Got some sweet, sexy young thing waitin' in your car?" She gave a merry guffaw. Bubba and Darryl joined in, and Hark flushed red. He is a bachelor, and notorious for his lack of success with the local females, a fact which probably dates back to his days as a heavyweight.

Hark glowered. "Some women," he muttered, "just can't keep a civil tongue in their heads."

As I was saying, small-town people let you know they've been thinking about you. I was turning into the courthouse square the very next day when I heard the furious blasts of a shrill whistle and glimpsed a uniformed person on the sidewalk, waving me to pull up.

Uh-oh, I thought. What have I done now? I stopped in front of the Sophie Briggs Historical Museum (named for one of Pecan Springs' founding mothers) and rolled down the window on my Datsun. A dozen remarkably docile kindergarten children were crossing the street in front of me, holding hands and looking both ways. They were probably on their way to the museum to see Sophie's collection of two hundred fifty-seven frogs, which she acquired during her travels across the United States. Sophie was a peripatetic woman, in part because she suffered from wanderlust and in part because her oldest son, John, was an official with the Missouri and Pacific Railroad. She would pack her black leather portmanteau and hit the rails whenever the spirit moved her, free as a breeze and free of charge. Her ashes are sealed in an urn in the garden behind the museum, which I have always thought to be an irony of some sort.

MaeBelle Battersby came toward me, looking as if she had been stuffed into her blue uniform and the seams sewn shut, like a pillow. A couple of years ago, the City Council decided to put meters on the square, then discovered that they'd have to hire somebody to enforce the time limit and collect the money. They're still debating whether the meters are paying their way or diverting people from the downtown shops to the mall, where there's free parking. In the meantime, MaeBelle is the town's official meter maid, and is also empowered to write tickets for minor traffic offenses — minor, that is, to everybody but MaeBelle, who takes her work seriously. She'll ticket you for making a turn from the wrong lane, or failing to yield to pedestrians, as well as overparking.

This time, however, I was apparently innocent. "Hi, Miz Bayles," MaeBelle said, bending over to talk through the open window. "I've bin meanin' to drop by the shop and find out how that man o' yers is gettin' along out at the Manor. How's he doin'?" There was no irony or accusation in "that man o' yers." The older folks in Pecan Springs might once have made negative judgments about a couple who lived together without benefit of clergy, but that was before their sons and daughters started doing it. Anyway, McQuaid and I had been together so long that most people take us for granted.

"Thanks for asking, MaeBelle," I said. "He's much better — goes to therapy three or four hours a day now."

MaeBelle's gap-toothed smile split her chubby pink face. "That right? Boy, am I glad. When I first heard whut happened, I figgered he was a goner. P'lice work can sure be dang'rous." She patted the foot-long truncheon that was hanging from her belt. It was issued to her after a surly German shepherd charged out of the back of the Ford pickup she was ticketing and ate the seat of her pants.

"It was a close call, all right."

"Well, you see him, you tell him Lester an' me have bin thinkin' 'bout him an' hopin' he gits well quick. I'll drop in an' say hi when I git a chance. Next week, mebbe. My Aunt Velma's out there, y'know. Miss Velma Mayfield. My mother's sister."

"Is that right?" I asked. "I wondered what had become of her." Velma Mayfield had been a fixture around town for years, especially at the courthouse. She had worked for Tom Perry, one of our home-grown lawyers, and was known as a very competent woman. I was a little surprised to hear that she was at the Manor, though. She couldn't be any more than sixty-five. "How does she like the place?"

"Hard to say. You cain't always get the straight skinny from Aunt Velma." She pulled a sad face. "Which is a durn shame, smart as she was. You know, she ran Mr. Perry's law office for forty years, more or less. Bet she could tell stories on half this town. Bet there are lots of folks just as glad she's lost a few of her marbles." MaeBelle took out a handkerchief and mopped her sweaty face. "But she's got a clean bed and three squares and a whirlpool bath twice a week." She gave a horsy laugh. "Wish I had a whirlpool twice a week. Might help my lower back. It gives me a lot of trouble these days." She glanced at me. "I bin meanin' to talk to you 'bout Aunt Velma. I hear there's some kinda weird plant that helps people with Alzheimer's. That so?"

"That's what the research seems to be saying. Ginkgo biloba, it's called. Chinese doctors have used it for over five thousand years and the Germans have been experimenting with it since the 1960s. But American medicine is just getting acquainted with it."

39

"Them Chinese, they're plenty smart," MaeBelle said admiringly. "Invented fireworks, I heard." She pulled her brows together. "Do you think that ginky-billy stuff would help Aunt Velma?"

"It's been shown to slow memory loss in some patients," I said. "I've got a couple of articles about it on file in the shop. But you'd need to try it for several months before you could decide whether it's having any effect." It's been my experience with herbs like ginkgo and St. John's wort, a popular herb used to treat depression, that people don't always stay with it long enough to see whether it works for them.

"Save me a coupla bottles," MaeBelle said, making up her mind. "Might do me some good too. I bin forgettin' things a lot lately. Like I forgot to git the inspection sticker on my car, and I got a ticket." She lifted her chin proudly. "And if you think they'd cut me a little slack, workin' in the department and all, you can think agin. I got to pay my ticket same as everybody else."

I nodded, then changed the subject. "I understand that there have been a few complaints about the Manor. How's the staff treating your aunt?"

MaeBelle's brief shrug might have been

acknowledgment or dismissal. "They do the best they can with whut they got. Hard to find good girls to work these days, whut with all the liftin' an' stuff an' havin' to put up with nasty old folks. And there's a lot of turnover. Now that the new Walmart's come in, paying good benefits and all, the Manor's lucky to git any warm bodies." She broke off as she glimpsed Ines Watson stopping her car in front of Pratt's Drugstore. "Am I seein' whut I'm seein?" she demanded incredulously. "Is that Ines Watson goin' to actually *double park,* in front of my very face?"

"That's what it looks like," I said. "Boy, has she got a nerve."

"Boy, has she ever," MaeBelle said, and galloped off, blowing a blast on her whistle that might have wakened Sophie Briggs.

The tourists hate it when it rains, and the Chamber of Commerce pretends it never happens except between midnight and four a.m. The natives, however, will tell you they love it. And did it rain, all through April, for days on end — a great blessing, because the last three years had been the driest in decades. The Highland Lakes in the Hill Country to the west of Pecan Springs rose to their highest levels

41

ever, fattening the purse of the Lower Colorado River Authority, which sells the water to rice farmers downstream. And the spring wildflowers — bluebonnets, paintbrush, poppies, pinks — were absolutely miraculous, filling the meadows and roadsides with brilliant swaths of color and attracting hordes of tourists, who booked every bed and breakfast in Pecan Springs.

Thankfully, the rain let up on weekends and business at the shop was brisk, especially in potted plants. We sold hundreds of two-inch pots of thyme, and almost as much rosemary and marjoram, basil and sage. Even the lesser-known herbs moved well — rue, Texas mint marigold, lemongrass, feverfew, fennel, and St. John's wort. And Laurel Wiley, my helper and a red-blooded, asbestos-tongued chilehead, had rounded up four-inch pots of the best and most fiery chile plants: poblano, jalapeño, orange habanero, Thai Dragon, even Red Savina habanero, which has recently been accepted into the *Guinness Book of Records* as the hottest pepper in the universe. (At a soul-searing 500,000 units, the Red Savina blows the lid off the Scoville heat scale, the standard measure of a pepper's incendiary temperament. Jalapeños, at a measly 55,000 units, are meek in comparison.)

Thanks to Laurel's efforts, to our spring advertising promotion, and to a growing interest in herbs in general, the shop was doing well enough to give me a raise — which I badly needed, under the present circumstances.

Centuries ago, I was a criminal attorney in a large Houston law firm. I argued a lot of cases, made a bundle of money, had few friends and no other life to speak of, except for tending the tiny garden on my patio. In fact, the only healthy passion in my life was probably my passion for plants, who responded to my loving care and never once argued back.

Then one weekend, on a drive through the Texas Hill Country, I chanced on the town of Pecan Springs, and on a hundred-year-old stone building with a For Sale sign out in front. The building had two shops in front and a four-room apartment in the back, and was surrounded by patches of hard-packed earth that I imagined as gardens. One of the stores was an herb shop — a going concern called Thyme and Seasons, with real, live customers and an exceedingly modest cash flow. I fell in love with it, came back the next week for a closer look, and that was that. I handed in my letter of resignation, packed my power suits off to Goodwill, and traded my flashy red Fiat for a Datsun hatchback. I didn't totally burn my bridges, however. I kept up my bar membership and stayed in touch with a few law-school friends, just in case business soured or small-town life felt too claustrophic, neither of which has happened. Herbs certainly won't make me a millionaire, but I'm still charmed by the lifestyle they support.

For five or six years, while I was learning the business, I went slow. I kept the shop pretty much the way I found it, making the most of the hand-cut limestone walls, the scarred pine floor, the cypress beams across the high ceiling. But last year, after I moved out of the apartment behind the shop and into the big Victorian house on Lime Kiln Road with McQuaid and Brian, I tore down several walls and added a couple of hundred square feet of retail space. Now, the shop is almost exactly the way I want it. Unpainted wood shelves and antique hutches and pine cupboards stocked with herbal jellies, mustards, teas, vinegars, soaps, shampoos, massage oils, bath herbs, incense, tinctures. Books, of course, and stationery and cards and gift baskets. Wreaths on every wall, and red-pepper *ristras* and garlic swags hang from the beams overhead. Baskets of yarrow, sweet Annie, larkspur, statice, tansy. Bunches of globe amaranth and straw-flowers, raffia-wrapped bundles of lavender, buckets of fragrant potpourri. And outside, there are racks of potted plants, barrels of green herbs and antique roses, and the gardens all around the shop, with meandering stone paths and a fountain McQuaid built for me, as well as a stone cottage (formerly a stable), which I use for craft demonstrations and herb workshops — and occasionally for guests. The only thing left to make it perfect would be the addition of a tearoom, something I've been wanting to do for a long time.

As the cash flow has permitted, I have hired a couple of helpers. Willow — a sturdy twenty-five-year-old with dark hair and deeply tanned arms and the high cheekbones that testify to her Cherokee heritage — works in the gardens with me, as I need her. Her older sister, Laurel, who wears her long brown hair in braids, has gone from part-time to full-time counter person in the last few months, minding the cash register while I stayed with McQuaid and taking my place in the herb classes I usually teach. And if I get in a jam, I can always count on Ruby Wilcox, bless her, my tenant and the best friend any woman ever had.

Ruby's shop — the Crystal Cave, the only New Age shop in Pecan Springs — occupies the other space at the front of my building. This proved a handy arrangement, particularly in the early days, when neither of us could afford to hire extra help and had to rely on one another to keep the shops open during lunch hours and when one of us had to run an errand.

Ruby is a truly memorable person, six feet tall in her sandals and stylishly thin, with a galaxy of freckles across her nose and crimped hair that is chile-pepper red. Her eyes vary from green to blue (depending on the color of her contacts), and her outfits are even more varied. They are always strange, bordering on the weird, and so is she, which is why I like her. It is the attraction of opposites.

Most of the time, you see, I tend to be structured, linear, and rational. These tendencies are partly due to my late lawyer-father's influence, partly to my own law-school training, and mostly (according to Ruby) to the unfortunate dominance of an overdeveloped left brain that specializes in logical equations. For me, it is an unquestionable fact that two and two equal four. Ruby, on the other hand, is bewitchingly right-brained, and in her canny kind of knowing, two and two might add up to just about anything, and often do. You can see her singular weirdness in the Crystal Cave, with its stock of incense, astrology books, magic wands, celestial music, spirit rattles, sun catchers, unicorns, and fantasy dragons. You can also see it in her hobbies — tarot, chanting, massage, yoga, and meditation — not to mention her eccentric costumes. You'd be mistaken, however, if you took Ruby's New Age follies lightly, or allowed yourself to be deceived by her unruly exterior. Her nonsense has saved my hide a time or two, and although her off-the-wall ideas often take me by surprise, I've learned to shut up and pay attention.

I certainly paid attention that evening in late April, when Ruby danced into the shop to tell me her sensational news. She was wearing a long-sleeved rose-print dress and a silk shawl, fastened with a cameo brooch, white stockings, and black ballet-style slippers. She's been letting her hair grow longer, and the soft red tendrils hung loose around her face. She pulled up a stool and sank down on it, as if her legs wouldn't hold her anymore.

47

"What's up?" I asked. "Have you got a date with John Travolta or something?"

"Better than that," she said. She clasped her knee and rolled her eyes heavenward. "Oh, China, you'll never guess!"

"Probably not," I said. "Why don't you tell me, and save us both the trouble?"

She did. It took only four words. But even though I heard them, I wasn't sure I'd heard right. I stopped counting the bank deposit and stared at her. "You've won the *what?*"

"The lottery," Ruby said. She shook her head, half-dazed. "It's okay if you don't believe it, China," she added unsteadily. "I don't believe it myself. But I just got the ticket validated. They say it's worth a *ton* of dollars."

I like specifics. "How many dollars are in a ton?"

"Two million dollars." Ruby took a deep breath. Her chest heaved and her nostrils flared. "Fifty thousand a year, after taxes. More or less."

I was dumbfounded. "Two million dollars!" I cried, when I could speak. "Fifty thousand a year!" I flung the cash register tape in the air, dashed around the counter, and pulled Ruby off the stool, dancing her around in an ecstatic circle. "You're rich,

Ruby! You are absolutely, unquestionably, unimaginably *rich!*"

"It must be a dream," she said in a whisper. "I'm asleep. You're in my dream, China."

"Well, if I'm in your dream, you're in mine," I retorted. "And we'd better arrange to wake up together or one of us is in deep trouble." I paused, and frowned. "How did you happen to play the lottery? It isn't something you usually do, is it?"

She shook her head. "It was the only time, and I only bought one ticket. I was filling up my car at the Texaco down the street from my house, and I kept hearing this little voice, telling me that if I bought a ticket, I'd win. It was entirely intuitive. I just *knew.*" She opened her eyes wide and gave me an earnest look. "And I know what I'm going to do with the money — this year's installment, anyway."

I thought of Ruby taking a trip to Nepal to meditate, investing in dozens of outrageous new outfits, or importing a couple of hundred of her wacky Southern California friends for a wild-woman retreat. Whatever she did, it would be fun to watch — almost as good as winning the lottery myself.

"So what are you going to do?" I asked.

"*We* are going to open the tearoom."

"*We?* As in you and me?" I leaned against the counter, staring at her. "Don't be an idiot, Ruby. You could take that fifty thousand and pay off your mortgage, or you could blow it on a new car or a trip to —"

"Or I could invest in a business," Ruby said, studying her nails.

"Of course. Now, *that* would be a sensible idea. You could put your money into a —" I stopped.

"There!" Ruby exclaimed triumphantly. "You see? Why should I squander my hard-earned winnings on a cruise or a car, when I can put it to work to earn more money? For *us.*"

I stepped back behind the counter again, picked the register tape up off the floor, and began to sort the cash. "Investing in a business doesn't guarantee that you'll *make* money," I said darkly. "You could lose every dollar."

"So what? There'll be fifty thousand more of them *next* year." She did a quick two-step, clapping her hands in delight. "Isn't it incredible, China? Fifty thousand a year!" She stopped dancing and whirled around. When she stopped, she added breathlessly, "Anyway, the tearoom is a money-making idea, and you know it as well as I do. You've been talking about it for years. What I'm suggesting is a partnership. And if that doesn't make sense, I don't know what does."

I put down the twenties and started counting the tens, not looking at her. "I don't have fifty thousand dollars to match your fifty."

"But you have the space, and the experience, and the reputation. People already come here from San Antonio, Dallas, Houston — why, from as far away as Oklahoma City and New Orleans!"

"That isn't very far. I haven't seen anybody coming from Paris or London."

"They will, as soon as they hear about China's Texas tearoom." She waved her arms energetically, as if she were conjuring up a room full of dreams. Her eyes, blue today, were sparkling with excitement. "It will be rustic, but elegantly eclectic, a blend of French Provincial, English Cottage, and American folk."

I groaned, but that did not deter her.

"Chintz curtains, cloth-topped tables and painted wood chairs, ferns in hanging baskets, some lovely pieces of antique furniture here and there, and artwork by our friends. Oh, yes, *lots* of artwork, wherever the eye comes to rest. There'll be an entrance from each of our shops, and of course, a dozen tables in a patio garden. The renovations surely couldn't cost all that much."

I finished counting the tens, riffled through the ones, and put the currency, such as it was, into the bank bag. "Oh, yes, they could." I zipped the bag so hard that I pulled off the zipper tab.

She regarded me thoughtfully. "How much?"

"Eight grand," I said. I wrote the amount of the currency on the deposit slip, and reached for the thin stack of checks. "Not counting the furnishings, which would probably amount to another couple of thousand if you're content with American flea-market. Double that if you're serious about French Provincial and English Cottage."

She frowned. "What's the eight thousand for?"

I ticked off the required items. "The Texas Department of Public Health insists on two new sinks, a new stove, new floor in the kitchen, laundry facilities, another storage closet for brooms, mops, buckets, etcetera. Plus electrical work, not to mention sealing the stone walls and the ceiling beams so that flakes of history do not land in the fruit soup."

She looked determined. "Well, I'm sure if we did all that, we would have a wonderful space."

"But that's not all," I said. "Don't forget the old rule — when you start a business, you need six months' operating expenses in the bank. That could come to twelve or fourteen thousand, maybe more, if you want a lot of fancy stuff, or if you're serious about advertising." I turned on the calculator and punched in the numbers. "Call it twenty-five thousand, minimum."

"For Pete's sake, where's the problem?" Ruby cried. "I have *twice* that much!"

"Good," I said. "Pay off your mortgage. Go to Nepal and meditate. Not that I don't appreciate the offer," I added, uneasily aware that my words might sound ungrateful. "Thank you, by the way. It's a generous offer."

She frowned. "China —"

"It's like this, Ruby. *You* may have the money for this wonderful project, but I don't. If it would cost China and Ruby twenty-five grand to open the tearoom and run it for six months, that means it would cost *China* twelve-fifty, and her pockets are unfortunately empty. She doesn't have a fraction of that amount, and she's not likely to get it anytime soon."

On that score, my argument was irrefutable. McQuaid's medical costs were covered by insurance, his disability insurance had kicked in, and CTSU had promised to give him the remainder of his sabbatical leave when the disability checks stopped coming. But while his department head had assured us that his teaching job would be there when McQuaid was on his feet again, nobody could predict when that might be. Maybe never. Meanwhile, the checking account balance was sinking rapidly, a situation that was already calling for creative financing. The raise I had given myself was not nearly enough. It was time to put pressure on Brian's mother to get current on her child support payments, or take on a little moonlight lawyering. This was definitely not the time for me to go out on a long, skinny financial limb.

Irrefutable as it might have been, my argument didn't carry any weight with Ruby. She straightened her shoulders. "Well, if a little bit of money is all that's holding you back," she said airily, "forget it. I'll put in the cash. You can contribute the space, the expertise, the —"

"No," I said.

"You're being obstinate."

"Yes. I'm sorry, but no."

She thrust out her lower lip in a childlike pout. "You don't trust me."

"Don't be ridiculous. Of course I trust you. But I couldn't let you bear the entire financial risk of this venture — that wouldn't be fair. Plus, I don't think that friends ought to go into business together. It might spoil the friendship."

"Good *grief.*" Ruby threw up her hands. "How long have I been your tenant? Five years? Six? We're *already* in business together, and I haven't noticed that our friendship has been spoiled."

She had a point, but I didn't want to tell her that. I said, "Sorry, Ruby. It's a good idea. It might even be a *great* idea. But this isn't the time for it."

Ruby pulled herself up with a calm dignity. "You're wrong, China Bayles, and I won't take no for an answer. I am going to nag you about this every single day until you say yes."

I sighed. When Ruby says something like that, she means it. I was in for a long siege.

She smiled and fluffed her hair. "And in the meantime, I'm going to spend some of my winnings on a perm and a new pair of shoes. I'm going out tonight."

"Oh, yeah?" I was glad for the change of

subject. "Who's standing in for John Travolta? Do I know him?" Of course I knew him. In a small town like Pecan Springs, everybody knows everybody else. Well, almost everybody.

"JJ Cody."

"JJ Cody?" I frowned. "As in Jerry Jeff?"

Ruby's giggle was almost self-conscious. "He likes his friends to call him JJ."

"His friends?" I leaned my elbows on the counter. "Forgive me for sounding like a mama hen, Ruby, but Jerry Jeff does have a reputation as a local playboy. A *married* playboy." His wife, Roxanne, is the office manager at the Cody & Clendennen Insurance Company, where her husband, Jerry Jeff, is a partner.

"They're separated," Ruby said. "Roxanne is filing next week."

"Gee, I hadn't heard that."

"You're not on the right branch of the grapevine, China." Ruby waved her hand airily. "She and Pokey Clendennen have been playing around together for months."

"But Pokey is Jerry Jeff's business partner!"

"It's not very smart," Ruby agreed, "and I'm sure it causes all kinds of tension at the office. But Jerry Jeff and I aren't involved romantically," she added. "Our dinner tonight is simply business."

"Well, I hope you weren't thinking of having dinner in Pecan Springs. If you do, it will be *everybody's* business." I looked at her curiously. "And just what kind of business do you and Jerry Jeff have?"

"Now that I have all this money, I was thinking that I ought to . . . well, you know." She made a vague gesture. "Become more fiscally responsible. Take care of some things I've been meaning to do for a while, and didn't have the money for. Like insurance."

"Not a bad idea," I said. "But mind what I say, or you'll be an item on the local grapevine tomorrow."

Ruby made a face. "That's the trouble with small towns. People feel like they've got a right to know every little detail of everybody else's life." She changed the subject briskly. "So how's McQuaid?"

"Better." I began jotting down the checks. There weren't that many of them. "He has full use of both arms now, and he can move his legs. Not much, but a little. He has quite a bit of pain, but Karen, his physical therapist, says he's making progress. She should know," I added. "They spend half the day together."

"He's making progress? Oh, China,

that's wonderful!" Ruby clapped her hands. "Maybe the two of you can get married soon."

"Maybe."

She sobered. "He's still resisting?"

"On the subject of marriage, he's the Rock of Gibraltar." The last time I had brought it up, McQuaid hadn't said no. He hadn't said anything, just looked out the window, pretending he didn't hear me.

Ruby gave an indignant *harrumph.* "Well, in my personal opinion, he's acting like a jerk. Here you are, being a mother to his child, managing the house, spending hours and hours at his bedside —"

"That has nothing to do with it."

"I don't know why not," Ruby retorted. "Doesn't it show how much you love him? I mean, isn't that what marriage is all about, in sickness and in health and all that?" She shook her head. "I just don't get it, China. For years, McQuaid has been after you to get married, and you kept saying no. Now you're willing, and he's —"

"Paralyzed," I said. "And if you don't get it, I do."

"Oh." She gave me a sidelong look. "The physical stuff, you mean. Sex." She paused. "It's not . . . working?"

"I can't personally testify to whether it's

working or not," I said. "There's only room in that bed for one, and anyway, his roommate is always around. It's hard to try anything under the beady eye of an eighty-seven-year-old chaperone." When McQuaid had first moved to the Manor, he'd had a private room. But the cost was high and he felt isolated, so he asked to be moved in with Jug Pratt, whom he had met in the dining room. Given the narrow range of options, Jug was a good choice. "His roommate is sort of a sit-down comic," I said. "He's always cracking bad jokes. It gives McQuaid something to do besides staring out the window."

"Is that what he does?" Ruby sighed heavily. "I guess I didn't . . . I mean, he's not always going to be . . . that way, is he?"

"If you mean, is he always going to be paralyzed, impotent, and clinically depressed," I said, "I doubt it. But the verdict is not in yet."

Ruby winced. "I don't know how you can be so matter-of-fact about it."

"What do you want me to do? Bang my heels on the floor and have a tantrum? Tear my clothes to shreds and run down the street screaming?"

Ruby took this seriously. "What you're doing is very bad, you know. You're stuffing all that anger and grief and suffering down inside you. You're like a volcano with a lid on it. You'd feel less pain if you let out some of your feelings."

"Well, maybe," I said. I finished adding up the deposit slip, stared at the disappointing total, and sighed. "But I'd probably feel a lot less pain if Brian's mother paid her back child support."

Chapter Three

For centuries, herbalists have recommended rubbing red pepper into the skin to treat muscle and joint pains. Medically, this is known as using a counterirritant — a treatment that causes minor superficial pain and distracts the person from the more severe, deeper pain. . . .

Michael Castleman,
The Healing Herbs

Neuroscientists believe that when a concentrated solution of capsaicin [the chief chemical compound in chiles] is rubbed on the skin, the resulting burning sensation causes pain messengers (Substance P) to notify the brain to start producing endorphins [natural painkillers]. Liniments [containing capsaicin] work on this principle, and capsaicin is the active ingredient of creams for painful skin and nerve conditions including shingles and neuralgia.

Carolyn Dille and Susan Belsinger
The Chile Pepper Book

It was May by now, and Leatha had been with us, off and on, since March. On the one hand, I really needed her help, especially in the evenings. Brian usually rode his bike out to the Manor to see his father after school, while I went for a couple of hours between dinner and bedtime. The boy was old enough to be trusted in the house alone, but it wasn't fair to abandon him for several hours every night. Leatha kept him occupied and happy while I was with McQuaid.

She also turned out to be an unexpected help around the house, cooking meals, doing laundry, and tackling the jobs I'd been meaning to do for months and just hadn't gotten around to: the kitchen floor, for instance, which was so cruddy it had to be scraped with a paint scraper before it could be scrubbed.

She had taken over the school chores, too, baking cookies for Brian's class and sitting in for me at his school play (which took place the same afternoon McQuaid got fitted for leg braces). After the play she took Brian shopping at the mall, where she bought him two pairs of the outrageously expensive designer jeans he covets and the most expensive sneakers they could find. All in all, she was the spitting image of grandmotherly benevolence and generosity. She and Brian had become great chums (he clearly knew which side his waffles were buttered on) and everybody kept telling me how lucky I was. To which I would growl something to the effect of "Yeah, the three of us are just one big happy family," and change the subject as fast as I could.

I know, I know. I can almost hear what you're thinking. Such a sweet deal you have, China. You should be ashamed of acting like a thankless twerp, an uncivil sorehead. Be grateful for your mother's help with the house, for what she's giving to Brian. You need her, and she's there for you. What more can you possibly want?

But that's the rub, don't you see? I don't want *more* from Leatha — I'd be delighted to settle for less. For Brian's sake, at least, it was good that she was there, and I appreciated her help. But anybody who's ever had a mother, especially if the relationship has been a troubled one, knows that this kind of help isn't free. There's a price to be paid, and I was the one who would have to fork it over. If I relied too heavily on her, how would I manage when she was gone? And worse, how was I going to repay her for the last couple of months? I was about to wind up with a big debt, emotional and otherwise, and no hope of settling it. Someday, when the old hurts had healed, Leatha and I might be able to connect more deeply, but I didn't want obligation or gratitude to be the bond that pulled us together.

So when my mother announced in mid-May that she planned to go back to the ranch in a couple of weeks, I was happy to hear it. Brian, however, wasn't glad at all. In fact, he and Leatha seemed to be hatching something between them. The suspicion came to me gradually, watching them whisper and laugh together as if they were sharing a secret. It was another week before I found out what it was.

One morning in late May when I was getting ready to go to the shop, Leatha came into the bedroom, in bathrobe, fuzzy slippers, and pink foam-rubber curlers, and told me that she wanted to take Brian to the ranch when school let out for the summer.

"No," I said, squatting down to look for my leather sandals under the dresser, where Howard Cosell invariably drags them in case he's lonesome during the night. He never chews them, only licks. McQuaid says he has a foot fetish, and he's sublimating.

"But it would be so *good* for him, China," Leatha persisted. "Sam can teach him to ride Rambo, and he can go swimming and fishing every day, and Jeannie is there with her new baby. We could be his family."

I found my sandals. The straps were limp and damp. In the night, Howard had graduated from licking to sucking. "Brian already has a family," I said firmly. "He has his dad. And me. I grant you that I am not his mother, but I'm the closest thing to a mom he has."

"China," Leatha said, "I must speak frankly."

"Don't you always?" I asked.

But that wasn't fair. One of our difficulties is that we almost never speak frankly. My mother and I have learned all sorts of interesting little gambits, clever defenses, quick feints, all for the purpose of concealing our true motives from one another. We're like lawyers for opposing sides, testing each other, each trying to scope out the other's vulnerable spots. Only in this case, we're not strangers, as most lawyers are. We are intimately related, and we've been perfecting our strategy for decades.

She ignored my remark. "Between the shop and the Manor, you have hardly any time for a small boy. And Brian spends only a few hours a week with his dad. Surely —"

Now, all this may be true, but I suspected that it wasn't the real reason behind Leatha's offer. Or behind her visit, for that matter. I wanted to be as independent of her as possible. She wanted to tie me more closely.

"Leatha," I said again, *"no."* I gave myself a quick glance. My shaggy brown hair needed a three-weeks-ago trim and I had to do something about the widening swath of gray at my left temple. But there wasn't time for anything more than a couple of quick licks with the hairbrush, which is about the limit of my patience with my hair. No time for makeup, either. But that was okay because I only wear it when the Queen comes to town.

She folded her arms and met my eyes, challenging. She had decided to be stubborn about this. "I really think you should give this more thought, China," she said. "A summer on the ranch will do wonderful things for the boy. When he comes back for school next fall, he will be a different child."

Her use of the declarative instead of the subjunctive was not lost on me. "I appreciate the offer," I said, "but Brian belongs here. He and I have to stick together. And he needs to be able to see his father every day."

"But that's just *it!*" She threw out her hands. "Haven't you noticed how deeply depressed the boy is? Seeing his poor father in that wheelchair, knowing that he may never walk again —"

"Nobody knows that for sure," I said quickly. "And anyway, a little depression isn't going to hurt Brian. His father's paralysis is a fact of his life, just as your alcoholism was a fact of mine. The sooner Brian learns to deal with the pain, the healthier he will be."

Leatha's mouth pulled down, and I knew I had gotten through. We hardly ever mention our mutual past unless we're quarreling about it. "I don't think the two situations are parallel," she said stiffly.

"They are exactly parallel," I said. I dropped the brush in the drawer and shoved it closed. "Long-term illness is just as likely as alcoholism to make a family dysfunctional."

Leatha is quick on the uptake, and she turned the argument around. "In that case, it would be good for him to get away. Anyway, a few weeks' vacation will be good for him. He'll make new friends, get plenty of sunshine and fresh air, and have a wonderful time."

"He needs to stay here." I stuffed my blouse into my jeans.

Leatha looked at me for a long moment. "You're jealous," she said wonderingly.

"Don't be ridiculous," I snapped. But I had to admit to myself (not to her, *never* to her) that somewhere in the complexities of my psyche, there was probably an ounce or two of jealousy, mixed with my instinct to hold Brian close in these moments of pain. Well, maybe more than an ounce. Maybe a couple of pounds.

It was a day or so after Leatha's invitation. I opened the door to McQuaid's room with my usual sprightly hello, which felt (as it usually did) terribly artificial. McQuaid shifted in his wheelchair to greet me, turning away from the window with its spectacular view of the goat pasture adjacent to the Manor. The field will someday sprout another wing of the main building, and the goats are not there for the amusement of the Manor's residents. They are gainfully employed in the business of eating the cedar trees that cover the building site. In our part of the country, it's cheaper

68

to rent a flock of goats than to hire a bull-dozer. The job gets done almost as fast, and nobody has to worry about burning the dead trees — which may also be a problem, if we're having a dry spell and the county commissioners have imposed a burning ban. All things considered, goats are much less hassle, and a lot more interesting to watch.

"Afternoon, China," Jug Pratt greeted me cheerily.

Jug is stooped and wizened, with a freckled scalp and sparse patches of gray hair that stick up over each ear, like a great horned owl. He'd lived in this room for a couple of years in apparent contentment, which I found hard to understand. How does a person — any person, of any age — become reconciled to such restrictions? The sight of Jug perched on the side of his bed reminded me of this question, which has a great deal of urgency for me, given McQuaid's situation.

"Hey," Jug said. "You heard the one about the guy who played golf after dark?" He was wearing a faded blue T-shirt with cereal stains on the front and gray wash pants held up with yellow suspenders. Beside him was a paper bag of peanuts which he was shelling and eating. He was tossing the hulls into the wastepaper basket, but Jug doesn't see very well, and the floor was littered with misses.

I grinned. "Yes," I said, going past him to McQuaid, who has the bed next to the window in the double room. "Yesterday."

Jug grinned back. "Then it oughta be better today. Practice makes perfect, y'know." He flexed his fingers. "My arthuritis is sure actin' up today. It's been real fierce since I had the shingles last winter."

"Every day and every way —" McQuaid said dryly.

"Better and better," I murmured, and bent over to kiss him, nuzzling his neck and slipping a hand inside his plaid shirt, feeling the warmth of his skin and the warm, soft tenderness that flooded through me. I wanted to fold him in my arms and hold him to me, hold him against all the hurt and fear. But McQuaid stopped me, stiffening under my touch, pulling my hand away.

"Feelin' him up, eh?" Jug asked amiably. He cracked a peanut. "Better watch out, young lady. Afore you know it, you'll be sittin' in his lap, same's that purty black-eyed nurse that comes trippin' around at bedtime, just to say a sweet good night to Mac here."

"Oh, yeah?" I straightened, pretending severity. "How about that, Mac?"

"I'm totally innocent," McQuaid said in a bored voice, but playing along. "Anyway, she's got blue eyes. You know I don't go for blue eyes."

I turned to Jug. "How much would I have to pay you to take notes?"

"Gimme a kiss 'n' we'll call it square," Jug said lecherously.

"How about if I give you some ointment that'll help your arthritis?"

He shook his head. "Tried everythin' under the sun. Nothin' works."

"Then you haven't tried hot peppers."

He squinted at me. "Listen, lady. I been eatin' peppers since I was weaned. They ain't done nothin' for my arthuritis. They shore made me horny, though." He cackled. "When I was a youngster, I'd stuff myself with jalapeños, primin' mesself for a Satiddy night." He grinned at McQuaid. "Say, that's whut you need, Mac. A good dose of hot peppers. Hotter the better." He cackled maliciously. "Rub 'em on yer pecker an' see if that don't make you get up outta that chair and dance a jig er two. Lot more fun than sittin' there, starin' out the window."

McQuaid shuddered. "Sounds like the

71

remedy's worse than the ailment."

"In an ointment, peppers might help your arthritis, Jug," I said hurriedly. "I'll bring you some."

The old man flexed his fingers. "If you hadn't already heard it, I was goin' to tell you about the guy who played golf after dark, and come in at two in the mornin'. His wife ast him how come he was out so late. He said —"

There was a tap on the door and a man's voice called, "Anybody home?"

"Stop poundin' on that door an' get yerself in here," Jug yelled. Two men came in, one in uniform. They filled the narrow space between the foot of the bed and the door, and Jug gave them a suspicious once-over. "Who're you?"

"I'm Chief of Police Harris," the uniformed man said in a surly, threatening voice. He rolled his cigar from one side of his face to the other, pulled his heavy black brows together, and hooked his thumbs over his belt. His belly sagged over the buckle, straining the buttons of his shirt. "I'm here to arrest this roommate of yours and haul him off to jail."

"Oh, yeah?" Jug was interested but hardly impressed. "He's a bad 'un, all right. Gives the aides reg'lar hell. So whut's he done that he's headed fer jail?"

The other man chuckled. "It's what he hasn't done that's the problem." He strode over to McQuaid, crunching on peanut hulls, and pumped his hand. "How ya doin', buddy?" he said, in a loud voice. Some people seem to think that people in wheelchairs have problems with their ears, too.

"Sure could be a lot worse," McQuaid said evenly. "Hello, Jerry Jeff." To the chief, he said, "Yo, Bubba." Bubba and McQuaid are not close friends but they both belong to the cop fraternity, which paradoxically makes them brothers. The fact that McQuaid is no longer officially a cop hardly matters, especially now that he's laid up with a service-related disability.

Jerry Jeff Cody turned light blue eyes on me, and grinned easily. "Well, hello. China Bayles, isn't it?" A blond, handsome man with powerful shoulders, he wore a white polo shirt, close-fitting slacks that showed off his narrow hips, and an expensive gold watch that advertised his success as Pecan Springs' leading insurance ("Covering the Longhorn State") broker. I've known him casually for several years, and known about him rather longer. That is, I've heard the

73

stories which circulate from time to time about his flings with various local ladies. Unfortunately, Ruby hadn't seen fit to heed my advice about going out to dinner with him somewhere outside of Pecan Springs. In the local imagination, she had been added to Jerry Jeff's conquest list.

"Right," I said briefly.

Jerry Jeff's teeth were very white, his smile friendly. "Your friend Ruby tells me that you and she are going into business together. Good idea."

McQuaid raised his eyebrows. "Oh, yeah? What kind of business?"

"Restaurant?" Jerry Jeff asked, trying to remember.

"Tearoom," I said shortly.

McQuaid raised his eyebrows. "I thought you'd given that up."

"I have," I said. "This is Ruby's idea, and I haven't been able to talk her out of it yet."

"Well, it sounds like the right combination to me," Jerry Jeff said with genial good cheer. "You've got a great location, and Ruby's got marketing smarts." His smile was patronizing. "You'll make a super team."

I grinned through clenched teeth.

Jug had been watching Jerry Jeff with a

quizzical look. Now he said, "Say, don't I know you, mister? Didn't I see you here a couple days ago, comin' out of Velma's room?" He glanced at Cody's wrist. "Don't recollect you, 'xactly, but I sure remember that watch. Sucker's big as a gold mine."

Jerry Jeff looked like he was going to say no, considered a split second, then shrugged. "Could have been me, I guess."

"Velma a friend of yours?" Jug asked curiously.

"No," Jerry Jeff said. "Not exactly." He looked uncomfortable.

Jug shook his head. "You don't want to mess around with Velma. She's nuttier'n a fruitcake. Chatters all the time but don't make no more sense 'n a prairie dog. Speakin' of nuts," he added, "have one on me." He cackled. " 'Member ol' Will Rogers? He was always eatin' peanuts and passin' 'em around." He threw Bubba a peanut.

"Thanks, Pop." Bubba picked it out of the air, cracked it, and ate it.

"Catch." Jug lobbed one to Jerry Jeff, who tossed it into the wastebasket.

"Thanks, I'll pass." Jerry Jeff turned to McQuaid. "Hot and cold running nurses, huh?" he asked, raising his voice. "Waiting on you hand and foot? Satisfying your every desire?"

McQuaid's answering smile was thin. "How come you're not out peddling life insurance to little old ladies?"

"Because I'm here to persuade you to do your civic duty." Jerry Jeff sat down on the corner of McQuaid's bed. "The Cedar Choppers Chili Cookoff is just around the corner, and we're short a judge. We tried to find somebody to take your place, but didn't have any luck. So the Honchos sent me to tell you you're it, and Bubba here came along to make sure you don't weasel out."

"Hell, *no*." McQuaid shook his head. "No way."

Bubba folded his arms over his belly. "Hey, fella. I got to scald my gut with that stuff once a year, you do too. You got to do your civic duty, same as me."

"You're able-bodied," McQuaid said. "You can run from the sore losers."

Jerry Jeff chuckled. "Nothing wrong with your sense of humor, pal."

Jug grinned. "Dang right. I told him one yesterday that tee-totally cracked him up. What room does a lion watch TV in?"

Jerry Jeff snapped his fingers. "His den," he said, and Jug's face fell. Jerry Jeff laughed and punched McQuaid's arm. "Hey, come on, guy. We're countin' on you. Remember the blast we had last year?"

"*You* had a blast," McQuaid growled. "You were drunk as a skunk. I had the trots for a week. Man, that stuff is *murder*."

"Was I drunk?" Jerry Jeff thought about that. "Yeah, well, maybe. I nearly char-broiled my tongue on the first sample, I remember that much for sure. I guess I spent the rest of the afternoon trying to put out the fire."

Bubba shifted his weight. "It'll do you good, McQuaid. You ain't been out and about for a while. Folks are askin' about you. You get out there, show 'em how good you're doin'."

"Anyway, China already said you'd do it," Jerry Jeff put in, not looking at me.

McQuaid slitted his eyes. "Is that right, China?"

Before I could answer, Jerry Jeff said smoothly, "She told Hark Hibler, and he ran your name in yesterday's paper right along with the other judges." He grinned at me, big and easy. "We've got all kinds of volunteer jobs, China. Glad to sign you up, too."

McQuaid looked at me, scowling. "Traitor."

"If Hark said I said that," I replied, "he's an out-and-out liar. *If* he said it," I added, with a pointed look at Jerry Jeff.

"Can't disappoint your public," Jerry Jeff said to McQuaid. "Everybody's expecting you to do your share. We're not putting this show on for fun, you know — the money goes to charity. We all have to pitch in."

"I gotta, you gotta," Bubba growled.

"Better do it, Mac," Jug said. "Nothin' else to do around here on a Sattidy, anyhoo."

"Well, *hell*," McQuaid said in disgust. "Why don't ya'll gang up on a guy?"

Jerry Jeff stood. "I knew you'd do your duty. Want us to send a van around for you?"

"Get outta here," McQuaid growled. "Before I sic my physical therapist on you."

"Nice guys," Jug said, when they had gone.

"One of them, anyway," McQuaid said. He glanced at me. "You didn't tell Hark I'd judge that cookoff, did you?"

"Of course not."

He relaxed a little. "Yeah. You can't trust Jerry Jeff. He tells you whatever he thinks will make the sale. Typical insurance salesman."

Jug pursed his thin lips. "Wonder what kinda bidness he's got with ol' Velma. A bubble short o' plumb, I call her. Light-fingered, too." He looked reflective. "She sure was a looker when she was younger, and smart too. Ol' Tom Perry, he was a lucky guy, havin' her work for him."

"What do you mean, light-fingered?" I asked.

Jug shrugged. "Aw, you know. She steals stuff." He grinned. "Say, you heard about the guy who stole three miles of elastic?"

"Yes," I said hastily.

"He was put away for a good long stretch."

"I'm outta here," I said, kissed McQuaid, and headed for the door.

"Rat fink," McQuaid said scathingly. "Desert a man when he's down."

"But not out," I said, and blew him a goodbye kiss.

"Speaking of out," Jug said, "do you know how the egg gets out of the hen?"

McQuaid gave a resigned sigh. "Okay, I'll bite. How does the egg get out of the hen?"

"Through the eggs-it," Jug said, and as McQuaid moaned loudly, he gave a triumphant crow.

Just outside the door, I ran into a stooped, white-haired man in red plastic moccasins, wrapped in a quilt that trailed behind him on the floor.

I was still shaking my head over Jug's foolishness. "Hello," I said.

He held up one hand, his fingers out-spread in Mr. Spock's Vulcan greeting. "Live long and prosper," he replied gravely. "Have you seen the Klingons?"

"Oh, there you are, Mr. Walton." Joyce Sanders, the nursing supervisor, had come up behind us, dressed in green scrubs and carrying a clipboard. "Aren't you a little lost?"

"Nope." Mr. Walton motioned toward the ceiling. "Ship's docked up there. They'll beam me up whenever I say."

"I'm afraid the transporter's not oper-ating," she said, and turned him around. "Come with me, and I'll see that some-body sends the shuttle." To me, she said, "Hi, China. How's Mike today?"

"Coping, more or less," I said, falling into slow step with the two of them. I won-dered how Joyce would react if I gave her the most recent report on the use of herbs to treat senile dementia and memory loss. Ginkgo and gotu kola have been shown to increase the blood supply to the brain, and rosemary contains chemical compounds that slow the breakdown of an essential

80

neurotransmitter. She probably had to do things by the book — the medical book — but I'd give it a try, anyway.

"Mike's physical therapist says he's doing quite well," Joyce said. "If he keeps improving at this rate, the prognosis looks good."

"I wish he could come home," I said.

"Don't be too anxious," she replied. "There's more to his care than you might think." An aide came toward us and took charge of Mr. Walton. Joyce turned back to me. "Did you know that you and I have a mutual friend? Dottie Riddle. She said you helped her out of a jam a while ago."

"With a lot of help from a couple of friends," I said. Ruby and Justine Wyzinski and I had pitched in to get Dottie — the Cat Lady of Pecan Springs — out of jail and clear her of a murder charge. It had been dicey there for a while.

"To hear Dottie tell it," Joyce said with a smile, "you're Kinsey Milhone and V. I. Warshawski rolled into one." She had a pleasant face, round and friendly, with a firm, no-nonsense chin.

"I wouldn't put it that way. I've had a bit of experience, but mostly on the other side. In a former incarnation, I was a criminal lawyer."

We had almost reached the nurses station. Joyce lowered her voice. "I'd like to speak to you confidentially, China. We have a problem here that I don't know how to deal with. I'd go to the police, but —"

"Telephone, Miss Sanders," a nurse called.

"In a minute." She was intent. "As I was saying, I'd talk to the police, but it's not exactly the kind of thing they can handle. It's too . . . well, delicate."

"You're making me curious," I said. What sort of problem would involve the police?

"It's Mrs. Rider," the nurse said urgently. "She says she wants to talk to you about her mother's diapers."

Joyce made a face. "Is it okay if I phone you, China?"

"Sure," I said. "Call anytime. And if you don't mind, I have a couple of articles I'd like to give you."

With a nod, Joyce hurried off to the phone, and I turned and headed for the lobby. The Colonial Manor is a U-shaped building that consists of three sections, each one named after a Texas river: the original center section, called Brazos; a new one-story wing on the left, called Colorado, and a new two-story wing on the right, called Rio Grande. McQuaid's room was in Colorado, the convalescent unit where the rehabilitation center — an equipment room, a whirlpool, a small exercise pool — is located. Brazos houses the dining room, the crafts room, and the administrative offices, as well as the rooms of residents who require more intensive nursing care, or who are suffering from dementia or early-stage Alzheimer's. Rio Grande, the new two-story unit, is an assisted living facility with one- and two-bedroom apartments designed for seniors who need a minimum of help and are still relatively ambulatory. The lobby, where people can gather to talk, watch television, or play cards, is located at the intersection of Rio Grande and Brazos.

I was in the lobby signing myself out when I looked up to see two women pushing through the double doors that led to Brazos. One was Fannie Couch, whose morning call-in talk show, "Fannie's Back Fence," is the hottest thing on Radio KPST. Along with the usual recipes and local gossip (cleaned up for airing on the radio), listeners get plenty of local controversy as well. It's not exactly *Frontline*, but every now and then Fannie gets her teeth into a story. She is our down-home version of Leslie Stahl.

But you wouldn't know that from look-ing at her. Fannie has blue-rinsed white hair, a sweet Southern belle smile, and a Texas twang that rivals Mollie Ivins's slow drawl. She favors little-old-lady dresses, sensible shoes, satchel-size purses, and Edwardian hats as elaborate as the speaker's table centerpiece at the Garden Club Fashion Brunch. Today, she was wearing a white straw with silk lilacs and plastic grapes spilling from a tulle-wrapped crown, matching the lilacs in her lace-trimmed print dress. In outfits like these, Fannie looks as if there's nothing more perilous on her mind than a mint julep.

Fannie's companion was Edna Lund, a woman in her early fifties with a disci-plined mouth and shrewd eyes. She looked trim and athletic in leather-belted khaki slacks and a sleeveless red blouse that showed tanned, hard arms. For most of her life, Edna lived with her father, Harmon, on the Lund family ranch, the H-Bar-S, out in Gillespie County. After the old man had a heart attack, father and daughter moved to Pecan Springs. She looked after him until he had to be moved to the Manor, where he died a couple of months ago.

Edna is pleasant, but she isn't exactly a

friendly person, which I suppose is the consequence of living most of her life on nearly six thousand acres of Texas ranchland. She remained isolated even after she and her father came to Pecan Springs, staying at home to manage an increasingly irascible old man who (by all reports) seemed to take a personal delight in making his daughter's life difficult. Old Mr. Lund's death had apparently left her pretty well fixed, although I'd heard there was a snag in probate and some confusion over the estate, which still hadn't been settled. Maybe it had to do with locating her brother, who'd been kicked out by his father some fifteen years before and now lived in Alaska — or so I'd heard. Anyway, after she moved Mr. Lund to the Manor, Edna began to participate more actively in community affairs, like the library's literacy program. Today, she was carrying a book under her arm, and I guessed that she'd been reading to residents.

Fannie greeted me with a hug and the standard question. "Hello, China. How's Mike doing these days?"

"Physically, he's getting stronger. Otherwise, he's a little depressed." I handed her the pen so she could sign herself out. "Jug Pratt is doing his best to entertain him."

"Jug Pratt could make a corpse giggle," Fannie said. "You and Edna know one another?"

"Of course," Edna said. "Hello, China." She consulted her watch, printed the time in precise numbers in the "Out" column, and silently corrected Fannie's time, which was different from hers by several minutes.

I don't suppose Edna can help it. For almost thirty years, she managed the complicated business of the six-thousand-acre H-Bar-S, where (according to Fannie, who's known Edna longer than I have) she was her father's first lieutenant.

"I understand that you're a regular visitor to the Manor, Edna," I said, as the three of us went out the door to the parking lot.

"My father died here a few months ago," she said, getting her car keys out of her shoulder bag. "Since then, I've been coming to read to some of the residents."

I thought of what Lila Jennings had told me a few weeks before, and also of Joyce's mysterious hint of trouble. "Well, then," I said casually, "I suppose you're up on the latest gossip about this place. You'd know if there are any problems."

"Gossip?" Edna's eyes went to Fannie. "You should talk to Fannie about that."

She paused beside a green Toyota pickup. "Don't forget that you're going to let me know what I'm supposed to do for the chili cookoff, Fannie."

"That's easy," Fannie said. "You're working in the check-in tent, where the cooks bring their samples. You'll be the one who gets the samples together and carries them over to the judging tent. Okay?"

"Fine," Edna said. "I'm glad to help."

"So?" I asked, when Edna had driven off.

"I suppose you're asking about problems at the Manor," Fannie said. A breeze came up, and she reached up to hold her hat. She gave me a mysterious smile. "Edna is my secret agent, you know."

I blinked. "Secret agent?"

"Oh, not really," Fannie said with a little laugh. "That's just what I call her. I'm doin' a program on this place in the next few weeks, and she's pretty much of a reg'lar here. I asked her to keep her ears open and collect the gossip for me. She's a pretty sharp-eyed gal, you know."

"So what has your secret agent found out?" I asked with a grin. "According to Lila Jennings, there's all sorts of trouble out here."

"In case you hadn't noticed," Fannie

said, "Lila's imagination tends toward disaster. It's true that folks aren't any too happy with Opal Hogge — she's the chief administrator — and there have been a few thefts and the usual grousing about the food. But the Manor's not bad, as nursing homes go." She stopped beside her dusty red two-door Ford. "Speaking of food, is Mike going to judge the chili cookoff? Jerry Jeff said he was going to ask him."

I nodded. "He wasn't crazy about the idea, but he says he'll do it."

"Good for him to get out, if he can," Fannie said, opening her car door. The hot air came out in a puff, and she took off her hat and tossed it onto the passenger seat. "I got stuck with judging the Sweet Heat competition again."

"Again? I thought you'd decided to give that up."

She sighed heavily. "I should. It's pure hell on this earth. Last year, Chuck Moffett's habanero marmalade nearly melted my dentures." She got into the car, lowering herself gingerly onto the hot plastic-covered seat, and pulled her lilac-print dress up over her knees. "But Jerry Jeff twisted my arm."

"He's a real arm-twister," I agreed conversationally, leaning against the open door.

"Oh, well. I guess it won't kill me to do it one more year. Then they can find a few other poor suckers to judge the damn thing." Fannie dug through her bag. "By the way, I hear that Jerry Jeff and Roxanne have agreed to a property settlement."

I raised my eyebrows. "Really?"

"Uh-huh." She pulled out a set of keys, which were suspended from a piece of red-white-and-blue plastic in the shape of Texas. She held the keys in her hand for a moment, as if she were weighing them. "But Roxanne's madder than a boiled squirrel about it. It seems that Jerry Jeff's financial picture isn't as rosy as she thought it ought to be."

"No kidding." Well, Jerry Jeff was slick. And Roxanne wouldn't be the first wife who discovered that the community property pot was empty when the divorce rolled around and it was time to go halfsies.

Fannie put the key into the ignition. "Of course, Roxanne hasn't been pure as the driven snow," she remarked obliquely. "She and Pokey Clendennen have been thick as thieves for over a year. I'm sure that didn't set real well with Jerry Jeff. Maybe he figured he'd get even."

"Sounds as if there's enough blame to go around," I said.

Fannie turned the key. "I hear Ruby's going out with him." She glanced up at me, and I read concern in her blue eyes. Fannie knows Ruby pretty well. "She's not serious about him, is she?"

"Ruby is *not* going out with him," I said. "He took her to dinner in order to sell her some insurance."

Fannie shook her head and got to the point. "Well, the way I hear it, Roxanne isn't any too happy with the current state of affairs. Which includes Jerry Jeff's girl-friends."

"Why am I not surprised? Just out of curiosity, who's on the current list — besides Ruby?"

Fannie raised her eyebrows. "You know I don't gossip."

I smiled, nodded, and waited.

"I only repeat what I can substantiate."

I waited a moment longer.

"He's seeing Felicia Travis."

Ah. Last year's Miss JuneFest, who can't be twenty yet. Jerry Jeff must be the envy of every teenaged, testosterone-driven male in Pecan Springs.

"And he's been seen with Lulu Burkhart."

"Maybe he's selling her insurance, too."

Fanny gave me a quick glance. "After

what happened between Jerry Jeff and Craig Burkhart, I don't think Craig would want Lulu to buy insurance from Cody and Clendennen." Jerry Jeff and Craig Burkhart had gone to court over something — a property deal of some sort, maybe — and Burkhart had lost.

"I wish Ruby had found another insurance salesman," I said.

Fannie sighed. "Can't say I blame you. It's not a pretty business. But maybe you ought to keep an eye on Ruby. I'm not saying Roxanne's going to make a fuss, but she might."

I frowned. "What kind of fuss?"

Fannie met my eyes. "With some people," she said, "you never know." She started the car. "Sorry. I don't mean to sound ominous." She put the car into gear. "All the same, you keep an eye on Ruby. You hear?"

Chapter Four

"Women have no business whatsoever trying to cook chili. It's a man's dish and a man's sport."

Don Russell
Chilympiad co-founder

As things turned out, I didn't have to worry about keeping an eye on Ruby that weekend, because she was in Dallas, visiting her sister. I didn't see her until the next Monday morning, and by that time, Fannie's warning seemed less urgent, hardly worth passing along, actually.

The shop is closed on Mondays, but that doesn't mean I take the day off. I spent the morning happily digging in the garden under the watchful eye of Khat, the large and elegant Siamese who lived with me until Howard Cosell came into the picture. After a couple of chaotic months, Khat decided he would be happier being a shop cat, a decision which has worked out well all the way around.

I was on my hands and knees, setting out Purple Ruffle basils in the space between the path and the fence, when Hark Hibler phoned with an offer. He and Arlene had liked the sample columns I gave him. They had decided it was time to fancy up the *Enterprise* by adding a Home and Garden page on Thursdays. I could start the week after the chili cookoff with a feature on chile peppers, including recipes. I considered the offer for all of two seconds and said yes.

Then Ruby stopped by. Her shop is closed on Mondays too, but she doesn't have a garden to keep her busy. She was looking cool and leggy in a short-short pink denim skirt with silver rivets down the side and a sleeveless pink top. When I told her about my new job, she suggested that we celebrate with lunch.

"It'll have to be someplace cheap," I said. "Sales were pretty slow last week." And summer stretched out ahead, the shop's slowest time of year. I'd been wondering whether I could afford to keep Laurel on full-time, or whether I'd have to cut back on her hours.

"Cheap?" Ruby raised her chin. "You forget. I am a wealthy woman. It's on me. Anyway, I owe you. You bought the last lunch."

I glanced at Khat, who was rubbing

against Ruby's ankles. "If you're in the mood to squander your ill-gotten gains, I know a certain someone who would be glad of a few chicken livers."

Ruby bent over and smoothed Khat's ears. (His rump is untouchable, which you will learn to your sorrow if you try to give him a full-body stroke.) "Later, my love," she cooed. "Aunt Ruby will bring you a whole pound of fresh chicken livers, sautéed in butter."

"Don't forget the garlic," I said.

She straightened up and looked at me. "This cat must have had great karma in his last nine lives. You're spoiling him."

"The garlic is as much for me as it is for Khat. It keeps the fleas off. They detest the odor."

On that note of herbal esoterica, I went to wash my hands and then we walked across the street to what used to be the Magnolia Kitchen, now called Casa de las Dos Amigas. We knew the restaurant had been sold, of course, but the new owners' upgrade had taken the neighborhood by complete surprise. Until a few months ago, the Kitchen had belonged to our friend Maggie Garrett, a former nun and a gifted chef. But Maggie had gone back to St. Theresa's and the restaurant had been purchased by two women from Indianapolis, Lois Alpern and Barbara Holland. They ripped out Maggie's casual country decor and replaced it with all the clichés of Sante Fe modern: clay tile floors, chrome-and-glass tables, indirect lighting, pink walls, pastel prints of idealized Native Americans, and stuffed fake cacti in large terra-cotta pots. They hadn't gotten around to changing the patio herb garden yet, but Lois had told me they were planning to turn it into additional parking. The news made me sad. The garden had provided the culinary herbs — cilantro, parsley, dill, garlic, fennel, lemon balm, lemongrass, marjoram, mint, thyme — that had distinguished Maggie's menu from all the others in town. I hoped it would be spared.

The new menu featured Southwest cuisine at New York prices. My choice was *poblanos rellenos,* a humble poblano chile which had been dignified with a stuffing made of ground chicken, beef, and pork, along with peanuts, carrots, and raisins, then baked and served with a peanut sauce — a concoction Barbara must have learned at the Santa Fe Culinary Academy, where she spent six months learning to cook. Ruby was having something called Goat-cheese *Crostini,* featuring shrimp and goat cheese on sourdough bread slices, along with a fluffy looking green salad with more varieties of lettuce than we could count. The service was slow (understandable in a new restaurant), but when the food finally came, it was almost good enough to make up for the orchestral version of "San Antonio Rose" that was playing in the background.

"Not bad!" Ruby bit into her *Crostini* with enthusiasm.

"It's good," I said, digging into my stuffed pepper. "But not for your ordinary Pecan Springer, who's addicted to sirloin and fried catfish."

Ruby looked around at the nearly empty dining room. "The place is just getting off the ground. It'll take a while."

"Be realistic, Ruby. How many natives can afford to pay these big-city prices for lunch? And how many tourists will opt for ersatz New Mexico when they can go to Bean's and get authentic Texas?" Bean's Bar & Grill is the real thing, with scuffed pool tables and chipped dart boards, a rusty wagon-wheel chandelier, the front half of a ratty buffalo sticking out of the wall, and the best Tex-Mex between Austin and Del Rio.

"Well," Ruby said judiciously, "I don't think it will be a threat to our tearoom, if that's what you mean."

"That's *not* what I mean," I said. "Ruby, I really don't think —"

She leaned forward, eyes intent, face serious. "China, I do not understand you. For the last twelve months, you have been talking about the tearoom — how attractive it could be, how much money it would make, how many customers it would bring in, how this, how that. Now you've got the chance, and all you can say is no. What is the *deal* with you?"

I poked at the remnants of my pepper. "I just don't think you ought to sink your lottery winnings into such a speculative project. It's too big a gamble."

Ruby rolled her eyes. "And just how did I get the money in the first place? If the lottery isn't gambling, I don't know what is."

That stopped me for a few seconds, but I recovered. "Think of the way you'll feel if you put all that money into the tearoom and it goes belly-up," I said. "You'll be disappointed. You'll be angry. It will come between us."

"What is going to come between us," Ruby said frostily, "is your inability to accept any help from your friends."

"That's it," I snapped, "blame it all on me. *I'm* the one who's at fault."

We glared at one another.

Lois Alpern, one of the new restaurant owners, chose this moment to stop by the table. Lois is a slender, graceful woman in her early fifties, quite attractive in a cool sort of way, with frosted hair shorn up the back like a boy's and fluffed out on top in an exuberance of frothy curls — definitely not a cut she had gotten from Bobby Rae at the House of Beauty. She was wearing trim-fitting cream-colored slacks, a thigh-length rosy-beige tunic the same shade as the walls, and gold hoop earrings big enough for Howard Cosell to jump through. Her face was carefully made up with deep blue shadows over her eyes, and her half-amused glance made me conscious of my shorts, T-shirt, and sandals and the garden dirt under my nails.

"I hope you ladies are enjoying your lunch," she said.

Pointedly, Ruby and I did not look at one another. "The food is very good," Ruby said.

"Tell Barbara we enjoyed it," I added.

Lois took the compliments with a graceful nod and turned to something else that was on her mind. "I've been wondering," she said, touching one earring with perfectly manicured rosy fingertips, "what you might tell me about the chili contest we've been hearing so much about."

"It's the biggest local event of the year," Ruby replied. "Of course, you know that it's just one part of JuneFest, which kicks off our summer tourist season. There's a beauty contest, street dancing, a parade, a watermelon-eating contest —"

"I know all *that*." Lois made a dismissive gesture. "It's the chili contest we're interested in."

Ruby gave me a cool glance. "You need to talk to China about that. She's a close friend of one of the judges. And she's going to be covering the event for the newspaper. She's the new Home and Garden editor for the paper, you know."

"Oh, no, I *didn't* know," Lois said, her eyebrows rising under her frosted fringe. "Home and Garden editor. How nice!" She smiled with a warm friendliness that exonerated my dirty nails, and I was suddenly One of the Girls. "Well, then, perhaps you can give us some insights into the competition, China. Barbara has a great vegetarian recipe, you see, that she plans to enter. It's a simply superb chili, quite mild, made with several different kinds of beans, peanuts, jalapeños, and her own secret spice blend." She rolled her eyes. "*So* elegant, presented in a lemon-glazed earthenware bowl and garnished with a swirl of yogurt, diced avocado, and lime wedges. Smart, tasty — and sure to win."

"But that's not possible, Lois," Ruby said. "You see, this particular cookoff is for —"

"We absolutely *covet* first prize, China." Ignoring Ruby, Lois leaned forward and lowered her voice. "It would be a simply *fabulous* advertisement for Casa de las Dos Amigas."

I frowned. "As Ruby was saying —" I began, but Lois cut me off.

"Please tell your friend that we'd be glad to do anything we could to . . . well, tip the scales in our favor," she said, and gave a significant little laugh. "Free lunches for a month, perhaps. Or maybe you'd rather tell me what's appropriate."

Ruby cleared her throat. "As I was saying, people here are possessive about chili. The legislature declared it the official state dish twenty years ago."

"Yeah," I said. "We like our chili cowboy style."

Lois's sniff was clearly audible. "Cowboy style?" She bit off the words as if they were synonymous with *ignorant aborigine.* "But superior flavor is bound to be recognized, even by a . . . cowboy. And of course, vegetarian chili has almost no fat."

Our disagreement forgotten, Ruby and I traded glances. Normally, neither of us is especially vicious. We try to go the extra mile, especially with folks who come from north of Dallas. But there are limits.

"Here in Texas, we like our chili greasy," I said. "And we don't care for beans. Maybe you haven't heard the National Chili Anthem. It's called 'If You Know Beans About Chili, You Know that Chili Has No Beans.' "

"No beans!" Lois asked, horrified. "But in Indiana, we *always* —"

"Beans," Ruby said sternly, "are actually against the rules."

"The *rules?*"

"Yep," I said. "Where CASI is concerned, chili is made with meat, not beans. Here in Texas, at least."

"What's a cassy?" Lois asked suspiciously.

"The Chili Appreciation Society International," I said. "This is a sanctioned event, you know."

"A sanctioned —"

"The meat is *extremely* important," Ruby

said, as if she were giving a lesson in brain surgery. "It's usually either Texas longhorn or venison. If it's longhorn, you want a cow with lots of character. The same goes for deer meat. In November, the guys shoot the biggest, oldest buck they can find and stick him in the freezer until it's time for the cookoff."

"Buffalo is good too," I said. "And emu's not bad, if you check for pinfeathers and cook it long enough to soften up the strings. Ostrich, too. Cracker Bob's Ostrich Chili could have been last year's big winner, if some joker hadn't dumped a pound of red worms in the pot when his back was turned."

"Red . . . worms?" Lois said faintly.

"Of course," I went on, "venison and buffalo and such don't make a very greasy chili, so folks usually throw in a pound or two of lard. And Cracker Bob has a neat idea — he renders the fat of an overweight possum and pours it in at the last minute. He ends up with about an inch of grease on top."

Lois was trying to speak, but Ruby had thought of something else. "And of course there's alligator. The team that won year before last cooked up a pot of something called Hot Swampy Chili, with alligator meat and crawdad tails." She paused thoughtfully. "You have to drive to East Texas to get alligator, though — it's scarce around here. Parks and Wildlife frowns on shooting the wild ones, but there are plenty of alligator farms. You could probably get enough for a couple of batches."

I nodded. "Of course, if you want local meat and you haven't shot a buck or don't have a Texas longhorn you can butcher, the very *best* thing is rattlesnake. And that's not at all hard to find."

Ruby nodded enthusiastically. "The chili that came in second last year — something called Roadkill Chili — was cooked up by a gang of Harley bikers on their way to Mexico. It had big hunks of rattlesnake in it. They said they scraped the snake off the road, but I never believed it. They probably got it at the landfill — that's the best place to go rattlesnake hunting."

"That's right," I said. "Rattlers aren't hard to catch first thing in the morning, when it's cool and they haven't had their coffee yet. But be sure to wear heavy boots and leather gloves and take a big burlap bag."

Lois's face had turned greenish-gray, an interesting contrast to the rosy-beige of her tunic. "I'm certainly glad we talked," she managed. "I'll convey your . . . suggestions to Barbara. Perhaps she'll want to rethink her entry."

Ruby held up her hand. "Oh, but you *can't* enter, Lois. I started to tell you, but I got interrupted. The Cedar Choppers Chili Cookoff is a men-only event."

"Men only?" Lois was incredulous. "But that's discrimination! Up north, we'd never stand for it."

I shook my head. "Wait a minute, Ruby," I said. "A woman can enter, if she's one hundred years old or older. It's in the rules."

"That's *double* discrimination!" Lois shrilled. "Sex discrimination *and* age discrimination."

"That's certainly what it sounds like," I remarked mildly.

"And you . . . you put up with it?" Lois sputtered.

I shrugged. Ruby smiled. "The boys have to do something with their weekends," she said.

If Lois had been civil, we might have told her that she and Barbara had other options. The Luckenbach Texas Ladies' State chili cookoff is open only to women, and the Terlingua World Championship is open to both women and men. And if they were really interested in local chile culture, they might join either the Salsa Queens or the Caliente Cooks. But these were things she could find out for herself.

As we walked back across the street, Ruby was shaking with exasperated laughter. "What a smug, patronizing . . . Yankee!"

"Do you think she got it?"

Ruby shook her head. "I doubt it."

"Maybe we were too rough on her."

"I doubt that, too. She's probably in the kitchen this very minute, telling Barbara that we're so country that we think a seven-course meal is a possum and a six-pack." Ruby glanced at me. "Do you have a few minutes to talk? As I recall, we were interrupted."

I pushed my hands into the pockets of my jeans. "Are you sure you want to get into it again? As I recall, we were having an argument."

"That's because you were being stubborn."

"Put that into the present tense. I am stubborn. And *you* are pushy."

We were halfway up the path to our shops. Ruby stopped and gave me a slit-eyed look. "Right on both counts, and it's ridiculous. I have all this money that I'm dying to put to work, and you won't let me —"

"I'm not keeping you from putting your money to work, Ruby." The sun was hot on my back and the bees were busy among the thyme blossoms on either side of the path. A hummingbird was poking its long beak into the orangey-gold bloom of the butterfly weed, pollinating while it harvested the nectar. "If you're looking for big bucks, buy stock in a Harrison Ford movie or invest in some lakefront real estate. But don't keep nagging me about —"

"Do you know what your problem is, China Bayles?" Ruby put her fists on her hips, her eyes narrowing. "You're afraid of being partners — with me, or anybody else."

"That's nonsense," I said. "Unwilling, perhaps, reluctant, maybe —"

"You are *afraid*. Why do you think you said no to McQuaid all those years?"

I scowled. "I said no because I . . . because —"

I stopped, my eye catching a tall, feathery fennel, covered by a dozen caterpillars striped in greenish white and black and dotted with yellow. They were stripping the fennel.

"You see?" Ruby demanded. "You're

saying no to me for the same reason. I realize that you need to have your own business, where you can call all the shots. But at some point in our lives we all have to admit that a partner can help share the risk. After all, we do get ourselves into tight spots now and then. And two heads are better than one when it comes to figuring things out." She looked at me. "Are you listening?"

I nodded absently. In a few days, stuffed with fennel and ready for a snooze, the caterpillars would spin themselves into cocoons. After a while, the cocoons would split and swallowtail butterflies would emerge into the sun, their new black wings handsomely chevroned in cream and blue. The fennel, meanwhile, would have sprouted fragrant flowers, ready to be pollinated by the newly hatched butterflies and play host to the next round of caterpillars. A joint venture, so to speak.

"Listen, China." Ruby looked at me steadily. "It's only money. Spend it, save it — either way, it'll soon be gone. But you and I can use it to build something neither of us can have on our own."

"Well," I said slowly. "Maybe."

Ruby's face broke into a broad grin. "Yes? Was that a 'yes' I heard?"

"You heard a *maybe*," I growled. "There you go again, Ruby, jumping to —"

"Oh, China, this is terrific!" Ruby cried. She grabbed my hands and began to dance around. "This is fabulous! This is —"

"Premature," I said firmly. "I haven't said yes. I don't want to rush into anything."

"Oh, we won't rush," Ruby assured me. She was breathless with excitement. "We'll go *very* slowly. I'll just talk to the Department of Health about the permit, and sketch out the kitchen, and put together some ideas for our menu. And then there are the furnishings, and the —" She stopped suddenly and looked at her watch. "Oops! Late for my hair appointment. I've got a date tonight."

"Ah," I said. I took my keys out of my pocket and unlocked the shop door. "I hear that Roxanne and Jerry Jeff have reached a property settlement." Maybe it was time to pass along Fannie's cautionary advice.

"I heard that too," Ruby said, "and if you ask me, it's about time they got their business straightened out." She gave me a straight look. "You didn't think it was JJ I'm seeing tonight, did you?"

"Well . . ."

"Well, it isn't. Haven't you heard that he's dating Felicia Travis?" She made a little mouth. "I understand that they're planning to get married and go on an around-the-world honeymoon."

"Off with the old, on with the new," I murmured, wondering where this left Lulu Burkhart. "And I think *my* love life is complicated."

"Yes, well, Felicia has many obvious charms," Ruby said dryly, "not the least of which is extreme youth. And big boobs, which in my humble, flat-chested opinion are more a liability than an asset."

I picked up my trowel and a flat of four-inch pots of rue, destined for the center of the front herb bed, where no one was likely to brush against them. The plants yield a juicy sap that can raise blisters if you get it on your skin and expose the skin to the sun. "So if our local insurance salesman is totally out of the picture, who is tonight's lucky guy?"

Ruby followed me out to the walk. "Guess," she said happily.

I knelt to my planting with a sigh. This is one of Ruby's favorite games, and she usually plays it for all it's worth — an irritation just now, since I was really curious. "Paul Newman? George W. Bush? The Pope?"

The corner of her mouth quirked. "I'll give you a hint. His name begins with *H*."

"*H?*" I was drawing a blank. "Okay, I give up. Who is it?"

"Oh, come on." She grinned, letting the suspense build. "He's your boss."

"My boss? I don't have a boss." And then I realized who it was. "Hark Hibler?" I asked, surprised. And then, because I was afraid she'd take it the wrong way, I added enthusiastically, "That's great! I like Hark."

"He's certainly no hunk," Ruby admitted. "But he's not bad-looking, now that he's lost so much weight. He may not be the most thrilling man in the world, but his psyche seems reasonably well-adjusted, he reads books instead of watching football, and he thinks it's neat that I have a brain." Ruby made a face. "Pecan Springs isn't Houston, you know. There aren't a dozen smart, sexy, reconstructed males lurking behind every bush."

I scraped the bark mulch to one side and began to make planting holes in the soft earth. "What makes you think there are a dozen of those anywhere in the world?" I asked. "Face it, Ruby. You and I are getting picky in our middle age."

Ruby nodded seriously. "Be glad you have McQuaid."

"Oh, yeah?" I sighed and shoved a plant into the ground. "So who says I've got him?"

Chapter Five

A number of other seasonings commonly find their way into chili. Here are a few of the most frequent contributors.

Cilantro
A fresh herb resembling broad-leafed Italian parsley, with a refreshingly spicy, astringent flavor.

Coriander
Used in the ground form for chili, this seasoning has an intriguingly sweet spiciness.

Cumin
Almost as integral to chili as chiles themselves, this spice — used as small whole seeds, or, more often, ground into a fine powder — has a distinctively pungent, slightly musty flavor.

Oregano
This very popular, aromatic dried herb beautifully complements the flavor of chili, particularly when it includes some form of tomatoes.

Norman Kolpas
The Chili Cookbook

My quip to Ruby wasn't just something I had tossed off. When I went out to the Manor late that afternoon, I found McQuaid stretched out on his bed, hands clasped under his head, looking up at the ceiling. Jug was playing Bingo in the recreation room, so we had the privacy for something a little more intimate than wordplay. I shut the door, lay down on the bed beside him, and touched his cheek with my fingers. When he didn't respond, I turned his head to mine and kissed him. His lips were cool and remote, and there was no pressure from his arms. Once upon a time, even a light touch had been enough to send currents of sweet, high-voltage desire pulsing through both of us. Now, it felt like the wires were shorted out, the batteries dead.

He turned his head away and said what was in both our minds. "Sorry." His voice was gruff.

"Yeah. Me too." I propped my head on my hand and traced the jagged scar that makes a white diagonal across his forehead. "But it'll get better soon." I spoke with more confidence than I felt.

"Maybe. Maybe not." He sounded resigned. "I'd like to think I'm just tired, China. Therapy for hours on end, trying to get some strength back, trying to make my legs work —" He shook his head. "But it's not just physical exhaustion. It's . . . everything else, everything on top of that. Not knowing whether I'll ever be able to have you. Or even want you." He lay still for a long moment, his chest rising and falling under my hand. "I don't . . . let's not talk about it anymore. This isn't something you can understand."

"Then *make* me understand," I said urgently. I had never been a star quarterback, or a tough cop, or a man, so I couldn't know what it felt like to lose the ability to run, to win a fight, to make love to a woman. I couldn't feel his pain, or fathom his fear. But what frightened me most was the idea of not talking.

"That won't help," he said. "It won't change anything."

"Of course it will. We need to get this out in the open before you come home." I could feel his heart beating under the flat of my hand. "Brian and I can't wait, McQuaid. We hope it's *soon*. Like tomorrow. Or next week."

"Yeah, I know. Brian is part of this, too. But I'm not sure . . . I don't think . . ." He fell silent. I could hear a woman's voice on the paging system out in the hall, and the muted sound of the air conditioning, and

McQuaid's breathing. After a few minutes, he spoke in a lighter voice, letting me know that the painful subject was closed, "So. What's new at the shop?"

I would rather have talked some more about us, but I answered, matching his tone as well as I could. "I finally told Ruby I would consider going into business with her."

"Well, that's good," he said. "I wondered what was holding you back. It's not every day of the week that somebody offers to bankroll a business." He grinned crookedly. "Most people would walk through fire to help Ruby spend her lottery money."

"I know," I said. I sat up and hooked my arms around my knees. "She's anxious to get started this afternoon, of course. Hire an architect, hunt for furnishings, plan menus. But that's out of the question."

He looked up at me. "Why?"

I gave his leg an affectionate pat. "Because my plate is already full, you dummy. There's the shop to manage, and the gardens, and Brian will soon be out of school. And there's you, and —"

His jaw tightened. "You don't have to come here every day, China. And I've already told Leatha she and Sam can take

Brian to the ranch for the summer. The kid deserves some fun — and *you* need some breathing space."

Startled, I twisted so that I could see his face. "You told Leatha — but didn't she tell you I'd already said no?"

He had the grace to look uncomfortable. "I don't know why you didn't want him to go," he muttered. "A summer on the ranch will be good for the boy, and a lot more fun than hanging around here. I can't play ball with him or go fishing or —" His voice was ragged. "Anyway, you need a break. He's not your kid, after all."

I felt as if I'd just been dunked in an icy tub. "Brian *is* my kid," I said sharply, "and I don't want a break."

"You know that isn't what I mean," he said testily. "I just mean that he isn't your responsibility. You don't have to give up —"

"I'm not giving up anything. I *like* being responsible for him."

His face had closed down. "What have you got against Leatha and Sam?"

"Nothing. But you should at least have consulted with me before you agreed." Now I was really angry. "And she had no business coming to you after I said no."

"I don't feel like arguing."

I turned to touch his face. "I'm not arguing," I said, more softly. "I'm just telling you how I feel. I know I'm not Brian's mother, but when you're not around, I'm responsible for him. I told Leatha I wanted him here for the summer, so he could visit with you every day."

He closed his eyes. "Look, China, this afternoon's workout took a lot out of me. I'd like to get some rest before dinner. Okay?"

It wasn't okay, but I couldn't tell him that. We traded a peck on the cheek and I left him lying on his back, staring at the ceiling.

I was walking past the nurses station, head down, when I collided with Joyce Sanders.

"Oops, sorry," I said. "I guess I was wool-gathering."

"Oh, China, hello." Relief was apparent in her voice. "I'm so glad to see you. If you've got a minute —"

She took me by the arm and tugged me into her small office, a narrow room that was mostly taken up by a long worktable with a computer and phone, a couple of office chairs, and bookshelves. The tiny cubicle would have been claustrophobic if it weren't for the large interior glass window over the desk, which looked out on the hallway and the nurses station. We sat down and Joyce pushed her brown plastic-rimmed glasses up on her nose.

"Do you recall that problem I mentioned to you last week?"

I nodded.

"Well, something's going to have to be done, and quick," Joyce said. She had turned so that she was facing me, with her back to the window. "Don't be obvious about it, please — but can you see that dark-haired aide in the blue scrubs, working at the nurses station?"

I glanced quickly over Joyce's shoulder. "The pretty one?" The girl, who was barely out of her teens, certainly was pretty, with dark eyes and olive-brown skin and a generous mouth.

"Her name is Carita Garza. I hired her about eight months ago, and she's done a very good job. She's bright, pays attention, and learns fast. Unfortunately, she has a dreadful situation at home — most of her paycheck goes to support a couple of younger sisters and an alcoholic mother. Her father is in prison, and she goes to visit him once a month. But she somehow manages to put all that trouble aside when she comes to work. She's quite amazing, actually."

Having grown up with an alcoholic mother, I could appreciate Carita's efforts. "She sounds like a jewel. So what's the problem?"

Joyce picked up a pencil, turned it in her fingers, dropped it. When she looked up, her brown eyes were troubled. "Mrs. Hogge — she's the Manor's chief administrator — suspects her of theft."

In its outlines, the story was simple, sad, and very troubling. Since Carita had come to work at the Manor, there had been a half-dozen thefts, mostly in Rio Grande, the assisted living facility. Those residents were wealthy enough to afford the pricey apartments and were discouraged but not prohibited from keeping cash in their suites. Many of the women kept valuable jewelry around too. "Her jewelry is often the only thing an elderly woman really treasures," Joyce said, "and it's something she can easily bring with her. You can't tell her it isn't a good idea. And you can't tell an eighty-year-old man that he shouldn't keep cash in his bureau drawer." She gave me a rueful smile. "I mean, you can *tell* them, but they don't listen."

"Don't people lock their doors?"

"Seniors are terribly forgetful, so we're sure that some of the doors in Rio Grande were unlocked. But the rooms in the convalescent unit can't be locked because we need constant access to them — there've been thefts there, too. And a couple of wallets were lifted from guests' purses left unattended in the dining room or lobby."

"That was what you wanted to tell me the other day?"

Joyce nodded. "The last theft, from an apartment in Rio Grande, was something over three hundred dollars. All told, several thousand dollars are missing. It's certainly a police matter, but it isn't the sort of situation where a police investigation after the fact would turn up much."

"You say that Carita is suspected. Did someone see her and report her?"

"I almost wish that's what happened — it would make things much easier. The trouble is that I like Carita, and I want her to be successful. I can't quite believe she would —" Joyce took off her glasses and polished them absently on her sleeve.

"Would what?"

"This morning, Mrs. Hogge noticed that the earrings Carita was wearing were identical to a pair that had been reported missing a few months ago. Carita says she bought them at a local flea market, but of course her statement can't be verified."

"Are they in fact the same earrings?"

"That's what makes this so awkward." Joyce rubbed her eyes with her hand, then put her glasses back on. "The woman from whom they were stolen is now . . . well, she's been transferred to the Alzheimer's section in Brazos. She *says* they're her earrings, but I wouldn't trust her recollection." She looked at me. "You see the problem."

I certainly did, and the criminal attorney part of me felt like making a motion for dismissal. There was no eyewitness testimony to tie the girl to the thefts, and not even any clear evidence that the earrings were actually those that had been taken. Not to mention that being fired on suspicion of theft would put a tragic end to a promising career — and pose a potential large liability for the Manor.

"I see the problem but I can't suggest a solution," I said. "Carita might be the thief, but it's at least equally possible that she isn't. In that case, firing her would do her a terrible injustice — and invite a messy lawsuit that could keep the Manor's lawyers busy for a long time."

"On the other hand," Joyce said gloomily, "we can't just allow the thefts to continue without taking *some* sort of action. Mrs. Hogge feels that if it isn't stopped, we'll lose residents."

"She might be right," I said. I glanced toward the nurses station and caught Carita's eye. She gave me an apprehensive look and turned away. How much did she guess about the topic of our conversation? "Sorry," I said. "Looks like you're in a real pickle. One of those damned if you do and damned if you don't situations."

Joyce gave me a pleading look. "You can't . . . well, do a little detective work for us? It might not be too hard to find out whether Carita has been spending money she can't have earned, or if somebody has seen her wearing some of the other jewelry that was taken. Or maybe you could poke around and find out who the thief really is."

"Really, I don't think —" I began, but Joyce put her hand on my arm.

"Don't say no, China. You're perfect for the job. You're here at the Manor every day, and you know most of our staff."

I shook my head. "I'm sorry. I'd like to help you, Joyce, but McQuaid and I are going through a difficult period. His injury has been hard on us, and we're trying to get on with our lives. Everything is so complicated just now — so many things mixed up together. I just can't take on another project."

"I was afraid you'd say that." Joyce gave me a small smile. "But I do understand. I know things must be tough for you and Mike just now. Can you suggest somebody else? Unfortunately, it would have to be somebody who knows us — somebody who's here pretty regularly."

I was shaking my head when suddenly I had an idea. "Actually, I might know somebody who could help, if you can give me a day or so to check it out."

Joyce's face brightened. "That's great!" she exclaimed. "Who are you thinking of?"

"I'll get back to you as soon as I can." I stood up. I didn't want to raise Joyce's hopes before I got an answer to my question. But if I were looking for a sharp-eyed person to do some undercover snooping into a tricky situation at the Manor, I knew exactly who I'd ask.

Edna Lund.

Chapter Six

You can always judge a town by the quality of its chili.
Will Rogers

Judging is the most dangerous part of a chili cookoff.
D. Lee McCullough
Chili Monthly, September 1984

Before you can understand what happens next, you have to know something about a Texas chili cookoff, which is nothing like the Pillsbury Bakeoff. In fact, it's not like any competition you've ever witnessed — except, maybe, for mud wrestling or rattlesnake sacking. It's more like a tailgate party in the parking lot prior to the UT-OU game, or the Oatmeal Festival in Bertram, Texas, where an airplane dumps flakes of instant oatmeal on the spectators. This is the Lone Star State, where chili was invented. If you take your chili straight, you'd better take your chili somewhere else.

As to exactly who in Texas actually came up with the dish, and when, there is a certain amount of disagreement. One theory pins it on the cowboys of the 1840s, who pounded together dried beef, beef fat, dried chile peppers, and salt into something like pemmican, which could later be hauled out of the saddle bag and boiled with whatever liquid was handy. Another suggests that the first chili chefs appeared in the 1850s, when the gaily dressed San Antonio chili queens set up their simmering pots over mesquite fires in the Plaza de Armas, hanging colored lanterns over their oilcloth-covered tables. Joe Cooper, author of *With or Without Beans*, thinks that the chili queens were predated by the Mexican *lavanderas* who washed the Republic of Texas's dirty socks and made extra money by turning their laundry buckets into chili pots when it came time for the soldiers to eat.

Scholars may argue about the origin of chili, but there's no disagreement as to why this dish is so popular. What does the trick is the chile pepper — the herb with an attitude. Dive into a bowl of red (as chili is familiarly known in Texas) and in a couple of minutes you'll know what I'm talking about.

Mucho pain.

Your eyes will be tearing, your nose will

be running, and your tongue will be on fire. But your sinuses and even your lungs will start clearing, courtesy of the chile's capsaicin (a natural decongestant) and you will have swallowed a good dose of vitamin C, beta-carotene, and quercetin, which is thought to lower cancer risk. A minute or two more, and you'll be feeling no pain at all — well, almost none. The capsaicin will have stimulated the production of endorphins, those friendly neurochemicals associated with a runner's high, and you'll smile happily while you dab away the tears. A cheap, healthy thrill. What more can you ask from a basic bowl of stew?

The first chili cookoff is legendary, pure Texas, the stuff of a chilehead's dreams. It was held in 1967, in a ghost town called Terlingua, once the site of mercury mines. Terlingua doesn't have much to recommend it but a few dust devils, a whole lot of short-tempered scorpions, and a wide-angle view of the Big Bend, off to the south. It was a good place to hold a cook-off because there weren't any law enforcement types in the immediate vicinity. Actually, there wasn't much of anything in the immediate vicinity, and the original contestants were encouraged to pack such survival items as a bottle of tequila, a shaker of salt, tarantula repellent, and a Terlingua first aid kit — a bottle of Jack Daniels and a bullet. Terlingua was, and is, one of the hotter hotspots in the entire United States. It was a fitting place for a bunch of good ol' chileheads to stoke up the chili-cookin' fires, uncork the tequila, and watch the world's biggest moon float across the world's biggest sky.

The fires of chili enthusiasm continue to burn hot in the hearts of Texans, and some sort of cookoff takes place here nearly every weekend between February and November. The last three decades have seen the flowering of the Chilympiad (in San Marcos), the Czhilispiel (in Flatonia), and the Howdy Roo (in Marble Falls), as well as the Cathedral Mountain Chili Cookoff and Easter Egg Hunt with Sunrise Services, the Caliente Classic, and the Fireant Chili Festival. Not to mention magazines — *Chili Pepper* is the current favorite of most chileheads — and the dozens of hot web sites on the Internet.

Now, all of this may strike you as a bit over the top, but it's the environment in which the Cedar Choppers Chili Cookoff has flourished since 1979. The cookoff itself is not as big as the Chilympiad in nearby San Marcos and not nearly as raunchy as Terlingua — after all, JuneFest is a family celebration, and Pecan Springs believes in family values. Still, the CCCC has a certain elemental rowdiness. Older residents, Methodists, and Baptists often skip the event, preferring to attend Friday night's crowning of Miss Pecan Springs and her court, the Saturday morning parade down LBJ Boulevard and around the courthouse square, and the traditional Saturday afternoon contests in Pecan Park: the lawnmower and wheelbarrow races, the horseshoe pitching tournament, the tortilla and cow pie toss, the rubber duck race. Of course, those who are interested in culture can stroll over to the Myrtle Masters Library and take in the exhibit on German Texas history (Pecan Springs was settled by German emigrants in the 1850s), or drop by the Myra Merryweather Herb Guild House and admire the gardens (especially the salvias and the yarrows, which put on quite a show in early June). The bored can listen to the Wilhelm Toepperwein Polka Band or the Freitag Fiddlin' Family (Mom and Dad, seven children, two cousins, and a nephew) and of course, watch the Chili Showmanship competition, which goes on for a couple of hours during the cookoff and consists of grown men making utter fools of themselves, to the chagrin of their spouses and the delight of everybody else. The hungry (and too faint-hearted to brave the chili booths) may sample the Kiwanis Club's bratwurst and sauerkraut; the Lions' barbecued brisket and funnel cakes; the Can-Do Club's fajitas, flautas, and curly fries; and the high school cheerleading team's Chocolate Covered Fruit.

But while Pecan Springs may be intent on celebrating its multicultural heritage, there is a certain contingent for whom the chili cookoff is the main attraction — in fact, the only attraction. This is the local pod of the Chili Appreciation Society, known as the Heart of Texas (HOT) Honchos. The HOT Honchos spend the week prior to the event building chili stands in the empty field across the river from the park, stringing extension cords, setting up the judging procedures, and bullying their children into working as parking lot attendants. For the past couple of years, the HOT Honchos (a male enclave) have been joined by two sister groups: the Salsa Queens, who sponsor the Hotter the Better Salsa Challenge; and the Caliente Cooks, who sponsor the Sweet Heat. Both of these cookoffs are open to men as well, just to show how generous the women are.

Thyme and Seasons is only a stone's throw from the square, and we're always busy on JuneFest weekend. This year, however, Laurel was taking care of the shop. I was McQuaid's official wheelchair pusher, and anyway, I was on assignment for the *Enterprise*. For my first Home and Garden page, Hark had put me in charge of collecting recipes from the winners of all three cookoffs. This would not be a piece of cake. Most cooks prefer to keep their recipes to themselves, or they've had too many longnecks and can't remember where they parked the pickup, much less how much of what went into the chili pot. Lore has it that most cooks don't know what went into the chili unless something turns up missing. (Cartoon: A cook asks his helper if he's seen the fuel for the cookstove. "Over there by the dog," the helper replies. The cook glances around. "Where's the dog?" They both peer into the chili pot and groan.)

But Hark wanted recipes, and I wasn't about to disappoint my new boss in my first big assignment. If I couldn't get them from the cooks, I'd pull some from my files or get them from Diana Finlay, Features editor at the San Marcos *Daily Record*.

Diana, whose husband, Kent, wrote the National Chili Anthem ("If You Know Beans About Chili, You Know that Chili Has No Beans") used to edit the *Chili Monthly*. It folded back in the mid-eighties, but copies should be around somewhere — in Diana's barn, probably. As I remembered, the magazine was full of great straightforward, no-nonsense chili recipes — real *Texas* chili, which is never gussied up with avocado, nuts, lime wedges, olives, cheese, or yogurt.

The Manor's van is available for residents' use, and at eleven on Saturday morning, I drove McQuaid to Pecan Park. We had not spent any time alone together since our argument over Brian's summer plans and I was determined that today — McQuaid's first public outing — was going to be a good one. I chattered gaily about the weather and the upcoming cookoff. McQuaid was morose.

"I feel like a freak at a sideshow," he muttered as the van's lift deposited him and his wheelchair on the ground. "Everybody's staring. They're feeling sorry for me."

"Bullfeathers," I said cheerfully, hooking my straw tote bag over the handles of his chair. "There are nothing *but* freaks at this sideshow. What makes you think you're anything special?"

McQuaid looked around. Maybe it's the smell of spicy chili sweetened by burning mesquite or the sight of fifty-plus teams of hairy-legged guys wearing shirts with such cerebral slogans as DEATH BY HABANERO and I'VE GOT THE HOTS FOR YOU, BABE. Whatever it is, there's something about a chili cookoff that has the power to transform even the gloomiest man into a fire-breathing, ripsnorting macho male. McQuaid was no exception, and the transformation from invalid to I'm-in-charge-here was immediate and interesting.

He pulled himself up straight in his chair and yanked the bill of his red cap down over his nose. "Shut up and push, Bayles," he growled. "It's time to get this show on the road."

"Push where?" I asked, looking around. We were standing on the outskirts of what looked like a five-acre hobo jungle, littered with cook tents, campers, lawn chairs, and Igloo coolers. Everywhere were little huddles of men with two-day beards, dressed in ragged blue-jean cutoffs and cowboy boots. They were hunched like Chuck-wagon Charlies over camp stoves, barbeque pits, and open fires, stirring the contents of fire-blackened Dutch ovens, the bottom half of rusty oil drums, olive-drab ammo cans, copper washboilers, and cast-iron kettles suspended from crooked tripods. The billowing smoke could probably be seen as far away as Dallas, and the hot air was redolent with the sweet-sour twang of local heroes George Strait, Willie Nelson, Waylon Jennings, Merle Haggard, Gary P. Nunn. It was Willie's picnic, Saturday night at the Gruene Dance Hall, and hamburgers at Dirty Martin's after the Rice blowout — all dumped into one crusty black iron pot, seasoned with serranos and habaneros, and cooked long and slow over a mesquite-and-dried-cow-pie fire under a blazing Texas sun.

"Where?" I repeated.

"Over there, on the other side of the porta-potties, past the EMS station." McQuaid pointed. "See that Honcho flag flying? That's the judging tent." He raised his arm, back in the saddle now, and enjoying it. "Mush, you husky! Home with the armadillos!"

I gritted my teeth and reminded myself that this was what I had wished for when I had left McQuaid lying on his back, staring dismally up at the ceiling. I mushed, shoving the wheelchair over the gravel as McQuaid smiled and waved to friends, exchanging greetings with people he hadn't seen since before the shooting. Somebody stuck a beer bottle in his hand and somebody else gave him a corn-dog on a stick, and he alternately swigged and munched while I kept pushing. He looked happy for the first time since February.

"Hey, Mike, glad t' see ya, ol' buddy."

Jerry Jeff Cody was sun-flushed, sweating, and heavily handsome in khaki shorts and a red T-shirt that boasted THE HOTTER THE BETTER, HONEY. He shifted a Coors from one hand to the other, giving me a dismissive glance and McQuaid's shoulder a solicitous pat. "C'n she handle that chair, fella, or you want me t' hunt up somebody with a little more muscle?"

McQuaid intercepted my snarl with a good-natured chuckle. "Believe China can handle it, ol' buddy. She's used to tryin' to push me around."

"Yeah. Ain't they all?" Jerry Jeff's smile went crooked. He paused, breathing heavily, and I could smell the beer from where I stood. "Say, M'Quaid, I need some advice. I've got this problem, y'see, an' you're an ex-cop. You could tell me what I ought to —"

"JJ, I want to talk to you."

The woman who had interrupted him was wearing the shortest of white shorts and the briefest of red halters. The earrings that dangled from her pretty ears were silver chile peppers, and a matching chile pepper nestled deep in her cleavage. She was blond, beautiful — and madder than a boiled squirrel.

Jerry Jeff frowned at her.

"Did you *hear* me, JJ?" Roxanne Cody demanded in a shrill, petulant voice. "I said we got things to talk about." She didn't even glance at McQuaid or me. In his wheelchair, he was probably below her line of sight, while the gray streak in my hair made me an older woman. The pair of us, a cripple and a crone, might as well have been invisible, for all the notice she took.

Jerry Jeff cleared his throat. "You wanna have a conversation, Roxie, you go see Charlie Lipman. I'm payin' him good money to talk to you."

Roxanne smiled, her lips like ripe habaneros. "You bet I'm talking to Charlie, sweetheart." Her voice dripped acid honey. "I been thinking 'bout what I found out last night, and I've decided that it throws a whole different light on our agreement."

She reached up, touched a red, saber-length fingernail to the tip of his nose and pushed, as if she were punching a button. "You tell that lawyer of yours that we're goin' back to square one on that measly little settlement you proposed. When we're finished, it's gonna be a whole lot bigger and richer and sweeter. Do you hear?"

Jerry Jeff stepped back, pale under his sun-flush. "Just a damn minute, Roxanne. You've already signed —"

"Have I?" Roxanne smiled sweetly. "But you wouldn't want me to go into court and tell the judge just how much income you failed to disclose, now, would you? I bet the first phone call you'd get would be from your friends at the IRS, wantin' their cut, plus penalties and interest. So you'd better tell Charlie Lipman that we've got ourselves a whole new ball game, and Roxie-baby's in charge of the rule book." Her voice hardened. "And while you're at it, you tell that little sexpot Felicia Travis to unpack her lace nighties. There's not going to be any around-the-world honeymoon cruise. When I get through with you, you'll be lucky if you've got enough left to get the two of you to Terlingua and back." With that parting shot, she sashayed away, hips swinging. Jerry Jeff stared after her, his jaw working. There was a tic in the corner of his eye, and I almost felt sorry for him. Almost, but not quite.

McQuaid chuckled dryly. "Yeah, ol' buddy. You got *some* problem." He glanced up at me, and I could read a quick affection in his look. Compared with the two of them, we were almost normal. "We'd better get over to the judging tent, China. It's almost noon."

"Roxanne?" With an effort, Jerry Jeff refocused his eyes on us. "Hell, she's not my problem."

"Oh, yeah?" McQuaid said. "Could've fooled me."

Jerry Jeff tried to laugh, but couldn't pull it off. "Yeah. Well, I've got a mess there, that's for sure. I've been thinkin' maybe the best way out is a hired gun. But that's not what's on my mind. Mike, buddy, I need some help."

McQuaid shifted in his chair. "Doesn't everybody?"

Jerry Jeff had the grace to look uncomfortable. "Listen, you used to be a cop. I need your advice."

"I'm retired." McQuaid looked down at the chair, and the good humor went out of his voice. "In more ways than one."

"Yeah, I know, but —" JJ stopped, swallowed, and tried again. "Listen, Mike, this is serious. Somebody is threatening me."

"No shit." McQuaid all but snorted. "What do you expect, Jer? I saw that look on her face. And to tell the truth, I don't blame her for being fed up. For Pete's sake, JJ, Felicia Travis can't be more than seventeen."

"Eighteen," Jerry Jeff said. "Listen, it's not Roxanne who's got it in for me."

"Who, then?"

Jerry Jeff suddenly remembered I was there. "After the judging," he said. "I'll buy you a beer and we can talk, alone. Okay?"

"Ask me later," McQuaid said. "I may not be able to talk after I've poured a gallon or two of the world's hottest chili down my throat. Come on, China. Get those dogies moving."

There were actually two Honcho flags (red chile peppers rampant on a green prickly pear pod) flying over two tents. One was the check-in tent, where the contestants were already bringing samples from their cook-pots to be logged in, with the help of a half-dozen women under Fannie's supervision. Edna Lund was organizing trays of samples, Lulu Burkhart was lending a hand, and even Roxanne Cody had been put to work, silver chiles and all.

The complicated procedures were established some years ago, after two or three untoward incidents demonstrated that a bunch of chileheads can't be trusted to play fair when the grown-ups aren't looking. At the meeting of head cooks that had taken place early that morning, each contestant received a 20-ounce foam cup (for chili), a quart jar (for salsa), or an eight-inch plate (for desserts). To the container was taped a coin envelope containing two slips of paper, each printed with the same number — the contestant's entry number. The contestant was supposed to sign and pocket one numbered slip, leaving the second in the coin envelope. As the filled containers were turned over to cookoff officials at the check-in tent, they were logged in by contestant number, renumbered with a felt-tip marker for easy reference, and placed in waiting boxes. When the boxes were filled, they were carried by table monitors to a nearby tent where the judges were at work.

The judging for all three contests was held in the second tent, where a horseshoe arrangement of tables had been set up under a trio of fans. Two teams of three chili judges (one for the preliminaries, one for the finals) were to be seated on one side of the horseshoe. Chairs were arranged for the three dessert judges on the other side, and for the three salsa judges at the end. Table monitors — Edna and Lulu Burkhart were two of them — were beginning to bring in the first round of entries but otherwise the tent was empty of spectators — except for me, and I had to show my press pass. Cookoff officials learned long ago that it's a good idea to keep the cooks out of the judging tent — behind a police line reinforced by rottweilers, if necessary. Judges face enough hazards without risking a confrontation with a cook whose chili they have spurned.

I pushed McQuaid to his appointed spot between the other two chili final judges, Darryl Perkins, the mayor's husband and a chilehead from way back, and Maude Porterfield. Maude has served as Justice of the Peace for well over half her seventy-five years and her impartiality — the most important quality in a judge — is beyond question. She has officiated at this event since most of the cooks were in high school and knows what to expect. She wore a red bib over her green print dress and presided with all the solemnity of traffic court.

A minute or two later, the last three

judges came straggling in — Bubba Harris, who looked like he'd much rather be out at the lake, catching bass; Fannie Couch, who had traded her post at the log-in station for a seat at the Sweet Heat table; and Jerry Jeff Cody, hot and bothered. I didn't wonder, after his sizzling encounter with Roxanne. I waved at Fannie and she gave me a salute.

When the judges were settled, it was time for the blessing, offered as always by the Reverend Roger Beadle, who was dressed in the rusty coat of an old-time circuit rider. Originally attributed to a black range cook named Bones Hooks, the prayer is a tradition at cookoffs from D.C. to L.A. Politically incorrect it may be, but the judges won't lift their tasting spoons without it.

The Reverend Beadle cleared his throat and raised both hands. "Lord God," he said, "you know us old cowhands is forgetful. Sometimes we cain't recollect whut happen yestiddy. We jes' know daylight an' dark, summer, fall, winter an' sprang. But we hope t'heaven we don't never forgit to thank you proper afore we eat a mess of good chili.

"We don't know why, in your wisdom, Lord, you been so doggone good to us.

The heathen Chinee don't have no red. The Frenchmens is left out. The Rooshians don't know no more 'bout chili than a hawg knows about a sidesaddle. Even the Meskins don't git a good whiff of chili less they lives round here. Chili-eaters is some of your chosen people, Lord. We don't know why you so good to us. But don't never think we ain't grateful for this here ver' fine chili we is 'bout to eat."

The Reverend Beadle's "Amen" was echoed around the tent, and it was time for the judges to pick up their pencils, study their judging sheets, and start tasting.

However pleasant such a job may sound, the judges are not out for a free lunch. They know the criteria (called the AATTA scale) by which the entries are evaluated — appearance, aroma, texture, taste, and aftertaste — and they know they're going to taste some pretty fine chili. But they also know that a few weird people enjoy putting bizarre ingredients into their chili, and that a certain percentage of the cups will contain an unsavory brew that smells like Mount St. Helen's, tastes like a toxic chemical dump, or has something swimming in it. These hazardous entries usually merit a quick stir with the tasting spoon, a hasty sniff, and a score of one or two on the ten-point scale. The salsa and Sweet Heat judges probably don't run the same risk as the chili judges because their cooks take their cooking a little more seriously. But by the end of the day even they would agree that you can have too much of a good thing — even chile peppers.

The judges began with enthusiasm, camaraderie, and a few unprintable remarks about the most unspeakable entries. A half hour later, they had settled doggedly to work, and all you could hear was pencils scratching and an occasional irate "What'n the Sam Hill is *this?*" I hung around to make notes for my newspaper article, and because I wanted to talk to Edna Lund, whom I had seen in the check-in tent, logging in the salsa and desserts and shuttling back and forth with boxes of entries to be judged.

I caught her when she wasn't busy and told her about the situation at the Manor. She was a little distracted by what was going on at the tables, but when I mentioned Carita's name, she gave me her full attention.

"Carita Garza?" She pushed her damp brown hair away from her face with the back of her hand. The judges were sitting under the fans, but it was hot as Hades everywhere else. My blouse was stuck to my back, and the sweat was running down my neck. "If that's true," Edna added, "I'm sorry. She's a good worker, and smart, too."

"Then maybe you'd like to help her out. You're at the Manor on a regular basis, and you know the staff. If Carita is innocent, you could do her a great favor by finding out who is really committing the thefts."

She looked uncertain. "How would I do that?"

"By asking questions and keeping your eyes open." She gave me a hesitant glance, and I reached for a strategy that might appeal to her experience. "Stay alert for anything suspicious, the way you would if one of your ranch employees had been stealing from you." It still sounded vague, and I felt uncomfortable. If Edna had been Ruby, I wouldn't have had to give her operating instructions. Ruby likes to think of herself as a detective. She would have jumped at the chance for an assignment like this, and would have come up with her own agenda in about thirty seconds.

Edna frowned. "The ranch was an entirely different situation," she said. "If one of the hands was stealing — and it happened, from time to time — I always knew it right away, and I gave the man exactly what he deserved, at the first opportunity. There was never any detective work involved." She hesitated. "Still, I hate to see Carita get into trouble. The Manor doesn't have enough good help. I suppose I can talk to Joyce about it."

"Thanks," I said, relieved. I had done my bit. Between them, Edna and Joyce could handle it. "I'm sure Joyce will be glad to —"

There was a commotion at one of the tables, and both of us turned. Jerry Jeff Cody was standing up, scrabbling with his hands at his throat, and gasping loudly. "Help!" he croaked. He did a clumsy backward two-step, and his chair fell over. "Help!"

Edna looked alarmed. "Is . . . is something wrong with him? Maybe we'd better call a doctor. It looks like he's *sick*."

"It's nothing," I said. "Every year, one of the judges gets up and jumps around like he's on fire. It's part of the show. Everybody thinks it's funny."

Edna stared for a moment longer, as if she didn't know whether to laugh or be worried. Then she turned away. "Grown men," she said disapprovingly.

"Musta bit on a chunk of chile pepper," Bubba Harris said. He slid a can of beer down the table in Jerry Jeff's direction.

"Wash it down afore it blisters your gizzard."

"Some of this stuff is hot enough to toast tonsils," Maude Porterfield said dourly. She blew her nose on a paper napkin. "Seems like it gets hotter every year."

"That's the problem," McQuaid said, making a note on his scoring sheet. "They think they lost last year because it wasn't hot enough, so they double up on the chiles."

Jerry Jeff's face was bright red and puffy, and his chest was heaving. He staggered backward and stumbled over his upended chair. He fell with a crash, beating his heels on the floor and grabbing at his throat, gasping and wheezing. One of the judges applauded, and another whistled. Edna started to say something, then stepped back.

Darryl Perkins looked down admiringly at the writhing figure. "That's some act, Jer old buddy." He turned to McQuaid. "Let's give this guy a showmanship prize, huh, Mac? You'd sure as hell think he'd scorched his gullet all the way down."

"Exaggerated, if you ask me," Maude said with an audible sniff. "Your performance last year was a lot more subtle, Mike."

Jerry Jeff squawked out something that sounded like "Aw, *nuts*," gave a last, profoundly disgusted kick, and lay still.

"Way to go, Cody," Bubba Harris said, and the rest of us laughed.

McQuaid frowned. "Nuts?"

"I wouldn't be surprised." Maude shuddered. "This is absolutely the last year I'm letting Jerry Jeff talk me into judging. After today, I quit. You guys can find another sucker."

McQuaid backed up his chair and wheeled over to the victim. "You okay, Jerry Jeff? Hey, get up."

"Yeah," Darryl Perkins said. "No fair you takin' a break while the rest of us are slavin' away." He got up and splashed half a bottle of Lone Star over the red-faced man on the floor.

Jerry Jeff didn't stir.

"Haul the sonofagun over by the door," one of the salsa judges said. "They can cart him out with the trash."

Somebody else guffawed. Then McQuaid suddenly shoved his chair around. "Medic!" he yelled. "Get somebody from the EMS in here, on the double! This is for real!"

I took two steps toward the door, but Edna had already beaten me to it. "I'll go," she tossed back over her shoulder.

The other judges jumped up and began to cluster around Jerry Jeff. Maude, an expert in such matters, knelt beside the prostrate man, her fingers on his carotid artery. "No pulse," she said calmly, after a moment. "He's not breathing."

"He's holdin' his breath," Darryl Perkins said. "When JJ was a kid, he could hold his breath under water longer'n any of us." He toed JJ with his cowboy boot. "Come on, fella. Get up."

Bubba helped Maude to her feet. "Looks like a heart attack to me," he said grimly. He looked around. "Where the hell are those medics?"

Darryl Perkins shook his head, chuckling. "Man oh man, he's good. He's got you guys fooled."

"We can't wait." McQuaid waved, galvanizing me into action. "China! Get over here and start CPR!"

I was on my knees over Jerry Jeff for the three or four minutes it took the volunteer medics to arrive on the scene, break out the defibrillator and the artificial airway, and get to work. But after three tries with the defibrillator — that horrible piece of equipment that looks and sounds like a medieval instrument of torture — the chief medic, a very young man, sat back on his heels and shook his head.

"Sorry," he said, to nobody in particular.

Maude looked at her watch. "For the record, we'll put it at 12:42. Somebody go get his wife. She was in the tent next door."

"Put what at twelve forty-two?" Darryl Perkins asked with a dazed look.

"The time of death, you idiot," Maude said sourly.

Chapter Seven

Ah, ha, Texas Red
Makes the heat devils dance in
  the brassy sky
The buzzards hover and circle and fly
They know pretty soon everybody's
  gonna die
From eatin' Texas Red
Try a bowl of Texas Red.

"Texas Red"
Ruby Allmond, 1977

"What a way to go," Bob Godwin remarked in a tone of lingering admiration. "Dead from a bowl of red." He took an order pad out of the back pocket of his faded jeans and glanced expectantly at the four of us gathered around the table. "So what'll you have?" He chuckled dryly. "Chili's real good today."

Hark leaned back in his chair. "A pitcher of beer and some nachos?" he asked the rest of us.

Ruby and I nodded, but McQuaid shook his head. "No nachos for me. I'll have a quart of milk. My tongue's scorched." He thumped his chest with his fist. "Heart-burn, too. Some of that stuff was down-right vile."

"Serves you right," Bob said cheerfully. "You want the best chili in town, you come here. Don't go foolin' around with them crazy amateurs. Remember whut happened to ol' JJ, God rest his ass." He cast an in-quiring glance around the table, checking for other orders, then pocketed his order pad. "Well, you know what they say about the bear."

"What do they say about the bear?" Ruby asked.

Bob shrugged. "Some days you get the bear, some days the bear gets you. Today it was the bear that got JJ." Having delivered that philosophical eulogy, he headed for the bar.

Bob is the proprietor of Bean's Bar and Grill, a tin-roofed stone building next to the MoPac tracks and across the street from the old firehouse. He sports a broken heart tattoo on one thick forearm and a coiled snake on the other and lives in a trailer with a yard full of goats. You can go to Bean's to play pool, throw darts at a poster of a former governor posed on a white Harley, watch the Aggies beat the 'Horns on the TV over the bar, or blow an entire week's ration of fat grams on one chicken-fried steak smothered in cream gravy, with a side of fries, onion rings, and Texas toast.

"I can't believe he's *dead*," Ruby said unevenly. She and Hark were going out later that evening, and she was dressed all in white, white gauzy skirt, off-the-shoulder gauzy blouse, white sandals. She looked cool and pretty, but flustered. "What *happened?* Was it the chili?"

"Yeah," Hark leaned forward on crossed arms, his round face serious. He had spent the day in Austin and, like Ruby, had just heard the news. "Did I get it right? You said he was poisoned?"

"I can't believe that," Ruby said. "Who in the world would want to kill JJ?"

"I didn't say anybody wanted to kill him," McQuaid replied carefully. "I'm guessing that he died of anaphylactic shock, an allergic reaction to some nuts that were in one of the chili samples. That's what I think he was trying to tell us, there at the end."

Aw, nuts, he had said. Or at least, that's what I had heard.

"Oh, so *that* was it." Ruby nodded, comprehending. "Poor JJ," she said. "I knew he was allergic to nuts. He mentioned it once."

"You knew him well?" Hark asked. He had his eyes on Ruby, and I read a real interest there — no jealousy, just curiosity. During the time I'd known Ruby, she'd had a couple of near-disastrous relationships with men and several casual ones that hadn't amounted to much. I found myself hoping that it would be different this time. There is a deep-down honesty in Hark, and a refusal to compromise his principles. I like him.

"No, not well," Ruby said absently. "Not enough to grieve, I mean." She was pleating one of Bob's cheap paper napkins between her fingers. "I guess it's not JJ's dying that bothers me so much," she went on after a moment. "It's more that . . . Well, you never dream that such a little thing can be fatal. To have your life snuffed out by a *peanut*. It sounds so . . . so trivial, somehow. Almost comic." She shook her head sadly and I shuddered, remembering the man writhing on the floor at our feet, clutching at his throat and gasping desperately for air, while we applauded his last agony. "It's too bad, really," she said, and put the napkin down. "Jerry Jeff Cody won't be remembered for what he did when he was alive. If it's true that he was killed by a peanut, that's what people will remember."

There was a long silence as we contemplated Ruby's remark. Finally, I said, "It certainly wasn't an easy way to go. I keep thinking that if we'd acted sooner, we might have saved him."

"Nobody knew what was really happening," McQuaid said quietly. "We all thought he was playacting, the way judges do sometimes. You've got to do something to break the tedium of sitting there all afternoon, dipping your spoon into that stuff."

"But . . . *how?*" Ruby asked. "I mean, how did he die? How does it . . . well, work?"

"The throat swells shut and the victim dies of asphyxiation," I said. A pinball player in the back of the room hit a jackpot, and the machine began to clang noisily. Somebody cheered. "It's a malfunction of the immune system. The body thinks it's being invaded and releases a large quantity of histamine. That's what does the damage. If the medics had shot him up with epinephrine, they might have saved him. But I asked afterward, and they said they didn't have it with them."

McQuaid cocked an inquiring eyebrow. "How do you know all that?"

"I read about it in a legal journal, in the

report of a suit against a restaurant. The victim had specifically told the waiter about her allergy, but nobody told *him* that the chicken had been cooked in peanut oil. She survived, and took home a whopping settlement from the restaurant's insurance company. The key evidence in the case was the waiter's note on the order he turned in to the kitchen. He wrote, 'allergic to nuts,' but nobody paid any attention."

Hark pushed his mouth in and out. "I've known Jerry Jeff for a lot of years," he said thoughtfully. "He developed that allergy way back when he was a kid. He'd bring it up every so often, so some well-meaning friend wouldn't accidentally hand him something with peanuts in it."

I looked at McQuaid, remembering something. "That's why he wouldn't accept a peanut from Jug, that time in your room at the Manor."

McQuaid nodded. "I don't suppose it ever occurred to him that anybody would put peanuts in chili."

"*Nobody* would put peanuts in chili," Hark said in a definitive tone.

"I know two people who would," Ruby said with a little laugh. She looked at me. "Lois Alpert —"

"And Barbara Holland," I added. "In fact, both of them were planning to enter the cookoff —"

"— until we told Lois it was only open to men." Ruby finished the sentence for me, leaning back so that Bob could put the beer and nachos on the table.

"Maybe they got some guy to enter their chili under his name," I said.

"Peanuts in chili?" McQuaid asked, amazed. "You've got to be kidding."

"Heck, no," Bob said. He took a bottle of hot sauce out of his back pocket and plunked it on the table. "I had chili once in San Diego with chopped-up peanuts sprinkled on top. Tasted Gawd-awful to me, but everybody else was slurpin' it up like it was good. And down in Mexico, folks dip whole peanuts in chile molido and eat 'em while they're drinkin' tequila." He looked at McQuaid. "I sent Budweiser to the Circle K for your milk. He'll be right back."

"Thanks," McQuaid said. Budweiser is Bob's golden retriever. He often runs errands to the Circle K on the other side of the tracks, wearing a leather saddlebag Bob stitched up for him and stamped with his name, with instructions and money in one of the pockets. Bob has taught him to stop and look both ways before he crosses the tracks, to make sure there's no train coming.

"You're welcome," Bob said. He looked around the table. "So what's all this about peanuts in chili?"

"That might have been what killed Jerry Jeff," McQuaid said. "He was allergic to them."

"No foolin'," Bob said, with interest. "Well, there ain't no peanuts in *my* chili, you're guaran-dam-teed."

Ruby pulled a cheese-covered nacho out of the pile and began to munch on it. "My Aunt Harriet used to work for the Oklahoma Peanut Commission. She always made chili with peanuts, and she'd put a jar of peanut butter on the table, in case it wasn't peanutty enough. Her chili won a contest in Tulsa once, and she got her picture in the paper."

"Oklahoma," Bob said with severity. "I knew it. It had to of been a Okie who killed poor Jerry Jeff." He wiped his hands on his apron and strode away, shaking his head.

Hark picked up the pitcher and began to pour. "So whose chili had the fatal nuts in it?" He handed me a mug, obviously waiting for an answer.

"You're asking me?" I said in surprise.

"How should I know?"

"Because you're the one who was supposed to collect recipes." Hark shoved my mug across the table, and pushed another toward Ruby. "Did you?"

"Oh," I said, in a small voice. "I guess I forgot. In all the excitement, I mean."

Hark rolled his eyes. "Some reporter you are, China Bayles. Give you an assignment and —"

"But I was only supposed to collect the *winning* recipes," I said. "As it turned out, nobody won. The surviving judges got nervous and called everything off. There's some talk about rescheduling, maybe in October."

"Still, we'd better have recipes," Hark said crisply. "Here we are, staring straight down the throat of the biggest Texas chili story anybody ever heard of, bigger than Terlingua, even. We have to cover it from every angle."

"Bigger than Terlingua?" McQuaid chuckled. "I doubt it."

Ruby leaned forward, her eyes narrowed. "What I want to know is whether anybody had the presence of mind to confiscate the chili samples Jerry Jeff had already tasted. It shouldn't be too hard to tell which one had the peanuts in it."

"Confiscate is not the right word," I said. "But yes, McQuaid did suggest to Bubba that the chili samples should be impounded and analyzed." Bubba, convinced that JJ had suffered a heart attack, hadn't seen any particular reason to go to the extra work. But to humor McQuaid, the cups had been gathered up.

Ruby cocked her head at McQuaid. "Did you have a special reason for suggesting it?"

"It just seemed like a good idea," McQuaid said slowly.

Ruby pounced. "*Why* did it seem like a good idea?"

McQuaid was silent for a minute. Then he glanced at me and shrugged. "I suggested it because Jerry Jeff told us that somebody was threatening him."

"Oh, yeah?" Hark swiveled around, suddenly intent. "Who?"

"Unfortunately," McQuaid said, "he didn't get around to naming names. He was saving that part for after the judging."

"But the murderer got to him first," Ruby said, and slammed her hand on the table. "I'll bet it was Roxanne! She hates him. He told me she thinks he's stashed a bunch of cash somewhere, just to keep it out of the divorce settlement."

"Nobody said anything about murder, Ruby," I said sternly.

"Where the hell is that dog with my milk?" McQuaid demanded. "Ah, there he is." He whistled and Budweiser trotted over and stood patiently while McQuaid undid the flaps of his saddlebag. He took out a quart of milk and rewarded the dog with a pat on the head and a nacho. "I could use somebody like you to retrieve for me, fella."

"You've got Howard Cosell," I reminded him.

McQuaid opened the carton and began to drink out of it. "Howard Cosell couldn't retrieve a dog biscuit if he and the biscuit were in the same phone booth. Besides, they won't let him into the Manor."

"Then come home," I said playfully. "I'll retrieve for you, if Howard Cosell won't." I gave him a more serious look. "It's going to be lonesome after Brian leaves tomorrow. I'll rattle around in the house, all by myself."

McQuaid didn't answer, and the silence was finally broken by Ruby, who asked of the table at large, "If nobody suspects murder, why did McQuaid confiscate the chili samples?"

McQuaid set down his milk carton. "You're jumping to conclusions, Ruby. Nobody *suspects* anything, let alone murder. The hypothesis is that the victim suffered an allergic reaction while he was eating chili. You don't need a degree in criminology to figure out that the chili should be analyzed and the victim should be autopsied. And that's all there is to it."

"But somebody put the peanuts into the chili," Ruby said. "That person is guilty of —"

"Bad taste," McQuaid said. "I vote we change the subject."

We ordered another plate of nachos and Hark told a couple of funny newspaper stories. McQuaid countered with one of Jug's jokes. Ruby reported that an architect friend wanted to draw up plans for the tearoom remodeling, and I reminded her that I had only said maybe, not yes and that we definitely needed to talk about it before getting other people involved.

"How about tomorrow afternoon?" she asked promptly.

"Fine by me," I said, and we agreed to four o'clock, at Ruby's house. After we finished the second round of nachos and beer, Hark and Ruby excused themselves. McQuaid looked suddenly gray with weariness, so I loaded him and his chair into the van and drove to the Manor. But be-

fore I opened the door, I turned to face him. Today's outing had been a good one, in spite of what had happened to Jerry Jeff. It was time to bring up the subject we'd been avoiding.

"You *could* come home, you know," I said, carefully casual. "You have the use of both arms now, and you're getting around really well in your chair. Maybe you'll even be walking in a few months. In the meantime, we could rent one of those beds that sings and dances and does massage, and put it in the downstairs guest room. And I'm sure we could locate a van with a lift, so I could drive you here for your therapy."

McQuaid said nothing for a long moment. "I wish I could come home," he said at last.

"Well, good." I managed a smile. "That's a first step."

"But I can't."

"Why not?"

He turned his head and looked out the window. A boat-tailed grackle, wings drooping, tail cocked at a ludicrous angle, was parading lustily in front of a group of watching females in the early evening sunlight. "Do you want the truth, China?"

"I —" I swallowed. Did I? "Yes. Yes, of course."

He spoke in an evenly measured tone that told me he'd already thought this through. "I can't come home because I can't face up to everything home means. Sleeping with you and not being able to make love. Watching Brian run around and not being able to run with him. Living in the house and not being able to do little chores. Having to . . ." He turned to look at me, not touching me, but holding my eyes. "Having to depend on you for everything — get out of bed, get dressed, go to the bathroom, even. I can't make you my caretaker."

That was it, then. I didn't know what to say, but I had to say something. "I don't mind," I replied inanely. "I want to help."

"*I* mind." His voice sharpened. "You don't understand everything that's involved in taking care of me, China. And as long as I'm here, I'm focused. I don't have to think about anything but doing the damn therapy and going to the bathroom and eating and sleeping." He pulled in a ragged breath. "I don't have to worry about what this is doing to you or Brian or Mom and Dad. I don't think about the past or the future. All I think about is right now, and legs that may never work right, and a body that —"

"But we have to think about the future. We have to talk —"

"Don't *push!*" he said angrily. "For God's sake, China, you ought to be able to understand without yanking the words out of me like bad teeth. You're the one who hates to be dependent. It kept you from marrying me."

"That was . . . different." I couldn't think how, but surely it was.

"I don't think so." He dropped his eyes. "Anyway, I think you ought to bail out."

"Bail out! You mean, break up?" I stared at him.

"It's not such a crazy idea. In fact, it makes good sense, all the way around." He put his hand on my arm, softening his tone. "Look. The way I am, the way I feel — it's not your fault, China. Nobody will blame you if you call it quits and get on with your life. We never got married, thank God, so we don't have to get a divorce."

I winced at his emphatic "thank God," and felt a deep, twisting regret. If I had married him when he asked, we wouldn't be having this conversation. He would be at home with me, where he belonged.

"It's not all that hard," he went on earnestly, "if we take it step by step. Brian will be at the ranch all summer. Next fall, he can move in with Mom and Dad and go to school in Seguine. You can find a smaller place for yourself, so you don't have that big house to take care of. Or you can move in with Ruby — she's got plenty of room, and she'd love to have you. I'll get somebody to pack up my stuff and put it in storage. Under the circumstances, the landlord isn't going to give us any trouble about the lease." His grin was crooked. "See? No big deal. No hard feelings. Just two people who have decided to call it quits."

"This is idiotic," I said flatly. "You're acting like you're the first man who's ever been disabled. The same thing has happened to other couples, and they've gone on with their lives, together."

"No hard feelings, no strings," he said, as if he hadn't heard me. "Just call the landlord and —"

I was suddenly, blisteringly angry. "No way, José," I snapped. "That house belongs to us, you and me and Brian. As soon as the doctor says it's okay, you're coming home. I don't care whether you're walking or crawling, or whether we make love or we don't." I spaced out the words. "You're coming *home*."

"But you don't understand, China." He

sounded despairing. "I don't want you feeling sorry for me. Or for yourself. I —"

"As soon as you can," I repeated fiercely. I leaned forward and kissed him, hard. "You stupid jerk."

Twenty minutes later, I was walking back to my Datsun, which had sat since morning under a cedar elm at the far side of the parking lot. It had been a long, hot, difficult day, and I was weary to the bone. I had laughed while a man died, and my lover had told me to get out of his life. I wanted to go home, make myself a stiff drink, and take it into a cool bath. I did *not* want to talk to Carita Garza, who was hunkered down beside my car, wearing rumpled green scrubs and dirty tennis shoes. She jumped to her feet when she saw me coming.

"Oh, Ms. Bayles," she said breathlessly, "I've been waiting to talk to you."

"Can't it wait until tomorrow?" I stuck the key in the door and turned it. "It's been a tough day."

"Please." Her voice was thick with tears. "Ms. Sanders says that you're a lawyer, and that you're very smart. That you help good people who are in trouble."

"I told Joyce Sanders I'd find somebody

165

else to help you." I saw the pain on the girl's face, and softened my tone. "And I did. I spoke to this lady about your situation this afternoon, and she's agreed to help." Well, not quite. But close enough.

Carita held herself tensely, her brown eyes large and dark above high cheekbones. "Who? Who did you talk to about me?"

I heard the half-fearful tone and wondered whether I should have been so free with Carita's story. "Edna Lund. You probably don't know her."

"Yes, I do." The fear seemed to lessen, but the tension did not ease. "How can she help me? She's just somebody who comes to read sometimes and talk to Miss Velma. She's not a lawyer." Carita said the word as if it were vested with some sort of magical power.

"I'm not, either."

Carita went on as if I hadn't spoken. "Ms. Sanders says you helped her friend. She says the lady would still be in jail if you hadn't found out who really killed that professor at the college." She looked at me, pleading. "I know you could find out who is stealing, and prove it's not me." Her brown eyes filled with tears. "If it's not too late."

"What do you mean, if it's not too late?"

She hung her head. "Mrs. Hogge fired me. She found a credit card in my purse. She said it belonged to one of the residents."

I frowned. "Where was your purse?"

"She got it out of my locker and took it to her office."

"She unlocked your locker?"

"She's got a master key, in case we lose ours." Carita became dreadfully earnest. "I didn't take the credit card, or anything else, Ms. Bayles, I swear it! My family depends on this job, and on me. I'd be a fool to risk losing it by doing something as stupid as stealing."

It was hard not to believe the girl's protests. If she were guilty, surely she wouldn't have appealed to me for help. And if her story was true, it raised several troubling questions. Why had the Manor's chief administrator decided to search Carita's locker at the very moment when the incriminating credit card lay in the girl's purse? Had somebody tipped her off? If so, who? Might the tipster have slipped the card into Carita's purse? And the search of Carita's locker, while not strictly illegal, was certainly unethical.

"She fired you — did she call the police?" I asked.

Carita shook her head. "I told her I wanted to talk to the police and get this thing straightened out. But she said she had enough evidence to prove to *her* that I was guilty and that it wouldn't look good for the Manor if the police got involved. She said they'd had enough trouble over the thefts already."

It sounded as if Mrs. Hogge needed a refresher course in employee rights. I looked at my watch. It was after seven. "I suppose she's already gone home."

Carita nodded tautly. "You *will* help me, won't you?"

"I'll do what I can," I said. "On Monday, I'll have a talk with Mrs. Hogge." In the meantime, I would check Carita's story with Joyce.

Carita sagged against the car in relief. "Oh, *thank* you, Ms. Bayles," she cried. "I know you'll make it all right."

Don't count on it, I wanted to say, but of course I didn't. I did what criminal lawyers always do to comfort their clients. I put on a confident smile, patted the girl on the shoulder, and told her to go home and get a good night's sleep and leave the worrying to me.

As if I didn't have enough to worry about.

Chapter Eight

Peppers range from brightly spicy little serranos and Thais to mysteriously smoky chipotles and dried fruit-flavored anchos. They can add an element of greater complexity to anything you cook, literally from soup to nuts, and they can be used as subtly or aggressively as any other spice once you understand how to cook with them.

Helene Siegel and Karen Gillingham
The Totally Chile Pepper Cookbook

Brian had wanted to hang around to enjoy JuneFest with his friends, but once the Saturday afternoon contests were over, he was anxious to leave. Leatha didn't make any secret of her eagerness to be gone, either. Since McQuaid had told me he'd given permission for Brian's summer at the ranch, I had felt betrayed, and she knew it.

But things didn't come to a head until the morning after the chili cookoff. Brian was getting the last of his gear together, and I was having a cup of mint tea in the kitchen, trying to decide which of my long list of chores I should tackle first. Laurel was taking care of the shop — we're open noon to five on Sundays, to catch the tourists — and I was meeting Ruby at four. Until then, I had the day to play catch-up.

Leatha came into the kitchen and set her cosmetic case on the counter. "I do hope you won't be lonely, here by yourself," she remarked in an offhand way.

"You might have thought of that," I said, "before you asked McQuaid to let Brian spend the summer with you. *After*," I added pointedly, "I had already said no."

Leatha looked apologetic. "I was only thinking of Brian. He is so deeply anxious about his father and —"

"I *know* he's anxious," I said. "That's why I want him here. So he can play a part in his dad's recovery. So he can cheer his dad up, help him get better."

"But I'm not sure Brian should take that kind of responsibility," she said quietly. "It's not fair to a child to saddle him — or her — with the task of making somebody else better." She paused for a moment. "I used you that way, when you were a child. It wasn't fair to you, either."

I was about to retort that the two situations were entirely different, when I remembered that not very long ago I had made exactly the opposite argument. This recollection took the words out of my mouth, and Leatha went on speaking.

"I think Brian will profit from a little distance on his father's disability. But he's not going to the South Pole — only to the ranch, which is less than ninety minutes away. Sam and I will make sure that he gets back for frequent visits, and Brian can phone whenever he wants to. Or he can e-mail his dad, if you can arrange for Mike to have a computer at the Manor."

"E-mail?" Brian said happily, from the door. "Cool!"

"We'll see," I said grudgingly.

Brian came to the back of my chair and hung around my neck. "I'm sorry I won't be here to take care of you," he said, in a troubled voice. "Maybe I shouldn't go. I know you'll be lonesome without me. And Dad, too. Especially Dad."

I heard it, then, very clearly, the same guilt and anxiety I used to feel when, in spite of all my efforts to take care of her, Leatha fell off the wagon again. I looked up and saw her watching, saw the concern in her face, and saw something else, too — regret, sadness, suffering. In that same split second, I saw myself, and all the ways I had punished my mother in retaliation for her abandonment of me, and I knew I didn't want to do that anymore.

I tugged Brian's arms loose and pulled him around so that I could see his face. "Lonesome?" I said. "Of course I'll be lonesome. And so will your dad. But every time we start to miss you, we'll think of you riding Rambo and swimming in that river, and we'll smile. And maybe before long, we can join you. We might even bring Howard Cosell," I added recklessly.

Brian brightened. "Really?" he asked. "You mean, Dad might be well enough to . . ." His voice trailed off. "I don't think so," he said, looking down. He ran his finger down the buttons of my blouse. "I don't think he *wants* to."

"I think he does." I touched his cheek tenderly. "Anyway, it's something to aim for. And in the meantime, I'll take the laptop out to your dad, so you can e-mail him whenever you feel like it."

His arms went around me, and I held him closely, this small, sweet, sweaty boy whom I loved more than I could ever have imagined possible. Then I gave him one last kiss, brushed the dark hair off his forehead, and stood up.

"Okay, kid, on your way," I said gruffly. "Promise you'll have fun."

"I promise." His grin was lopsided and his pale blue eyes — his dad's eyes — were wet. "Promise you'll call me if you need me," he said, in a very adult way. "I'll come home right away."

"Sure," I said. "But fun is more important."

"Don't worry," Leatha said, as he ran out of the room. "We'll take good care of him."

"Yeah," I said. "Thanks. Thanks for . . . everything." And then, not planning it, not thinking about it, I reached for her, and we stood there for a long moment, holding one another, not saying anything. When we let go, she was sniffling, and my throat hurt.

"I *do* love you, China," she said.

"Yeah," I said, feeling awkward but okay. "I love you, too." I couldn't quite bring myself to call her Mom, but I wanted to.

Leatha and Brian left about nine, and then I did what mothers usually do when the kids go away to summer camp. In the interests of health and safety, I cleaned Brian's room. I stripped his bed and filled a laundry hamper with the sheets and the clothes I picked up off the closet floor. Under Ivan's thoughtful gaze, I vacuumed the dust bunnies under the bed, raked Brian's sports cards into a box in the corner, and removed Einstein from his imprisonment in the closet to his preferred roost on the drapes. Cleaning the rodent cages on the shelf under the window is something I have to work myself up to. They weren't smelly enough yet.

I went downstairs to call Joyce Sanders, but drew a blank. She didn't come in on Sundays, and the woman at the nurses station flatly refused to give me her home number — with good reason, I thought. Well, there were other things I could do. I had just settled down at the kitchen table with a pile of invoices and the checkbook in front of me and Howard Cosell dozing on my feet, when the phone rang.

"Hi, China," McQuaid said, and then, without preamble, "I've been thinking." His voice held more energy than it had the night before, and he almost sounded like his old self. Had it been my adamant refusal to let him off the hook, or his reflections about JJ's death? My answer came in the next sentence. "I've been kicking myself all morning for not being smart enough to get JJ's score sheet so we could see which of the cups he had already sampled."

174

JJ's score sheet. I put down my pencil and leaned back in the chair. "Do you suppose Bubba took it when he cleared away the sample cups?"

"I doubt that he was interested enough to bother. He wouldn't have rounded up the cups if I hadn't pushed him."

McQuaid was right. As far as Bubba was concerned, JJ had come to a natural end. "The score sheet won't be much good without the log-in sheets and entry forms," I said. "If you're looking for the contestants' names, that is."

McQuaid thought for a moment. "Yeah, I guess that's right. The entries are double-numbered, so the judges won't know who cooked what chili."

"I'm not doing much until about four," I lied. Or rather, I was, but this took top priority. Top priority was anything that stirred McQuaid's imagination and jacked up his energy level. I switched off the calculator. The invoices could wait. "Want me to poke around and see if I can find any of that stuff?"

"Sure, if it's not too much trouble." His voice became tentative, hesitant again. "Did Brian and Leatha get off to the ranch this morning?"

"Yeah, about an hour ago. I'm going to

bring you the laptop so you two can do e-mail." I paused. "Actually, I've decided that it's a good idea for Brian to go. He needs to get away from both of us. And I'm sure he'll have a good time."

There was a moment's silence. "I hope you're not just saying that to make me feel better. I shouldn't have gone behind your back in the first place."

"I should have said yes in the first place," I replied. But if I'd said yes, I might not have learned what I learned this morning, about Leatha and me. Sometimes you have to make a mistake in order to get it right. Sometimes it's *only* your mistakes that lead you to get it right, sooner or later. I might have said all this to McQuaid, but it was complicated. Anyway, it was a very personal enlightenment. You have to make your own mistakes to appreciate the revelation — somebody else's mistakes just seem dumb.

I heard him let his breath out. He sounded relieved. "Yeah. Listen, China. About last night —"

"The only thing we have to know about last night," I said, "is that I love you. Brian loves you. We want you home, as soon as you can get here."

I could almost hear the grin. "I'm a jerk."

I chuckled. "Well, we're agreed on one thing."

"Okay, Sherlock. Let me know when you find that score sheet."

"Will do," I said cheerily. I hung up and went to look for the laptop computer. It had once belonged to Roy Adcock, a former Texas Ranger whose suicide had been the precipitating event leading to McQuaid's shooting. His widow had given it to me before she left Pecan Springs for a new life on an herb farm in New Mexico. I put it in the car and headed out to the park to look for the score sheets.

But a half-hour later, I was calling McQuaid on the cell phone (a device of the devil, but necessary in emergencies and often handy otherwise) to say that the clean-up crew was already at work. The tents were gone. All I could see were trash cans surrounded by drifts of litter.

"Actually, the place looks like it was slammed by a tornado," I said, glancing around. "Not a sign of a score sheet any-where."

"It was a long shot." he said, matter-of-factly. "Thanks for making the effort."

"I'm not finished yet," I said. "I'll give Fannie Couch a call. She was in charge of the tent where the cooks were logging in.

Maybe she knows what happened to the score sheets."

Fannie wasn't home, but her husband, Clyde, knew where she was. "I took her over to the station a little while ago," he growled in his gravelly voice. "If you'll turn on your radio, you can listen to her. She's sitting in for the guy who reads the Sunday paper on the air. His wife is having a baby." He paused. "Hey, if you talk to her, remind her that she's supposed to be in San Antonio by twelve-thirty, and it's an hour's drive down there. I'll pick her up out front."

When I turned the car radio on, Fannie was indeed reading. In fact, she was already several paragraphs into the *Enterprise*'s story on the death of Jerry Jeff Cody.

"Mr. Cody, one of Pecan Springs' leading citizens," she read in her dry Texas twang, "expired despite Herculean efforts to revive him. The tragic event occurred during the judging of the Cedar Choppers Chili Cookoff on Saturday, before a startled group of Mr. Cody's friends and other intimates." (I guessed that the article had been written by one of the CTSU student reporters who do their journalism internships at the paper.) "Police Chief Bubba Harris, who was on the scene at the time of death, is quoted as saying that Mr. Cody died of a heart attack. Several other witnesses said that medical attention was delayed because everyone thought the victim was pretending to be ill. 'We all thought it was part of the fun,' one grieving friend said sadly. 'Jerry Jeff, he was a born practical joker — loved gettin' under people's hide and watchin' 'em squirm.' Justice of the Peace Maude Porterfield, who was also present when Mr. Cody died, is deferring her determination of the cause of death, pending autopsy results."

Fannie coughed delicately. "Mr. Cody, who was thirty-eight, was a partner in Cody and Clendennen Insurance Company and was widely respected for his dynamic participation in many affairs throughout our city, including the HOT Honchos, who sponsored yesterday's chili cookoff. He is survived by his grieving wife, Roxanne Cody, and his parents, of Texarkana. Arrangements are pending at the Mortimer Brothers Funeral Home."

You might fault the style, but the reporter got most of the facts straight. It was true that Bubba believed the death to be a natural one, that people had thought it was part of the fun, and that JJ was known for his dynamic participation in affairs. Fannie paused, then cleared her throat and went on to a lighter subject, the outcome of the tortilla and cow pie toss that took place at the very moment of Jerry Jeff's untimely death. By the time I drove into the parking lot a few minutes before eleven, she was wrapping up the show with one last article, a report on the triumphant conclusion of JuneFest and the crowning of the new queen.

KPST Radio, Your Friendly Hill Country Family Station, is housed in a green concrete block building surrounded by sprawling cedar shrubs and youpon holly bushes, at the end of Imogene Lane. Nothing much happens there on week-ends, and the tiny reception room was dark and empty. I opened a door and went down a low-ceilinged corridor toward a lighted control room. I waved through the glass at Henry Morris (KPST's station manager, sound engineer, newscaster, and weatherman, as well as bookkeeper and oc-casional lawn-mower). Henry gave me a thumbs-up, indicating that it was okay to go into the sound room next door, where Fannie was taking off her earphones.

She looked surprised to see me. "What brings you to the station on a Sunday, China?" she asked. She was dressed in mauve today — a silky mauve print dress trimmed in lace, pale mauve stockings, mauve suede shoes. A man's straw hat garnished with purple and pink pansies hung from the mike boom. A little old lady with a difference.

"McQuaid asked me to hunt up the score sheets from yesterday's judging," I said. "Do you happen to know where they are?"

Fannie cocked an eyebrow. "Matter of fact, I do. I collected them before they could get scattered and lost, and they're still in my bag." She began to rummage. "Mind my asking why Mike wants them?"

"Well —" I said.

She stopped searching and looked at me. "I thought so. When Jerry Jeff was a kid, his mama didn't dare keep a jar of peanut butter in the house for fear he'd get into it and have one of his wheezing spells. Face swelling up like a horny toad, choking in his throat. You ask me, that's what killed him. Nuts in the chili."

"Did any of the contestants mention using nuts as a secret ingredient when they gave you their samples?"

She laughed shortly. "If somebody put peanuts in chili, he wouldn't be likely to say so out loud. Folks might do that north of the Red River, but not down here." She dove into her bag again and came up with a manila envelope. Handing it to me, she said, "You know the entries are double-numbered?"

I nodded. "To figure out who cooked what chili, we need to look at the cup number on the score sheet, then trace it back to the log-in sheet."

"Right. The log-in sheet has the contestant's number on it. The entry form has the number and all the other stuff — name, address, and so on." Her shrewd gray eyes were inquiring. "So McQuaid's looking for the chili with the nuts in it?"

"I think that's what he has in mind," I said. "But I have another purpose. I'm supposed to come up with some recipes for the new Thursday Home and Garden page. I thought I'd give some of these guys a call."

"Good luck," she said. She took the hat off the mike boom and set it on her head at a rakish angle. A cluster of silk pansies hung down over one ear. "By the way, Edna Lund called me this morning. She said that Carita Garza is in some kind of trouble out at the Manor." Fannie looked grave. "Too bad if she is. She's a good girl, in a tough family situation. Daddy in prison, mama on the bottle. The kid needs a helping hand."

I sighed. I'd been trying to forget that I had planned to talk to both Joyce and Mrs. Hogge about Carita. "I'm afraid it's going to take more than a helping hand," I said. "Mrs. Hogge, the Manor's chief administrator, fired her yesterday."

"No!"

"Yes. Hogge searched the girl's locker and found a stolen credit card in her purse."

"Oh, my," Fannie said sadly. "Sounds bad."

"It *is* bad. Carita denied that she had taken the card and asked Mrs. Hogge to call the police. Hogge refused, and fired her. The whole thing struck me as basically unfair, and I promised Carita I'd look into it."

Fannie sighed. "Well, I understand why Opal Hogge doesn't want the police messing around out there. She's probably afraid —" She stopped, frowning. "On the other hand, maybe I shouldn't —"

"Yes, you should," I said. "And don't tell me to wait for your radio program. What is Opal Hogge afraid of?"

She was about to tell me, but Henry Morris chose that moment to open the sound room door. "Hey, Fannie, Clyde's here to pick you up. He says for you to get out to the car on the double. You've got to get to San Antonio."

"Oops!" Fannie grabbed her bag. "I forgot all about San Antonio. I've got to give a talk at an AARP meeting. Call me this evening, China."

"Wait a minute," I said urgently. "What is Opal Hogge afraid of?"

But Fannie was on her way out the door, mauve pansies bobbing excitedly over the brim of her hat. "Sorry," she called over her shoulder. "It'll have to wait."

Chapter Nine

Chili Queen Chili
traditional Texas chili recipe
from the Institute of Texan Cultures

2 lb beef shoulder cut into
$1/2$ in. cubes
1 lb pork shoulder cut into
$1/2$ in. cubes
$1/4$ cup suet
$1/4$ cup pork fat
3 medium onions, chopped
6 cloves garlic, minced
1 qt water
4 ancho chiles
1 serrano chile
6 dried red chiles
1 tbsp comino seeds,
freshly ground
1 tbsp Mexican oregano
salt to taste

Place lightly floured beef and pork cubes with suet and pork fat in heavy chili pot and cook quickly, stirring often. Add onions and garlic and cook until they are tender and limp. Add water to mixture and simmer slowly while preparing chiles. Remove stems and seeds from chiles and chop very finely. Grind chiles in molcajete *(mortar and pestle). After meat, onion, and garlic have simmered about one hour, add chiles. Grind comino seeds in* molcajete *and add oregano with salt to mixture. Simmer another 2 hours. Remove suet and skim off some fat. Serve.*

I stopped at the Diner for a bowl of tomato soup, a ham sandwich, and a few words with Docia — Lila's daughter and the lunchtime cook — about the hazards of eating unidentified chili made with alien ingredients. Docia is a short, plump woman in her forties with a cheerful face, red from being toasted over the grill, and a quick, alert glance. If this had been *Murder She Wrote,* she would have given me some sort of lead that I could pass along to McQuaid, but it wasn't and she didn't. We traded regrets about Jerry Jeff's untimely and unusual death, I asked about her mother's health, and that was that. Except that I happened to remark that the tomato soup was very good. She said she'd put basil in it, I said I'd give the soup a plug in my newspaper column, and she said in that case, it was on the house. When I left, I was beginning to see that there might be some reward for writing the column after all.

Jug Pratt had gone to visit his brother for the day, and McQuaid was alone in the room, watching a golf tournament on television. He switched it off when I came in, shortly after noon. I had phoned him from the car, so he knew I had the score sheets.

"Good job, China," he said, as I opened the envelope and began to sort papers into stacks on the bed, score sheets in one pile, log-in sheets in another, entry forms in a third.

"Fannie said she gathered up the papers because she didn't want them to get lost," I said, "but I think she suspected something." I glanced at him. "Do *you?*"

He leaned back in his wheelchair. "If it hadn't been for Jerry Jeff's remark," he said, "I might chalk up his death to an unfortunate accident. But he did say that somebody was threatening him, and I don't think he was joking." McQuaid quirked an eyebrow. "Still . . . peanuts in the chili? Seems like a haphazard sort of way to knock somebody off."

"But that's what's interesting about it," I said. "It could be the perfect crime."

"Unless we can find out whose chili had the peanuts in it."

"Even then," I said, "the State would have to uncover the motive and prove intent."

He gave me an amused glance. "It's a case that some bright defense lawyer could have all kinds of fun with."

"Well, here are Exhibits A through Z," I said, gesturing at the piles of papers on the bed. I handed him Jerry Jeff's score sheet. "And here's the list of what JJ sampled before he died, with his comments. He wasn't terribly impressed by the quality of the entries, I gather."

"Most of the stuff was pretty bad," McQuaid said. He studied the score sheet, and I came around behind him and looked over his shoulder.

In the half hour or so he had worked, Jerry Jeff had sampled fifteen different cups of chili. He hadn't scored any of them above a seven on the AATTA scale. In the "Comments" section, he had written general remarks like "awful!!!" and "mediocre." Nowhere had he written the word "nut" or "nutty," or commented on the texture of a particular sample.

"Not much help here," McQuaid said, "except to narrow down the field. At least we know which of the cups he sampled."

I grinned. "Surely you weren't expecting

him to write something like 'This stuff will be the death of me.' "

"Smart ass," McQuaid said. He pushed himself over to the bed, where the papers were stacked. "Let's go through the registration forms and match up these fifteen samples with the contestants, to see if we recognize anybody connected with Jerry Jeff."

It took a little while, but when we were finished, we had fifteen entry forms, cross-matched through the log-in sheets to the numbered sample cups listed on Jerry Jeff's score sheet. The entry forms included the contestants' names, addresses, and phone numbers.

"Here's Pokey Clendennen," I said, leafing through the stack.

"Oh, yeah?" McQuaid said. "I didn't know he was a chilehead. I don't think he's entered the cookoff before."

"Maybe he had another reason for entering," I remarked. I handed McQuaid the forms and watched him shuffle them. His eyes were intent, his face full of interest. I was sorry that Jerry Jeff was dead, but glad that McQuaid was coming to life. "Find anybody else you know?"

"Several guys from the Honchos, most of them friends of JJ's. Otherwise, I don't

—" McQuaid stopped and tapped one of the forms. "Wait a minute. Here's Craig Burkhart. He and Jerry Jeff mixed it up in a lawsuit a year or so ago. I think there's still bad blood between them."

I frowned. "Wasn't it something about a piece of property?" I paused. "There might be another connection between them, too. Lulu Burkhart."

"Oh, yeah?" McQuaid shook his head. "Jerry Jeff got around, didn't he? I wonder who else's wife he was involved with."

"Fannie Couch is the one who told me about Lulu," I said. "I can ask her if she's heard any other names in the past year or so. And for information about the lawsuit, we can talk to Charlie Lipman. He's Jerry Jeff's lawyer."

"Oh, yeah? Where'd you hear that?"

"Don't you remember? Jerry Jeff told Roxanne to talk to Charlie about the divorce settlement. If Charlie didn't handle the lawsuit, he'll probably know who did."

"Okay," McQuaid said, "I'll phone Charlie. I'll also talk to Pokey Clendennen and Craig Burkhart. Burkhart tried to sell me some investment property once, and our paths have crossed from time to time." He pulled out two forms and handed me the rest. "You take these."

I sighed. "I was afraid you were going to say that. Thirteen calls? I'll be on the phone all afternoon." I looked at my watch. "Scratch that. I have to be at Ruby's by four."

"Sorry, China." McQuaid gave me an apologetic look. "I'd do it, but you've got the cover. Just tell them you're collecting recipes for your column in Thursday's paper. They'll be glad to hand them over, just so they can see their names in print."

"Except for the killer, who will probably lie. However," I added thoughtfully, "if somebody tells me there's no peanuts in his entry and the analysis turns up peanuts in his chili, he's a pretty good candidate, wouldn't you think?" I put the rest of the papers back into the manila envelope and laid it on top of McQuaid's chest of drawers. "Oh, by the way," I remarked casually, "Brian says he'll e-mail us from the ranch. I've got the laptop out in the car. Want me to bring it in?"

"That'd be good," McQuaid said. He was reaching for the phone beside his bed. "Surfing the web doesn't take a lot of muscle, and it'll give me something to do when I'm not torturing my legs on those damned machines."

I smiled. The exercise machines were

only part of it. Getting McQuaid involved with the computer again would help to pull him back into real life. Things were looking up.

All of the calls I had to make were local, so I went out to the car to use the cell phone, opened both doors to let the breeze through, propped both feet on the dash, and settled down to my chore. Half an hour later, I stopped to make a tally. I'd done pretty well. I had struck out on two (ten rings, no answer), left one message on an answering machine, and managed to talk to ten of the thirteen contestants.

Of the ten, eight promised without hesitation to phone, fax, or mail me their recipes, expressing eagerness to have their chili immortalized in the newspaper. The other two confessed that they didn't have recipes but would give the matter some thought and reconstruct a list of the ingredients. One sounded particularly troubled. It turned out that he'd celebrated a bit too enthusiastically the night before the cookoff and hadn't been able to crawl out of his sleeping bag, much less stand over a bubbling cauldron all morning. His nephew had done the actual cooking, and he had no idea what might have jumped into the pot. The nephew had lost his wristwatch, and he himself was missing a T-shirt.

None of the ten laid claim to any exotic ingredients, except for one guy who used a mixture of ground buffalo and beef kidney suet, another who admitted that he'd thrown in a package of moldy cream cheese he found at the bottom of the cooler, and a third who claimed that he always threw in what was left of the breakfast coffee, including the grounds. Nobody mentioned anything about peanuts until I prompted them with a casual question and got in return a volley of hoots and hollers and an incredulous "Peanuts? In chili? Who you tryin' to kid?" If peanuts or peanut butter had been somebody's secret ingredient, he was not going to share that fact with the masses.

I was on my way back to McQuaid's room with the entry forms and the laptop when I thought of Carita Garza. I turned around and went back to the hallway where the administrative offices were located, but Opal Hogge's door was locked and nobody answered my knock. As I went past the nurses station, I was stopped by a short, dark young woman with long hair braided into two plaits down her back and tied at the ends with green yarn. Like the other aides, she was dressed in green scrubs and tennis shoes.

"Excuse me," she said in a low voice, "but aren't you Ms. Bayles?"

I nodded. "I signed in once already, earlier, if that's what you're asking."

"No, nothing like that." She glanced over her shoulder, put her hand on my arm, and pulled me into a small room that held a refrigerator, a sink, and a microwave. On the door of the refrigerator was a hand-lettered sign that exclaimed, "Do NOT Steal Food From People's Lunches!!!"

"My name is Angie," she said. "I'm Carita's cousin. She said you promised you'd help her get out of trouble, and I wondered . . . have you talked to Mrs. Hogge yet?"

"I won't see her before tomorrow." I studied the girl. With her narrow face, high forehead, and olive skin, she resembled Carita, although she wasn't quite as pretty. "Do you have any information?"

"I'm not sure." Her face was troubled, her eyes half-fearful. "If you mean, do I know who's stealing, no. But I thought if you were going to see Mrs. Hogge . . . that is, it might help if you knew . . ." She managed a tiny smile. "Excuse me," she said. "I'm a little nervous."

"I'm sure you want to help Carita," I said, to prompt her.

"Oh, yes, I do!" she exclaimed. "But if Mrs. Hogge found out that I was the one who told you, she'd fire me, too. And if you mention it to her, or confront her about it, she's just going to deny it. So I'm not sure that telling you this will do any good."

"Telling me what?" I asked, feeling frustrated. "Look, Angie, if you want to help Carita, you're going to have to give it to me straight. With specifics."

She considered for a moment, then seemed to decide that I could be trusted. She took a deep breath and plunged in. "It's about Miss Velma. Velma Mayfield. She has early-stage Alzheimer's. Half the time she can't remember where she is or what's going on. And if she wants something, she thinks it's hers." She shook her head. "It's enough to break your heart. She's really not that old, and she used to be very smart. She still tries to read, but most of the time she's holding the book upside down."

Light-fingered, Jug had called her. "Do you suspect Miss Velma of the thefts?"

"She might have taken a few things," Angie said hesitantly. "Mr. Purtle's Walkman, maybe, or Miss Curlew's bath bag —

stuff that's missing from this wing. But I don't think she could have wandered around in Rio Grande without being noticed. And if she took things, what did she do with them? Her room has been searched a time or two and nothing's turned up."

"Well, then, what's the problem?"

Her eyes darkened. "Miss Velma has an ornery streak, you see, and she talks back to people. She makes . . . well, personal remarks, some of them pretty nasty. Most of us just brush it off, because Alzheimer's sometimes works that way, and you can't be mad at a person for what they can't help. But Mrs. Hogge really gets furious. They must have known one another a long time ago, because Miss Velma is more familiar with her than with the rest of us."

"Familiar?"

Angie cleared her throat. "Well, yes. Miss Velma calls her Opal, which is Mrs. Hogge's first name, and sometimes she calls her Bunny, which must be a nickname or something. And she says things like, 'If you're not good, I'll tell your daddy what you did' — you know, stuff like that, in a childish, taunting kind of way."

"And that makes Mrs. Hogge angry?"

"Oh, yes! Friday morning — day before

yesterday — I opened Miss Velma's door and saw Mrs. Hogge *shaking* her. She had her by the shoulders and she was jerking her like a rag doll. Miss Velma was crying and her roommate was trying to get out of bed and make her stop." She grimaced. "I guess Mrs. Hogge didn't hurt Miss Velma, but she might have."

You bet. I had read of far too many cases of serious injuries to the brains of children and elderly people caused by the relatively simple act of shaking them. It could be a deadly act. "What did you do?" I asked quietly.

"She turned around and I was afraid she saw me. But I shut the door fast, and I don't think she knew who it was. If she did, I'm sure I would have heard about it already."

I regarded Angie thoughtfully. It was possible — just marginally possible, I thought — that she was making this up to cause trouble for Opal Hogge, who had fired her cousin. "You mentioned the roommate. Would she be able to say what she saw?"

"Mrs. Rogers?" Angie frowned. "Well, maybe. She has Alzheimer's too, but she has moments when she's fairly lucid."

"Have you reported the incident to Ms. Sanders?"

Angie shook her head. "I . . . I haven't told anybody. Even if Miss Velma could tell what happened, nobody would believe her. And if Mrs. Hogge found out I was making accusations, she'd fire me, for sure! Just like Deena, who worked in the kitchen. One of the freezers went out and the food thawed, and Mrs. Hogge fired her for failing to report faulty equipment."

Not a woman your heart might warm to, I thought. "Still, it would be a good idea if you told Ms. Sanders."

Angie nodded miserably. "I'm sure you're right. But Mrs. Hogge pretty much has the last word around here, and nobody wants to get in her way." She chewed a corner of her lip. "I was trying to figure out what to do when Carita told me about you and how you got that lady out of jail, and I thought . . ." She pondered a moment. "Well, I thought if you knew what Mrs. Hogge had done, you might be able to put some pressure on her or something. She can't fire *you*."

Pressure? That would be blackmail. But I don't think that was the way Angie meant it. She wasn't exactly in a position of power, and it was probably the only way she could think of dealing with a supervisor who seemed to her both irrational and vindictive. I was beginning to be very curious about Opal Hogge.

"Anyway," Angie said, looking at me with something close to relief. "I feel better now that I've talked to you. I mean, maybe you can't do anything, but I feel better."

"Thanks," I said dryly. "You're going to be here tomorrow morning?"

"I come in at seven."

"Good. I'll think about what you've said. If I decide that Ms. Sanders should hear it, will you tell her?"

She pulled one braid over her shoulder, twisting it in her fingers. "I . . . suppose," she said reluctantly. "If you say so. But I don't want to get into trouble with Mrs. Hogge."

"I understand," I said. "One more thing. What's the number of Miss Velma's room? I might want to stop in and see her."

"She's in Brazos, Number 33."

"Thanks," I said, and patted her on the shoulder. But I refrained from telling her that I would do the worrying for her. I already had enough worrying to do.

Chapter Ten

The Aztecs believed the chile pepper to be a powerful sexual stimulant, and early Spanish priests cautioned against its use, claiming that it "inciteth to lust."

Elizabeth Rozin
Blue Corn and Chocolate

Chile has long been the source of laughter for us in these rugged [Sangre de Cristo] mountains where a well-honed sense of humor is a survival skill. The popular identification of chile with the male member has spawned a plethora of chistes *[jokes], like the joke about the* politico *who takes a bathroom break during a campaign rally on one of our bitterly cold nights. When the man using the urinal next to him remarks, "Pretty chilly, Senator," the* politico *replies, "Gracias."*

Jim Sagel
"Chile del Norte"
New Mexico Magazine

McQuaid hit the mute button on the remote control when I came into the room. "What took you so long?" he demanded.

"Hey," I said. "I had thirteen confessions to hear, plus one nurse's aide to absolve. You didn't expect me to finish in fifteen minutes, did you?"

"What's this about a nurse's aide?"

"Later." I put the laptop on the floor, perched on the corner of his bed, and propped my feet on the arm of his wheelchair. "How'd you do?"

"Well, I talked to Charlie Lipman. Turns out that he was Cody's lawyer in that suit. It was a dispute over some commercial property. Burkhart lost, but not graciously. He threatened to get even." McQuaid paused meaningfully. "Charlie said he didn't think the animosity had died down any. I kept my mouth shut about Lulu, but I wondered if that had something to do with it."

"I suppose he was curious about your interest in Jerry Jeff's affairs. What did you tell him?"

"The truth. Jerry Jeff told me that somebody had threatened him, and forty-five minutes later he was dead. Charlie said he might have some information he could share, but he'd like to think about it until tomorrow."

"Typical lawyer's response," I said.

"Never make a statement today that you can put off until tomorrow."

"Yeah. Well, that's as far as we got. But there's no hurry. This isn't the kind of case where the murderer is likely to hop a plane for Mexico." His face grew serious. "I don't know. Maybe I'm bored and grabbing at something to do. Maybe I'm making a mountain out of a molehill."

"I don't think so," I said. I didn't want to lose the momentum. I loved the energy in his voice, the interest he was showing. Maybe we were spinning our wheels, but who cared? We were headed in the right direction. "How about Burkhart and Clendennen? Did you connect with them?"

"Clendennen said he'd get you that recipe if you'd stop by the insurance office and pick it up after noon tomorrow. He's got to go to Austin, and won't be back until then." He paused. "Lulu Burkhart says Craig is in Houston and won't be back until tomorrow afternoon. Actually, his chili recipe turns out to be *her* recipe, because this was his first cookoff and he had no idea how to go about it. She'll be happy to give you a copy for your column." He gave me a glance. "She also volunteered the information that Craig doesn't eat chiles and has never been all that crazy about the chili cookoff."

"Interesting," I said. I took out my notes and gave him a quick rundown on my telephone calls. "I didn't find out anything of particular value," I concluded, "but if these guys come through, at least I'll have enough recipes for my newspaper page. And as you pointed out, this gives us some baseline data. If one of those samples turns out to have nuts in it —"

"Yeah," McQuaid said. "Nothing to do but wait for the results of the analysis, I guess. And the autopsy, of course. It might just turn out that Jerry Jeff choked to death on a chunk of hot pepper. Or that Bubba was right, and he suffered a heart attack."

"Speaking of Bubba," I said, "are you going to tell him about those threats?"

His look was mildly incredulous. "You don't think I'd obstruct justice, do you?" I laughed, and he added, "But there's no point in complicating Bubba's life until we see the autopsy report. He's in no mood for frivolity, believe me. The Council hired some big-city consultant to come in this week and do sensitivity training with the force."

There was a sympathy in McQuaid's voice that I did not entirely share. I don't exactly dislike Bubba Harris, especially since I found out that he keeps bees for a hobby, and I certainly have my reservations about the Council's getting tangled up in police business. But Bubba's had things his way for fifteen years, which means fifteen years of a mostly white, mostly male police force in a town that is at least half female and one-fifth Hispanic. There are quite a few people who would like to hire a police chief who could be responsive to the entire community. I'm one of them.

"While we're waiting for the results," McQuaid went on, "maybe you could have a talk with Jerry Jeff's widow."

"I suppose you're interested in the fallout from the divorce settlement," I said thoughtfully. That was what interested me, anyway, especially Roxanne's charge that Jerry Jeff had failed to report all his income. It isn't unusual for an about-to-be-ex to hide a big hunk of his (usually his but not always) assets from the other party. The situation has a little more resonance, though, when the income has been concealed from the avaricious eyes of the Internal Revenue Service.

"The settlement, plus anything else you can dig up," McQuaid said. "Roxanne might also be able to give you the names of people who had it in for him."

"From the tone of her voice during their confrontation, I'd say *she* had it in for him. There won't be any settlement now, of course. And Roxanne will get at least double from his death what she would have gotten in a divorce — not counting the life insurance. And don't forget that he was an insurance salesman. Probably insured up to his eyeballs. Charlie will know something about the size of the estate."

"Okay. You get Roxanne's story. I'll get back to Charlie, and we can compare notes."

"You're the boss," I said. "Anything else?"

"Yeah. About last night."

I grinned. "I thought we agreed that you were a jerk and let it go at that." I picked up his hand and kissed it.

"That aside —" He chuckled, then sobered and touched my cheek. "I owe you an apology, China. I've been depressed lately, and I've been taking it out on you."

I shook my head. "You've had a rough time. I'm proud of the effort you're making. I understand why you feel the way you do. Really, it's okay."

"No, it isn't. But it's hard to make plans for the future when I can't even go to the bathroom by myself." His voice hardened. "I hate the idea of depending on you for everything. And I meant at least part of what I said last night. I still think you'd be better off without me."

"Hey. That's enough." I put my finger on his lips. "I don't want to hear any more of that nonsense, McQuaid. I don't care what you think, I'm not going to —"

He batted my hand away. "Damn it, China!" he exploded. "Will you shut up and let me talk?" He grabbed my hand and held it, hard, and the line of his mouth softened. "I still think you're better off without me. A woman would have to be nuts to commit herself under these circumstances. But if you really mean what you said last night about not caring whether I walk or crawl, I'd be a blithering idiot not to take you up on it." He gave me a crooked grin. "I may not be functioning worth a damn below the belt, but the brain still works."

I frowned. "You mean —"

"I know I'm not very romantic. I should tell you that I'm sorry I've been such a miserable shit for the last few months. I ought to tell you how much I respect and admire and love you — more than I can ever imagine loving anyone. I ought to say how much I want to be back in your bed. But I'm not very good at sweet talk. Hell, if you still want me, let's go for it. Let's get married."

"Still want you?" I laughed, a little hysterically, and leaned forward to kiss him, hard. "You *jerk!*" He pulled me awkwardly into his wheelchair, and my arms went around him.

Five minutes later, Jug trudged in, pushing his walker. McQuaid and I hurriedly broke apart, and he grunted. "Yep, I figgered I'd see you in his lap sooner or later." He shook his head, the corners of his mouth turned down, and lowered himself painfully into his chair with a long sigh. "Damn. I'm gittin' too old to go gallivantin' around on Sundays. Think I'll tell that brother of mine to come here if he wants to see me." He leaned his head back wearily. "What y'all been up to?"

"We're getting married," McQuaid said.

Jug raised his head. "That right? Well, I figgered that chili you ate yestiddy would change things. Nothin' like a couple of bowls of Texas red to fire up a man's private parts." He grinned. "I'll have to save up my strength so's I kin be first in line to kiss the bride. When's the big day?"

"I don't know," McQuaid said. "We

haven't got that far." He gave me a questioning glance. "I suppose we ought to wait until I can walk back up the aisle with you, China. In fact, maybe it would be a good idea to hold off on setting the date until we see how the therapy —"

"Forget *that*," I said firmly. I turned to Jug. "A couple of months at the outside." I patted McQuaid's hand. "As soon as we can clear the groom's calendar."

"Yeah." Jug smiled amiably. "Better land the sucker while you got him hooked. He could be like the fish that jumped into the boat and then jumped out again." He looked at us. "You heard that one?"

"Yes," we chorused in unison, and I said to McQuaid, "How about going along with me to the lobby? I've got something else I need to talk to you about."

"Yeah, folks gettin' married got lots of private talkin' to do," Jug said reflectively. He reached for the TV remote control and flicked the set on to ESPN. "You figgered on how many kids yer gonna have yet?"

"We have all the kid we can handle," McQuaid said without hesitation, and I felt a surge of relief. I'm past the age when starting a family is easy, but McQuaid is five years younger. I've always thought that a younger woman would give him a chance at another family.

I fetched cans of soda from a machine in the hall, and we found a quiet corner in the lobby next to a large aquarium which bore the sign, Do NOT Feed the Fish!!! Now that we'd finally agreed to get married, I found it hard to believe. But there were so many questions that had to be answered. When should we tell Brian? Did McQuaid want to phone his folks, or should we wait until they came for a visit? Was it okay to tell Ruby? What kind of ceremony should we have? When? And above all, when could we plan on his coming home?

We had time to settle those questions, however. Right now, I was feeling urgent about my conversation with Angela, and I wanted to tell McQuaid about it. It took only a few minutes to give him a condensed narrative version, including Carita's firing and the potentially deadly encounter Angela had witnessed. By the time I finished, he was shaking his head.

"Bad news," he said emphatically, in his cop's voice. "Unfortunately, it's the sort of thing that's hard to investigate unless the victim is capable of being interrogated or a credible witness is willing to come forward."

"That's the problem," I said. "According to all reports, Velma Mayfield suffers from increasing dementia. And the girl, Angie, may not be a credible witness. Hogge fired her cousin."

"A tough situation." He eyed me. "What are you going to do?"

"I thought I'd do some digging into Opal Hogge's background. When I told Fannie Couch that Hogge had fired Carita Garza, she remarked that Hogge might not have asked the police to investigate the thefts because she doesn't want them out here."

"What's she afraid of?"

"I don't know. Fannie had to leave before I got the details. But I'll find out."

McQuaid nodded. "The Manor is a locally owned facility, you know. In fact, one of the board members — Colin Gaskill — teaches in the Sociology Department at the university. If you can substantiate the aide's claim that Hogge abused Velma Mayfield, I'm sure Colin would take it seriously." He looked grim. "Elder abuse isn't just a crime, it's bad for business."

"Good idea. Thanks." Of course — the board. Why hadn't I thought of that? "I also wondered if you'd stop in and see Velma Mayfield — she's in Brazos, Number 33 — and tell me what you think about her competence. Maybe she remembers what happened. Even if she doesn't, she might be able to tell you something about her relationship with Opal Hogge. Bunny — that's what she calls Hogge — sounds like a kid's nickname. They must have known one another for quite a while."

He nodded. "You're going to talk to the nursing supervisor, aren't you? Somebody should examine the old woman for bruises. And it might be a good idea for her to make sure that Velma isn't left alone with Mrs. Hogge."

"I plan to talk to Joyce tomorrow," I said, "after I've filled in some of the background." I looked at the clock on the wall over the aquarium. "I promised Ruby I'd meet her at four. I'll push you back to your room."

"I can push myself," McQuaid said. "I need to work on my upper arm strength. On the way, I'll stop and see Miss Velma." He looked at me. "I hope you're planning to give Ruby the go-ahead. That money is burning a hole in her pocket. And you've been wanting to open a tearoom."

I sat down again. "But it's *complicated*," I protested. "I've been in business by myself for a long time. I'm not sure I want to get involved in a partnership."

The corners of McQuaid's mouth quirked. "But Ruby's your best friend."

"All the more reason not to be her partner," I said firmly. "Friendship doesn't automatically qualify two people to be in business together. Anyway, I don't know enough about Ruby's business ability to make such a major commitment."

The amusement went from his mouth to his eyes. "She's always paid the rent, hasn't she? Have her checks ever bounced? And don't you rely on her for other kinds of advice?"

"Well yes," I conceded, "but I've never seen her books or her bank statements. For all I know, she's a really lousy businesswoman. And what happens if the partnership doesn't survive? Most of them don't, you know. Then you've got a hell of a mess to clean up — legally, financially, and otherwise. I might wind up losing a friend, as well as a partner and a tenant."

"A lot of marriages don't survive, either, but that doesn't keep people from trying." McQuaid paused for a moment, regarding me thoughtfully. "What are you afraid of, China? Losing your independence on two fronts at once?"

"Hey," I protested, "that's not fair. Not to mention tacky."

"Think about it." He pushed his chair backward and wheeled it around. "Are you going to tell Ruby about our getting married?"

"Is that okay?"

"It's up to you. I think it would please her."

The news did more than just please her, it made her ecstatic. "Oh, China, that's wonderful!" she cried, when I told her. She turned around from the kitchen counter where she was sprinkling peanuts over a chocolate-frosted cake. "It's perfect, absolutely perfect, for both of you. I couldn't be happier if I were getting married myself!" She held me out at arm's length and studied me. "How do you feel?"

"Stunned," I said. "Bewildered. Dizzy, daft, dazed —"

"Sit," Ruby commanded, pushing me down onto one of her green kitchen chairs. "Relax and get hold of yourself. Comfort food, coming up."

Ruby's kitchen is not exactly a spot to relax in. The wallpaper is red and white striped with a watermelon border above the white beadboard wainscot. A green lamp hangs over a red table and four green chairs. The cabinets and floor and window shutters are white, like the wainscot, but there's a green and red watermelon rug under the table, the curtains are vintage tea towels in a hodgepodge of designs, and the windowsills are lined with cobalt blue bottles in all shapes and sizes. The room is a cheerful riot of bright colors and lively patterns, and Ruby — in a yellow tunic, red shorts, and blue sandals — looked right at home.

"When's the wedding?" she asked eagerly, over her shoulder, as she poured glasses of cold lemonade. "Will there be a lot of guests, or just a few? Maybe you should have it in the garden behind the shop." She paused, and I could almost see the lightbulb turning on. "If you did that, we could hold the reception in our new tearoom." She whirled excitedly, ideas popping like popcorn. "We could even combine the wedding reception with our grand opening! That should get *everybody's* attention!"

It got mine. "Stop right there," I said. "Haven't I got enough to handle, without you whipping around like a hurricane, making all my plans for me, telling me what to —"

"There, there." Ruby set my glass and a plate of cake in front of me and gave my shoulder a motherly pat. "Everything will be all right. Drink your lemonade and eat your cake and we'll talk about dates and —"

"No dates," I said, leaning back in the chair. "Give me a day or two to let it sink in, please. My gosh, Ruby, we haven't even told Brian yet. You're the first."

"I'm flattered," she said, and sat down across from me with lemonade and cake. She pointed at my plate. "That is called Peanutty Pepper Cake. I made it especially for you, so you can see that peanuts and chiles really *do* go together." She eyed me. "You're not allergic to peanuts, I suppose, but you'd better take it slow until you see how hot it is."

Ruby's Hot Lips Cookie Crisps are incendiary, so I took her advice. But the creamy chocolate frosting mellowed the heat, and the cake had a rich peanutty taste. "Great!" I said, around a mouthful. "Can I have the recipe for my column this week?"

"Would you believe? All you have to do is make up a yellow cake mix, add a half cup of crunchy peanut butter, and throw in a half teaspoon of cayenne pepper — more, if you want it hotter. The frosting comes out of a can. Of course, if you'd rather have chocolate cake, you'd start with a chocolate cake mix. Nothing easier." She forked up a bite herself. "Since you don't want to talk about your wedding, let's talk about the tearoom. If we got the ball rolling on the renovations right away, we could be open by early September."

It might have been the chocolate, the chile, or just plain Ruby, but I was already feeling better. And Ruby's voice was determined, which suggested that this was a discussion of major significance. "Open for what, exactly?" I asked. "Are you thinking of offering a daily menu? We're talking hypotheticals, now, not plans," I added hastily, so she wouldn't get the idea I was agreeing to anything just yet. "Nothing concrete."

She pushed her plate aside and leaned forward. "Hypothetically," she said with a glint of something like amusement, "we wouldn't be open every day. At least, not until we've got all the bugs ironed out and we see what kind of traffic we get. Let me tell you what I have in mind."

What Ruby had in mind, I had to admit, sounded very practical. The tearoom, a separate business from our two shops, would be open on Wednesdays, Fridays, and Saturdays from twelve to four and by special arrangement. Since I had my hands full this summer, Ruby would be responsible for getting the permit and arranging for the necessary renovations. Meanwhile, we would plan the decor and the menu together. Ruby's friend Caitlin was interested in managing the food, and Caitlin's partner Gina, who works for an ad agency in Austin, had volunteered to do publicity. Ruby herself had drawn up a projected business plan, including start-up expenses and a six-month operating budget. The costs would be split fifty-fifty, with Ruby loaning me my share at a very reasonable rate of interest. The tearoom would pay rent to me. Within a year, according to the plan, my share of the profits would allow me to begin repaying my debt to Ruby. Her numbers looked solid, and I had to admit that the whole thing was very businesslike.

"Well, what do you think?" Ruby asked, when we'd finished going over the papers she'd laid out on the table.

"I'm impressed," I said sincerely. "You came up with this all yourself?" I looked down at the columns of numbers. "All this figuring and stuff?"

Ruby made a huffy noise. "Of course I did. What do you think? I paid a bunch of merry elves to do it? I conjured up a troop of fairies with calculators? I waved my magic wand and —"

"I just mean . . ." I gestured around the kitchen. "I've always been impressed by your creativity and imagination, Ruby. I guess I've never seen the *other* side of you before."

"That's because you've never looked." She gathered up the papers and put them back into their folder. "For heaven's sake, China," she added irritably, "I've been making a living at the Crystal Cave for over five years now. I couldn't do that without *some* business brains." She looked at me, frowning. "I'll accept your apology."

"I grovel at your feet," I said. "I lick your toes. I —"

"Yuck." She put the papers into a plastic file box marked TEAROOM and her tone became brisk. "Well? What do you think? Is this a partnership or isn't it? Are you in or are you out?"

I frowned. This was a Ruby I had never met before, a crisp and efficient Ruby. Had her found money totally changed her personality? Or had this management-type person been concealed somewhere inside my best friend for all the years I'd known her and was just now emerging, like a butterfly out of a chrysalis, empowered by a fat checking account?

"Well?" Ruby demanded. She bent over, put both hands on the table, and looked me squarely in the eye.

"I'm . . . in," I said. "I guess."

"I'll ignore that last bit." Ruby straightened and thrust out her hand, smiling. "Shall we shake on it, partner? One for all and all for one, and all that stuff?"

We shook. The earth did not open. The sky did not fall. We drank some more lemonade, ate some more cake, and talked for a while about colors and fabrics and what we might call our new enterprise. I offered Teatotally Terrific, but she rejected it as not having the right ambiance. She proposed Magnolia Tea Room, but I objected on the grounds that it was too close to the name of Maggie's defunct restaurant. Then we both came up with A Tea Room of Our Own, which many of our friends would recognize as a play on the title of Virginia Woolf's famous essay, and Just Our Cup of Tea. We were debating the merits of these, when Ruby casually suggested Thyme for Tea.

"That's it!" I said, snapping my fingers. "Thyme for Tea — Ruby, it's perfect! It alliterates, it's memorable, it ties beautifully into herbs and the shop. You see? I *said* you were creative." For the first time, I felt enthusiastic about the project. Somehow, the name had made it real. We weren't just playing teashop in my dollhouse with Ruby's Monopoly money.

"Thank you," Ruby replied solemnly, as if she too were struck by the symbolism of this decision. Then she shook herself. "Well, now that we have a name, I can get Gina to work on a logo and a design for our sign, and I'll see the architect and get started on the Health Department stuff. You'll need to go over it, though. There's a lot of fine print."

"And I'll get a DBA and a new sales tax number and draw up our partnership papers," I said. "We need to make sure that both our interests are protected." I looked at Ruby. "Maybe you should get Charlie Lipman to review the partnership stuff for you. You know, make sure I'm not trying to pull a fast one."

She rolled her eyes. "For pity's sake, China. If I can't trust you to look out for my business interests, who can I trust?"

We talked for a little longer, then I said good-bye and drove to the shop to check on Laurel, pick up the cash bag, and see what kind of ordering I'd have to do for the coming week. For someone who valued her personal independence above all other worldly attributes, it had been a momentous few hours. I had acquired a spouse, a business partner, and a new business, all in one short, life-changing afternoon.

It would take some getting used to.

Chapter Eleven

In Texas, where it is a sign of machismo to eat any hot pepper with no visible signs of regret, there is a superspicy kind that nobody eats. If the jalapeño is considered hot, this, the chili petin, is HOT! It's a wilding, seldom seen in home gardens. Just one will flavor a pot of stew. You cannot abide having one in your mouth. Reference books sometimes call it a bird pepper: birds, especially mockingbirds, seem to favor them without burning their bills. This tiny, ovoid bundle of heat is also called chiltecpin, and a longer, pointed variety is called chilipiquin.

Russell Webber
"Chilipetin: The Hottest"
The Herb Companion,
Aug.-Sept. 1989

I spent a half-hour with Laurel, talking business, then drove home. I had almost gotten used to McQuaid not being there, but the house seemed hugely empty without Brian and — I had to admit it — Leatha. I went upstairs to check on Einstein and found him frisky, having basked warmly in the sunlight on Brian's drape all afternoon. I checked on Ivan and the various reptilian oddities in the cages under the window, then went downstairs to feed Howard Cosell, who roused himself with an effort from his favorite napping spot under my old Home Comfort kitchen stove.

"It's just you and me, babe," I said, adding a little wet dog food to the dry, along with a generous sprinkling of garlic powder. I squatted down beside him as he wolfed down his dinner. "Hey, did you hear the big news?" I asked him. "McQuaid and I are getting married."

Howard Cosell did not answer, being otherwise engaged. In the silence that followed my announcement, I was suddenly struck by a new thought. Would I still call him McQuaid after we were married? The name had come easily when we met — he was a detective with the Houston PD, I was a criminal attorney — and it had seemed right for our determinedly casual relationship. But marriage was different, and I might feel differently about calling my husband by his last name. And what about my own? Would I be China Bayles? China McQuaid? Some combination of the two?

These questions about names might seem simple, almost trivial, but they aren't. I have had a law degree under my name, and a career, and a thriving business. What happens to *me* — my identity, my essential self, as Ruby would say — if I change it?

That wasn't a question I could dismiss lightly, and it brought up an even bigger one. I sat down on the floor beside Howard Cosell to think about it. I loved McQuaid, and part of me (the domesticated part that loves herbs and gardens and enjoys nest building) wanted to be married and live happily ever after, or to at least cohabit contentedly. But a different part of me — the logical part, that got her law degree and spent fifteen years in hand-to-hand combat in the legal system — wondered whether marriage and contentment (let alone happiness) were compatible concepts. Marriage was a *big deal*. What if I couldn't handle it? What if I began feeling trapped? What if I just needed to be alone? In fact, now that I considered all the ramifications, I wondered whether I could actually bring myself to —

Slurp.

Howard Cosell had finished his meal and, in an uncharacteristic burst of doggy affection, was licking my ear with a rough, garlicky tongue. I gave him a hug and stood up. I hadn't come to any definitive conclusion because this wasn't the kind of thing that could be definitively concluded.

Howard Cosell looked up at me and gave his tail two mournful wags. I looked down at him and said, "Thank you, Howard Cosell. Shall we get back to business?"

I let Howard out to do his in the backyard, and I went to the phone. Roxanne Cody answered cheerfully enough, I thought, for someone whose husband had died the day before. But theirs had obviously not been a happy marriage, and who am I to judge? When I gave my name and suggested that we get together that evening, however, she replied that her out-of-town in-laws were there and that they had family business to discuss. What did I want to see her about, and would tomorrow do as well?

I answered without hesitation, having already chosen my strategy. "Before he died, your husband said something to a friend that raises some questions about his death. And yes, tomorrow will be fine. Can we try for early in the morning?"

"Oh." There was a silence. Then, sharply, "What kind of questions?"

"I'll be glad to go over that with you in detail," I said in a lawyer-ish tone. "Is eight o'clock too early?"

"I'm in the gym at that hour."

"The Health Spa? I'd be glad to meet you there. How about eight-thirty?"

"I won't have a lot of time." She was getting more wary by the minute. "I have to be at the office at nine-thirty. Who did you say you are?"

"China Bayles," I said. "Shall we say eight forty-five, then?" We did, and I hung up. Michelle's Health and Fitness Spa is on Silver Creek Road, only a couple of miles away. I know the place well, because from time to time I have forced myself to work out on the machines. In fact, it might not be a bad idea for me to sign up for an exercise class while I was out there — I could stand to lose a few pounds. I straightened up and looked at my dumpy image in the mirror on the back of the hallway door, trying to imagine myself in something a little dressier than jeans and a T-shirt. Something like a wedding dress. I turned from the front view to the side and sighed. It had better be more than a few pounds, unless I wanted the *Enterprise* to report that the bride had been casually attired in a loose denim smock. The *bride*.

The logical part of me cringed and I turned hastily back to the phone, to call Fannie Couch.

"Sure, come on over," she said, when I reminded her that our morning conversation had been interrupted. "In fact, come for supper. I made potato salad and marinated some chicken. Clyde's gonna put it on the grill so's I can take a load off my tired feet. We won't have a thing in the world to do but sit in the yard and criticize his cooking."

It was an offer I couldn't refuse. When I came up the walk, the mouthwatering odor of mesquite-grilled chicken made me remember that a couple of pieces of Ruby's cake was all that stood between me and a long-ago lunch. Fannie and I settled ourselves with tall glasses of iced tea in low-slung canvas chairs under the weeping willow tree in the Couches' pleasant backyard and prepared to critique Clyde's performance at the grill. The blue blooms of a head-high clump of Indigo Spire salvia near the fence attracted a squadron of bumblebees and butterflies, and a hummingbird feeder hung in a nearby cedar elm. Ruby-throats and black-chinned hummers whirred noisily around it, the males bossing the females and juveniles and engaging in what looked like near-fatal aerial combat with their competitors. It was a hot evening, with the temperature still in the upper eighties and only a whisper of a breeze stirring the willow, but the heat was nothing new. The thermometer had registered ninety-plus almost every day since mid-May, and the mercury would stay up there until mid-October. Texas summers are like the Dallas Cowboys — hard-charging well into the fourth quarter, with no sign of let-up.

"So." Fannie adjusted the pillow under her head and lay back comfortably, hitching up her dress to cool her pale, pudgy knees. "What's on your mind?"

"Opal Hogge," I said. "You were going to tell me what she's afraid of."

She clinked the ice in her glass. "I hope I didn't exaggerate. You have to remember a lot of this is just gossip I've picked up here and there. No way can I put it in the program. If I can't attribute my sources, I can't put it on the air, and that's all there is to it. Unless I want to end up on the business end of a lawsuit."

"What didn't you exaggerate?"

She waved away a curious yellow jacket. "Well, you might say that Opal Hogge is in way over her head and isn't smart enough to know it. Or you could say she's a sly puss with a hot temper who knows she can't hack it and is doing her level best to pull the wool over everybody's eyes. The way she treated Carita Garza is downright nasty, but there's more like it. She's fired some, and others quit first, before she got to them. The turnover out there lately has been *fierce*. Now, that is one thing I *do* aim to point out as a problem," she added. "If they can't keep good workers, there's a skunk in the woodpile somewhere."

"Why did you make the remark about the police, Fannie? What reason might Hogge have to keep them away?"

"Well, that's simple enough," Fannie replied. "It sure as shootin' wouldn't look good to the board of directors if the chief administrator fired an employee for stealing and the police came and said the employee didn't do it after all. It sounds to me like Hogge wasn't any too sure of her grounds and she didn't want some policeman telling her she was wrong."

That was what it sounded like to me, too. "So you think a serious investigation might turn up a different thief?"

"I should hope so," Fannie said. "That girl has worked miracles for that Garza family. I'd have to see some pretty strong proof before I felt right about accusing her. Didn't you say the purse was in her locker? I hear myself wondering whether somebody put the credit card there and then put a bee in Opal Hogge's bonnet. Somebody with a grudge against the girl, maybe."

"I wondered that myself." I paused. "How long has Opal Hogge been running the show out there?"

"A couple of years, at least." Fannie picked up her iced tea and raised her voice. "Hey, Clyde, don't forget to baste that chicken real good, you hear? Otherwise, it'll fry up just like shoe leather." To me, she added, "Her nephew's on the board — some professor or such over at the university. Edna says that's how she got the job."

"Her nephew wouldn't be Colin Gaskill?" I asked warily.

"That's right." She gave me a curious glance over the rim of the glass. "How'd you know?"

"A lucky guess." So much for going to the board — at least, to that particular board member. McQuaid would have to dig up somebody who might be more neutral on the subject of Hogge's performance. "Where was she before she came here?"

"She directed a private nursing home in San Antonio," Fannie said, "something to do with a church. That's according to my friend Rosie Montgomery, who had a sister in the home. There was some kind of problem and Opal Hogge left. I can give you Rosie's phone number if you want to dig a little deeper."

"Sounds like the board didn't take a very good look at Hogge before they hired her."

Fannie peered at her watch. "That man doesn't pay the least attention," she said. "Clyde," she said more loudly, "you better yank that corn off the grill before it puckers up." She sipped her tea and pushed her lips in and out, frowning. "Well, they had a mess on their hands — the Manor's board, I mean. They sacked the previous director in a big hurry. That was Howard Dunaway, who got caught with both hands in the till. At the same time, they had a bunch of construction in the works, the new wing an' all, an' the State breathin' down their neck about some problem or other that turned up on inspection. So I guess they took the first person that looked halfway decent on paper, without going into her background too deep. Especially since one of their own vouched for her."

A male hummer buzzed me, his scarlet throat splendid in the sun. "Sounds like a dumb way to do business," I said.

Fannie shrugged. "That board never did pay much attention to what was goin' on. It let Howard Dunaway manage until he just about managed them into a hole in the ground. It probably won't do any different by Opal Hogge." She drew her white eyebrows together. "But if what you say is true about Hogge abusing Miss Velma — well, now, that's something they'll have to pay attention to, unless they want somebody to file criminal —" She stopped. "Clyde Couch! Did you hear what I said about that corn? Get it out of that fire before it parches, or we'll be gnawing grits off those cobs!"

We watched as Clyde hurriedly fished a foil-wrapped package out of the coals; then Fannie put her feet back up and said, sadly, "My heart bleeds for Miss Velma, it really does. She's not old at all, you know, not much over sixty-five. She worked for old Tom Perry for over forty years, right up to the day he got killed, and for a few months after, winding up this and that. In fact, if the truth be known, it was Velma kept his practice together the last year or two. Tom was failin' long before that gravel truck flattened him last October, but he just wouldn't admit it. And now —" She shook her head again, mournfully. "Well, it's pitiful, is what it is."

"What's the connection between Velma Mayfield and Opal Hogge?"

"Now, that I can't tell you," Fannie said. She chuckled. "They sure weren't girlhood friends. Velma's got a good twenty years on Opal Hogge. S'pose they're related?"

"Maybe." I had just thought of something. "If so, MaeBelle Battersby will know. She's Miss Velma's niece."

"That's right, I'd forgotten. MaeBelle's mother was a Mayfield before she married into those shiftless Claypools. The Battersbys don't live too far from here, you know."

"One more thing," I said. "You mentioned that Lulu Burkhart was rumored to be involved with Jerry Jeff Cody. Has his name been connected with anybody else?"

"Well, there's Ruby," Fannie said with a dry chuckle.

"Other than Ruby," I said. "And Felicia Travis."

"Not lately," Fannie said. She heaved herself out of her sling chair. "Clyde's wavin' at us. Let's go see if that chicken's fit to eat."

I could have waited and caught MaeBelle on the courthouse square, policing the parking meters, but since she lived nearby, I figured I might as well stop and see her.

It was still daylight when I parked in front of the Battersby house, a gray frame cottage with red shutters, neatly set behind a thick, prickly border of Texas lantana that was already blooming calico red and yellow. The Latin name of this attractive plant is *Lantana horrida*, because some people think the leaves smell awful, and because you have to arm yourself with elbow-length leather gauntlets to prune its thick, prickly branches. And also because its berries are toxic. But *horrida* or not, lantana doesn't take a lot of water and butterflies grow giddy over it, which in my book is enough to earn its keep.

MaeBelle opened the front door. She was clad in a loose, hibiscus-print muumuu and she was fanning her sweaty face with a folded *Enterprise*. The door opened directly into a very small, very warm living room that smelled richly of onions. I sidestepped a fully extended recliner in which lay a heavy-set man with several days' worth of stubble, a small fan whirring on the lamp table beside him. Two bare-legged preschoolers, their hair so blond it was white, were eating watermelon at an oilcloth-covered table in the adjacent dining room.

"That's Lester," MaeBelle said, gesturing at the man in the recliner. Lester didn't move. "The kids belong to my youngest, Jamie. She works on Sundays and the day care is closed, so they come here."

"I'm Lissa," the little girl informed me, kicking her legs very fast. She jabbed the boy with her spoon. "He's Peter. He's a dork."

"Not," Peter replied placidly. He was fat and short, and his elbows were propped on the table, chin almost resting on his watermelon, eyes half closed.

"You are too a dork," Melissa retorted. "I said so." She spooned some watermelon into her mouth and spit a seed, expertly, onto Peter's plate.

"Who cares?" Slowly, deliberately, Peter put the tip of his spoon on the seed, flipped it off his plate, and went on eating. His eyelids didn't even flicker.

"That kid'll never get ulcers," I said to MaeBelle. "He has the gift of ignoring interruptions."

"Like his grandpop." MaeBelle sighed,

with a glance at Lester. "Surely t' God it musta been harder when I had three of my own this size, but I guess I forgot. I do love 'em, God bless, but they wear me plumb out. Can't hardly wait for Monday so's I kin put on my uniform an' go back to givin' parkin' tickets." Still fanning herself, she led the way through a small, hot kitchen, the counter cluttered with a day's worth of dirty dishes and a skillet that had held fried onions, and opened a screen door. "Let's sit on the porch. The durn air conditioner went out yesterday — allus on a weekend, you know."

On the west side of the house, the porch was only marginally cooler than the stuffy indoors. MaeBelle went to a spigot and turned it on and a sprinkler out in the yard began to arc spray back and forth. She sank down into a plastic chair and motioned to me to take the other one. "Whut can I do for you, Miz Bayles? Information, you said you was after?"

"Yes. I'm doing a little project on some of the old folks at the Manor, and I was curious about your Aunt Velma." My explanation (partly a lie, mostly an evasion) might be vague, but I didn't think MaeBelle would question it.

"Well, I'm glad you picked Aunt Velma."

MaeBelle's tone was reminiscent. "She was a corker, she was, in her day. Mind like a whip. An old maid, you know. My mother used to say Aunt Velma was married to her job. Mr. Perry couldn't of got along without her. Kept his office straight, records in order."

"Did she grow up around here?"

"Over in New Braunfels. Got two years at the teacher's college in San Marcos and taught grade school there for a while, then moved to Pecan Springs an' started workin' in Mr. Perry's law office. I was just a little thing, no bigger'n Lissa, but I remember she bought me a doll out of her first paycheck. She always told me I'd grow up an' amount to somethin'." MaeBelle's round face beamed. "An' now I got me this job as parkin' meter attendant, which pays a real good salary, plus hospital insurance an' retirement an' my uniform." She gestured proudly. "An' you know what, Miz Bayles? I paid off this house last month. All by myself, too, 'cause Lester hurt his back liftin' a case of beer an' hasn't worked in a couple years."

"I'm sure your aunt would be proud of you," I said, meaning it. I didn't know very many people who could boast that they'd paid off their mortgage.

MaeBelle's face saddened. "I told her

about the house, but she didn't act like she knew what I was sayin'. The Alzheimer's came on her real sudden, you know, after Thanksgivin' last year. She was livin' alone, but she got so she couldn't remember how to get home from downtown. Then she'd forget about takin' a bath and eatin', an' she got real thin an' had trouble with her bowels. Had to start wearin' one of those diaper things. I started givin' her B-12 shots an' that helped some for a while, but it wasn't long until we had to put her into the Manor."

"It's a good thing she had you to help," I said. "What do people do when they don't have family?"

"I'm here t' tell you," MaeBelle replied emphatically. "Cleanin' out that house was a lot of work, believe you me. We brought some of the furniture here — that recliner Lester's stretched out in, for one — an' we had us a big yard sale. But the garage was full of old books and papers and stuff from the law office. Aunt Velma wouldn't let us throw away a single piece of it for fear somebody might want it." She laughed shortly. "That was one thing Lester didn't mind doin'. He thought there might be money hid, an' he sorted like the devil was eggin' him on. But there wasn't, of course

— money, I mean. Aunt Velma had enough to live on, but not much more."

"It must have been hard on everyone," I said sympathetically.

MaeBelle sighed heavily. "I tell you, Miz Bayles, movin' Aunt Velma out to the Manor like to of broke my heart. She was the most independent person I ever saw. Did ever' little thing for herself, bar none. 'Cause she never had a man around to help, you know." She laughed a little. "Not that havin' a man around is any guarantee you'll get help when you need it."

"Was she upset by the move?"

MaeBelle nodded. "I'd say. But she was never one to dwell on grief. She gets her bed changed ever' week an' good food, an' people stop in, though she don't always know 'em. Miss Lund reads to her. Opal Hogge keeps a eye on her. Opal is Aunt Velma's second cousin, on Mama's daddy's side."

"I was going to ask you about that," I said. "Somebody mentioned that your aunt called Mrs. Hogge Bunny."

"She did?" Grinning, MaeBelle slapped her hand on her knee. "Good for Aunt Velma! Shows she remembers some things, anyway. But I bet Opal didn't like that very durn much."

"Is that right? Why?"

She leaned forward. "Well, when they was little, Opal's brother had a old horse named Bunny that was meaner'n a skilletful of rattlesnakes an' stubborn as all git-out. Opal'd throw a tantrum over some little thing, an' her momma would call her Bunny, after that horse. That'd make Opal hot as a little bird pepper, an' she'd stomp an' fling herself around. Her brother got so he'd call her Bunny just to get her mad." She sighed. "Not too diff'rent from my grandkids, I guess. Maybe the world ain't changed that much, after all."

I agreed that maybe it hadn't. We sat chatting for a while longer, discussing the situation in the police department and other such urgent small-town matters. MaeBelle told me that the chief — "the boss," she called him — was on a very short fuse where the consultant was concerned. When I asked if she had to take part in the sensitivity training, she shook her head and allowed that everybody figured she was sensitive enough already. Then the grandkids came out and began to romp around the back yard. MaeBelle got up and turned the sprinkler off so they wouldn't get wet. I looked at my watch. It wasn't nine yet, and McQuaid would still be up. I'd stop at the corner store and get a pint of Double Chocolate Fudge ice cream. We might not be able to go to bed together, but that didn't mean we couldn't enjoy a little bedtime indulgence.

The white duck curtain that was pulled around Jug's bed didn't do much to muffle his stentorian snores. The light was turned low and McQuaid had parked his wheelchair close to the television set. He'd been watching a cop show with the volume turned way down so he wouldn't disturb Jug. He grinned when he saw me with the ice cream, and turned off the sound. I rooted around in the drawer of his bedside table and found one plastic spoon, which we shared.

"What have you been up to?" he asked, digging into the ice cream container.

I kicked off my shoes and sat crosslegged on the end of his bed. "Well, I took the plunge," I said.

"You and Ruby are going into business together? That's great, China!"

"We'll see how great it is," I said. "It feels like going into partnership with a hurricane. Anyway, after I saw Ruby, I went to the shop for a bit, then I went home and fed Howard Cosell and called

Roxanne to make a date to see her in the morning. Then I went to Fannie and Clyde's for grilled chicken and gossip, and then I dropped in on MaeBelle Battersby, who is baby-sitting her grandchildren." I took the spoon and the ice cream he handed me. "MaeBelle says she doesn't have to take sensitivity training because everybody figures she's sensitive enough." I dipped the spoon into the ice cream. "Sunday night in a small town. Not very exciting."

"Did you learn anything?"

I summarized the various conversations, while he ate and listened. The television set flickered, casting shadows around the room.

"MaeBelle's information about Bunny is interesting," he said, when I'd finished.

"It was a long time ago, but it tells us something about her personality." I paused. "Did you see Miss Velma?"

He turned his head, listening for Jug's next snore. When it came, assuring us that Jug was dead to the world, he handed the ice cream to me and said, "Yes, I saw her. After you left, I went to her room. She was sitting in a wooden rocker beside her window, watching the goats. There was another woman in the bed by the wall."

"How did she seem?"

"Physically, she's a small woman, and pretty frail. Her dress was on inside out and her house slippers were on the wrong feet. She had a kind of vacant, wandering look, but every now and then something would click and her eyes would snap back into focus, and she'd be reasonably sharp for a minute or two."

"Could you see any bruises?"

"No, but her dress had long sleeves." He took the ice cream from me. "I told her my name. I said, 'I live here.' So she'd know I wasn't a visitor or something like that." He grinned. "Then she focused on me and said, very carefully, 'No, *I* live here. You're lost.' She pointed at the door and said, 'Go ask one of the nurses. They'll tell you where *you* live.' "

I laughed. "A woman with a sense of humor."

"She might not have thought it was funny. I told her I'd come to see her especially, and asked her how she was feeling. She said she was better, and then she got this flirtatious smile and said, 'You're a good-looking boy. What are they keeping you here for?' I told her I had to learn to walk again, and asked her whether she liked it here, and whether the nurses were good to her."

"What did she say?"

"She shrugged and said some were better than others. Then she looked down at her feet and said, 'Some of them don't know one foot from another. They put my feet in the wrong slippers.' She looked up at me and giggled, and I could tell she knew she was making a joke. She seemed lucid at that point, so I said, 'How about Bunny? Is she good to you?' "

I leaned forward. "How did she respond?"

"Her shoulders stiffened and her mouth got tight. 'Bunny,' she said. She sounded almost contemptuous. Then she asked me my name again, and I told her. I told her she could trust me, and she asked me why I was in the wheelchair. I said I'd been on special assignment for the Texas Rangers, and I'd been shot. That seemed to get her attention. 'You're a Texas Ranger?' she said, and she seemed interested. She wanted to know if I'd come to see her about the papers."

"The papers?"

He shrugged. "We were on the wrong track, so I tried again. I asked her if Opal Hogge was good to her, and whether there had been any problems. This time, though, the question seemed to distress her. Her eyes got teary and her lower lip trembled, and the vacant look came back. I asked a couple more questions — whether Hogge had come to her room, whether there had been any trouble. But all I got was a stare, and that trembling lip."

I don't know what I had expected, but I felt disappointed. "It doesn't sound as if she'd be a very good witness."

"She has flickers of understanding. If somebody put the right questions at the right moments, she might be able to report whether she's been abused, and by whom. But it could be argued that she's susceptible to suggestion, and I doubt if her testimony would stand up all by itself, without corroboration."

"Well, at least we know that much. Thank you for seeing her."

He ate the last of the ice cream, tossed the empty carton in the wastebasket, and leaned back in his chair. "China, I've been thinking. If we're really going to get married, we might as well do it right."

I eyed him warily. "What do you mean, 'do it right'? You're not talking about a big wedding, are you? That's what Ruby seems to have in mind. If she had her way, she'd probably turn it into a three-ring event."

He grinned. "Well, I was actually

thinking about one ring. An engagement ring. How about if I get Grandma's garnet ring from Mom and have it reset for you?" He hesitated. "But maybe a garnet is too old-fashioned. Maybe you'd rather choose a new ring."

I swallowed. A ring? There were too many decisions to make, too fast. But then I glanced at his face. He was watching me carefully, waiting for my reaction. Testing me? Measuring my commitment? I made myself smile.

"Your grandmother's ring sounds lovely. But won't your mom mind parting with it?"

He grinned. "Are you kidding? Mom would give up anything — even her membership in the Brazos Belles Bridge Club — to see us married at last."

"Well," I said, "I guess we shouldn't disappoint her, then." I stood up.

The light from the television flickered across his craggy face. "You haven't changed your mind, have you? I mean, I still don't understand why you want to tie yourself to somebody who can't even —"

I put my hand on his lips. "Hush," I said. "You just *hush*."

Chapter Twelve

Chiles have become a popular alternative to tear gas and mace to repel muggers in the city and mean moose on the mountain trail. The Mayans hurled chiles at their enemies to blind them. Pueblo Indians burned chile seeds to fumigate their dwellings. Organic gardeners make a spray of dried chiles steeped in water to repel insects. Enterprising boat owners add powdered chiles to boat bottom paint to ward off barnacles, vets use it to treat horses with chest ailments, and it has been employed to dissuade critters from chewing on electrical wires and pizza poachers from raiding the office refrigerator. And if you're a nail-biter, you might try dabbing a tiny bit of chile oil on your cuticles. That will teach you to keep your hands in your pockets.

China Bayles
"Hot Pods and Fired-up Fare"
Pecan Springs *Enterprise*

I had just stepped out of the shower on Monday morning when the phone rang. It was Bubba Harris. He was gruffer than usual. Either he was still annoyed at the prospect of spending all week doing sensitivity training, or the crow he was eating had gone down the wrong way.

"Thought I'd get you to pass a message on to McQuaid for me. The doc at the hospital sent over that autopsy report early this mornin'." Bubba coughed. "You tell McQuaid that Doc Jamison says Cody died of anaphylactic shock. The stomach contents included traces of peanuts." He got grimmer. "I still can't figger why anybody'd be fool enough to put peanuts in chili. I guess there's no accounting for tastes."

I asked the question that would be on McQuaid's mind. "What about the samples?"

"They went to Austin. I can put in a call, but it'll be a couple days before we hear anything." He got even gruffer. "Listen, Miz Bayles. The way McQuaid went on about those samples makes me think he thinks there's more in this than meets the eye. If that's so, and he's got reason to believe this was a crime, I want to know about it, pronto. But I don't want a lot of wild-hair speculation. Far as I'm concerned, Jerry Jeff accidentally bit down on a peanut that some idiot put in his chili. If

McQuaid's got any hard facts to contradict this, I want to hear 'em." He paused. "But they better be facts and they better be *hard*. You hear? I got my hands full this week with that goldurned consultant the Council hired." He snorted disgustedly. "Sensitivity training. I'll show 'em who's sensitive."

"Yessir," I said. "Hard facts. McQuaid will be in touch." We hung up, and I dialed McQuaid.

"I just got off the phone with Bubba," I said. "According to Doc Jamison, it was anaphylactic shock that killed Jerry Jeff. Bubba thinks this was accidental, and he's busy with sensitivity training this week. But he told me to tell you that if you've got any hard facts to support a suspicion that this is something more than what it looks like, he wants to know about them. Pronto."

"The trouble with Bubba," McQuaid said, "is that he somehow never got it that hard facts aren't the only facts worth considering." His tone changed, and I heard a smile in it. "Hey. Mom called this morning, and I couldn't wait to break the news. She says to tell you she is tickled pink. She'll bring the ring over today."

I laughed. "Not in much of a hurry, is she?"

"Listen, baby. This is the answer to her prayers. You don't think she's going to give God a chance to change his mind, do you? What time are you seeing Roxanne?"

I glanced at the clock. "As soon as I comb my hair and throw some clothes on my naked body."

"Totally naked?"

I glanced in the mirror. "Totally."

"Bring some chiles when you come. I need to get in shape."

I smiled. It felt good to hear him joke about sex again. "I'll stop by and get a couple of bottles of Lila's salsa," I said.

"And I'll call Charlie Lipman and see if he's available this morning. If he is, why don't you pick him up and bring him out here so we can have a talk. I've got a physical therapy session first thing this morning, but I'll probably be finished before ten."

When we hung up, I went to the closet. Roxanne might need to be coaxed into telling her story, or maybe pushed a little, which meant that I should be appropriately costumed. I sorted through the stuff at the back of the closet until I found what I was looking for. Some days, you need to look like you're capable of pushing people around.

Michelle's Health and Fitness Spa has gone through several incarnations in the last few years. The building began life as a warehouse, then became an auto-parts store. Then it was remodeled into a gym by a woman named Jerri, who died in an unfortunate automobile accident on Devil's Backbone. Michelle took it over last year and has totally redone the place, painting it adobe tan with pink trim and cutting back the spiny agarito that grows beside the door. (As a security hedge, agarito will give even the most determined intruder second thoughts. And if you see people in a field, flailing away at an agarito with sticks, they're not trying to decapitate it, they're harvesting the berries by knocking them onto newspapers or a ground-cloth so they can take them home and make jelly.)

"Good morning!" The artificially cheerful girl behind the counter was wearing silver tights and a neon-blue leotard cut to the hips. She surveyed me critically, as if she were gauging how many sessions it would take to get me in shape. "Which class didja wanna sign up for?"

"I'm meeting someone," I said, sneaking a glance at my side view in the mirror at the end of the counter. I was a bit thick across the hips, but the gray pin-striped suit didn't look too bad, especially considering that I hadn't worn it in quite a while. The jacket hid most of my sins of indulgence, its businesslike cut softened, but not much, by a white notched-collared blouse. It was my last remaining court costume.

"Havaseat." The girl motioned me to a chair next to a pile of magazines featuring svelte females baring bronzed muscles and bleached teeth. I put my gray leather briefcase (empty, but Roxanne wouldn't know that) on the floor and sat down, idly choosing a bride's magazine. On the cover was a model with a swanlike neck and a waist the size of my wrist. The dress, which I might purchase for the contents of my cash register in an entire year, was a froth of white lace, trimmed in seed pearls and sequins. On an inside page, I found an article on the informal garden wedding, which advised me that this season's best-dressed bride would walk down the aisle in pink flowered columnar georgette, ankle-length, with a cartwheel hat swathed in green tulle, carrying pink and green hydrangeas.

"You're waiting for me?"

Roxanne Cody, dressed for work, was wearing more clothes than the last time I had seen her: a sleeveless, silky yellow shell tucked into the waistband of a matching tight-fitting skirt, and dangling earrings in the shape of the state of Texas. Her blond hair curled in damp tendrils over her ears and her face was newly made-up.

"Good morning, Mrs. Cody." I picked up my briefcase, stood, and extended my hand. "My name is China Bayles. I'm an attorney. Is there a place nearby where we can talk?" I wasn't lying. I may not practice law, but I'm still a member of the legal fraternity.

Frowning a little, she shook my hand. "Well, I don't know. There's a pancake place down the road, but —"

"How about your car?" I picked up my briefcase. "This won't take long."

Roxanne's car was a white Lexus GS300, fully loaded. The insurance business must be more profitable than I thought. We got in, leaving the doors open to let the breeze through, and I remarked, "This is a very nice car."

"It belonged to my husband," she said. "Which I guess makes it mine now." She laughed harshly. "Or the bank's."

"When is his funeral?"

She leaned forward to check her lipstick in the mirror, was not completely satisfied with what she saw, and began fishing in her purse. "There isn't going to be one. Not here, anyway. His parents are taking the body to East Texas. They're making those arrangements." Once she got launched into a sentence, her voice was breathy and nasal, Marilyn Monroe with a Texas accent. She found her lipstick and set to work. "What's all this about?"

A large tractor-trailer rig thundered by on Silver Springs Road in front of us. When it was gone and we could hear again, I said, "I was standing beside your husband when you spoke to him on Saturday, just before the judging. There was a man with me, a former homicide detective. A friend of Jerry Jeff's."

Recollection began to dawn. "A guy in a wheelchair, right? Kind of good-looking? An ex-cop, huh?" She studied me more closely. "Funny, I don't remember seeing you."

I wasn't surprised. "You spoke to your husband about a certain problem you were having with the divorce settlement," I said. "He suggested that you talk with Charlie Lipman to resolve it."

She frowned at her reflection, and I could see her searching hurriedly through the data banks for the tape of Saturday's conversation. She wanted to tell me to get out of the car and leave her alone. But she was trying to remember what and how much she had said, and she'd probably keep talking to me until she found out how much I knew.

"Okay, so you were there," she said in a challenging voice. "So what's that got to do with the price of cotton?" She dropped her lipstick into her bag.

I met her eyes and held them. "As I said, the man in the wheelchair, Mike McQuaid, is a former homicide detective. After you left, your husband asked for Mr. Mc-Quaid's help. He'd been threatened. He said he was afraid."

"Afraid? Well, I certainly hope so. Afraid of losing the whole shebang — the property, the business, that tarty little girlfriend of his. And of going to jail, too. I told him —"

"I know what you told him, Mrs. Cody," I said quietly. "When you had gone, your husband told Mr. McQuaid he felt threatened, and an hour later he was dead." I paused. "Have you been notified yet of the results of the autopsy?"

Her eyes slid away. "Jerry Jeff died of a heart attack. That's what the police chief said after it happened, and the medic. He said so too."

"You know your husband's medical history, Mrs. Cody. I think you know it wasn't a heart attack."

She looked at me. A muscle was twitching under one eye. She opened her mouth as if she were going to deny my charge, thought better of it, and closed it again. Her eyes had darkened.

"According to Police Chief Harris," I said, "the autopsy report shows that your husband died of anaphylactic shock, the result of eating peanuts. The chili samples are being tested to determine which of them contained the nuts."

"Tested?" Under her makeup, her face had gone pale and her brightly varnished nails were digging into her palms. "You're making it sound like the police suspect . . ." She stopped.

"I am sure the police will tell you what they suspect. When they come to talk to you."

"To me? But I —" She blinked rapidly, her lashes leaving traces of mascara under her eyes. "Why should they come to me? I can't tell them anything, not a thing. I didn't cook up any of that chili. I wasn't involved in —"

"In cases like this," I said, "it is standard procedure for the authorities to begin their investigation with the person who stands to benefit the most from a death." I paused. "I assume that you are your husband's chief beneficiary, not only to his share of the business, but to any personal property and life insurance?"

She caught her lower lip between her teeth. Her chin quivered. She was beginning to understand her position more clearly.

I leaned forward, sympathetic. "Look, Mrs. Cody, I know this is very hard. But if you have any information, however insignificant it might seem to you, it might be to your advantage to share it. If the police view you as their chief suspect —" I let the sentence hang in midair.

She gripped the steering wheel with both hands and leaned forward to rest her forehead on it, while she debated with herself. Finally, not looking up at me, she said, "I didn't take it seriously, you know. He was always coming up with big stories about this and that, dramatizing things to make himself look important." Her voice was muffled. "With JJ, it was hard to know what to believe."

"Didn't take what seriously?"

She raised her head. Her lipstick was smeared where she had bit her lip. "What he told Charlie Lipman on the phone. About those notes, I mean."

Once started, she seemed anxious to tell the story. One day a couple of months ago, she'd picked up her office phone and heard Jerry Jeff on the line, talking to Charlie Lipman about his tax situation. She said she didn't actually intend to eavesdrop on her soon-to-be-ex's phone conversations, but the words "income tax" got her attention. She had suspected for more than a year that JJ was siphoning off some of the business income — she didn't know how much — and that he had a stash of private funds cached away somewhere. This idea bothered her for a couple of reasons. One, because it was money that she wouldn't get if it came to a divorce; and two, because her name was on Form 1040, right beside her husband's. If Jerry Jeff was playing dodgeball with the IRS, she could be in it as deep as he was. So she listened, but all she caught was JJ's almost hysterical report to Charlie that somebody was writing letters to him, threatening to blow the whistle if he didn't do . . . something. She didn't know what. As I listened, I decided that she was probably telling the truth — at this moment, anyway. Of course, she had to know that her story would be checked with Charlie Lipman.

"Who? Who was threatening him?"

She shook her head. "He didn't say, at least, not while I was listening. But I had the impression that the letters came from somebody he knew pretty well."

"If you were guessing, Mrs. Cody, who do you think it might have been? And is it possible that the person who wrote the letters might have killed him?"

For some reason, the questions seemed to make her feel easier, and she thought about them for a moment. "JJ wasn't exactly Mr. Clean, you know. There were always people who were upset with him, clients, mostly. I could probably dig up some names, if that would help." She hesitated. "But the name that comes first to mind is Craig Burkhart. He and JJ were joint-venture partners in a strip center. They were pretty good friends, too, until JJ backed out of the deal. Craig claimed he was cheated. He still carries a grudge, big time."

"Did you know that your husband's name has been linked with Lulu Burkhart?" I asked.

"His name has been linked with a lot of

women over the years. The latest is Felicia Travis." She gave a sarcastic chuckle. "I'll bet Felicia is disappointed that her lover boy has checked out. No round-the-world honeymoon cruise for her."

"How about your husband's partner?" I asked.

She seemed to stiffen. "Pokey? What about him?"

"Does he have any reason to want Jerry Jeff dead?"

"Of course not," she snapped. She stopped, becoming wary. "I mean, I can't think of anything. They always got along real well. You can forget about Pokey."

I left it alone. "The threats — Jerry Jeff didn't describe them as death threats?"

"It didn't sound that way." Away from the subject of Pokey Clendennen, she felt better. She tapped a curved red nail on the steering wheel, considering. "It sounded more like blackmail, actually. Like, if you don't do what I want, I'll rat on you." She tapped some more. "That was when I really got scared, you know? I got to thinking, what if this person actually has evidence? What if JJ doesn't do what he's told, and this guy — whoever he is — decides to go to the IRS? I can't *prove* I didn't know what he was doing. After all,

260

I'm the office manager, right? Except that I didn't have that much to do with the bookkeeping. Jerry Jeff mostly took care of that. But he might lie to the IRS, just to get me in trouble."

I nodded. "I'm not a tax lawyer, but those sound to me like legitimate worries." She didn't realize it, but it also sounded like a very legitimate reason to want him dead.

"Exactly. So I got busy and dug around and I found out where he put it." Feeling much more confident, she glanced in the mirror, saw what she had done to her mouth, and reached for her purse. "It didn't take all that much work, actually. I guess Jerry Jeff never thought I'd go looking for it. He never did give me much credit for having brains."

I looked at her in surprise. "You found it?"

Her small, breathy voice was much calmer now, and there was a more determined note to it. "Well, I don't mean to say that I actually found the money itself, and of course I have no idea how much is there. But I know where he put it. I can get to it any time."

This interesting declaration raised several new questions, chief among them her reason for telling me. "I see," I said. "So now that you know, what are you going to do?"

She took a tissue and wiped away the lipstick smear. "Here's the way I look at it, Ms. Bayles. If anybody's got the right to blow the whistle to the IRS, it's me, right? If I go to them and tell them where it is and how much it is and where he got it, I'll be in the clear, won't I?" She drew color on her mouth, blotted it, and disposed of the lipstick again. Her face fixed, she turned to confront me. "Won't I?" she demanded.

"Probably," I said.

She gave a short nod. "Well, that's what I'm going to do," she said, almost as if she were thinking out loud. "I'm going straight to the IRS and throw myself on their mercy." Her lips curled at the corners and her voice became even more breathy and childlike, as if she were rehearsing. "I'll be this sweet, brainless thing who doesn't have a clue. I've just found out that my big, bad hubby was cheating on our income tax. I'm scared to death and just want to get everything straightened out as quick as possible, so here's the money I've found. Take it all, and do whatever is necessary." She looked up, and her voice sharpened. "In fact, I don't even think I'll get a lawyer. It'll look more natural if I do it myself."

Roxanne was right. She could handle the IRS just fine. In fact, if she played her cards right, she might end up owing only the interest on the unpaid taxes. And I'd noticed something else, too.

There was a lot more to this woman than I had suspected.

Charlie Lipman's office is in a Victorian cottage painted gray with green and maroon trim, in a newly gentrified section of professional offices just down the street from Thyme and Seasons. He specializes in divorces, wills, property — domestic matters, mostly. He and McQuaid sometimes play poker together, and we've occasionally gotten together with him for beer and nachos at Bean's.

Charlie must have seen me pull into the lot from his office window, because I was just getting out of the car when he came heavily down the steps, already puffing a little in the heat. He was wearing baggy suit pants and a white shirt with the sleeves rolled up, and his suit jacket was slung over his shoulder. Charlie isn't as attractive as he used to be. He's too heavy for his own good, the pouches under his eyes are saggy, and his cheeks are mottled. This morning, he was wearing a small Band-Aid on his right cheek, and his usual dour look. But he smiles sometimes, and when he does, you suspect that he's basically a nice guy who's gotten stuck in a life that has somehow disappointed him.

"Mornin', China." He eyed my suit and gray pumps as he got into the car. "You're spiffed up. You been out doin' bidness already this mornin'?" Charlie is bidialectal. He talks Texas when he's fishing, hunting, drinking coffee, or transacting business with Pecan Springers. Otherwise, he has the dialect-free speech of a CNN anchorman and the vocabulary of a Harvard law professor.

"I'll tell you about it when we get where we're going," I said, and pulled out of the lot.

We got to McQuaid's room just a few minutes after he'd returned from his first therapy session of the morning. He was lying on his bed, wearing dark blue sweatpants and a white T-shirt. His pale blue eyes lit up when he saw me and he grinned, but his hair was damp with sweat, his face was gray, and he was breathing heavily.

We had passed Jug in the hall, on his way to the rec room for the weekly domino tournament, so the three of us had the room to ourselves. "Hey," Charlie said, pulling up a chair. "You're looking good. When you goin' home?"

"I look like shit," McQuaid said. "That damn therapist is a sadist. But I told her this morning to have no mercy — put me on those machines and make me work till I drop. I'm in training for the big day." He paused. "China tell you about us getting married?"

There it was, big as life — Charlie's grin. It nearly split his face. "Is *that* right?" he said incredulously. He looked from McQuaid to me and back. "Well, congratulations, you two. Swear to God, I thought you'd never make it."

"She wouldn't say yes," McQuaid said, at the same time I said, "He kept putting me off." We both laughed, and I squeezed his hand. "So you're heading home, huh?" I said to McQuaid. "I guess that means I'd better turn out my toy boys and get somebody to haul away all those empties."

Charlie loosened his tie. "So. What's the subject of conversation this morning? Ol' Jerry Jeff Cody's sad demise, I reckon?"

"That's right," McQuaid said. "We've

got some questions for you."

"One thing you got to remember," Charlie said. "Cody may be dead, but I'm his executor and I'm still representing his interests. So I've got a question for you. Yesterday's newspaper said he died of a heart attack. According to Hark Hibler at the Diner this morning, it was an allergy attack — peanuts, was what he said. Anybody know for sure which it is?"

I told him about the autopsy report, which settled the cause of death, and about Bubba Harris's invitation to share any hard facts we uncovered. McQuaid reported that Jerry Jeff had mentioned a threat, which had prompted him to ask that the cups be analyzed.

Charlie let out a long, sour sigh. "I knew it was gonna be a bad day when I cut myself shavin' this morning. You thinkin' foul play?"

"There's no real evidence," McQuaid said. "But something's going on here and I'd like to know what it is. For the sake of argument, let's say that somebody slipped peanuts into one of those chili cups with the intention of killing him. Who might it have been?"

"Well, the classic motives are money and sex," Charlie said slowly. "Which brings at least two people to mind. *If* this was murder, which I'm not yet prepared to concede."

"Money and sex," McQuaid said thoughtfully. "That would be the wife and the business partner?"

"Right the first time," Charlie said. He lifted one heavy leg and crossed it over his thigh, and I saw that he was wearing mismatched socks, one navy, one brown. "Roxanne gets Cody's estate, which includes a hefty pot of life insurance as well as a bunch of ranch land. And the way I been hearin' it round town for the last few months, Pokey gets Roxanne."

"Will there be any estate," I asked, "when the feds get through with it?"

Charlie raised both eyebrows. "My stars. You *do* get around."

"Roxanne mentioned it," McQuaid said. "She hit Jerry Jeff with the revelation on Saturday, just before he died."

"And she told me a little more about it this morning," I said. "She says she overheard her husband talking to you about his income tax situation and realized that he'd been skimming — something she'd suspected for some time. She did some quick research on her own and figured out where the loot is stashed. Now that Cody is dead, she plans to personally inform the feds and turn the money over to them."

"I'll be damned," Charlie said. "I *told* Cody that wife of his had brains." He scratched his cheek. "In fact, listenin' to you, I'm askin' myself just how much she knew *before* she overheard that conversation. Pokey's ignorance I can buy. When it comes to finances, that boy is about as sharp as a rusty hoe. But I did wonder how Jerry Jeff could've siphoned money out of the business without catchin' Roxanne's eye."

"What was your impression of her, China?" McQuaid asked.

"From her reaction, I'd say she already knew how he died, but for reasons of her own was hoping that people would think it was a heart attack. She was frightened by the idea that she might be questioned by the police."

"Maybe because she has designs on that money," McQuaid said.

"Maybe," I said. "It even occurred to me to wonder whether she might be planning a private trip to visit that stash — before she calls in the feds."

Charlie looked morose. "Well, hell. I reckon I'll have to beat her to it."

"You know where, and how much?" McQuaid asked.

"I know where it *was*," Charlie said pointedly. "And, yes, I made Jerry Jeff tell me how much he'd salted away, and I documented my knowledge. I sure as shootin' wasn't going to the feds without knowing where the body was buried and how much it stank. So to speak," he added.

McQuaid eyed him curiously. "How much are we talking about?"

Charlie shook his head slowly, not answering.

"Okay, then," McQuaid said, "how about those blackmail letters? Did you ever see them, Charlie?"

"Nope. The only time he ever mentioned them to me was in that phone conversation, and then it was only as background to the main feature, which was the tax problem."

"Roxanne told me that the writer seemed to be somebody he knew," I said. "Was that the impression you got?"

"Yeah. There were apparently two letters, and he got them over a period of a couple of weeks. The writer threatened to go to the IRS unless Cody did what he was told."

"What was he supposed to do in return for the blackmailer's silence?"

"Don't know, sorry." Charlie rubbed his

cheek thoughtfully, encountered the Band-Aid, and dropped his hand. "But those letters — they were the handwriting on the wall, as far as he was concerned. He said that even if he did what the writer wanted, he'd still have to live with the possibility of being turned in. I think maybe he figured the person would do it anyway, just for spite. And with the divorce coming up, he could see that he was gonna fork over a big chunk of the business to Roxanne — which amounted to giving it to Pokey. At least, that was the way things looked to him, and it gave him a bad case of heartburn. He decided he might as well let the feds take what they wanted, which would pretty well screw Roxanne and Pokey. And I can't say as I blame him."

"So Jerry Jeff was looking for advice on how to turn himself in?" McQuaid asked.

Charlie nodded. "I told him that if he paid what was owing, plus the penalty and interest, he could figure on three to five, of which he'd serve eighteen to twenty-four months, probably at the minimum security unit in Bastrop. It's no island paradise, but I can think of worse things. When he got out, he could start over."

"Altogether, not a bad deal," I said.

"As I say," Charlie replied, "there's

worse." He looked at McQuaid, frowning, trying to sort it all out. "Are you thinking maybe the blackmailer got pissed off because Jerry Jeff wouldn't play, and decided to kill him instead? Seems like kind of a stretch to me."

McQuaid pressed his fingers together, frowning, pushing his mouth in and out. "To tell the truth, I don't know what I think. Maybe I'm jumping the gun. There's no evidence that Jerry Jeff was murdered."

"Except for one thing," I said. "I'd have to check this out, but it's my understanding that anaphylactic shock usually sets in within a minute or two after the victim eats the food — in this case, peanuts. We know for a fact that Jerry Jeff was in the judging tent for at least a half-hour before he suffered the attack, and that during that time he ate nothing but those fifteen chili samples. But not one of those fifteen cooks owns up to putting nuts in his chili."

"Somebody could be lying," Charlie said.

"Sure. But why? Unless, of course, the same somebody had a motive for murder."

Charlie gnawed at his thumbnail. "Damn," he said gloomily.

"There's something else, too," I said. "It's just an impression, but I got the idea this morning that Roxanne definitely did not want Pokey considered as a suspect. The minute his name came up, she became distinctly wary. When the conversation moved away, she got comfortable again."

McQuaid thought for a minute. "What's Pokey's situation, Charlie? Realistically speaking, what's likely to happen to the business, when the feds start digging into things?"

Charlie's round face was glum. "There'll be an audit, that's what, and everything will be tied up for a couple of years."

"Which might give Pokey a compelling reason to dislike his thieving partner," I said, "who also happens to be the husband of his lover." It was a situation rife with potential motive.

"And if Roxanne believed that her husband was going to implicate her in the tax fraud," McQuaid remarked, "she might be desperate to shut him up. Especially if he could prove her complicity."

"Not to mention," I said, "that a dead husband returns a lot higher yield than a live ex-husband. As a divorcee, she only gets half. As a widow, she gets it all."

Charlie gnawed the other thumb.

"Damn," he said again.

"But still," McQuaid said, "we don't have any evidence of a crime."

All three of us sat, considering these facts, until our private reflections were interrupted by the phone. McQuaid picked up the receiver, listened for a moment, then reached for a pen, and jotted something down on his sheet. "Thanks," he said briefly. "We'll check into it."

"Check into what?" I asked, as he hung up the phone.

There was a glint of excitement in his eyes. "That was Dorrie, the dispatcher at the police station. The lab didn't have anything else to do this morning, and got the analysis done. Turns out that one of those cups had a substantial amount of finely chopped peanuts in it."

"Do you suppose that qualifies as a hard fact?" I asked.

"Maybe, although there's still no way to tell how the peanuts got there. Anyway, Bubba's closeted with the consultant and the mayor, so he doesn't know about it yet." McQuaid looked down at the number he'd written on his sheet. "Number twenty-two. Where are those entry forms, China?"

I got the envelope from the top of the

chest of drawers, where I'd left it the day before, took out the forms, and began leafing. Twenty-two was almost at the bottom of the stack.

I looked up. McQuaid and Charlie were watching me, expectant.

"Well?" Charlie demanded. "Who's the lucky guy?"

"Pokey Clendennen," I said. "Now, *that's* a hard fact."

Charlie sighed. "I knew I shoulda gone back to bed."

"The perfect crime," McQuaid said.

I looked from one of them to the other. "Who's going to tell Bubba?" Then, at the looks on their faces, I said, in alarm, "Oh, no, you don't. Not *me*."

"Okay, I'll tell him," McQuaid said, "when he gets out of his session with the consultant. You can talk to Pokey."

"But Pokey's a suspect," I objected. "This is a police matter now. Bubba ought to talk to him."

"That may be the case," Charlie said, examining his socks with a slightly puzzled air. "But the fact that the peanuts turned up in Pokey's chili probably isn't going to persuade this particular police chief that the whole thing is anything more than a colossal culinary blunder — or somebody's warped idea of a joke." He shook his head. "Gotta stop dressing in the dark," he muttered.

"Charlie's right, China." McQuaid reached for the phone. "Anyway, you've got a good reason to talk to Pokey. You need that chili recipe for your column."

This was true. I could hardly deny it. But Charlie came up with the clincher.

"You're just being coy," he said to me, as McQuaid waited for Bubba to come on the line. "Deep in your heart of hearts, you want more than anything else in the world to find out whether Pokey Clendennen had the imagination to kill his partner with peanuts." He smiled.

Chapter Thirteen

After Jack Smith, the Los Angeles Times *columnist, let it drop that his secret chili ingredient is peanuts, the* Goat Gap Gazette *took sharp editorial note of the disclosure. "Please stay in L.A., Jack. Texas is not ready for you."*

> Bill Bridges
> *The Great American Chili Book*

As Charlie and I walked down the hall, I remembered that I had intended to see Opal Hogge this morning — that I *needed* to see her, in fact, before I could decide what ought to be done on behalf of Carita Garza and Velma Mayfield. It wouldn't take long. I was about to ask Charlie if he minded waiting for a few moments, when we happened to meet a client of his who'd been visiting a friend. I mentioned that I wanted to drop in on Mrs. Hogge, and the client offered to give Charlie a lift to town.

Before I went in search of Opal Hogge, I stopped at the nurses station and asked for Angie. The nurse on duty shook her head. "She phoned in sick this morning."

"Nothing serious, I hope," I said casually.

"I hope so too," the nurse said. "She's a smart gal. And heaven knows, we need to keep the good ones." She pushed a notepad across the counter to me. "Want to leave a message? I'll put it in her box."

I wrote down my name and phone number, and two words: "Call me." Now that I'd had time to think about it, I knew she needed to tell Joyce Sanders what she had seen in Miss Velma's room — and the sooner the better. But why hadn't she come in today? I felt a prickle at the back of my neck. Was something wrong?

I found Opal Hogge in her office, standing in front of an open file cabinet. She was a tall woman with large shoulders and a head that seemed almost too small for her body. Her faded blond hair was twisted into a tight bun at the nape of her neck, escaping tendrils captured by large tortoise shell combs above her ears. She was dressed in a dark blue shirtwaist dress, with epaulettes that exaggerated the boxiness of her shoulders. She glanced at me when I came to the door.

"Yes? May I help you?" Her tone was cool and businesslike, but not unwelcoming, and she gave me a small smile.

Matching her crispness, I got straight to the point. "My name is China Bayles. I'm a friend of Mike McQuaid's, one of your residents." I paused. "I am also acquainted with Carita Garza. She spoke with me on Saturday night about her dismissal. She's terribly concerned about it."

At Carita's name, Opal Hogge's shoulders tensed. She turned back to the file drawer and pulled out a folder, opened it, and began leafing through it. "I don't think it's appropriate for me to discuss the matter with you," she said. Her voice was high and taut. Horizontal creases crossed her forehead, intersected by vertical creases between her eyes. I tried to imagine her as a small child that everyone called Bunny, but couldn't quite bring it off.

I sat down in a straight chair in front of the desk. "I'm a lawyer, Mrs. Hogge. I've told Carita I would help her decide how best to resolve this problem. I hoped that you and I might discuss —"

She strode around the desk and sat down in her leather chair, folding her hands on the desk. "There's nothing to discuss," she said flatly. "I've had my eye on the girl for some time, and I knew she was stealing. She was discovered wearing earrings that had been taken from one of the residents, and then I found the credit card. I was perfectly justified in discharging her." The lines around her mouth had become crevasses and there was a brittle hardness in her voice.

"I wondered how you happened to pick that particular time to open Carita's locker and search her purse," I said speculatively. "Did someone suggest that you might find the missing credit card there?"

Her nostrils flared. "Nobody had to suggest anything to me, Ms. Bayles. I know a thief when I see one."

She hurled the word *thief* like a bullet. I waited a moment, then said, very quietly: "But an accused employee has the right to ask for a police —"

"A thief has no rights." Her voice came up a notch. "I have made it plain to all of the staff that there is zero tolerance for such behavior. If I made an exception in the case of Carita Garza, I should have to make an exception in every case. There would be no discipline around here, none at all."

"I see," I said softly.

She sat back in her chair and pulled in her breath. Her outburst had clearly been out of proportion to my questions. Why? Was this the ghost of Bunny, exhibiting a childish temper that should have been out-grown long ago? Or had I stepped over the line by challenging her authority, by questioning her right to rule the roost here? Or was it more sinister than that, even? Was she hiding something, and feared that she might be found out?

It took a moment and cost her something, but Mrs. Hogge managed to find, somewhere inside, a modicum of self-control. Her voice was softer when she spoke again. "I am very sorry that Carita has seen fit to involve you in this, Ms. Bayles. Please tell her that I will see to it that her employee record does not reflect the fact that she was dismissed. I will enter it as a resignation. I think that would be best for her, under the circumstances."

"I would like to examine the record and speak with Ms. Garza before a decision is made," I said.

She clasped her hands tighter, but kept her voice even. "Of course. I'll have Joyce Sanders, our nursing supervisor, make a copy for you." She stood. "Now, if that's all you wanted —"

"A copy will be fine." I reached into my bag and took out one of the business cards that have only my name, address, and phone number — not the name of the shop. I stood and placed it on the corner of her desk. "Please mail it to me. With it, please include the name and telephone number of the board's attorney."

I turned on my heel. I was halfway to the door when it opened and a nurse put her head in, spoiling my snappy exit.

"Mrs. Hogge," she said, breathlessly, "Ms. Sanders sent me to tell you that we've had a death. In Brazos. She'd like to know if you can come."

I turned. Opal Hogge was staring at the nurse. The corner of her mouth was twitching. After what seemed a very long time, she said, "Yes, of course. What room?"

"Thirty-three. The doctor has been called, and Ms. Sanders is trying to reach the niece, but she's at work and can't be located just now."

"Thirty-three," Mrs. Hogge said in a strangled voice. Her face was very white. "I'll be there immediately." She all but ran around her desk, forgetting all about me, and fled down the hall.

Brazos, Room 33. It was Velma Mayfield's room.

It took a little while to get everything sorted out. In the meantime, I have to confess that — just like Opal Hogge — I made the assumption that the dead woman in Brazos 33 was Miss Velma. My conclusion was reasonable, with a 50-50 chance of being accurate, but I was wrong. It was Mrs. Rachel Rogers who had died: Velma's roommate, the one who slept in the bed next to the wall and had snored during McQuaid's visit; the one, Angie said, who had tried to climb out of her bed to stop Opal Hogge from shaking Miss Velma.

I only learned this fact, however, after I followed Opal Hogge down the long hallway and around the corner to Number 33. I shouldn't have, of course, but Angie's confession had given me a sense of responsibility where Miss Velma was concerned, and Mrs. Hogge's sudden, stark pallor had captured my attention. I expected to be noticed and sent away, but there was a lot of confusion at that end of the hall. I was just another one of the residents and visitors who were witnesses to this drama, no doubt a familiar one in this section of the Manor.

I stood for a moment in the open door. The room was crowded. A nurse was moving an equipment cart away from the bed where the dead woman lay, and I wondered whether there had been some attempt at resuscitation. Another was standing by with a clean nightgown and hairbrush, perhaps with the aim of making the body presentable. In a hushed and harried voice, Opal Hogge was telling someone to fetch a gurney so that Mrs. Rogers could be moved to the nursing-home chapel, down the hall. The staff probably tried to handle deaths with as little fuss as possible, so that the other residents wouldn't be affected by this reminder of their own mortality.

I turned away from the room. Down the hallway a few paces sat a woman in a wheelchair, clutching a doll. A padded vinyl bar across her lap locked her into the chair, and the expression of deep sadness on her face tugged at me. She was white-haired and her face was lined, but she wasn't that old — not much over sixty-five, I guessed.

I knelt down beside her. "Miss Velma?"

"She's dead." Her reedy voice quavered and broke, but the words were quite clear. "Rachel's dead."

I took her hand. "I'm very sorry. It's hard to lose a friend."

"She was a nice person when she was awake." Miss Velma half-giggled, but the giggle turned into a fierce sob. She flung the doll, hard, onto the floor. "I'll miss her, damn it."

I thought of Opal Hogge's white face. "How did Rachel die?"

For a moment she just sat there, holding herself tense, as if she were trying to summon the memory. Then she whimpered, a baby-soft cry, and her eyes brimmed with tears. She sagged into the chair, and the light went out of her eyes.

My question wasn't appropriate, I realized ruefully, wishing I could take it back. Rachel Rogers was older than Miss Velma, probably in her eighties. She had no doubt died in her sleep — or perhaps Velma had watched, stricken and helpless, unable to do anything but push the red button to summon the nurse. I stroked the damp, straggly silver hair off her forehead. "It's hard when our friends leave us," I said, trying to comfort her. "Please cry, if you want to."

"Crying won't . . . bring her back." She looked up at me, then past me, catching a glimpse of Mrs. Hogge, coming out of the room. Her eyes suddenly held something more compelling than grief: a sharply focused hatred.

"Bunny." She spit the word out.

"Bunny!" she cried, and raised her fist.

Opal Hogge turned and saw me kneeling beside Miss Velma's chair. Her eyes slitted and her whole frame seemed to tense. To me, she said nothing. To the nurse with her, she said, "Put Miss Mayfield to bed, and see that she gets a sedative if she needs it. She's obviously disturbed by all this."

Miss Velma dropped her hand and began to shiver. She slid down in the chair, her blue-veined hands coming up to cover her face. "Oh, no, Bunny!" she cried, and began to sob.

Driving into Pecan Springs, I had plenty to think about. I had been driving this road since McQuaid came to the Manor in March, and the Hill Country landscapes always make me wish I could do watercolors. In April and May, the rocky meadows are swept with the blue and scarlet of bluebonnets and paintbrush, brightened by tall white prickly poppy and smudged with the dark purple of prairie verbena. In June, the palette changes to yellow, orange, and red: waves of Indian blanket, clasping coneflower, coreopsis, black-eyed Susan, with here and there purple patches of monarda, which the natives call horsemint, and a few early spires of standing cypress, glowing like scarlet tapers. This month's wildflower display was almost brilliant enough to distract me from what had happened this morning, but not quite.

The conversation with Opal Hogge had not yielded any new facts, but it had given me a much clearer picture of the woman and sharpened my apprehensions. In fact, I had stopped at Joyce Sanders's office, with the intention of telling her what Angie claimed to have seen. But she was busy with the dead woman's niece, and the morning was wearing on. I picked up the cell phone, dialed McQuaid, and told him what had happened.

"Hogge sounds like a piece of work," he said. "Maybe I should go over to Brazos and check on Miss Velma."

"You read my mind," I replied. "I don't think she can give you any information, but one of the floor nurses should be able to tell you how Rachel Rogers died."

"I'll try to talk to Joyce Sanders, too."

"It's time she knew about what Angie claims to have seen," I said, "even if Angie isn't there. You could also ask her to examine Miss Velma for bruises."

"Where's Angie?"

"She didn't show up for work this

morning." I paused. "Maybe we should be worrying about *her*."

My next call, a quick one, was to KPST, where Fannie was doing her daily radio broadcast. I caught her during a commercial and got the phone number of her friend Rosie Montgomery, the woman who was supposed to know something about why Opal Hogge had left her previous job in San Antonio. I phoned, got an answering machine, and left a message. While I talked, my Datsun had cleverly driven itself into town (that's the way it seems, when I'm using the cell phone), turned left on Lampasas Street, right on San Antonio, and pulled up to the curb in front of Cody and Clendennen Insurance. It was just about noon, when Pokey was supposed to get back from his trip to Austin. If I was lucky . . .

I was. I was just getting out of the car when I saw Pokey's red pickup truck turn the corner into the alley around back. I slung my purse over my shoulder and went after it, hoping to catch him before Roxanne had a chance to clue him in. I wanted to see his reaction when he learned how his partner had died.

"Hi!" I said, with a breathless smile. "I'm China Bayles, the editor of the *Enter-*

prise's Home and Garden section. Mike McQuaid mentioned to you that I'd like to get your chili recipe for the newspaper. Did you remember to bring it?"

Pokey Clendennen is in his late thirties but he has that forever-young Jimmy Stewart look: gray Stetson, Western shirt, jeans, and boots, which goes with gingery hair, blue eyes, and a fetching gee-whiz grin. Appearances are deceiving, however. Word has it that this slow-talking, slow-walking all-American boy (he earned his nickname by always being late for school) has had more than his share of problems with alcohol, drugs, and women, including, most recently, his partner's wife — now his deceased partner's widow. Still, Pokey is definitely a world-class charmer, and I wouldn't be surprised to discover that he's a card-carrying member of the Million Dollar Sales Club. Some clients, particularly single women over forty, might be willing to fork over a sizable premium just so they could call on Pokey in time of need. (It is whispered around town that the nickname describes habits other than tardiness.)

He gave me an engaging grin as he got out of the truck. "China Bayles? Yeah, sure. I've got the recipe here somewhere."

He came around the truck to the passenger's side, where the seat was stacked with papers. He fished through, found it, and handed it to me. It was clipped from an old newspaper. He frowned a little. "It's not supposed to be totally original, is it?"

"Not necessarily," I said. I looked at it. "Did you follow it exactly?"

He folded his arms, leaned against the truck, and tipped back his Stetson in a classic Western pose. "Yeah, I did," he said amiably. "I've made chili myself, of course, but I never do it the same way twice, and I always forget exactly what I did. This is a recipe my cousin had, and he said it was pretty good. It was my first time to enter, so I thought I'd use his, rather than try to remember mine." There was an attractive dimple to the left of Pokey's mouth. It came and went as he spoke. He smiled. "I'd hate to poison anybody."

I smiled back. "What made you decide to enter the cookoff? If you don't mind my asking, that is. I thought I'd include a little bit of human interest along with the recipes."

"Oh, that was Roxanne's idea. Roxanne Cody. She's our office manager. Every year, she nags all the guys in the office to enter. Says it's our civic duty. This year, she got on my case and wouldn't let up until I agreed."

I glanced down at the recipe, then up at him. "Roxanne. Wasn't it her husband who died?"

He shifted his weight against the truck and the smile faded. "Yeah. My partner. Too bad. You know, to look at the guy, you'd never know Jerry Jeff had a bad heart. Ran a couple of miles a day, didn't smoke, ate healthy, more or less. He maybe drank a little, but no more than the rest of us. Too damn bad."

"Right." I looked back down at the recipe, studying it, and frowned. "Are you positive you followed this exactly?"

He took the recipe out of my fingers, looked at it, and handed it back. "Yep, I sure did, down to the mountain oysters." He gave me a boyish grin. "You know what those are?"

"I don't think so," I lied.

"They're . . ." He blushed. "They're what comes off a bull calf when he's . . . you know." His face was red.

"Castrated?" I asked pleasantly.

He cleared his throat. "Uh, yeah. That's right." He shuddered. "I gotta admit, cuttin' them durn things up made me a little queasy."

"I'll bet," I said. I gave him a puzzled look. "But I'm *sure* there's something missing from this recipe."

"What?"

"Peanuts."

"Peanuts?" He chuckled. "I get it — this is some kind of joke. Mike McQuaid said something on the phone yesterday about peanuts."

"A joke?" I shook my head soberly. "I don't think so. Your entry number — it was twenty-two, right?"

"Yeah, that's right." He looked at me narrowly. "Yeah, twenty-two. How'd you know that? I thought the entry number was supposed to be such a big mystery."

"I guess you haven't talked to anybody at the office today." I put the recipe in my purse.

"No, I've been in Austin all morning."

"Well, I suppose you'll find out quick enough. You see, the police gathered up the chili samples that Jerry Jeff tasted before he died and got them tested. The results came back this morning, only a couple of hours after the autopsy report. Jerry Jeff died of anaphylactic shock. He was allergic to the chopped peanuts that were found in one of the sample cups."

"Well, I'll be damned." Pokey straight-

291

ened. "So his allergy finally caught up with him, after all! Is that why you're interested in —"

"In the missing ingredient in this recipe," I said.

He lowered his head like a bull, his face darkening. "Wait a minute. I don't get it. What missing ingredient?"

"In fact," I continued, as if he had not spoken, "if the judges had been able to finish their job, you might have won the prize for the weirdest combination of ingredients." I paused. "Entry Number Twenty-two was the only sample that had chopped peanuts in it — along with the mountain oysters, of course."

For a long, drawn-out moment, Pokey stared at me with the horrified look of a cowboy trapped in a loading chute, watching twelve hundred pounds of red-eyed, sharp-horned snorting bull charging at him. Sweat popped out on his freckled forehead.

"You're not . . ." He gulped, blinked, and gulped again. "You're not saying —"

I nodded. "According to the police report, it was *your* chili that killed Jerry Jeff, Pokey."

That did it. He looked at me wildly, then took two steps away from the truck and started to run, stumbling across the uneven pavement of the lot.

"Roxanne!" he bawled, flinging open the back door to the Cody and Clendennen Insurance. "I gotta talk to you, Roxanne!"

Lunchtime on the Pecan Springs Square is the social event of the working day. There are several options to choose from, but if you find yourself on the town square when the fire station whistle blows at noon, I suggest that you join the crowd at Krautzenheimer's German Restaurant, which occupies the narrow building between the Sophie Briggs Historical Museum and the Ben Franklin Store.

That was where I was headed, anyway — partly because breakfast had been about a quarter-century earlier, partly because I wanted to locate MaeBelle Battersby, and partly because Hark Hibler usually eats lunch at one of the front-window tables, on the theory that if a courthouse story breaks, the press will be front row center.

Today, Ruby had joined Hark, and he was more interested in her than he was in the breaking news from the courthouse. I couldn't blame him, because she was dressed to brighten a cloudy day: lime-green and yellow batik-print top, matching patio pants, gauzy yellow scarf tied around her mop of red hair, yellow and green wedgies that looked like they might have come out of the Andrews Sisters' closet, yellow and green plastic bangle bracelets and matching dangle earrings.

I sat down. "My, we are colorful today."

"I've been to see our architect," Ruby said happily. "She'll have the drawings in a few days."

"What architect?"

Ruby gave me a sliver of Mona Lisa smile. "I told you I was going to get an architect to draw up the plans." She studied my face, beginning to frown. "Really, China. I'm going to have to keep a better eye on you. You *do* remember, don't you? The shop is called Thyme for Tea. It's located behind Thyme and Seasons. My name is Ruby Wilcox, and I'm your partner. Your name is —"

"Writing the checks does not confer on you the right to be tacky in public," I said severely. "I've had other things on my mind."

"Thelma and Louise," Hark said. He handed me a handwritten menu enclosed in greasy plastic. "Did I ever tell you about this guy I know down around Fredericksburg? He had these two female ostriches on his ranch, named Thelma and Louise. But Thelma was such a stupid bird that she hung herself in the gate and Louise got lonesome and ran away from home, and he decided he wasn't cut out for the ostrich business."

"I fail to see the relevance," Ruby said. She folded her menu. "I'll have the turkey Reuben with sauerkraut and German potato salad."

Hark looked at me. "Are you working for me today?"

I reached into my purse and pulled out Pokey Clendennen's recipe. "You bet," I said, putting it down in the center of the table.

"Then I'll buy. What are you having?"

One of the numerous Krautzenheimer granddaughters — there are more than I've ever been able to count — came to take our orders. I dittoed Ruby's Reuben but subtracted the potato salad, which would only make my skirt even snugger than it already was.

When the girl had gone, Ruby said, "I've got a front-page story for you, Hark." She glanced knowingly at me. "It's a romance."

"Then it goes on the society page," Hark said.

"This is different," Ruby said. She

stirred sugar into her iced tea. "I mean, it's *news*. 'Home and Garden Editor Announces Engagement to Local Hero.' "

"China and Mike?" Hark swiveled to look at me. "No kidding. I had you figured for an old maid." He grinned, to show me he didn't mean it. "Congratulations. When's the big event?"

"As soon as McQuaid feels like it. But —" I frowned at Ruby. "It will *not* be big news. McQuaid and I have no desire to make a public spectacle out of our private —"

"We hope to coordinate the event with the grand opening of Thyme for Tea," Ruby said. She put her hand on Hark's arm. "Will you see what you can do to help us get the *best* media coverage?" she asked sweetly.

"You see?" I said. "The woman wins a little money, gets a little power, and thinks she's a CEO from the Fortune Five Hundred."

"What I think is," Ruby said thoughtfully, "that we should give our grand opening a name. That's what publicists do to create interest in an event. How about the Lavender and Lace High Tea? That sounds very *bridal*. We could use lavender as the theme of the menu, as well as our theme color. And lace, of course —"

"Ruby! I'm so glad I've run into you." It was Pauline Perkins, Pecan Springs's eternal mayor, who is campaigning for election to a fifth term on the platform of more responsive law enforcement. She gave Hark a warm pat on the shoulder and me a friendly see-you-at-the-polls hand-shake, and turned back to Ruby. "I was hoping you would volunteer to help me organize a —"

I let Pauline go to work on Ruby, and turned to Hark. "One of the things I wanted to talk to you about," I said, speaking *sotto voce,* "has to do with the Manor. You said you did a piece on it last year. What was it about?"

"Oh, the usual," Hark said. "It covered the history of the place, its organization, the role of the board, their plans for the new wing, stuff like that. There'd been a problem with the former administration, and the board was anxious to put a new face on things when they hired Opal Hogge. I interviewed her too, of course."

"What do you think of her?"

His mouth twitched. "Do you want to know what I wrote in the paper, or what I *think?*"

"I can go back and read what you wrote. Tell me what you think."

"I think she is an insecure, vulnerable woman who knows her business but feels threatened as hell by anybody who is remotely competent — except for Joyce Sanders, who maybe gets along with her because she doesn't rock the boat. I think the board made a lousy decision when they hired Hogge. I think they should fire her this afternoon, if not sooner. But none of the above alters my opinion that the Manor's therapy unit is one of the best in the state. Does that cover it?"

"Just about." I sat back while one of the Krautzenheimer grandsons put my plate in front of me. The sharp odor of sauerkraut seasoned with caraway seeds made my mouth water. "How about Velma Mayfield? What do you know about her?"

"New subject?" Appreciatively, Hark eyed his plate of bratwurst, potato salad, and cole slaw. He picked up the catsup bottle and laced a thick red ribbon down the middle of the sausage.

"Not entirely. It seems that Hogge and Miss Velma are distantly related. Second cousin, or something like that."

"I suppose I know what everybody knows about Miss Velma." He nodded toward the courthouse. "She was a fixture in that place for quite a while. She was old man Perry's law clerk, you know, except he never called her that. Called her his 'girl' and never let on that he appreciated what she did. She rewrote his briefs, filed all his court papers, ran messages to the judge, wrote wills and probated them, even negotiated out-of-court settlements with opposing attorneys, especially later on."

"Sounds like she did everything but plead and argue," I said.

"You got it. If you ask me, she was a better lawyer, hands down, than Tom Perry. That old rascal didn't give a damn about anybody. She had a heart." He sliced into the sausage and the juice squirted. "MaeBelle tells me she's failing. Too bad."

"Did you ever hear of Miss Velma being involved in a legal case with Opal Hogge? Property, probate, anything like that?"

Shaking his head, he speared a hunk of sausage and ate it enthusiastically. "Sounds like you're fishing for a connection between them — other than bein' cousins, I mean."

"In a word, yes," I said, and on impulse, decided to tell him. "One of the aides at the Manor told me she saw Hogge roughing Miss Velma up."

He stopped chewing and stared at me. "No kidding. If the board got wind of that,

Hogge would be out on her butt in two minutes." He chewed once or twice, then stopped again. "We got a story here?"

"Not hardly," I said. "No hard facts, as Bubba would say." Just a girl's word for what she had seen, and an old lady's fiercely raised fist. And another old lady, dead in her bed. I shivered.

"No hard facts, huh?" He grunted. "Well, you sure as hell ain't gonna have much of a career in journalism."

I grinned. "Aw, heck. And I've been collecting all these great chili recipes." I put my finger on the one in the middle of the table. "This one's made with mountain oysters."

Hark rolled his eyes. The freckled Krautzenheimer granddaughter came over to refill our iced tea glasses. Through the window, I saw MaeBelle Battersby, checking parking meters on the other side of the square. Pauline finished her conversation with Ruby, tossed a quick, polished smile around the table, and strode off in search of another volunteer victim.

"Speaking of chili," Hark said, taking care of the last of his sausage, "we heard over at the paper this morning that Jerry Jeff actually died from anaphylactic shock."

Ruby leaned forward. "Did any of those

recipes have peanuts in them?"

"Not a one," I said.

Hark frowned. "Then where the hell did the peanuts come from?"

"You got me," I said. Apparently, Hark had gotten only part of the news. He didn't know which sample the peanuts were in. "Actually," I said, "I've been wondering about Cody and Clendennen — the insurance company, I mean. What do you know about it?"

"As I recall," Hark replied, "those guys have been in business since they got out of college. JJ and Roxanne got married about that time, too, so the three of them have been in it, together, for about fifteen years."

"Jerry Jeff has always had a reputation as a womanizer?" I asked. "Pardon, Ruby."

Ruby tossed her head with an exaggerated carelessness. "We were just friends, nothing more."

"Pretty much," Hark said diplomatically. "Pokey too, of course — although I heard that he settled on Roxanne a while back, and she's kept him busy, more or less."

"Do you know if any of Jerry Jeff's women friends might have had resentful husbands?" I was thinking, of course, about the blackmail letters. Maybe it was as simple, and sordid, as adultery.

"I doubt it," Hark said. "His taste tended toward single women — unlike Pokey's, which goes the other way."

"What about the company's reputation? Any problems, employee difficulties, disaffected clients, outraged competitors — stuff like that?"

"Not that I know of," Hark said. "They were just two good old boys, making a pretty fair living off people's worries." His chuckle was dry. "I don't know why, but insurance people rub me the wrong way. We buy insurance because we're scared we'll lose what we've got. Why are we scared? Because the insurance companies keep reminding us how much we've got to lose. Then, when you've got a claim, they send somebody out to tell you why they can't pay." He was warming to his subject. "Look at what happened in California. Get a good earthquake, and the insurance companies close up shop. Or Florida. Comes a hurricane, the insurance companies are the first to head for high ground. Not to mention all the pension funds tied up in —"

"Right," I said. "Are you sure *you* didn't slip Jerry Jeff a few peanuts?"

Hark laughed. "Oh, hell, I've got an opinion like that on just about everything. I usually save it for the editorial page, but you asked." He shrugged. "Of course, not everybody thinks the way I do. Some folks feel like their insurance man is their best friend. And some of 'em are. Pokey was named as godfather to the Shaws' last baby, after he helped them straighten out their big hospital bill. Old man Lund made Jerry Jeff his executor."

"Old man Lund. Edna's father?" Somehow, that seemed incongruous. But maybe JJ and the Lunds had been long-time friends.

"Yeah. And both Jerry Jeff and Pokey are joiners. Lions Club, Rotary, Chamber of Commerce, Honchos — you name it, they belong." He grinned. "Now, a skeptic like me might say that membership in all those organizations is part of their public image. Maybe they do it because their hearts are pure."

I looked out the window and saw MaeBelle making her way around the third side of the square. "Thanks for the lunch — and the information." I pushed back my empty plate, grabbed Pokey's mountain oyster chili recipe, and stood up. "I hate to eat and run, but I have to see somebody."

"Better hurry," Ruby said, following my glance. "MaeBelle's a tough lady. She doesn't take bribes."

303

Chapter Fourteen

*It doesn't matter who you are, or what
you've done, or what you think you can do.
There's a confrontation with destiny
awaiting you. Somewhere, there's a chile
pepper you cannot eat.*
                    Daniel Pinkwater
                    "A Hot Time in Nairobi"

"Have you heard from the Manor today?"

MaeBelle ripped off the ticket she'd
written and deftly inserted it under the
wiper blade — not my wiper blade. My car
was a block over, still parked in front of
Cody and Clendennen. "Nary a word," she
said cheerfully. She turned and saw my
face. "Why? Somethin' happen?"

"Your aunt's roommate died this morning."

"Rachel Rogers? Aw, gee, that's too
bad." MaeBelle's round face grew sad.
"She was a sweet little thing. Her'n Aunt
Velma was real attached. They didn't talk
much, of course, but they looked out for
each other, in small ways."

"Your aunt seemed pretty upset by her

death," I said. "It might be a good idea if you stopped in to see her later today."

I hesitated. I hadn't intended to tell MaeBelle about the violent scene between Opal Hogge and her aunt until I knew more about the situation, but now — after the roommate's death — I was having second thoughts. If I didn't warn MaeBelle and something happened to Miss Velma, I'd feel responsible.

"I wonder," I said, "whether you've ever considered a different place for Miss Velma to live — the Oaks, maybe." The Oaks is an older nursing home on the east side of town, across I-35. It isn't as upscale as the Manor, but it has a reputation for caring treatment.

"A diff'rent place?" MaeBelle's forehead puckered. "Is somethin' goin' on I oughta know about?"

"Well, I don't have anything very concrete," I said, "and I certainly don't want to alarm you. But I happened to be at the Manor this morning when Mrs. Rogers was discovered dead, and your aunt — well, she seemed afraid."

MaeBelle opened her eyes wide. "Afraid? Afraid of what?"

I gave her a direct look. "Opal Hogge." I paused, then came out with it. "Look,

MaeBelle. I heard from one of the aides that she saw Mrs. Hogge shaking your aunt. I don't know whether she's telling the truth, but —"

"Shaking!" MaeBelle's eyes bulged. "Bunny Hogge, shaking Aunt Velma! Why . . . why, that's elder abuse! I saw a piece on *Sixty Minutes* about that just last week! Old people can die that way, same as little babies."

"Remember," I said cautiously, "it's only a report. It hasn't been confirmed."

"That don't make no difference." MaeBelle's eyes narrowed. "Mrs. Rogers is dead? You don't suppose somebody shook *her*, do you? I better —" But that was as far as she got.

"MaeBelle," a voice called urgently, and both of us turned around. Flying across the street toward us was Dorrie Hull, in blue jeans and cowboy shirt, blond hair loose around her shoulders. Dorrie is the day-shift dispatcher in the police department, and a regular customer at Thyme and Seasons. She gave me a quick smile and a hello, then turned breathlessly to MaeBelle.

"MaeBelle," she said, "you gotta come quick. The boss has called an emergency staff meeting."

MaeBelle tipped her uniform cap forward. "An emergency meeting? *Today?* Why, everybody but you and me is gettin' sensitized! Must be something big happened. What's it about?"

Dorrie's blue eyes were big in her pale face. "He's quit," she said, "effective soon as the Council can find somebody to take the job." She dropped her voice. "But don't let on you know it when you get back to headquarters, MaeBelle. It's supposed to be a big shock." She looked at me. "And don't let on you heard it from me, China. He's gonna make a public announcement soon's he tells the staff, but it wouldn't do for word to get out before."

"Bubba Harris has *quit?*" I asked incredulously.

"Sure as shootin'," Dorrie replied, glum. "He says it's more'n he can do to keep the peace in this town an' keep the Council happy at the same time."

"You don't suppose he got *fired,* do you?" MaeBelle's voice was low and shuddery. "Maybe he wasn't sensitive enough to suit 'em."

"Maybe it's a case of snatchin' the pan off the fire when you smell the bacon burnin'," Dorrie said sagely.

MaeBelle's face was dark. "Well, I've

allus believed in leavin' with the one that brung ya. Guess I should be thinkin' about findin' myself another job."

"You better think about gettin' your tail to the meetin'," Dorrie said, taking Mae-Belle's arm. "This is happenin' *now*, and if we don't git ourselves back to the office, we'll miss the show."

Torn between two loyalties, MaeBelle looked at me. "I'll head out to the Manor as soon as my shift ends. And if I don't like the look of things, I'll haul Aunt Velma out of there tonight, if I have to take her home with me."

She and Dorrie scurried off.

I stood still for a moment, wondering who the Council would hire to fill Bubba's scuffed boots and how his resignation would affect the current situation with regard to the goings-on at Cody and Clendennen — probably not at all, since there was still no evidence of a crime. Anyway, the resignation might be just a ploy, a big stick Bubba was brandishing in an attempt to get the Council to call off their sensitivity consultant. Maybe it would work, and they'd back off. Maybe it wouldn't, and we'd be breaking in a new police chief.

But Monday is not a day for loitering on the town square, even if it is my day off.

The courthouse clock had just struck one-thirty and I was only a couple of blocks from Thyme and Seasons. If I didn't do another thing today, I had to fax a couple of orders so they'd be delivered by the end of the week.

When you go into an herb shop, you're likely to see entire shelves lined with big glass jars of dried plant material. Some of these herbs — lavender, mint, lemongrass, rosemary, sage, thyme, to name a few common examples — are probably grown in the owner's garden and harvested, under duress, by the owner's kids (or long-suffering spouse or crazy friends who pretend to enjoy bending and stooping in the sun). Other herbs, however, are purchased from one of the big wholesalers — like Frontier Herbs, which grows forty-plus herbs on its sixty-acre organic farm and imports thousands of other varieties of herbs and spices from around the world. Look in the Frontier wholesale catalog, for instance, and you'll see ten different whole chile peppers, ranging from 2,000 units to 200,000 on the Scoville heat scale — ancho, arbol, birdseye, chipotle, gualjillo, habanero, Morita smoked, New Mexico, pasilla, red — and almost two dozen crushed chiles, ground chiles, and chile blends, from all over the world.

The first order of business when I got to the shop was to feed Khat and reassure him that he was top puss in my menagerie, no matter what nasty rumors Howard Cosell floated. Having polished off lunch in a flash, he leapt lightly to the counter for his postprandial nap while I dug out my Frontier order form, added a few last-minute items, and faxed it. While I worked to the background music of a contented cat's furry purr, my mind kept flipping back through the various conversations I'd had today and I began making a mental list of the things I had to tell McQuaid. I was picking up the phone to dial him when the door to Ruby's shop opened and Ruby came in, carrying a smart new leather briefcase and several sheets of paper.

"You ran out of Krautzenheimer's so fast that I didn't have time to ask you to sign these." She put the papers on the counter next to Khat and held out a pen. "I hope you didn't get a ticket."

"I wasn't overparked. I needed to talk to MaeBelle." I looked at the papers. "What's all this?"

"Bank stuff," Ruby said carelessly. "Signature card, checking account authorization, consent to the kidnapping of our first-born unless we follow the rules. If you're in a hurry, don't bother to read. Just sign at the X."

I gave her a suspicious glance. I distrust people who tell me not to read what I'm about to sign, and then make a joke about it. "How much did you deposit?"

"Enough to get us started." She thrust the pen into my fingers. "Hurry up, China. The bank closes at two."

"It'll open again in the morning," I said. "How much?"

"Twenty thousand," Ruby said. She eyed me. "Now, don't start yell—"

"Twenty thousand!" I squawked. "Ruby, that's *real* money!" Khat woke up and yawned, showing a pink tongue and sharp ivory fangs.

"Of course it's real money." Ruby was nettled. "What do you expect to pay architects and contractors with? Vanilla beans?"

"But that means I owe you ten thousand dollars, and we haven't poured a single cup of tea!" I was beginning to feel like the captain of the *Titanic*, confronting the horrifying evidence left by his first major iceberg. What was happening to the independent China who had bootstrapped her own business without anybody's help, not even the bank's? What about the woman who insisted on being responsible only to and for herself? She owed a big pot of money, had entered a partnership with a suddenly assertive friend, and had agreed to get married. Good grief!

"We'll worry about that when the time comes," Ruby said authoritatively. She took my hand and bent my loose fingers around the pen. "Don't think, sign."

Mrrow, Khat remarked. He stood, put his front paws on the papers and elongated himself in an elegant stretch, then leapt from the counter to the windowsill. *Mrrow,* he said again, with greater emphasis.

"You see," Ruby said sagely, "even your cat is telling you to do it."

"After he was bribed with the promise of fresh chicken livers sautéed in butter and garlic." I sighed. At some point or another, everyone encounters the inevitable. Closing my eyes to the sinister fine print, I signed at the X's.

"Thank you," Ruby said. "Now you can go back to that call you were making when I came in. Was it important?"

"Only a conversation with McQuaid."

She picked up the papers and put them into the briefcase, which was impressively stamped with her initials in gold. "Don't you think you could break down and call him Mike, now that you're actually going to marry him?"

"Listen, Ruby," I said heatedly, "I am caving in on big-time issues here, and it's not an entirely delightful experience. Don't push me on the small stuff. Okay?"

Whatever she said was drowned out by the loud jangle of the cowbell that hangs on the front door handle. The door opened a few inches, and a girl's face appeared.

"Ms. Bayles?" The voice was tentative, almost apprehensive. "We know you're closed today, but we saw your car out front and we wondered if —"

"Angie!" I said, more than a little relieved. "And Carita. Come in!"

On the job, in scrubs and with their hair pulled back, Angie and Carita had looked like cool, crisp nursing professionals. Now, mops of shiny dark hair artfully tangled, slender and petite in close-fitting shorts and sandals and pastel crop-tops that bared their brown midriffs, they looked more like teen models. Standing side by side, they looked remarkably alike, too. But of course — Angie had said they were cousins. They came into the shop quickly, one after the other, and almost apprehensively, glancing over their shoulders as if to make sure that they weren't seen.

"Gosh," Angie said, glancing around, "this is a *great* place."

Carita sniffed. "It smells good."

"I think so," I said. I introduced them to Ruby as aides from the Manor, and Ruby as my friend and business partner.

"I asked for you this morning at the nurses station," I told Angie, "but you weren't at work."

"I didn't go in," Angie said. "Carita needed somebody to talk to. It's been pretty bad for her, since Saturday night."

Carita swallowed. "Angie and I, we've been talking, all day yesterday and all this morning. We think we've got it figured out, about the thefts and the credit card." She glanced apprehensively at Ruby. "But maybe . . ." She tugged at Angie's arm, turning toward the door. "We'll come back later, when you're not busy."

"Wait," I said. "Why don't we let Ruby hear your story? She's every bit as good as Jessica Fletcher when it comes to figuring things out. Remember the cat lady? It was Ruby who did the detective work that got her out of jail." At the question in their eyes, I added, "And don't worry. You can trust her not to share your story with anybody. How about if I fill her in?"

The two girls gazed at Ruby, in her variegated costume, then held a silent consultation with their eyes. Carita gave a doubtful nod and Angie said, "Okay, if it'll help."

The story took only a few minutes. Ruby asked a couple of questions, and I had to go back over a point or two, but there really wasn't much to it. Employee suspected of theft, stolen item discovered in employee's possession, employee fired. Pretty simple.

"But simple things are often complicated," Ruby said sympathetically. She looked from one girl to the other. "What do you mean when you say you've got it figured out? What do you think happened?"

"It's all tangled up," Angie began, "but we think we know who put the credit card into Carita's purse."

"We know who, but we can't figure out *why*," Carita said, frowning. "And we sort of don't believe what we think we know." She shook her head. "It just doesn't make any sense."

"So we hoped maybe you'd have an idea," Angie added. "We thought you might be able to help us decide what to do."

"Okay." I leaned on the counter. "So who did it?"

The girls stepped closer together, almost as if for protection, and I thought again how alike they were. There was a quiet shyness about them, too, that I found attractive — unlike some teenagers, who are so in-your-face that you're glad to get away from them.

"We don't know for sure about the other stuff that was stolen," Carita said. Almost unconsciously, she reached for Angie's hand and they hooked little fingers, like two kids with a magic talisman. "Some of the staff think maybe it was Deena."

"Deena?" I frowned, trying to remember. "Oh, yes. The one who got fired for not reporting the faulty kitchen equipment."

"Excuse me?" Ruby asked, and I explained what Angie had told me earlier.

"Except that some people think Deena *really* got fired for stealing," Carita said, "not for the other thing. They say Mrs. Hogge didn't tell anybody the real reason — not even Deena herself — because she wanted to see if the thefts would stop. It was like a test, or something."

"It makes sense," Ruby said. "And if Deena was the thief, she would know why she was fired. She wouldn't make a fuss over it, either, because she wouldn't want stealing on her employee record."

The girls nodded in concert.

"Did the thefts stop after Deena left?" I asked.

"Yes," Angie said. "Everybody noticed it. All the aides, I mean. They talked about it in the break room. To tell the truth, people were relieved, because the rest of us weren't under suspicion any longer. There was one little problem, though."

"The earrings," Carita said, taking up the story. "Deena gave them to me after she got fired, and I wore them to work. Mrs. Hogge accused me of taking them."

"So you didn't get them from the flea market, after all," I remarked.

"No. I didn't want to get anybody in trouble. I said the first thing that came into my head. It was a lie."

"So." I looked from one of them to the other. "How did the stolen credit card get into Carita's purse?"

Their faces were sober and somehow more adult. They traded looks again, perhaps for reassurance.

"We think," Angie said, "that Mrs. Hogge put it there."

"Mrs. Hogge?" Ruby arched skeptical

eyebrows up under her fringe of gingery hair.

"We know it's a terrible thing to say," Carita replied earnestly, "but this is what happened. Last Saturday, I worked the three to eleven shift. I took my break at six and got my purse out of the locker so I could give Marguerite — she's one of the nurses — the two dollars I owed her from lunch the day before. The credit card wasn't in my wallet then. I would have seen it." She blushed. "When I gave Marguerite the money, the wallet was empty. But five minutes after I put my purse back in the locker and went back to work, Mrs. Hogge called me to her office. My purse was on her desk. She told me to open my wallet, and there it was."

Ruby frowned. "Five minutes doesn't seem like much time for —"

"Exactly!" Angie exclaimed. "There wasn't time for anybody else to put the credit card in Carita's purse and tell Mrs. Hogge it was there — and then for Mrs. Hogge to find it. The only way it could have happened was for Mrs. Hogge to get the purse herself and put the credit card in it, so she could accuse Carita."

"But why would she do such a thing?" Ruby asked.

"That's the part we don't understand," Carita said helplessly. "It doesn't make any sense at all. Nobody's ever complained about me."

"In fact," Angie said, "just last week, Mrs. Hogge herself told Carita that she was doing a good job."

"It's like she all of a sudden had to get rid of me," Carita said. Her large dark eyes were filled with unhappiness. "I don't know why."

I looked at one cousin and then the other. If the girls couldn't see why Mrs. Hogge had to get rid of Carita, I could. "Maybe it's a case of mistaken identity," I said.

Carita stared at me. "Mistaken — ?"

Angie was quicker. "You mean, she got the two of us mixed up?" She frowned. "But that doesn't make any sense, either. I haven't done anything to get fired for. There was that business with Miss Velma, but I didn't tell anybody but you."

"Pardon me," Ruby said in a puzzled tone, "but I think I'm missing a piece. Can somebody fill me in?"

Haltingly, Angie reconstructed what she had witnessed in Miss Velma's room. "But I don't see what that's got to do with Carita," she concluded.

"If Mrs. Hogge only got a glimpse of you," Ruby said, "she might have thought you were Carita. So it was Carita she fired."

"See?" I said. "Jessica Fletcher."

"But Angie and I don't look *anything* like each other," Carita objected. "Angie's much prettier, and she's got that little mole on her chin, and her hair is longer and —"

"Minor differences," Ruby said confidently. "To a stranger, or someone in a hurry, or scared, you're the Bobbsey twins."

"The Bobbsey twins?" Carita looked puzzled. "I don't think I've met them."

"Maybe they work in the kitchen," Angie said.

"Really." Ruby rolled her eyes at me. "Am I that old?"

I could have said they were that young, but I didn't want to insult them. "Ruby just means," I explained, "that you two look very much alike."

"You know," Angie said thoughtfully, "I'll bet Mrs. Hogge *did* mix us up. She planted that credit card so she could fire Carita and keep her from telling."

"And to discredit her," Ruby said. Her eyes narrowed and her voice crackled. "That woman has no business running the

Manor. As long as she's in that job, patients and employees both are vulnerable. Why, she could have *killed* Miss Velma, shaking her like that!"

"But what can *we* do?" Angie asked helplessly. "Mrs. Hogge is the boss. She runs things the way she wants and nobody dares to question her. And neither Carita nor I can prove anything. She'll just say we made it up."

"I wish we knew somebody on the board of directors who would back us," I said. "Somebody with some clout. McQuaid thought he had a contact, but it turns out that the guy is Opal Hogge's nephew. He helped her get the job in the first place, so I don't think we can count on him for anything."

"We do know somebody," Ruby said, unexpectedly. "She's the president of the board, in fact. Her name is Liz McKenzie. I met her at a workshop a couple of years ago, and we see one another every few months. We can trust her to help without putting Angie into jeopardy. She might even be able to see that Carita gets her job back."

"She said *might,*" I cautioned, but Carita gave a joyful yelp anyway, and Angie's arm went around her shoulders.

"That would be wonderful." Angie wore a wide grin. "Carita needs her job worse than anything. Her family needs it, too. Gosh, thanks, Ms. Wilcox."

"The old girls network strikes again," Ruby said, smiling modestly. "Behind every great woman is another great woman. We'll see Liz as soon as we can."

The girls left a few minutes later, and Ruby looked down at her watch. "Well, I'm glad I hung around, but now it's after two and the bank has closed. I guess that paperwork will have to wait until tomorrow."

"Do you have anything else to do today?" I asked.

Ruby eyed me. "That depends. What's on your mind?"

"Behind every great woman is another great woman," I said humbly. "I'm tired of trying to figure this out for myself. I'm going out to the Manor to talk to McQuaid, and I'd like you to go along."

Ruby leaned forward. "It's about Jerry Jeff, isn't it?" she said. "You're onto something. You think somebody actually *murdered* him."

"Maybe," I said, "although to tell the truth, it's hard to know how much I really know, and how much I'm making up. If you take my meaning."

"I do." Ruby sighed. "Sometimes I have the same problem."

"The thing is," I said, "that there's no *evidence*. I mean, if I were an attorney in this case, I'd have no trouble coming up with two or three different theories. Any one of them might be true, but which one? And Cody's death isn't the only thing I'm not sure about. Miss Velma's roommate died this morning."

"Oh?" Ruby sighed. "Well, I don't suppose that's an unusual event at the Manor — in the Alzheimer's unit, anyway."

"No," I said. "But something about it is making me uneasy. You see, Angie wasn't the only person who saw what happened between Opal Hogge and Miss Velma. According to Angie, Mrs. Rogers — Miss Velma's roommate — witnessed it too. In fact, she tried to get out of bed to stop it."

Ruby thought about this for a moment. Then she stiffened. "You don't think Opal Hogge could have —" She pulled in her breath. "You're not saying she *killed* her!"

"I don't know what I'm saying," I replied. "Mrs. Rogers must have been eighty, maybe more. Most likely, she died of simple old age. But it's easy enough to kill an old person without leaving any traces, and Opal Hogge has been in her line of work long enough to know how it's done."

"That's right," Ruby said. Her voice became taut. "Remember that nurse who killed all those old people with insulin injections? And I read about somebody else, too — somebody who used potassium. China, this is *serious*. Hogge has managed to discredit one witness by charging her with theft. Now the only other witness turns up dead! Velma Mayfield might be in danger, too."

"I spoke to MaeBelle about it," I said. "She said she'd see about moving her aunt. Meanwhile, I've got a call in to a woman in San Antonio who is supposed to know why Opal Hogge left her position there."

Ruby was pacing back and forth, agitated. "But we have to *do* something, China! We can't just stand back and let —"

"Do what? There's no evidence of an assault, unless an examination turns up bruises. And even then, it's probably impossible to say for sure how she got them. We have a victim who can't make a reliable report, a witness who —"

"That's it!" Ruby stopped pacing and snapped her fingers. "We have Angie. She's a good witness."

"Not so fast. She's comfortable with us, but she probably wouldn't do very well in

324

court. Hogge's lawyer would start by asking why she didn't report the abuse to her supervisor, then suggest that she's lying in order to tarnish Hogge's reputation and redeem her friend. And there's something else, too. We can't act until we understand her motive. What does Opal Hogge have against Velma Mayfield? Did Velma simply get under her skin, or is there more to it than that?"

"Well, we're not going to figure it out standing here," Ruby said. "Come on. Let's go see McQuaid."

Chapter Fifteen

If you can't stand the heat, it may be because you have too much taste. Literally. Some people can't eat hot chiles because they have nearly twice the average number of taste buds per centimeter of tongue area. Approximately one quarter of the population are these "supertasters." Another quarter are "nontasters," with fewer than average taste buds. The rest of us are — well, average. Some tasteless people may be able to chomp their way through a peck of peppers without shedding a tear, while the thought of even one small jalapeño is enough to steam up a supertaster's glasses.

China Bayles
"Hot Pods and Fired-Up Fare"
Pecan Springs *Enterprise*

McQuaid, in his wheelchair, was waiting for us in the lobby. "Jug's having a nap," he said. "The domino game this morning wore him out."

"It must be a new experience, having an eighty-year-old roommate," Ruby remarked, as we settled into the corner behind the aquarium. "I don't know if I could handle that."

McQuaid grinned. "I'm learning that the world doesn't revolve around me. Probably qualifies as a learner's permit for marriage."

Which led to Ruby's congratulating McQuaid on our getting married and saying how coincidental it was that our wedding reception would take place at the same time as the grand opening of Thyme for Tea. McQuaid raised his eyebrows at me, and I shrugged.

"What can I say? She has the checkbook."

We didn't have time to debate the question, because an old woman shuffled up, bent over an ornately carved wooden cane. She was wearing four or five long, silky petticoats in shades of neon red and orange and purple, layered one over the other and anchored by a dozen loops of plastic Mardi Gras beads hitched around her waist. Her drawn-on eyebrows and lipsticked mouth gave her a clownish look, but there was a mischievous glint in her eye. She bent over and dropped a kiss on McQuaid's forehead.

"What would you say to black-eyed peas an' okra for supper tonight, sugar?" she asked gaily.

"Hot diggity," McQuaid said, and smiled up at her.

She patted his shoulder. "Well, don't you be late, now, y'hear? The girls'll be disappointed if you don't get there in time to give each of 'em some of your sweet, in-dee-vi-jual attention." She looked at Ruby and smiled hugely, showing perfect dentures. "My, honey, I surely do admire them pants. You'll be a big hit with the boys tonight." She patted Ruby's cheek, then off she went, twirling her beads. In a moment, she was bending over to stroke the bald head of an old man in a yellow plaid sport coat.

"When I grow old," Ruby remarked appreciatively, "I shall wear purple. And red. And orange."

"Her name is Madame Iris LeBeaux," McQuaid said, as if that explained everything. Maybe it did. "Now, where were we?"

In the midst of another interruption, that's where. At that moment, eight Sweet Adelines arrived, wearing bouncy red petticoats, red vests over white peasant blouses, and red felt Swiss hats perched on poufed hair. Giggling and chattering among themselves, they began the melodious process of tuning up while seniors gathered expectantly and aides began pushing chairs toward the middle of the room. Edna Lund came in and hung a big paper banner announcing "!!The Sound of Music!!" at the front of the room, and the Ladies Guild started setting up a snack table in the back.

Bowing to the inevitable, we turned down an offer of strawberry Kool-Aid and relocated to the patio, under the deep shade of the huge live oak that overhangs the building. It was nicer outside, anyway. The sky was a cloud-dappled blue and the temperature was in the upper eighties — one of those afternoons when you'd rather be sailing on Canyon Lake — but a breeze lifted the shiny oak leaves, and the muted sound of women singing close harmony was a pleasant background. McQuaid and I started off by bringing Ruby up to date on everything we knew, and I concluded by reporting what I had learned from Pokey, finishing my narration to the distant tune of "Down By the Old Mill Stream."

McQuaid rearranged himself in his wheelchair, as if he were reorganizing his thoughts. "You're saying you think Pokey Clendennen is an innocent bystander?"

"I can't swear to it," I said, "but that was my impression. The idea that Jerry Jeff had been murdered seemed to come as a genuine surprise to him. But — this is how I've got it figured, anyway — after a moment's thought, it occurred to him that Roxanne might have done it, with the intention of implicating *him*." The Sweet Adelines swung into a spirited version of "The Sidewalks of New York."

"Maybe he has a reason to suspect her." Ruby brushed a misguided bee from the leg of her flowered pants. "Anybody could come along and toss something into those open chili pots, you know. Maybe Pokey saw Roxanne dump in a bag or two of Planters, and only remembered it when you told him how Jerry Jeff died."

"That could be," I agreed. "It would certainly explain his knee-jerk reaction. But if she wanted to be sure that Jerry Jeff got a good dose, that wasn't her only opportunity. The cups were assembled in the check-in tent before they were taken to the judging tent. Roxanne was working there. I saw her myself."

"She certainly stands to benefit," Ruby said thoughtfully. "Jerry Jeff told me that he carried over a million dollars in term insurance. He sold it to himself and got a commission on it, so it was cheap."

"A million bucks!" I exclaimed. "Now,

that's what I call motive."

"In a way," McQuaid said reflectively, "Roxanne not only stands to benefit, she can't lose. Let's assume that it was Roxanne who put the peanuts into sample number twenty-two. If everybody thinks that Jerry Jeff died of natural causes, she's home free, a rich widow. If the cops figure out how he died, decide he was murdered, and trace the nuts to Pokey's chili, she's *still* a rich widow and Pokey's the guy who takes the fall."

"How clever," Ruby murmured. Inside, the Adelines held the last "New York" until it was drowned out by enthusiastic applause, some shrill whistling, and the thumping of canes.

"But nobody's going to take the fall," I said. "Let's be practical, you guys. So what if there are a few peanuts in Pokey's chili? Nobody can prove *he* put them there. The same goes for Roxanne, only more so. You know as well as I do that no prosecutor in his right mind would take either one of them before a grand jury. Motive and opportunity don't add up to a conviction." I sat back, listening to the plaintive notes of "Bury Me Not on the Lone Prairie."

McQuaid's fingers drummed on the arm of his wheelchair. "What we need is an eyewitness who saw Roxanne or Pokey doctor that chili."

"What would that prove?" I asked with a shrug. "This is not like a case in which party A bashes party B with a blunt instrument. So Pokey or Roxanne put peanuts in the chili. There is certainly room to argue that it was done without any ill intention. The perfect crime — unless one of them confesses."

"That's not very likely," McQuaid said.

Ruby wore a musing look. "I wonder how Pokey is feeling right now. He must be pretty upset. Angry, too."

"You're probably right." I spoke slowly, thinking it through. "In fact, if Pokey suspects that Roxanne deliberately implicated him by using his sample, he might be angry or scared enough to spit it out. I'll have another conversation with him, and see if I can dig up anything more."

Ruby frowned. "Pokey and Roxanne — is there any chance that they'll do a flit?"

I tried not to smile. "Do a flit?"

Ruby waved her hand. "That's what some crook called it in a crime novel I read last week. It means to fly from justice. Run away."

"I doubt it," McQuaid said. "Why should they flee? They're not charged with anything. They both have homes here, and business connections."

"Yes, but maybe Pokey knows something and he doesn't want to lie," Ruby persisted. "Running away would be the easiest way to avoid it. Or maybe he was taking money out of the business, too, and he's afraid an IRS audit will catch him." She cocked her head and frowned, as if she were listening to an inner voice, maybe. "Really, China. I'm getting a hunch. I have the strangest feeling that Roxanne and Pokey might just fly off —"

"I agree with McQuaid," I said, thinking back on my conversations with both Roxanne and Pokey. "They're not the type. But I'll consider that as I talk to Pokey," I added more mildly, not wanting to discourage Ruby.

Actually, it is very difficult to discourage Ruby. "I could go with you," she offered helpfully. "We could both talk to him."

"I've got a better idea," McQuaid said. "How about if you interview the people who were working in the check-in tent, Ruby? One of them might have noticed something — like Roxanne putting peanuts into a sample cup."

"Check with Fannie Couch," I said. "She recruited the helpers. She'll give you a list of the people who were there."

"Well —" Ruby frowned to express her preference for a more prominent role in the investigation, but she didn't want to be left out. "Okay."

"Good," McQuaid said. "I'll reconnect with Charlie Lipman. He was going to make sure that Cody's stash, wherever it is, is still intact." He glanced at me. "What about Craig Burkhart?"

"But Roxanne and Pokey are the ones who stand to gain," I protested.

"Maybe," McQuaid said. "But you're forgetting about those blackmail letters. So far, we have no idea who may have written them, or how that person is connected with all this. Burkhart is a pretty good candidate. He lost that lawsuit — and he may have been afraid that he'd lose his wife as well."

"And they used to be partners, didn't they?" Ruby asked. "Burkhart might have known that Jerry Jeff wasn't reporting all his income."

"Burkhart's wife said he'd be back home this afternoon," McQuaid reminded me. "Go over there and see what you can dig up. If something comes of this and we hand it over to Bubba, I want to be sure we've covered all the bases."

"We won't be handing it over to Bubba," I said, and broke the news.

"Bubba Harris has *quit?*" Ruby was incredulous. "Why . . . why, that's like saying the sun's stopped shining!"

"It's true," I said. "I was talking to MaeBelle when Dorrie the dispatcher came rushing out to fetch her for a staff meeting. The chief was about to break the news to his team."

McQuaid's face was grim. "I've never been Bubba's biggest fan, but I'm sorry to see him forced out. The job is tough enough, damn it, without City Hall kicking sand in your face." He paused, tapping his teeth with his thumbnail. "I wonder who will replace him. There's nobody in the department who has enough experience to step into the job — or rather, nobody that the City Council will trust. They'll have to do an outside search."

"Maybe they'll hire a woman," Ruby offered hopefully.

"In this town?" McQuaid was vastly amused. "Come on, Ruby, get real. This Council isn't ready for a woman."

"What *are* they ready for?" I asked. "A sensitized male?"

"Kerrville's got a woman chief," Ruby said with dignity. "If Kerrville's City

Council can bring themselves to hire a woman, I fail to see why Pecan Springs can't. I personally intend to phone the councilwoman for my precinct and let her know that —"

"Before we get off on that subject," I said hastily, "what happened with Joyce Sanders this morning, McQuaid? You were going to talk to her about Miss Velma."

"I did," McQuaid said. His face was serious. "I reported Angie's claim of abuse, and asked her to check into it. She said she'd talk to Angie as soon as the girl could be located. When I went off for my second session with the physical therapist, she was on her way to examine Miss Velma herself. I stopped at her office just before you came, to see what she had learned. But she's apparently gone to San Antonio for a meeting."

"How did she respond?" Ruby asked. "Did she seem to take it seriously?"

"You bet. In fact, I thought she was expecting something of the sort. She didn't seem totally surprised."

The barbershoppers were repeating the last, mournful verse of "Bury Me Not," and the line "Fling a handful of roses over my grave" trembled in the air. At that moment, the sun went behind a cloud, and the afternoon's brightness was dimmed.

"What did Joyce say about Mrs. Rogers's death?" I asked.

"The woman had a history of heart trouble," McQuaid said. "That's what's listed as the cause of death."

"The famous cardiac arrest," I said dryly. "The victim died when her heart stopped beating."

"I suppose there'll be an autopsy," Ruby said, brushing at the insistent bee.

"Uh-uh." McQuaid shook his head. "The funeral home has already taken the body for cremation. That's what the family wanted."

Ruby made a protesting noise. "But that means that Opal Hogge might be getting away with —"

"It's possible," McQuaid said. "But Joyce had no legitimate reason to interfere with the family's arrangements. Anyway, by the time she and I talked, Mrs. Rogers was on her way."

"To a narrow grave, just six by three," I said quietly.

"What?" Ruby asked, startled.

"Bury me not on the lone prairie," I said. "Haven't you been listening to the song?"

McQuaid turned to me. "Any new developments on your end of this Opal Hogge business?"

"Yes, actually," I said. And to the lilting tune of "I Want a Girl Just Like the Girl that Married Dear Old Dad," Ruby and I told him about our conversation with Angie and Carita, and Ruby's idea about talking to Liz McKenzie. I reported MaeBelle's plan to move her aunt out of the Manor. "Once that's done," I said, "I don't think there's a great deal of urgency about the situation."

"That's probably true," McQuaid said. He reached for my hand. "I'm glad you thought of getting Velma moved, China. When I stopped in to check on her, she was upset and almost incoherent. Crying and carrying on about Mrs. Rogers and those papers she mentioned the other night."

"Papers?" I asked. "I wonder what that's all about."

"It could be anything," Ruby said. "When we moved my grandmother to the nursing home in Waco, her house was full of old letters. Until the day she died, she'd beg people to go back to her house and find a letter from Dahlia or Daisy or whoever, so she could read it. Never mind that her son had sold her house to pay her nursing home bills and her letters had long since been burned. Afterward, my mother said she was sorry we hadn't kept them."

"Did Miss Velma mention Opal Hogge in connection with Mrs. Rogers's death?" I asked.

McQuaid shook his head. "She mentioned her, but it's hard to say what the context was." He glanced at me. "Why don't you talk to her, China? You might pick up something I'm missing."

Ruby lifted her hands and ran them through her gingery hair. "How about me? I don't know if she would remember me, but it might be worth a try." McQuaid and I nodded.

Inside, the Sweet Adelines had flung themselves exuberantly into "The Yellow Rose of Texas."

"Gosh, McQuaid looks good, China," Ruby said, as we walked back to the car. "Almost back to normal. How is the therapy coming along?"

"I don't know all the details," I said, "but the therapist has him on some sort of apparatus that supports him while his legs learn to move." I unlocked the car door, got in, and opened Ruby's door. "The important thing, though, is the change in his attitude. Last week, he seemed so . . . defeated. Now, he seems determined."

"It's getting married," Ruby said knowingly. "It gives him something to occupy his mind."

"If you ask me, it's the investigation into Jerry Jeff Cody's death," I said, putting the key into the ignition. "*That's* what's occupying his mind. Not to mention the problems at the Manor. I —"

The rest of my response was cut off by the insistent buzz of the car phone. It was Rosie Montgomery. I mentioned Fannie's name, briefly explained what I wanted to know, and listened. She was not reluctant to talk. In fact, she was anxious. She was an old lady with a very loud voice, and she talked in circles.

"Well, you've certainly asked the right person," she said. "My sister Hilda lived out her last years in that home. It's a church home, you know, private. I was very well acquainted with the situation at the time, and I have some definite opinions, if you want to hear them." Her pause for breath barely slowed her. "Of course, you have to remember that this is just my opinion, although I have to say that it's shared by a lot of people. And I do mean a *whole* lot," she added, with emphasis. "The whole thing left us with a bad taste in our mouths."

"I do want to hear," I said sincerely. "What exactly was the situation?"

Mrs. Montgomery's voice was tinny, and so shrill I was tempted to turn down the volume. Instead, I held the phone away from my ear, so Ruby could hear too. "Of course," she said, "I'm just one person, but to my way of thinking, it was just a crime what that Hogge woman did. Robbery, plain and simple. Though to give the devil her due, so to speak, it wasn't all her fault. The board was to blame, too. They set the standard, you might say. If you know what I mean."

"Not exactly," I said, before she could begin a new paragraph. "To blame for what?"

"For the way they raised that money. Of course, the new building was terribly, terribly expensive and the operating expenses were just going higher and higher. I'm sure they had to do something desperate to make ends meet. And since the residents were church members, they must have felt they could get away with it." She paused momentarily. "You still there?"

"Oh, yes," I said. "In fact, I was wondering what they might have tried to get away with."

"Good. I thought maybe we got disconnected." She took a quick breath, then plunged ahead. "The families didn't like it one bit, I'll tell you. It made for such hard feelings that it split the church. Right down the middle, and things have never been the same since and never will. Some people were so sick at heart that they left and started their own —"

"Get away with *what?*" I asked. I was beginning to feel desperate, and beside me, Ruby was rolling her eyes. "What *are* we talking about, Mrs. Montgomery, if you don't mind my asking?"

"Why, the solicitations," she said, surprised. "The fundraising. Wasn't that what you called about?"

"I don't exactly know why I called," I admitted, "except that Fannie Couch thought you might be able to tell me why Opal Hogge left her position. Mrs. Hogge was involved in some sort of solicitation?"

"Was she involved? Was she *involved?*" Mrs. Montgomery gave a sarcastic laugh. "I'm here to tell you she was involved! Now, I'm not saying she did this on her own hook, mind you. The board gave her a green light to use any old methods she wanted, and somebody on the board even helped her make up a list of the residents' property and —"

"So she approached the patients with a request for money, on behalf of the nursing home's board?"

Mrs. Montgomery was beginning to run out of patience with me. "That's what I'm saying, isn't it?" she retorted indignantly. "With never a word to the families, not one single word! And offered to have the church lawyer draw up an entirely new will! Did you ever hear of such a nerve? Some of the residents, of course, were so far gone that they could be persuaded to do anything if you just petted them up a little, and of course, Opal Hogge was very good at that. Petting, I mean. She'd stroke and smile and then pounce, just like a cat, trying to get her claws on that money. My poor, dear sister —" Mrs. Montgomery interrupted herself with several mournful clucks, and was then moved to blow her nose.

"Your sister?" I prompted, when she was finished.

"— was completely taken in." Mrs. Montgomery blew her nose again. "Totally."

"She changed her will? In favor of the nursing home?"

"Gave them most of her money."

"Ah," I said. "I see."

"Not that I cared for myself, of course," Mrs. Montgomery said quickly. "Gerald and I are well enough fixed that we didn't need any of Hilda's money, although it would have been nice to put a new roof on the house and maybe go to Disney World before we get too old to enjoy it. But it wasn't the money, don't you go thinking that! It was the principle of the thing, pure and simple. It was the idea of that Hogge woman, bold as a brass monkey with a stick in its hand, marching in on my sister when she was flat on her back, too sick to know what she was doing, and talking the poor thing into signing all her money over to —"

"How much?" I asked.

The silence was the longest in the conversation so far. Finally, Mrs. Montgomery drew a long, shaky breath and said, "Fifty thousand dollars, more or less, split between me and my two older sisters. Gerald and I would've gone to court, but Sarah and Sadie just wouldn't hear of it — Sadie's ninety-two and stubborn as an old nanny goat — so what could we do? Anyway, we're church members, and we hated to act like the grinch who stole

Christmas, if you know what I mean."

"I'm sure," I said.

"But we weren't the only ones who were unhappy. Oh, no, not by a long shot, and some of them stood to lose a lot more than we did. When the families began to figure out what was going on — which mostly didn't happen until after their dear one had departed, of course — they went to the board and gave them a piece of their minds. First the board tried to say that they'd written a piece about it in the home newsletter, which of course none of the families ever read. Then they said they never meant to interfere in people's financial affairs, it was only a way of helping the church pay the bills. *Then* they said it was Opal Hogge's fault that the campaign got out of hand, that she must have gotten carried away and didn't stop to think how families would feel about it."

"So the board blamed Mrs. Hogge?"

"Yes, although most folks said it was purely hypocritical, because Opal Hogge was smart as a tack — you had to give her that much, regardless of how you felt about her — and she wouldn't have stuck her neck out without somebody on the board egging her on. But she just wasn't real well liked, and of course she wasn't a member of the church, so she got all the blame and the board just looked stupid, rather than devious. Like she had pulled the wool over their eyes or something."

"And they fired her?"

"Yes, which pleased Gerald no end, believe you me." Her voice became pious. "But I told him, I said, 'Gerald, the Lord tells us to forgive our enemies,' I said, and anyway, the damage was already done. The ones who were dead were dead, and their money went to the nursing home because most families felt like Gerald and me. They didn't want to cause an uproar in the church, and they didn't want people thinking they were stingy cheapskates." Sarcasm edged the piety. "We're supposed to give until it hurts. Although like I said, we've got this bad taste in our mouths about it."

"Well, yes," I said. "I can certainly see how there would be hard feelings against Mrs. Hogge."

"Hard feelings!" Mrs. Montgomery snorted a laugh. "Hard feelings! Believe you me, if she ever shows her face over here again, there are some people — God-fearing Christians, too, who go to church every Sunday — who would tar and feather her. Tar and *feather!*"

I managed to get the name of the board

president and the name and address of the church, and then said good-bye. I put the phone down and looked at Ruby, who was shaking her head incredulously.

"What a scam," she said. "Do you think it's the truth?"

"It's not a scam," I said, "at least, not from the church's point of view. And I'm quite sure it *is* the truth. There was a very similar circumstance in Oregon a few years ago. In that case, a jury convicted the nursing home director of extortion and fraud, and he went to prison." I thought for a moment. "As I understood it, he had a clause in his contract with the nursing home, which gave him a percentage of whatever money he raised. That was why he was so eager to do a good job."

Ruby made a face. "So," she said, "now we know."

"Know what?" I asked. "We know what Opal Hogge was up to in San Antonio, but that doesn't necessarily shed any light on what's going on here. According to Mae-Belle, her aunt was poor as a church mouse when they brought her here. She's probably on Medicaid by now. I doubt if Bunny was shaking her down for a few odd quarters."

"Well, then, how about other residents?

Mrs. Rogers, for instance?" Ruby cocked her head thoughtfully. "Maybe Mrs. Rogers rewrote her will in favor of the nursing home."

"Maybe," I said. "But we'd have to ask the niece, and I don't think we ought to do it while the family is still dealing with the death. After I've talked to Burkhart, I'll let McQuaid know what Rosie Montgomery told us, so he's up to speed. As you said, we have plenty of other things to do."

I turned the key in the ignition. That being the case, it was time to start doing them.

Lulu Burkhart had told McQuaid that her husband would be back from Houston on Monday afternoon. I decided not to phone ahead, thinking that I might learn more by surprising the Burkharts with a few off-the-cuff questions. So I let Ruby off at the shop to call Fannie and get names, and drove to the Burkhart house, in one of the newer subdivisions on the outskirts of Pecan Springs. I pulled up in front shortly after five. I caught Craig Burkhart, all right, but his wife wasn't there.

"Sorry," Burkhart said when he answered the door, an ornately carved, varnished oak affair with a large oval panel of stained glass. "You just missed Lulu. She took Pete to play soccer over at Johnson Field." He grinned easily. "She's one of those soccer moms this year. Out there every week, giving the coach hell if her boy doesn't get out on the field." He was in a dress shirt and dark slacks, tie off, sleeves rolled up, a heavy gold watch on his wrist. On the hallway table behind him, I could see a folded jacket and briefcase. "Want to leave a note or something?" he added pleasantly. "She won't be back until after seven, and then we're going out to dinner."

"Actually, I've come to talk to you, Mr. Burkhart." I shifted my briefcase to my left hand and held out my right. "My name is China Bayles. I'm a friend of Mike McQuaid's."

"Yeah, Mike, sure." He took my hand in a grip that was strong and self-assured. "How the hell is that old rascal? Somebody said he was one of the judges at the chili cookoff, so he must be getting around a bit. Too bad, what happened. I hope he's better. You tell him I said so, y'hear?"

"I will. In fact, it was McQuaid who asked me to stop by and have a chat with you. He's working on a case for a friend and he had a couple of questions he thought you might be able to clear up for him. May I come in?"

Burkhart's face — a handsomely rugged face, darkened with a late-afternoon beard — registered slight surprise, and some mystification. But he stepped back and ushered me into the high-ceilinged hall. As I came in, I handed him one of my cards. He glanced at it and dropped it into his shirt pocket.

Although the Burkharts' house still hadn't settled into its sparse foundation shrubbery or lost its new-house smell, it was built to look a century old, with enough vintage trim and turnings, balusters and newel posts, molded casings and fretwork spandrels, beaded wainscot paneling, flocked wallpaper, and glass chandeliers to have pleased even the most opulent of Victorian tastes. The living room furnishings were Victorian, too: a tufted red velvet love seat, carved antique tables, Tiffany-style lamps, fringed damask draperies, silk-flower bouquets in large Chinese vases. A cut-glass dish of rose potpourri sat on the table, filling the room with a heavy fragrance. I almost smiled, thinking that Madame Iris LeBeaux and her girls would feel right at home here.

Burkhart, however, looked distinctly out of place. He shoved a footstool aside and lowered himself gingerly onto one of the chairs, motioning me to take the love seat.

"My wife is into Victorian," he said, waving his hand around vaguely.

"She certainly is," I murmured.

"To my taste, she overdoes it. But she spends more time at home, so I tell her to do what she likes." He dismissed the decor and focused on me. "You said you wanted to see me?"

"You've been out of town since yesterday, I understand."

He nodded briefly.

"You're in commercial real estate?"

"Strip center development." He quirked an eyebrow at me and smiled. We were moving onto his turf. "I've got some outstanding pieces of property, a number of fine locations anywhere between Austin and San Antonio. You in the market?" He cocked his head. "Or Mike, maybe? I brought him a sweet deal a couple of years ago, but he said he wasn't ready to take the plunge." He was regretful. "Too bad. He could've made a bundle on it. We're out of the bust and into the boom again. Good strip locations are getting to be as rare as horny toads, but I've still got a few of the best. You tell him I said so. Anytime he's ready —"

"I understand that you and Jerry Jeff Cody were involved in a disagreement over a joint-venture commercial property."

"Yeah." Burkhart's head came up and his shoulders went stiff. There was a moment's silence, followed by, "What was it you said Mike wanted?" He frowned, thinking. "What case?"

"You know, I suppose, that Jerry Jeff Cody is dead?"

His eyes flickered. "Yeah. I heard that Saturday afternoon, when they cancelled the chili cookoff. Kind of threw a damper over the rest of the day."

"McQuaid said this was your first chili cookoff. So you are a chile enthusiast?"

He grunted. "Not hardly. I'm one of those people who can't stand them. They burn my mouth like hell." He grimaced. "I never can understand how chileheads eat those things raw. I'd be blistered in five seconds."

I was surprised. "If you don't like chiles, what prompted you to enter?"

He grunted. "Wasn't a what, it was a who. An investor from New York, who thought it would be a blast. You know, dress like a drugstore cowboy, brag to his

Big Apple buddies about how he cooked up this fantastic chili in an old iron pot over a mesquite fire. I felt like a fool, but I got Lulu to dig up a recipe and went to a lot of trouble to set things up. The client was drunk by noon and passed out by two. Which I guess must have been about the time JJ cashed it in."

"Cody was a friend of yours, I take it."

"I wouldn't call him a friend, exactly." He looked away. "Still, it's hard to think of him being dead. His birthday and mine were the same week." There was a long pause. "Kind of brings it home when you say it that way, you know? He worked out, ran four or five miles a day, looked healthy as a horse. I never even knew he had a heart problem."

"He didn't have a heart problem," I said. "The medical examiner says he died of anaphylactic shock. Somebody put peanuts into one of the chili samples."

"Peanuts!" Burkhart looked back at me, his face registering a blank, unfeigned astonishment. "*Peanuts,* you said?" To my nod, he muttered, "Well, I'll be damned." He mulled it over for a minute, his jaw working.

"You knew that he had an allergy?"

"I never actually saw him have an attack,

353

but I guess he'd had a bad scare or two, sometime in his life. When we'd go out for lunch, he'd never eat anything fancy or weird, only steak or fish or chicken. No nuts, not even a sesame seed. And he always pestered the waiter about soups, sauces, salad dressings, stuff like that. I'm sure he never figured that some idiot would put nuts in chili. Seems almost funny, when you think about it." He paused for a moment, reflecting, and while his guard was down, I asked my first real question.

"What can you tell me about the two letters?"

"Letters?" Still immersed in the irony of Jerry Jeff's death, he raised his eyes to mine. "What letters?"

"Charlie Lipman says there were blackmail letters."

"Blackmail —" He stared. "What's Lipman got to do with — ?" His eyes narrowed. "McQuaid used to be a cop. Is he doing some sort of —"

I interrupted him with the second question. "Can you tell me the source and the amount of the unreported income Cody was holding back?"

"Unreported income?" The half-shouted words pulled him out of his chair. "Blackmail letters? What the devil *is* this? What are you trying to — ?" He scowled and fished in his shirt pocket for my card. He pulled it out, looked at it, and found himself no wiser. "Bayles?" he snapped. "Never heard of you. You a lawyer? You working for Lipman?"

"Mr. Lipman and I are associated," I said.

His voice roughened and he raised his hand, pointing his finger at me. His hand was shaking. "Well, you listen to me, Ms. Bayles, and you listen good. If Charlie Lipman and Mike McQuaid are trying to tangle me up in Jerry Jeff Cody's dirty doings, you can tell them I'm not their patsy. Do you understand?" His face twisted and he punched a hole in the air with his finger. "Cody and I split the sheets a year ago, and that was the end of it."

"You lost a lawsuit to him."

Still standing, he folded his arms, glowering down at me. "Yeah. We went to court, and I lost. But I wouldn't waste two minutes writing blackmail letters to that lying bastard. I don't know anything about blackmail or tax holdouts or anything else that sonofabitch might have been up to."

"Did you know that your wife has been

reported to have had a relationship with him?"

He stared at me. There was a bright pink streak beneath the stubble on each cheek. His nostrils were pinched and white. I waited. For a long moment, all I could hear was the raspy sound of his breathing.

"My wife —" he said. He swallowed. His hands were clenched into fists. "My wife never had anything to do with him. It was all gossip. Dirty, rotten gossip." His voice rose, taking on a corroded edge. "This town is full of people who don't have anything better to do than —"

"So the answer is yes," I said quietly. "You knew what people were saying."

He closed his eyes, half swaying. His jaw worked convulsively. He sank back into the chair and put his hands over his face. His silence, his retreat behind his hands, told me what I needed to know.

I let him sit for a moment. Then I said, in a conversational tone, "Now that we've established that, Mr. Burkhart, perhaps you'd be willing to tell me what else you might know. Who would have had a reason to want Jerry Jeff Cody dead?"

He dropped his hands. "Want him . . . dead?"

"According to Jerry Jeff, somebody was

trying to blackmail him. Now he's dead. The inference should be obvious. Can you think of anybody who might have wanted to get something from him — something that might be worth killing for?"

His face was white. "You can't be . . . You're saying it's . . . murder?" He stretched the word out, incredulous.

"I'm asking you who might have wanted something from Jerry Jeff, and who would have been very angry if it couldn't be gotten."

"Who might have wanted —" His breathing was ragged, and I could see the dawning of a horrible new thought in his mind. "Murder," he whispered. He rubbed his temples with his fingers.

"I suppose you've heard that Cody and his wife were getting a divorce," I said.

"Yeah, I —" His Adam's apple bobbed as he swallowed. "Yes. I knew."

"And that he was planning to marry Felicia Travis, and take an around-the-world honeymoon cruise."

His eyes were fixed on mine. He nodded without speaking.

"Did your wife know?" I asked.

He understood the question behind my question, and it seemed to pull him together. "Yeah, she knew," he said. "She's the one who told me."

"And where was your wife during the chili cookoff, Mr. Burkhart?"

My question was soft and casual, like idle conversation, but it slammed him like a fist. He rocked with the punch. "I . . . don't know where she was," he said. "Helping out somewhere, I guess. She's a . . . she's a volunteer." He gripped the arms of his chair and sat forward. "You've got to believe me, Ms. Bayles," he said, and I could hear the desperation in his voice. "Lulu never had anything to do with Cody. It was all gossip, just people talking, you hear? There wasn't a shred of truth to it. Not a shred." Despite his effort to keep it even, his voice cracked.

It was time to back off. "Thank you," I said. "Now, about my earlier question. Can you think of anyone who might have had a motive?"

I watched him telling himself that he was off the hook, forcing himself to relax. "Who? Oh, hell, I don't know. Lots, I guess. Jerry Jeff never played a clean hand in his life. He was the greediest guy I ever met. There were plenty of people who'd had run-ins with him." He stopped, thought for a minute, and offered me an alternative to his wife. "But if you're asking who wanted something from Cody, you don't have to look any farther than you can throw a rock. His partner wanted his wife. His wife wanted his hide nailed to the barn, and his money to boot. If I had to go looking for suspects, I'd start with the two of them." He stopped, closed his eyes, and shook his head. "Peanuts in chili," he said wearily, and opened his eyes again. "It sounds like a stupid joke that went wrong. You're sure that wasn't the way it was?"

A good question. A *very* good question, one that I wished I had an answer for. I sighed, picked up my briefcase, and stood. "To tell the truth, Mr. Burkhart, we're not sure of anything."

This was not exactly true. Judging from Craig Burkhart's reaction, I was virtually certain that he had not known how Jerry Jeff Cody died before I gave him the details, and that my information about the blackmail letters had been news to him, as well. I was sure that Craig Burkhart was not a murderer.

But I was also sure that he was afraid, deathly afraid, not for himself, but for his wife. He suspected — and with good reason, I thought — that she had killed Jerry Jeff Cody.

Chapter Sixteen

Peter Piper picked a peck of pickled peppers;
A peck of pickled peppers Peter Piper picked.
If Peter Piper picked a peck of
   pickled peppers,
Where's the peck of pickled peppers
   Peter Piper picked?
                  Traditional nursery rhyme

A few minutes later, I was back in the car and on the phone to McQuaid, who had just returned from an early supper of meatloaf, mashed potatoes, and corn. Not exactly a gourmet meal, but the menu reminded me that the dinner hour was creeping up on me.

"Sounds like you got more than you went for," he said, when I'd finished the brief sketch of my conversation with Craig Burkhart.

"Yes," I said. "In my opinion, we can scratch Burkhart off the list. But he's scared to death that his wife was somehow involved." I hesitated. "Come to think of it, Lulu was working in the log-in tent, too. I saw her. She would have had easy access to those samples. And if she'd been close to

Jerry Jeff, she would have known about his allergy."

"And her motive?"

"That's easy," I said. "Jerry Jeff was getting a divorce — but not to be closer to her. He was about to go off with Felicia Travis." A rejected mistress, a spurned and angry lover, a jealous woman with revenge burning in her heart. This had been a crime of passion, and now I could see — oh, so clearly — the flame of desire, of anger, of jealousy, that had lit it.

"A very strong assumption," McQuaid said thoughtfully. "Still, it's all speculation, built on the rumor of a relationship. You say Craig denied it?"

"Sure — but what else could he do? He could see that her relationship with Jerry Jeff implicated her, and that Cody's plan to go off with Felicia gave her an excellent motive. She's gone to a soccer match at Johnson Field. If I hurry —"

"Ruby is going to talk to the women who worked in that tent," McQuaid broke in, "which will include Lulu. I think you'd better stick with the original plan and talk to Pokey."

I thought about that for a moment. Roxanne was a very likely suspect, although I was puzzled about those letters.

She would have threatened Cody to his face, rather than writing to him. Still, McQuaid was right. Roxanne and Pokey — either acting alone or as a team — were at the top of my suspect list.

"You're right," I said. "The next question is, where will I find Pokey at this hour of the day?"

"Try the Ranchero. That's his happy hour spot. Failing that, Beans."

I started the car. "Okay, chief, we're off to the Ranchero — after a pit stop at home to change clothes. Oh, by the way," I added, as I pulled around the corner onto San Jacinto, "I had a phone conversation with Rosie Montgomery, the lady with the lowdown on Opal Hogge. It was pretty low down, too." I summarized Rosie's long lament in several short sentences: "Opal Hogge got fired from her job in San Antonio. At the nursing home board's apparent instigation and without consulting the families, she solicited sizable bequests from residents. The families objected, the board reconsidered its fundraising strategies, and Opal got her walking papers."

McQuaid thought about that. "Very interesting," he said finally, "but I'm not sure it takes us anywhere."

"I agree. Certainly, Hogge wasn't after

money when she went after Miss Velma. MaeBelle says her aunt doesn't have anything." I stopped for the short red light at San Jacinto and Pecos. "Have you talked to Joyce yet? Did she examine Miss Velma?"

"Yeah. She came down to my room just before supper to tell me that she had found evidence of bruising on both upper arms. She asked another nurse to make an independent evaluation, and they both wrote up their findings." He hesitated. "But it seems there's a problem," he added.

I slowed to let two small boys and their dog cross the street. One of the boys — a leggy, awkward kid of twelve or so, dark-haired, wearing cutoffs, dirty T-shirt, and sloppy sneakers — reminded me of Brian, and I suddenly missed him. Mothering hadn't been my career of choice (in fact, it was pretty far down on my priority list), and mothering somebody else's child presents some fairly strenuous challenges. But Brian and I had managed to build a comfortable relationship before Leatha enticed him away with promises of horseback riding and daily swims in the river. I smothered a faint spark of jealousy and promised myself I'd call the boy tonight or first thing in the morning.

"What kind of problem?" I asked, still watching the kids as they slipped through a fence and cut across a yard.

McQuaid replied dryly. "The dragon herself — Mrs. Hogge — came in while the nurse was doing her evaluation of Miss Velma. Hogge questioned the nurse, who had no idea that her boss might be the demon in disguise. Unfortunately," he added, "the nurse told her that there was some suspicion of abuse, and that the supervisor was writing a report."

"Oh, no!" I exclaimed in dismay.

"Oh, yes. But it's even more complicated than that, because after Hogge left the room, Miss Velma, in a sudden flash of lucidity, said to the nurse, 'She's the one.' "

"Terrific!" I said. "That's the corroboration we were hoping for. And thank God she didn't speak up in front of Hogge."

"Yes, but we're not home free. You see, when MaeBelle showed up to fetch her aunt, Hogge informed her that an Alzheimer's resident may not be discharged from the Manor until her doctor has done an examination and approved a transfer to an appropriate facility. Miss Velma's doctor is out of town for several days. Which means that Miss Velma is still here, and that Hogge has been alerted to the suspicion of abuse. She probably sees Miss Velma as an even greater threat than before."

"Hogge can actually refuse to discharge somebody?" I asked, aghast.

"The rule is designed to protect the Manor from a lawsuit," McQuaid said. "They can't very well have senior citizens of diminished capacity sauntering in and out on their own recognizance. Apparently, Hogge *could* let Miss Velma go, but she also has the right to insist on the doctor's examination. It's all perfectly legal, since it's spelled out in the admission contract."

"So Miss Velma has to stay where Hogge can get to her," I said angrily. "Isn't there *something* we can do to make sure she's safe?"

"Actually, there is." There was a chuckle in McQuaid's voice. "They're doing it at this very moment. Joyce and Edna, that is."

"Edna Lund? What are they doing?"

"Transferring her to my room," McQuaid said. "Jug is moving in with Mr. Lewis for the duration, and Miss Velma is taking his bed. Hogge won't be informed of the swap unless she asks, and if she does, she'll be told that the family urgently requested it. I'll ask Charlie Lipman to write a lawyer-type letter that will get Joyce off the hook." I could hear voices in the background. "Co-ed roommates might be a little irregular, but Miss Velma seems to consider this an adventure. She thinks I'm a Texas Ranger, and I've been assigned to protect her."

I was relieved. "It sounds like you've got the situation under control."

"I hope so," McQuaid said. "I wouldn't be much good in hand-to-hand combat, but I doubt if Hogge is going to try anything with me here."

"I'll send warm thoughts," I said.

"Send cookies," McQuaid replied. "The meat loaf was adequate taste-wise, but there wasn't enough of it."

Happy hour isn't the big event in Pecan Springs that it is in the cities. There are no traffic jams to wait out and even the singles have things to do at home — water the grass, walk the dog, slap a steak on the grill. But there are a couple of places where people gather after work to discuss the weather, cuss the Cowboys, and grumble about the legislature. Beans is one, of course. The Ranchero, on the Staples Road, is another.

I was feeling cooler and much less rumpled in khaki pants, a sleeveless plaid shirt, and sandals. I'd wolfed down a peanut butter-and-banana sandwich and a glass of milk, too, which blunted my hunger. The answering machine had offered me several messages, one from Brian, one from Leatha, and two from Ruby. I tried to call Ruby at her house and her shop without success, but I postponed the other calls. I wanted to catch Pokey, if I could.

The sun was still high when I walked into the Ranchero, and after the early-evening brightness outside, it took a few minutes for my eyes to adjust to the smoky gloom, illuminated by dim hanging lights over the bar and the glare of a neon Coors sign.

The Ranchero is a large, low-ceilinged cave of a place, with a dance floor and room for a few local musicians to get together for an evening of pickin' and grinnin'. Nights and weekends, the place is jammed and the noise level is so high that it's a good idea to plug your ears with cotton and forget about conversation. But at this time of day, the patrons gather along the bar and you can actually hear people talk, even if it's almost too dark to see their faces. I sauntered to the end of the long bar, then back again, surveying the clientele, mostly pink- and white-collar folks in their twenties and early thirties.

The ratio was three guys to one gal — normal for a place like this. None of the guys was Pokey.

The bartender broke away from a conversation with two young women in short skirts and high heels and swiped the bar in front of my stool with a rag. "Hi," he said laconically, past the wad of chewing gum in his mouth. He was at least a dozen years younger than me and not particularly interested in older women. "Whatcha drinkin', ma'am?"

I tried to pretend that I hadn't heard the "ma'am," which always makes me feel that I've slid into a post-menopausal era without realizing it. "Actually," I said, "I'm looking for somebody. Pokey Clendennen." I opened my purse and pulled a five-dollar bill out of my wallet. "Know him?"

"Sure," the bartender said. He dropped the five into the tip glass and scratched his head with a vague air. "Seems t' me I saw him tonight. But he was goin' . . . somewhere. With . . . a coupla people." He paused significantly.

Another five followed the first, and the bartender became more forthcoming.

"It was ten, maybe twenty minutes ago. Pokey was with Roxie Cody and Joey Holman. You know Roxie?"

I nodded. I recognized Joey Holman's name, too, or I thought I did, although I couldn't place who he was. "Do they come here often?"

"Coupla times a week." He picked up a glass and polished it. "You c'n prob'bly still catch 'em. If you hurry."

"Hurry where?"

"Lamar Field. That's where they was headed."

No kidding. Lamar Field is our local airstrip — one concrete and a couple of grass runways, a cluster of metal hangars, and some gas pumps. There was talk a few years back about turning it into a regional hub to service Austin and San Antonio, which would have fed a cancer of commercial development and changed life in Pecan Springs (in my opinion) for the worse. But that particular crisis had been fended off and Lamar Field remains a home for cropdusters, sports aviators, and the local wing of the Confederate Air Force. It is also the takeoff spot for private flights to Mexico.

I looked at the bartender, a formless suspicion beginning to stir at the back of my mind. "Remind me. Who is Joey Holman?"

The bartender considered whether it was worth the trouble to hit me up for another five and decided to be generous. "Commercial pilot. Runs a charter service." He grinned, showing a wide gap between two chipped front teeth. "You wanna take a quick trip to Monterey, Saltillo, Piedras Negras — I can set you up with Joey." Ah, it wasn't generosity, after all. "He don't advertise, see. Only works through word of mouth, like." He looked at me speculatively. "Referrals. From friends. He don't feel obliged to stick with no flight plan. If you got private business, I mean." The juke box cranked up "Mamas, Don't Let Your Babies Grow Up to Be Cowboys," and he dropped his voice. "Joey, he's lined up a bunch of little bitty airstrips where he puts down. Don't call no attention to the flight that way."

I wondered briefly if I looked like the kind of person who might have private business in Mexico, but decided it didn't matter.

"Sorry, I'm not in the market right now," I said. I could forget Lulu Burkhart, and any of the other disappointed lovers and angry husbands that Jerry Jeff Cody might have left in his wake. Pokey, Roxanne, and a charter pilot with Mexican connections who didn't feel obligated to stick with his flight plan. The three of them added up to only one thing.

The bartender shifted his chewing gum from one side of his mouth to the other, philosophical in his disappointment. "Yeah, well, pass it along."

I slung my bag over my shoulder and slid from the stool. "You bet I will," I said, and headed for the door.

Lamar Field is another two or three miles out toward Staples, on the rich blackland prairie that stretches from I-35 and the Balcones Escarpment eastward to the Gulf. There was a scattering of vehicles in the airport's gravel parking lot; Pokey's pickup wasn't one of them, nor was Jerry Jeff's white Lexus. They must have driven out with the pilot. I pulled in fast and skidded to a stop in front of the pink concrete-block building that houses the aviation service, a couple of charters, and the Confederate Air Force office, with its flag insignia painted prominently on the wall. I jumped out and sprinted around back, through a gate in a chain-link fence. Two guys in zip-front coveralls, one gray, one blue, stood on the concrete apron. They were gazing southward, watching a small red plane as it climbed steeply away from the field.

"I'm looking for Pokey Clendennen," I

said breathlessly. "And Roxanne Cody."

The guy in the blue coveralls — a gray-haired, mustached man wearing a name badge that announced he was Charlie — turned to me, grinning. "Well, you'll hafta look sharp, missy." He jerked his head. "That's them up there. In that red Cessna."

"Oh, no!" I gasped. My pulse was racing, my breath came fast, my brain was in overdrive. Pokey and Roxanne, heading south. And since Roxanne had undoubtedly made a quick visit to Jerry Jeff's stash before she and her boyfriend boarded the plane, they were carrying a couple of duffle bags stuffed with Cody's unreported income. Enough to make it a very long, very luxurious Mexican holiday.

"Damn," I muttered. Why hadn't I anticipated something like this? I'd dealt with plenty of fugitives, back in the bad old days. I knew how easy it was to disappear into the wild blue yonder, especially when the vanishing act was as well-funded as this one. In fact, Ruby had even warned me that this pair might do a flit, and I'd pooh-poohed her intuition. What an arrogant, self-assured jerk I was, thinking I was on top of this thing when all the time, Roxanne and Pokey were one jump ahead of me!

Charlie laughed and patted my shoulder. "Hey now, hon, don't you be so consternated," he said, in a paternal tone. "Your friends ain't gone forever, you know. They'll be back."

"Like hell," I said disgustedly. I stared up at the plane, now not much bigger than a fly. It was circling the airport, still climbing, finding the right altitude for its southward flight. Its passengers had plotted a murder, executed it with cold-blooded competence, plundered their victim's stash, and chartered themselves a getaway airplane. Of course they wouldn't be back. In a couple of hours, they'd be safely on the ground in Mexico.

The guy in the gray suit chuckled at my obvious distress. "What's the matter, sugar? You don't think old Pokey can bring it off? Roxanne, too. The pair of 'em's too good to mess up somethin' as easy as this, wouldn't you say, Charlie?"

"Oh, heck fire, yes," Charlie agreed vigorously. "This ain't nothin', compared to what that pair's done in the past." He pulled a pair of small binoculars out of his coverall pocket and lifted them to his eyes. "Okay, boys 'n' girls, show us what you're made of. Let's see that Lover's Leap."

And with that, two small specks separated from the fly and began to plummet toward the earth. I gave a startled, half-stifled yelp. "It's a suicide pact!"

Gray-suit guffawed heartily. "Suicide pact? Hey, that's good. Ain't that good, Charlie? Suicide pact. Ol' Pokey'll get a kick outta that."

Charlie handed the binoculars to me with a friendly smile. "Whazza matter, babe? You never seen skydivers before? Here, have a look." He made a clucking noise with his tongue. "Boy, what technique. Ask me, that pair is world-class."

I took the binoculars. In clear, bright detail, I saw a slender figure in a red suit, another in a yellow outfit, hands clasped, legs splayed, falling facedown toward earth from something like ten thousand feet. The seconds stretched out as I clutched the binoculars, my gaze frozen to the falling bodies, not realizing I was holding my breath until the skydivers released their grip, moved apart, and, first one, then the other, pulled their ripcords. Red and yellow silk billowed into graceful wings over their heads and they swung, human pendulums, beneath the parachutes.

"I gotta tell you, that's a pretty sight," Charlie said, with satisfied emphasis. "A damn pretty sight."

A few minutes later, first Roxanne, then Pokey, landed on the grass beyond the concrete strip. They came down on their feet, each with a light thud, as light and graceful as birds. As if they had done this a hundred times — maybe they had — they tugged on the lines, collapsing the chutes into piles of fluid silk.

"Toldja they'd be back, didn't I?" Gray-suit said, and chuckled.

The rest of the scene was pure anti-climax. Pokey and Roxanne registered an appropriate surprise when they saw me standing there with their skydiving buddies. Joey Holman landed the red Cessna and taxied onto the apron in front of us. Charlie and his friend shrugged into their parachute packs, picked up their helmets, and headed for the plane to take their turn falling out of the sky. Roxanne carried both chutes inside to repack them, leaving Pokey outside with me, smoking a cigarette and answering my stammered questions with apparent candor and not an ounce of obvious resentment.

No, he hadn't seen anybody, and certainly not Roxanne, messing with his chili before he ladled it into the sample cup. What under the sun gave me that ridiculous idea?

No, he had no reason to suspect that Roxanne or anybody else, for that matter, had tried to frame him — pretty silly notion, when you got right down to it, wasn't it? If you asked him, it sounded like something some TV scriptwriter would come up with to pad out a plot.

Letters, blackmail letters? Hey, what kind of a weird joke was that? No, he couldn't even hazard a guess as to which of Jerry Jeff's many enemies — too many to count, even if you took your boots off — might try that kind of dumb trick. And if ol' Jerry Jeff was playing fast and loose with the IRS, he for one didn't know a thing about it and didn't want to, thank you very much. If his partner had been robbing the till and forgetting to tell Uncle Sam, he just guessed he'd have to forgive the dead and forget the debt. He'd never been one to hold a grudge, anybody could tell me that.

Now if I would excuse him (this said with a shy Jimmy Stewart grin), he'd just step in that door and help Roxanne, who always volunteered to do things other people didn't want to do, like packing parachutes and stuff. God knows, that sweet little girl needed cheering up, and that's why he'd suggested that they keep their regular weekly skydiving date, the way they'd been doing for about six months now. It was just about Roxanne's only recreation and it would be a shame to take it away from her, even though her heart was broken in two by her poor husband's untimely death.

By the time I got back into the car, I was feeling about as deflated as one of those red and yellow parachutes that sweet Roxanne was unselfishly packing away. It was entirely possible that she and Pokey were guilty of doctoring Jerry Jeff's chili — in fact, I remained convinced of it, in spite of Pokey's outstanding performance. But I had totally blown any chance to coax him to give the truth away. The way things stood now, they could live happily ever after and there was not a single thing I could do to prevent it. If justice was going to be served, somebody else would have to dish it up.

With a sigh, I reached for the cell phone and keyed in McQuaid's number. The sooner I told him about my ridiculous blunder, the sooner I could begin to forget it.

Chapter Seventeen

The longer a chile is cooked, the hotter the flavor. Simmering results in a dish that is hot overall; stir-frying adds flavor and a bit of spice. To lessen the heat, soak fresh chiles in a solution of three parts mild wine vinegar to one part salt for an hour.

Habeeb Salloum
The Herb Quarterly
Fall, 1993

To my surprise, McQuaid gave my report nothing more than a quick "Don't be so rough on yourself, China." He added, consolingly, "Every cop knows that investigation is mostly a matter of cold trails and blind alleys." He switched to a different subject. "I need you to look for something — tonight, if possible."

I sagged back into the seat. "Can't it wait?" I asked wearily.

There was a moment's silence, then he said, sympathetically, "I understand. You must be tired, chasing all over town after red herrings. Edna Lund has volunteered to look for it. Or maybe I can reach Ruby.

She's always anxious to help."

"What've you lost?" I asked, with a resigned sigh. It isn't that I feel competitive with Ruby or anybody else, it's just that . . . well, if McQuaid needs something, *I* should be the one to respond.

"It's not me," McQuaid said quickly. "It's Miss Velma."

"Okay, so what has Miss Velma lost?"

"Her will."

That brought me up short. "I thought she didn't have any money to leave."

"Maybe, maybe not. But Joyce and Edna and I have been talking to her, and her garbled statements are beginning to make some sense to us. She's pretty mixed up, but it's clear that she's desperately concerned about her will, and about Bunny. Actually, the two seem confused in her mind."

"Ah!" I exclaimed. "So Opal Hogge really *is* after Miss Velma's money!"

"Not necessarily," McQuaid replied cautiously. "There might not *be* any money. But then again there might. Or there might be other property — land, maybe, or securities — that nobody knows anything about. In fact, it's possible that the will lists the whereabouts of a safety deposit box where she was keeping her valuables.

It bears checking out, don't you think?"

"It certainly does," I said. The way things were shaping up, it might not be possible to bring Jerry Jeff's killers to justice, or even to prove that there had been a crime. But this was something I could handle without screwing up. If there was a will to be found, surely I could find it. Anyway, I'd feel better if I had something to do, no matter how unimportant. Left to my own devices, I'd probably sit around and stew about what a moron I'd been. Suicide pact, indeed! "Where should I start looking?" I asked, chastened.

"It's a little hard to tell, but Miss Velma seems to think it's stored with the other papers from Perry's law office. I suppose Perry drafted it for her, and probably also witnessed it. She seems to be saying that MaeBelle might know where they are."

"It's possible," I said. "MaeBelle told me that Lester hauled boxes of Tom Perry's papers out of Miss Velma's garage. Lester thought she could have hidden cash, so he went through everything pretty carefully. He probably didn't check for a will, though."

There was a moment's pause. "I hope he didn't burn the lot when he was finished."

"MaeBelle said Miss Velma made them

promise not to throw any of it away," I replied. "It's probably in the Battersbys' garage." I glanced at my watch. "Their house is on my way home. Why don't I stop and take a look? I can also let MaeBelle know that her aunt has been moved and that she's being watched."

"Good," McQuaid said. "If Miss Velma knew her will was safe, she might be less agitated."

"And if we knew what was in it, we might be closer to understanding the relationship between Miss Velma and Opal, and why Opal assaulted her."

"Precisely," McQuaid said. "If you have to take the matter to the Manor's board, the will might turn out to be a useful piece of evidence."

"Okay," I said with a new energy, and turned on the ignition. "You've talked me into it."

Lester answered the door with a longneck in his hand. Over his shoulder, I could see the television set tuned to a baseball game. Beside Miss Velma's recliner was a cooler full of ice and beer, and a giant bag of chips.

"She ain't here," Lester said. "Jamie's in the hospital with her 'pendix. MaeBelle won't be back for a coupla days." He began to push the door shut.

I pushed the door open again. "I'm not here to see MaeBelle, exactly. I wondered if I could look through the papers you took out of Miss Velma's garage. An important legal document has been lost." I was not going to tell *him* that I was looking for MaeBelle's aunt's will. "It's probably with the papers that came from Mr. Perry's law office."

Lester belched beerily. "Legal stuff, huh?" There was a roar of crowd approval on the television, and he turned around to check the action. "Well, them papers ain't here no more."

Bad news. "Where are they?"

"Out to my cousin's," he said. He was turned away from me now, his eyes on the batter sprinting toward first base.

"Your cousin's what?"

"Yer out!" he yelled, stamping his foot and lifting his beer bottle in salute. He turned back to me, jubilant. "Damn fool oughta know better'n bunt with Marvel behind the plate and a runner on first. Ain't got a snowball's chance."

"Absolutely," I said. "Your cousin's what?"

"My cousin's —" It took him a moment

to refocus and find his place in the conversation. "Oh, yeah. Arlie's deer lease. There's a old barn out there, and that's where Arlie an' me put them boxes." He eyed me defensively, as if I had accused him of something. "Hell's bells, you didn't 'spect me to leave 'em stacked up round here, didja? Wouldn't a bin room fer anythin' else. There's a *ton* of that stuff."

"No," I said in a conciliatory tone. "I'm sure you found a safe, dry place to store them."

"We-e-ll," he said, dragging it out, "I don't know about dry. That roof ain't too good. Floor neither. But hell, they're just papers. Velma hadn't made such a stink, I woulda put a match to 'em."

"Where is Arlie's deer lease?" I asked.

The crowd erupted again and Lester decided to get rid of me and get back to his solitary beer party. "Take Lime Kiln Road to Stassney Junction," he said. "Turn left three miles, go over a cattle crossin' and through a broken gate, an' yer there. Barn's on the right when you drive in." He began to close the door again.

I stuck out my foot. "May I have your permission to look through the papers? That may mean taking them where they can be examined."

"My permission?" This seemed to amuse him momentarily, then he shrugged. "Far as I'm concerned, you can do whut you want with that junk. Makes me no never mind." He lifted his beer and took a swig. "Ol' Arlie, he shot himself in the foot a couple weeks ago, so I don't reckon he'll care, neither." He started to shut the door once more, then thought of something else.

"You go out there, you keep a eye out fer snakes, y'hear? I shot one humongous mama rattler inside that barn, and a bunch of her babies got away."

What happened next is a little hard to explain. What I wanted was a long, hot bath and a cup of my special-blend bedtime tea. I intended to call Brian and hear that he'd been horseback riding and swimming in the river. I intended to talk to McQuaid again, about our wedding — no, about our *marriage,* to help quiet the jitters. I definitely did *not* intend to drive out to Arlie's deer lease and brave a pack of orphaned rattlers just to look for Miss Velma's misplaced will, which would still be there in the morning, if it was there at all.

But our house is located just off Lime

Kiln Road, only a couple of miles from Stassney Junction. And this was June, the month of long, bright twilights, when the evening air is clear as spring water and the Hill Country is so green and beautiful that you want to store away its sights, not-to-be-forgotten snapshots, in your memory. The twenty-minute drive out to the deer lease might be just what I needed to wind down after a day when I'd shuttled from one place to another, trying to fit together the pieces of an elusive truth. With any luck, the cartons would be labeled and I could find what I wanted right away. Or I could pick out likely boxes, load them in the car, and haul them home for a more thorough search. I might even be able to report success to McQuaid tonight.

So, with the sun hanging like a fat orange lollipop in a crystalline sky, my Datsun and I rattled over the cattle guard, coasted down a long, steep hill, and drove through a rusted metal gate that sagged open on a broken hinge. The cedars were a thick green hedge on both sides of the rutted caliche road. Between the trees I could see skunkbush and sage-green agarito and mounds of prickly pear cactus, which you don't want to step into without calf-high leather boots, and maybe not even then. These shrubs had managed to take root in the thin soil of the uneven slopes, and eroded slabs of limestone rock littered the ground. This is scrubland, unfit for farming or running cattle or even feeding goats, although that fact hasn't kept people from occasionally trying to do all three.

But its commercial worthlessness doesn't mean that the land is unproductive or without value — not by a long shot. It's a wonderful wildlife habitat, perfectly engineered and designed by nature to provide a rich livelihood to scorpions and lizards; to snakes and the small furry creatures on which they feed; for wild turkey and turkey vultures and road runners and great horned owls; for armadillos, squirrels, jack rabbits, skunk, possum, raccoons, bobcat, feral pigs, coyotes.

And deer. There are reported to be nearly four million white-tailed deer in Texas, in addition to the mule deer of the Trans-Pecos and Staked Plains and the little Del Carmen deer that roam the Chisos Mountains. There are so many, in fact, that Texas Parks and Wildlife annually encourages hunters to harvest their limit in order to keep down the population and reduce the winter migration into the suburbs, where deer delight in dining on expensive shrubbery. Last year, there were close to three-quarters of a million deer taken in Texas. In fact, many rural land-owners pay their taxes by leasing exclusive hunting rights to people like Lester's cousin Arlie. Beginning in late summer, these hunters put out shelled corn — deer corn, which you can buy in fifty-pound bags — to lure the deer close to camou-flaged wooden huts called deer blinds, sometimes built on stilts, sometimes erected in trees. There, after the season opens in November, hunters crouch, hop-ing for a clear shot at a trophy buck but settling for a spike (an immature buck), a doe, or a turkey. On the large ranches, which cater to the big-money boys from Houston and Dallas, a deer hunt is more like an expensive safari, with hunters pay-ing by the gun ($100 a day and up, plus kill fee); by the animal (a white-tail doe might go for $400, a buck for $2000); or even by the acre, depending on the terrain and the available wildlife. That kind of hunting is big business, and a tasty hunk of ground venison for a wintertime bowl of chili can cost upwards of $100 a pound, not counting room, board, and bar privi-leges.

But small, close-in leases like Arlie's don't involve a lot of money. Four or five buddies often pool their money to lease the same land year after year. They don't hunt very earnestly, using the trip as an excuse to escape the wife and kids, dress up in camouflage gear and leather boots, and play poker all night. They might camp out in tents or even rent an RV equipped with a generator, microwave oven, and satellite television for afternoon football or a VCR for stag movies. If the lease has a cabin or bunkhouse or a barn on it, they might sleep there.

The barn on Arlie's lease, however, wasn't fit for even the most macho sleepover. I parked the Datsun on the steep slope, set the emergency brake, and climbed out. As I surveyed the old building, I understood why Lester had hesitated when I asked him whether it was dry. The barn — maybe twenty by thirty, partially open on the side facing me — wore a sad and abandoned look. The siding was weathered cedar, splintered in places, the roof was rusty metal, and half the floor was dirt. It had been built against the slope, so that the right half of the building had two levels, and the limestone foundation was crumbling. Once, the area below had probably sheltered goats or pigs. Now, it was piled with old cedar posts and a tangle of barbed wire.

I looked away from the barn. On the downslope side stood a metal barrel on welded angle-iron legs, five feet off the ground — an old gasoline tank, probably. Beside it were rolls of hog fencing, a rusted watering trough, and the rear end of a derelict truck, made into a two-wheeled trailer. A mound of silver-gray horehound testified to the fact that a woman had once lived and worked here, perhaps in a nearby house that was now only a heap of rubble. Somewhere in the cedar brake I heard a mockingbird call, its song a tumble of melody that struck me as somehow melancholy. It came to me that an old barn on a Texas hillside was a strange place for a lawyer's files to end up, but not an extraordinary one, and perhaps not even inappropriate. Tom Perry had died suddenly, his legal secretary had become incompetent shortly afterward, and her family had no interest in the boxes of stuff she'd been storing until she had a chance to properly dispose of them. That the records were here was odd, probably, but no less inexplicable than this abandoned barn.

I looked up at the sky. The sun had

dipped behind the cedars, which meant I had a half-hour of daylight left. But the inside of the barn was dusky, and I would just as soon see where I was putting my feet. I reached under the seat and pulled out the big flashlight I keep there in case I have a flat on my way home from the shop late at night. Carrying it in one hand, I stepped inside the barn and glanced around.

The back two-thirds of the structure was stuffed to the roof with old-fashioned square hay bales, probably stored there for decades. Old license plates were nailed to the walls. Heaps of rusting farm debris filled the corners — wooden crates, a row of chicken boxes, scythes, pitchforks, a grain scoop, an old horse-drawn harrow, a plow, a wooden wagon wheel. My eyes widened at the sight of the harrow. On the Houston antique market, it would probably fetch more than my car. The barn held the heat of the day, its air rich with the smells of dried hay, rotting wood, bat guano. I could hear rustling in the corners. Mice maybe, or squirrels, or Mexican free-tailed bats, which fly out of caves and old barns by the millions each night to feast on hapless bugs. Or Lester's rattlesnake babies, grown up into six-foot adults, and their many close friends and relations. The thought was not comforting. I'd better locate those boxes, retrieve Miss Velma's will, and go home.

But where *were* the boxes? Not out in plain sight, certainly. I turned to my right and saw that a storeroom of sorts had been constructed on that side of the barn. In the center of the wood wall was a heavy plank door, fastened shut by a stick wedged into a rusty hasp. Next to the door hung a kerosene lantern, cobwebbed and dusty, but with its glass globe still intact. Under it was a metal matchbox, a rack hung with small tools, a coiled rope, and a rusty shovel leaning on the floor. With an effort, I yanked the stick out of the hasp and pushed the door open. It swung inward, creaking, on resistant iron hinges.

The storeroom was much darker than the barn, and I flicked on the flashlight. The cardboard boxes were there, a couple of dozen or more, in three head-high stacks against the wall. They leaned outward at a precarious angle, and as I shone the light around, I saw why. This part of the building overhung the livestock shelter beneath, and the support — a cedar post, probably — must have rotted. The floor slanted sharply to the right. I could see daylight between the splintery floorboards, and one was broken — I'd have to watch my step. A cobweb draped over the door was now stuck to my cheek and I brushed it off, hoping that the resident spider was not a black widow or a brown recluse. This was definitely not a place you'd want to linger.

I shone the flashlight on the boxes and saw that they weren't in much better shape than the structure itself. They looked damp-stained and moldy, and those on the bottom were collapsing under the weight of those on top. Some appeared to be labeled, but I couldn't easily make out the words. I set the flashlight, still lit, on the floor, and took down one of the top boxes, trying not to pull the whole tottering stack over. No label on this one, and a quick glance inside showed me what I was up against. The box was crammed with file folders and loose papers, so tightly jammed together that it was impossible to identify their contents. To find what I was looking for, I would have to pull everything out and sort through it. I wasn't going to do that job here, in the company of rattlesnakes and spiders. This was something better done at home.

Hands on hips, I stepped back and estimated the size of the job. With a little maneuvering, half of the boxes would probably fit into my car. I picked up the opened carton, carried it out, and stowed it in the Datsun. Back in the storeroom, I took the top box from the second stack, thinking that I could shorten my work by carrying two cartons at a time. I was reaching up to get another box when I saw the label. "Velma's Personal Files," it read, in neat black letters. "Private Documents."

Eureka! If I were Velma Mayfield's last will and testament, I would be in a box with her personal files, wouldn't I? I knelt beside the box, pulled up the top flaps of the carton, and looked inside. Under one or two loose classification folders — the kind legal secretaries use for client files — there were a couple of dozen manila folders, each marked "Velma, Personal." Promising, definitely. When I got home, I'd start with this box.

As I put the classification folder back into the box, I glanced at it. On the file label was typed the name Harmon Lund, and clipped to the file was a handwritten note that said, "For Edna." Harmon Lund. Edna Lund's father. I frowned. Somewhere, I'd picked up the information that even though the old man had died some months ago, his will had not yet been probated. Some snag in the legal proceedings, some confusion about his estate, was holding it up.

I weighed the folder in my hand, uneasily. It might contain papers that should be in the hands of the probate judge, or Edna's lawyer. She was her father's heir, I'd heard, although I had no idea who the executor was. Anyway, the folder had been meant for her. And it was in the wrong carton. Why wasn't it boxed with the rest of the client files, instead of being stuck in with Miss Velma's personal papers? Still kneeling, I flipped it open to have a look.

The top document, held in place with a double-prong fastener, was a file memo from Tom Perry, dated the previous September, just a month before he was killed. The subject heading was terse and straightforward: "Notes for probate judge re: defense of Lund codicil against possible challenge by daughter."

Challenge by daughter? What was that supposed to mean? I answered these questions with one quick scan of the page. Tom Perry had written this memo to be read by the court when Harmon Lund's will was presented for probate, in the event a challenge was raised against the will itself. The first paragraph set out the circumstances clearly, without evaluation. On September 15th of the previous year, Harmon Lund had executed a codicil to his existing will, specifically disinheriting his daughter, Edna, and leaving his entire estate to his son, James, last known to be living in Alaska. The second paragraph was an evaluation. "It is my personal opinion," Perry had written (and Miss Velma had presumably typed), "having known Harmon Lund for twenty-two years, that he is competent to make the codicil and that it fully reflects his current intentions with regard to the disposition of his property. He is an aged man with increasing physical disabilities and of irascible temper. He is now confined to a nursing facility. At the time of the execution of this codicil, he was quite rational. I wish the court to be informed of this opinion, in the event that Mr. Lund dies with this will in force and Miss Lund challenges it."

I stared at the memo. It was common knowledge in Pecan Springs that Edna Lund, who had managed the family ranch and cared for her father during his declining years, was to have inherited the Lund estate. But this memo suggested that

Edna was not going to receive a red cent — that her brother, whom old man Lund had rejected some fifteen years before — would get the whole thing.

This was all clear enough, if startling, and I immediately felt sorry for Edna. It was sad to think that she might have denied herself a life in order to care for a demanding old man, and in the end, had been turned away with nothing. What had she done to deserve such shabby treatment? Had there been arguments between them? Had Edna been unkind to him, or unsympathetic to his needs, or even physically abusive? I doubted that, though. She was a reserved person and I didn't know her well, but she certainly seemed caring enough in her volunteer work at the Manor and elsewhere. No, more likely, she had done nothing, and her father, who had a reputation for obstinate perversity, had simply decided to favor a long-forgotten son over a dutiful daughter.

But there were other questions to be answered. Why hadn't this thing already been settled? Had the executor not been able to locate the heir? But the executor had not even probated Lund's will — or at least that's what I had understood. Who *was* the executor, anyway? Who was the poor sucker that Harmon Lund had appointed to break the news to his daughter that the family estate was going to her brother?

I lifted the memo. The next item in the file was a copy of the codicil, signed by Harmon Lund in a firm, decisive hand and witnessed by Miss Velma and Tom Perry. No executor listed there — not unusual, if the testator intended to keep the original executor. The next item was the will itself, which, as I had expected, named Edna Lund as her father's sole beneficiary. The executor? I leafed to the section titled "Appointments" and had my answer, in three easy words.

Jerry Jeff Cody.

I raised my eyebrows. Jerry Jeff was Harmon Lund's executor? That was a surprise. No, come to think of it, I had picked up that information already. Where? I thought for a moment, then remembered that I had heard it from Hark at lunch today, when he was ticking off the civic contributions of the partners in Cody and Clendennen Insurance. At the time, I hadn't paid any special attention. Why should I? In small towns and rural areas, it isn't unusual for people to get cozy with the insurance man and consider that person as a valued financial advisor. Jerry

Jeff had probably been a long-time friend of the Lund family, and Harmon naturally thought of him when it came to carrying out his last wishes.

But now that I knew about the codicil, I saw a major complication. For whatever reason, Harmon Lund's estate hadn't yet been settled. The executor was dead, and somebody else was going to have to bring the will to probate, which would mean even further annoying delays for Edna, who must want to bring this drawn-out affair to a conclusion so she could get on with her life. Who was it? Out of curiosity, I read to the end of the paragraph and had my answer.

The alternate executor was Edna Lund.

Chapter Eighteen

Chiles have a tough skin that should be removed. The best way to do this is to roast them over the flame of your gas range or an outdoor grill. Wearing rubber gloves to keep the juices from burning your hands, cut a slit at the stem end to keep them from popping. Lay the peppers on the burner grates or the grill. Turn them frequently with tongs, roasting them until the skin is blistered and wrinkles easily. Place them in a paper bag to steam and cool. When cool, remove the skin, seeds, and stem.

China Bayles
"Hot Pods and Fired-up Fare"
Pecan Springs *Enterprise*

Edna Lund?

I sat back on my heels, dismayed by the sloppy lawyering. When the old man decided to disinherit his daughter, Tom Perry should have instructed him to name a different alternate executor, somebody who wasn't connected to the estate and wouldn't be hurt when she didn't get what she had been led, by the previous will, to expect. On the other hand, maybe the lawyer had tried to reason with him and Lund had refused because he didn't want anyone outside Perry's office to know about the change in his will, including the executor and the alternate. Maybe Perry had decided that it didn't matter, since Jerry Jeff was young and strong and likely to be around for a long time. Whatever the case, Jerry Jeff was dead, and it was Edna's job to probate the codicil that disinherited her. What a lousy trick! If I were her, I'd dig in my heels. I'd refuse. Now that Jerry Jeff was dead, the court could find somebody else to do the old man's dirty work.

Now that Jerry Jeff was dead.

I rocked back and forward, thinking. The documents in this file were copies. Where were the originals? Among Harmon Lund's papers, most likely, where Edna would have found them after her father died. Say, for the sake of argument, that's what had happened. How had she felt when she discovered that codicil and read it? Disappointed, hurt, cheated, indignant — then angry, furious, even enraged? I could imagine myself feeling that way, and I doubted that Edna was very different.

Say, then, that she *had* felt hurt and cheated and so enraged that she had impulsively put a match to that original, or torn it into tiny pieces and flushed it. Unethical behavior, maybe, unscrupulous, unprincipled — but it wouldn't be the first time somebody did it. Say, as well, that she never bothered to tell her brother about his inheritance, or perhaps even that their father was dead. Her father's lawyer was out of the picture, and Perry's secretary was mentally failing. If Jerry Jeff was also ignorant of the codicil, she would be home free. The executor would probate her father's old will, she would inherit, and nobody would be the wiser. Even if Jerry Jeff had known about the existence of a codicil but didn't have a copy, she would *still* be home free, wouldn't she?

Of course she would.

And now that Jerry Jeff was dead . . .

I stopped rocking and sat very still, my mind sifting through a hodgepodge of vague memories and fleeting impressions. Edna asking Fannie what she was supposed to do as a cookoff volunteer, and Fannie telling her that she would be working in the check-in tent, where the cooks brought their samples. Edna at the check-in table, logging in the cups. Edna in the judging tent, with a tray of cups, a few minutes before Jerry Jeff was stricken, looking nervously on as he staggered to his feet. "Is something wrong with him?" she had asked, and I had assured her that nothing was wrong, that he was pretending to be burned by the chili, that it was all part of the show. "Grown men," she had said, in a disapproving tone, and I had laughed.

I shivered. Was it possible? It was. Means, opportunity, and now, here was the motive, clear and basic as water: her father's cruel codicil, the will naming her alternate executor, after Jerry Jeff. It was all falling into place. But I wasn't sure that I trusted myself to draw valid conclusions. No, scratch that. I *didn't* trust myself. I had already behaved like a blithering idiot more than once tonight. I'd made a very good case against Lulu Burkhart, and an equally strong case against Roxanne and Pokey. In fact, I'd been so sure that the two of them were guilty that I'd thought they were attempting escape. Even though the evidence seemed to point clearly to Edna Lund, I felt uneasy about it.

I got hurriedly to my feet and stuck the Lund file under my arm. Forget Miss Velma's will. It had waited this long, it could wait another twelve hours. I picked up the flashlight and turned toward the door. I would drive to the Manor right now and get McQuaid's opinion. He'd been a cop, he'd know if my suspicions were way off base. He could check through all my what-ifs and tell me whether I had overstated some of them. He'd —

I felt the broken board snap. My right leg crashed through the floor midway up the thigh, my left knee smashed against the floor, and I pitched forward, so suddenly and unexpectedly that I didn't have time to fling out my arms to take the shock. My chest and face slammed against wood. My nose snapped, my teeth sliced into my upper lip and I tasted sudden blood. There was a sickening pain in my legs. I knew one of them was broken, but both hurt so much I couldn't tell which. I heard somebody making foolish yelping whimpers, wondered who and why, then realized that they were mine.

Seconds later, a brick wall fell on me.

It isn't a brick wall, I realize uncountable moments later, as I swim groggily upward out of the heavy darkness. It's a ton of cardboard boxes, and it has landed on me with the full weight of the law. The full weight of the law — get it? I hear somebody giggling hysterically, a little-girl giggle, punctuated by gurgling hiccups.

"Stop that," I command sternly, and the giggling stops. But my lip is as mushy as an overripe banana, my nose is spouting blood, and my face hurts like hell. I feel as if I've gone twelve rounds with Mohammed Ali, every round ending in a KO, with me flat on my bloody face on the canvas and my manager yelling at me to get up before Ali kills me. "No more talking," I tell my manager, and the talking stops.

No moving, either, or not much. Laboriously, I inch my left arm out from under a box as big as the Astrodome. Only one arm, only an inch or three, but even this minuscule movement makes me gulp for air, and I can't gulp. My head is twisted to the left, a box is balanced on my shoulder blades, and the cartons that have crashed like the Empire State Building across my back must have cracked about a hundred ribs. They are flattening me like bricks flattening a sponge, pressing the breath out of me like air bubbles pressed out of bread dough. It is entirely possible that they have shattered my spine. My right arm is fastened to the floor with giant staples, pinned under a couple of ten-ton boxes filled with the granite they used to build the Capitol building in Austin. My legs feel like —

Scratch that. My legs have no feeling. Mercifully, I can only imagine what's going on with them, because I am numb from the waist down. If I were to guess what has happened, I would say that I have stepped into a sabertoothed dinosaur trap, cleverly rigged to seize my right leg twelve inches above the knee and bite through the flesh to the femur. Since I remember having gone down like a 747 belly-flopping on a concrete runway, and I can picture my left kneecap, smashed in a trillion pieces. I wonder vaguely when I had my last tetanus booster, but rational thought hurts almost as bad as breathing. "Stop thinking," I admonish myself thickly, and close my eyes.

But the thoughts don't stop coming, and after a moment my eyes open again. I am nailed to the floor of a forgotten storeroom in a derelict barn on an abandoned farm that won't see another human until Lester's cousin Arlie comes out to scatter deer corn the first of September. This is June. After that comes July, then August. September comes later. Much later.

But surely I won't have to hold out quite that long. When I don't show up to open the shop tomorrow morning, Ruby will start worrying. She'll call McQuaid, who will remember that the last time he heard from me, I was headed for MaeBelle's house. He will reach MaeBelle when she gets off duty at five, and when she goes home to supper, she will ask Lester, who will —

Nope, wrong. MaeBelle has gone to see to Jamie, and won't be home for a couple of days. And Lester was embarking on a glorious drunk when he talked to me. He may not recall giving me directions to the lease. In fact, he may not remember me at all. It may be days before they —

I shudder. Even if they find me tomorrow night, it won't matter a whole hell of a lot. My right leg will be the size of a bloated rhinoceros, my lungs will be as flat as Eeyore's balloon, and after my rescuers have removed the boxes, they can scrape my torso off the floor with that antique grain scoop out there in the barn. They won't have to bother with EMS. They can call Maude Porterfield, she can sign my death certificate on the spot, and they can ship me straight off to the medical examiner for autopsy.

Two large tears of pain and self-pity — at this point, it's hard to know the difference — squeeze out of my eyes. But I can't cry, because that will stop up my nose and then I won't be able to breathe at all.

"Don't cry," I tell myself. "Be calm." I think of Ruby, meditating for hours on end, legs crossed in the lotus position. Can I do that? Not the legs-crossed part, of course. I try meditating, anyway. Face down, eyes closed, I listen to the breath moving in and out. I feel the beat of the pulse in my throat, concentrating on the breath, in-out, in-out. I listen to the rustle of rats in the corners, the flurry of bat wings, the raspy footsteps of the scorpion —

Scorpion! My eyes pop open, my breath flutters like a flag, my heart seizes up. Then, just as I am about to give in to panic, I hear the sound of an engine, tires on gravel, a car door slamming, hurried footsteps.

Somebody is out there! Rescue is on the way. I'll be saved. I am suddenly weak with relief. But then it dawns on me that I have to be found before I can be rescued, and I open my mouth to yell.

"Help!" I shout. The word comes out as an embarrassing mousey squeak. I suck in my breath, summon all my available strength, and try again. "Help! Help, please!" More squeaks, a cageful of mice.

"China Bayles?" It is a woman's voice. "China! Where are you?"

My mouth is open to shout again. I close it.

That voice belongs to Edna Lund.

The silence seemed to stretch on forever. I was caught in an internal dispute, torn between wanting like hell to get out of there and hoping Edna would go away without finding me. It was dark by this time. She might not notice the wooden door, or if she pushed it open, she might see only a jumble of old cardboard boxes. Maybe she'd go away. I sighed. Fat chance. My car was out there. And if she went away, where would that leave me? Dead, that's where. I opened my mouth to call, but nothing came out.

"China?" she cried. She was standing just outside the door. "Where *are* you?" A second or two later, the heavy wooden door creaked open. "China? Are you in *here?*"

A flashlight shone down on me, bright as a spotlight from a prison wall. I couldn't lift my head to look at the beam but the light hurt anyway. I shut my eyes, trying to think. If I acted cool, played dumb, didn't give her any reason to suspect that I had found that incriminating file, she would call for help — wouldn't she? Of course she would. Anything else was unthinkable.

The beam seized me. "China!" Edna cried, sounding frantic. "China, my God, what's *happened* to you? Are you all right?"

Was I all right? What a stupid question. But I was buoyed by the concern in her voice. "I'm super," I said. My tongue was furry, my lips as dry as old saddle leather. "My leg isn't so good, though. It's . . . I stepped through the floor. It's probably broken. My leg, I mean. The floor is broken too, obviously." I was babbling, but I couldn't stop. "That's how my leg got —"

"Broken?" She moved, and I could see her feet, stepping into the pool of light. She was wearing black pants and sneakers. She came around behind me, picking her way through spilled boxes.

"Yeah. Right." I tried to laugh, but didn't quite bring it off. "Half of me is down there in the basement, with a bunch of old cedar posts and barbed wire." And rattlesnakes. "The other half is under these boxes. Maybe you could move —"

She bent over and picked up the box that was balanced on my butt. "How in the world did this *happen?*" she asked sharply. The implication was unmistakable: if I'd been smarter or more cautious or just plain quicker, it wouldn't have happened at all.

Unfortunately, I agreed with her. "Carelessness," I said. "Not paying attention. I zigged when I should have zagged." I giggled again. The laugh ended in a gurgle, and I felt something hot and salty in my mouth. Was it blood? "Listen, Edna," I whispered, "can you do something about these boxes? I think I've got a couple of . . . cracked ribs."

She took a box off my back and set it on the floor, and I sucked in a deep breath. But breathing brought pain, thick, throbbing waves of pain surfing through me, and a spiraling vortex of dizziness. A dozen or so of those cracked ribs, sharp as knives, must be poking into my lungs.

Edna shone the light on my lower torso and knelt down to assess the situation. After a moment she stood. "I don't think I ought to try to get you out of here by myself, China," she said. "That broken floorboard is clamped on your leg like a vise, and your left leg is twisted at an odd angle. I hate to leave you, but I'd better go for help."

"There's a cell phone in my car," I said.

"Oh, good," she said, relief strong in her voice. She knelt over and patted my shoulder. There was a smear of dust on her black pants, and a small spider was making its way across the toe of her sneaker. "I've got a bottle of Scotch in my car, dear. I'm sure you can use a drink while we wait for help to come."

"Wonderful," I said, meaning it. Thank God, I was going to get out of this in one piece. And sooner than the first week of September. "Please hurry."

She turned to go, but the edge of her light caught the label on one of the cartons and she stopped, studying it. After a moment, she swung the light around the litter of fallen cartons, reading more labels. When she spoke, it was more to herself than to me. "These boxes . . . they're from Perry's law office."

Among the needles of pain, I suddenly found a clear voice. "I was looking for Miss Velma's will," I said. "McQuaid sent me out here to find it. He seemed to think it was urgent that I locate it tonight." I took a breath, coughed, and said, "When you call EMS, would you mind calling him, too? He knows I'm out here, Edna. He's going to worry if I don't check in with him and let him know that I've —"

But it was too late. Her light had found the file. She went down on her knees to look at it, and I heard the rustle of turning pages. The silence stretched out. A mouse scratched in the corner. Somewhere startlingly close, a great horned owl called, once, twice, three times.

Edna let the file slip to the floor. "You've read this, I suppose." Her voice was heavy, sad, old. "You know?" She waited a minute for me to confirm her suspicion, then sighed and answered her own question. "But of course you do. You're a lawyer." The words trailed off in another sigh.

I lay still, trying to think. A long time ago, in another life, I learned to lie professionally. In my heyday, I was among the very best — maybe not in the same category as Johnny Cochran and F. Lee Bailey, but pretty damn close. But lying took more energy than I could spare, and I probably wouldn't be convincing. I only had strength for the truth.

"Did you kill him?" I asked.

"Kill who?" she asked, almost absently. She stood. "My father?"

This opened up a line of inquiry that I hadn't even considered. But that would have to come later — if there was a later. She held the best hand, and I couldn't know how she was going to play it.

"Jerry Jeff," I said. "He was the executor

412

of your father's estate. With him gone, you could do as you liked with the will."

"I didn't intend to kill him, if that's what you're thinking," she said, almost testily. "I knew he was allergic, but I had no idea —" She stopped, reflecting, choosing her words with some care. "I don't think I really believed, at that moment, that a few chopped peanuts could actually *kill* him. The nuts were loose, on some cookies somebody had entered. All I did was shake them off the cookie and into the chili." She shook her head sadly. "I was as surprised as everybody else when he *died*. At first, I thought of trying to get help — but then I realized that this was the way out of my problem, and I just . . . well, I just let it happen."

"You could plead temporary insanity," I said. "You'd probably get off with a light sentence."

Her mouth was bitter. "And after prison, then what? Jimmy would have made off with the money, and I'd have nothing. Nothing worth living for." She shook her head regretfully. "I wish you hadn't gotten mixed up in this, China."

"It's too late now," I said.

She sighed. "Yes. Well, since you know the most important part, I suppose I might as well tell you everything, so you'll understand and not blame me too much. I tried to get Jerry Jeff to be reasonable about the estate. I told him I would give him half the ranch. He could keep it or sell it, whatever he decided to do with it. All I wanted was the oil royalties, sixty thousand or so a year after taxes." Her mouth hardened and her voice rose angrily. "That was *my* money! It wasn't fair that Dad gave it all to Jimmy, and the ranch, too. Jimmy didn't give a damn whether Dad was alive or dead. I was the one who took care of him for all those years!"

"Why did your father do it?" I asked.

"Why?" Her laugh grated. "Why did that crazy old man do anything? He didn't need a real reason — only to belittle me, hurt me, make me suffer. All those years, all those petty little punishments, all of them adding up to misery. He was a hateful, terrible old man, and I despised him. Living with him was sheer *hell*."

This was no doubt all very true, and I wondered briefly whether it was a motive for *his* murder, as well. But we were getting sidetracked. "I'm curious," I said. "Why didn't you come looking for the codicil before tonight?"

She paused, appearing to give this serious

thought. "I didn't know for sure there was a copy. I found the original when I was going through Dad's papers after he died, and I burned it. After a while, I began to wonder whether there might be a copy, but by that time, Perry was dead and Velma's mind had deteriorated to the point where she only made sense in snatches. I spent as much time with her as I could, hoping to catch her in a lucid moment. But I figured that if she couldn't tell me, she couldn't tell anybody else, either. And if there was a copy, it had to be lost among all the other records. I was willing to take my chances."

It all seemed very complicated, and I was almost too tired to care. "How much did Jerry Jeff know?" I asked blurrily.

"With the original, I found a copy of a note Dad had written to Jerry Jeff, telling him that he was planning to change his beneficiary. After Dad died, Jerry Jeff came looking for the codicil. But I told him I didn't know anything about it, and of course he couldn't find it. So the note was all he had to go on."

"And that was enough for him to hold up probate?" I asked, vaguely surprised. "Why would he bother? Why not just get on with it?"

Her chuckle was corrosive. "Apparently,

Dad hinted to him that there was something in it for him. It was a lie, of course. That was one of the old man's tricks. He'd promise you anything, dangle any sort of carrot, and then when you did what he wanted, he'd jerk it away. Like Opal Hogge. She gave him all kinds of special treatment in return for his promise to leave a big bundle of money to the Manor. That was one of the ways Dad manipulated people and got them to do what he wanted."

"But Jerry Jeff couldn't know that."

A smile ghosted across her mouth. "He did what Opal did. He tried to get Velma to tell him where the original was — only I don't think he was as rough with Velma as Opal was."

Well, that explained Bunny's treatment of Miss Velma. But as for the rest of it — it was terribly confusing, and pain was wrapping me like a choking fog. But I was thinking of something else, and after a minute I managed to get the words out.

"I suppose you also wrote to Jerry Jeff, threatening to turn him in to the IRS if he didn't probate the original will."

"The let—" She seemed momentarily taken aback. "How did you find out about —" And then, with a steely edge, "Who else knows?"

Ah. "Who else knows?" I asked, and answered myself, cheerily. "Why, *lots* of people. McQuaid knows, Charlie Lipman knows, Roxanne Cody —"

"You're lying," she snapped. "Mike McQuaid doesn't know. I was in his room tonight. If he knew, he would have given some hint."

"He was a cop for a lot of years," I said. "He wouldn't let you know he knew. And Charlie knows about the codicil. Jerry Jeff told him." I was covering, of course. Edna had to be wondering what to do with me. The more people that seemed to know, the less likely it was that she'd try something lethal.

She considered this for a moment. "You're lying," she said. "Mike doesn't know anything. If he had, he would've realized that Velma was talking about my father's codicil, not her will. The poor old thing probably doesn't even *have* a will. And I saw Charlie Lipman just this afternoon — he doesn't know, either. He couldn't have kept it from me if he had."

Edna swung her flashlight around the room. After a moment, she bent over, opened the flaps of one of the boxes, and began spilling papers across the floor, crumpling some of them into loose balls.

I regarded this odd behavior through a wave of dizziness. "What are you doing?"

Her voice seemed to echo hollowly, as if she were speaking from the bottom of a well. "Don't be a fool. I can't let you go back to town and tell everybody what you know." She tumbled another box of papers onto the floor.

Good grief. She sounded exactly like one of Jessica Fletcher's TV villains.

"I think you're too smart to do anything silly," I said thickly. But just in case I'd misjudged her, I tried easing my left leg forward. If I could get up on one knee, I might be able to get enough leverage to yank — There was a flash of gritty pain, as if the knee joint were full of broken glass. *Forget that.*

"Sorry, China," she said shortly. "It was one thing to scrape a few peanuts into a cup of chili. It's quite another to —" She stopped and straightened up. "Don't go anywhere. I'll be right back."

"That's not funny," I said, with dignity.

"You're right," she said. "I apologize."

She left, taking the flashlight. But I had no time to consider any other escape strategies, because she was gone less than thirty seconds. When she stepped back into the storeroom, she was carrying the kerosene

lantern she had taken from the wall outside the door, and the tin matchbox. My
heart jumped up into my throat.

"What are you doing?" I croaked, although I knew, perfectly well.

She put the lantern on the floor, shone
the flashlight on it, and turned it until she
found the cap to the fuel tank. She un-
screwed the cap and tipped the lantern
over onto the papers. Nothing came out. It
was empty.

My mouth had gone cottony. My hands
were icy. I could feel myself beginning to
shake, inside and out. "Out of gas. Too
bad. Guess you'll have to go back to town
and get some."

She didn't answer. Instead, she rose,
picked up the lantern and the flashlight,
and left again. This time, she was gone for a
much longer period — long enough for me
to figure out what she was up to. She was
getting gasoline from the gas tank on the
downhill slope beneath the barn. If that
tank was empty, she would siphon it out of
one of the cars. She would spill gasoline on
the floor and the papers, then light the lantern and tip it over. In two minutes, the
hay-stuffed barn would be a blazing in-
ferno. I wouldn't be cold any longer.

The door opened, and she came back in.

This time, I could smell the gasoline.

I opened my mouth to say something, but my teeth were chattering so that I could scarcely speak. Finally, I managed to get it out. "They'll know it wasn't k-k-kerosene," I said. "They'll s-s-suspect s-s-something." I wasn't sure this was true, though. Maybe they wouldn't know. Maybe the fire would be hot enough to destroy all traces of —

"Actually, this gas is so stale that there's not a lot of difference between it and kerosene," she replied, with the authority born of long experience as a ranch manager. She propped the flashlight on a box so she could see what she was doing, then spilled a goodly quantity of gasoline on one of the boxes and more on the heap of papers beside it. She dropped her father's file on top. "Even if they do notice, they'll figure it was you. They'll think you filled the lantern at the gas tank so you could poke around for Velma's will, and knocked it over when you went through the floor." She sighed heavily. "I'm sorry it turned out like this, China. If there had been any other way —"

Broiled. Grilled. Roasted alive. I clenched my teeth against the wave of nauseating fear. "They'll know you were here too. Lester will remember that he sent you out here."

"I'll tell them myself." She opened the tin matchbox, reached inside, and took out a match. "But by the time I got here, looking for you, it was already too late. The barn was completely engulfed in flames. I saw your car, and I knew you were inside, but there was nothing I could do except watch, horrified." She struck the match. It broke in her fingers and she stared at it. "That will be the truth," she whispered.

I pushed myself up on my forearms, sliding the left knee forward against the pain, desperately trying to pull my right leg out of the jaws of the broken board. A hideous memory came to me of a gray wolf that gnawed off her leg to free herself from a trap. If I could find an ax or a knife —

She took another match. "I'd knock you out," she said raggedly, "but I'm not sure I could do it without cracking your skull. And then they'd know." She paused. "I'm *really* sorry, China."

The match flared and snuffed out. She struck another, cupping it. The flame flickered, steadied.

"I can't believe you're doing this." I licked my lips. "Peanuts in chili — that's one thing. It might or might not have worked. But to light a funeral pyre and watch while it burns . . ."

"I know," she said thinly. "Jerry Jeff was a bad man. He deserved what he got. But killing you is unforgivable. It will be on my conscience for the rest of my life."

"Then don't do it," I said. "Don't —"

"Be quiet." She held out her hand to drop the match. I closed my eyes. I was not going to torture myself by watching the flame crawl across the papers, bloom into a fiery red rose. Eyes squeezed shut, fists clenched against the terror, I heard a step, another, and then a dull, heavy *bong,* like the ringing of a cracked bell.

My eyes flew open. Edna was pitching heavily forward, a dead weight, the match and flashlight falling with her, into a pool of gasoline. With my left hand, I reached out and swatted the match. It went out.

"China?" somebody yelled in the darkness. "China? Are you all right, China?"

"Ruby!" I cried. "What are *you* doing here!"

A foot scraped across the floor. A flashlight clicked on. Light fell across me like a blessing.

"I'm keeping an eye on my business investment," Ruby said. "What else?"

Chapter Nineteen

Chile Pepper Liniment
Mix together and use externally as a lini-
ment for sprains, bruises, rheumatism, and
neuralgia:

tincture of capsicum (chile pepper),
   2 fluid oz.
extract of lobelia, 2 fluid oz.
oil of wormwood, 1 fluid dram
oil of rosemary, 1 fluid dram
oil of spearmint, 1 fluid dram
               Alma R. Hutchens
               A Handbook of
               Native American Herbs

"What can I get you?" Ruby asked in a solicitous tone. "Shall I straighten your sheets or
plump up your pillow? Would you like a
glass of juice? Some ice cream? Shall I rub
your —"

"Oh, quit," I snapped crossly, pulling
away. Out in the hospital hallway, I heard
the incessant ding-ding of somebody's call
bell. Why the hell didn't the nurses come
and put the poor sinner out of his misery?

"She's going to be a grumpy invalid," McQuaid said from his wheelchair, parked at the foot of my bed. "You might as well go home and let her snap at me, Ruby. She's been doing it ever since she came out of the anesthesia."

I shifted my shoulders. I could feel the hair matted at the back of my head. I needed a bath. But none of this was Ruby's fault. "No, please don't go home," I said wearily. "I'm sorry, Ruby. I'll do better, I promise. It's just that everything hurts and —"

I bit my lip. A tear was running down the side of my face and into my damp and untidy hair. I was whining. I hate whiners. V. I. Warshawski never whines when she gets beat up.

"I know, dear," Ruby said, patting the cast on my right leg, which was suspended in midair. "Your leg must hurt terribly." She used the soft, syrupy voice that mothers use to soothe kids with the measles, that whole, healthy people use to console people with various broken and missing parts. "It'll be all better. Soon."

"Not soon enough," I said grimly. The doctor was predicting three weeks in this ridiculous rig, a week here in the hospital and two at the Manor, where — irony of ironies — I'd probably get to share McQuaid's room. Plus another six, at least, in a cast. I looked up at the malevolent trapeze of ropes and pulleys that cranked my leg in the direction of the ceiling, supposedly holding my broken right femur so it would mend correctly. "To tell the truth," I added, trying to be objective, "that leg doesn't hurt, it itches like fury. It's my left leg that *hurts*."

And no wonder. The left ankle was sprained, the socket bone cracked, and a bundle of ligaments had come unraveled. My rib cage felt as if I'd been on the working end of a medieval battering ram, but miraculously, my ribs were only bruised, not broken. My nose hadn't been broken, either, just bent a little, but my eyes were puffy and both cheeks were badly abraded. I wasn't complaining, though, considering how close I had come to being incinerated. If Ruby hadn't showed up, they might be shoveling my ashes out with the rest of the burned rubble. I could have been reduced to clinkers and melted-down gold fillings.

I reached for Ruby's hand. "Thank you," I said. "You saved my life. At the risk of sounding clichéd, I don't know how I can ever repay you."

"According to our partnership agreement, you'll start repaying me in a year," Ruby said briskly. "What I did Monday night simply ensured that you'd be around to keep your bargain." She smoothed the damp hair off my forehead and softened her tone. "Anyway, if I'd been the one stuck in the barn floor, you would have done exactly the same for me."

I considered for a moment. "Actually," I said, "if you'd been stuck and I'd been hovering on the outskirts, I believe I would have given you a signal. I'm not criticizing, mind you — just saying that I might have managed to give you some teensy, tiny hint to relieve your anxiety and let you know that you weren't all alone in a dark barn with a crazy woman who was planning to charbroil you."

"I did give you a signal," Ruby said. "I hooted."

McQuaid's eyebrows went up. "You *hooted?*"

"Three times."

And then I remembered. The mouse scratching in the shadowy corner, the rustle of rattlesnakes, the great horned owl hooting from a nearby tree. But it hadn't been an owl after all. It had been Ruby — which would have made me feel much less anxious, had I but known.

"Yes, you did hoot," I said. "I suppose I wasn't paying sufficient attention. But it was a very *little* hoot. And you did sound very much like an owl."

Ruby looked defensive. "So what was I supposed to do? Send up flares?"

McQuaid began to laugh, then to roar. I started to giggle. But giggling hurt my battered ribs, and I started to cry. The tears got inside my nose and made me cough. Coughing rattled the ribs, and I cried harder. Making loud soothing sounds, Ruby jumped up and rushed to the bathroom for a wet washcloth. Charlie Lipman, bearing a giant-sized pizza in a cardboard box and a cold six-pack in a shopping bag, walked into the middle of this cacophony. The cause of the merriment had to be explained to him, which kicked off the uproar all over again. It also brought a starched white nurse, who looked at us disapprovingly over her glasses and put a finger to her lips.

"This place is full of sick people," she said.

"I'm glad I'm not one of them," I said under my breath — not too loudly, just in case she was the one who would shortly reappear with a needle.

When we had all simmered down, Charlie put the pizza on the rolling table at the foot of my hospital bed and opened the box, filling the room with the heady aroma of mozzarella cheese and pepperoni. Ruby pulled the pizza slices apart and handed them around on napkins. McQuaid popped the can tabs. Charlie took off his suit jacket, took off his shoes, and put his feet up on the arm of McQuaid's chair. He was wearing one brown sock and one blue one. The blue one had a hole in the heel. He looked at Ruby.

"Well?" he asked. "Are you going to tell me how you ferreted out the ferocious peanut poisoner and foiled a dastardly attempt to barbecue our China? Hark's story in this morning's paper gave a good general impression but was wanting in substantive detail."

I smiled at the mention of Hark. He'd been very sweet when he heard what happened and had even promised that I could turn in my chile pepper story whenever I felt like typing it up. But he had also hinted that I might want to make a *real* story out of it, sort of a true crime piece, with recipes.

"China can tell the first part, about solving the mystery," Ruby said helpfully.

"I'll do the bit about the barbecue."

So, between bites of the best pizza I had ever tasted and sips of the most incredible beer ever brewed (it's interesting how a little threat of dying can hone your taste buds), I told what had happened, to the point where Ruby arrived on the scene, snatched up the rusty shovel, and whacked Edna Lund over the head.

Charlie gave Ruby an admiring look. "Great presence of mind," he said. "A strong woman, game and plucky. The sort I lust after. Why haven't we ever been to bed together?"

Ruby ignored his lechery. "I wasn't strong. I was scared to death." She shuddered. "That lantern was like a Molotov cocktail. And China was seriously stuck. It took two volunteer firemen with crowbars to rip up the floorboards and free her. I could never have gotten her out of there by myself, especially if Edna had managed to set the place on fire."

"We could have hacked off my leg," I offered. "I was definitely considering it."

Ruby blanched. "I probably should have slugged Edna a lot sooner than I did. But I couldn't bring myself to do it until I knew she really meant to torch the barn. Violence does terrible things to your karma."

"Torching would have done terrible things to China," McQuaid remarked. He looked at me. "I prefer her the way she is — rare."

Charlie picked a piece of pepperoni off his tie, leaving a smear of tomato paste. "What karma took you there in the first place, Ruby?"

"I followed Edna," Ruby explained. "You see, I went to the soccer match to talk to Lulu Burkhart, because McQuaid told me that China thought that Lulu might have a motive to kill Jerry Jeff, and —"

"Excuse me?" Charlie said, surprised. He looked at me questioningly. "You thought *Lulu* had a motive?"

"Fannie Couch told me about the rumors that have been going around the grapevine," I said. "About Lulu Burkhart and Jerry Jeff."

Charlie grunted. "Fannie Couch ought to be ashamed of herself. Lulu and Jerry Jeff may have been seen together a time or two, but it was because I was using her as an intermediary. In that messy deal between Cody and Burkhart, Lulu was the only one who had a lick of sense. I asked her to sit down with Jerry Jeff and see if they couldn't reach some sort of settlement. But Jerry Jeff was a horse's ass, as usual, and the case went to trial."

"That's okay, China," Ruby said, patting my hand. "It's good that you suspected Lulu. If you hadn't, I might not have talked to her so soon. While I was asking her about what she had been doing during the judging at the chili cookoff, she told me what she saw. Kind of as an aside." She stopped to bite the tip off her second slice of pizza.

"You know what they say about police work," McQuaid remarked, sipping his beer. "Ninety-nine percent of it is a waste of time. It's that lucky one-in-a-hundred shot that pays off."

"It wasn't luck," I said. "It was Ruby's skill in questioning a witness."

"It wasn't skill, either," Ruby retorted. "It was the Universe, pointing me in the right direction, so that you wouldn't get roasted to death."

"Hey," Charlie said. "Cut the suspense and tell already. What exactly did Lulu see?"

"She saw Edna Lund," Ruby said, "tapping chopped peanuts off the top of a cookie and into one of the chili samples. Lulu said she thought it was weird, and she started to ask Edna why she was doing it.

But something else distracted her attention. And then Jerry Jeff died — of a heart attack, she thought — and that distracted *everybody's* attention. She didn't know the real cause of Jerry Jeff's death until I told her, and she remembered what she had seen. I knew in a flash that Edna Lund was the killer — although I had no idea why she had done it."

"Blessings on you, Miss Marple," I murmured. "I shudder to think of where I'd be right now if you hadn't read so many murder mysteries."

McQuaid took a swig of beer and addressed himself to Charlie. "When Ruby realized that it was Edna we were after, she called me, very excited. I told her that Edna had just left here, on her way to the Battersby house to see if she could help China find Miss Velma's will."

"I got to the Battersby place just as Edna was driving away," Ruby said. "I figured she must be on China's trail, so I decided to stay with her."

"That must not have been easy," I said. "How did you keep her from seeing you?"

"I had to hang back quite a way," Ruby replied, "especially after she got to the turnoff at Stassney Junction and started down that unpaved road. But she was driving like a bat out of hell. I'll bet she didn't even bother to look in the rearview mirror. I could see her lights on the side of the hill, and when she switched them off, I figured she'd got where she was going. So I parked and hiked the rest of the way."

"Well done, Ruby," McQuaid said approvingly. "You saved China's bacon."

"Good grief," I groaned, as Ruby and Charlie laughed. "You could have gone all week without saying that."

"He might have said, 'You pulled China's chestnuts out of the fire,' " Charlie remarked wickedly.

"How about 'You pulled her fat out of the fire?' " McQuaid said.

I held up my hand, where McQuaid's grandmother's garnet ring glinted on my third finger. "Would you like your ring back?" I asked pointedly. "It's not too late to call the wedding off."

"I'd like to see you try it," McQuaid said fiercely. Ruby snickered.

"I just got back from visiting Jerry Jeff's stash," Charlie remarked, in a mediatory tone. "Would you like to hear what I found? Besides the money, that is."

"Was the money all there?" McQuaid asked. "Had Roxanne made a withdrawal?"

"The money was there," Charlie said. "Roxanne hadn't touched a dime. In fact, I've talked with her about the situation, and she's asked me to represent her with the IRS." He tipped the can back and drank, wiping his mouth on the back of his hand. "I'm sure we can work out some sort of deal. It'll be complicated, though. Some of the money may have come from Pokey's side of the business. But we'll let the feds straighten it out when they do their audit."

"Where *was* the money?" Ruby asked.

"In a garage in Waco," Charlie said. "In a safe that belonged to Jerry Jeff's uncle."

"Waco is a long way to go to hide your money," McQuaid said.

"Not if you want to keep it from your about-to-be-ex," Charlie replied pragmatically.

"You said you found something else in the stash," I reminded him, "besides the money."

"Yeah. Two letters. Blackmail letters. Written by Edna Lund to Jerry Jeff Cody."

"Wow!" McQuaid straightened up. "Have you got them with you?"

"Are you kidding?" Charlie gave him a look. "I've already dropped them off at the county attorney's office. But I can tell you what's in them. The first is a polite offer of half of the ranch if Jerry Jeff will probate the original will. The second letter, which was written a few weeks later, is a trifle nastier. Lund threatens to turn him in to the IRS if he doesn't go ahead with probate."

"Well," I said, "that ought to just about nail it. I'm sure the county prosecutor is jumping for joy. He'll use it to argue that it wasn't a crime of impulse, after all, and go for first degree."

"What I want to know is how Edna found out that JJ was cheating on his taxes," Ruby said.

"I'm guessing that her father knew about it and told her," Charlie said, "out of spite. Old man Lund was that sort of guy."

Ruby folded up the empty cardboard pizza box and pushed it into the wastebasket. "What's going to happen to Edna, do you think?"

"She's already been charged with attempted murder in China's case," McQuaid said, "and she'll no doubt be charged with the Cody killing in the next day or so. Her father's death will probably be investigated, as well. Edna said something that made China think she might have had a hand in that."

"There's something I'm still curious

about, China," Charlie said. "Did you ever find Miss Velma's will?"

"Talk about wild goose chases," I said.

McQuaid chuckled. "That's one of the interesting ironies of this case. Miss Velma is like a three-year-old with an attention deficit disorder. When China and Joyce and I got everything sorted out, we realized that the old lady hadn't been talking about *her* will. She was trying to tell us about Harmon Lund's will — about that codicil."

"You see," I said, "Lund's will wasn't with all the other client files. It was in a separate carton with Miss Velma's private papers. She seems to have put it there to keep it for Edna."

"For Edna?" Charlie asked, surprised.

"We're guessing, of course," I said, "but we think Miss Velma must have been sympathetic toward Edna, who was going to lose her inheritance through her father's irrational act. Velma very likely expected Edna to destroy the codicil, and she didn't intend that the file copy be found. So she hid it in a box of her personal papers, intending to hand it over to Edna when the time came. By the time Edna began looking for it, however, Miss Velma's memory was no longer reliable."

"But Monday night, when she was being moved into my room for safekeeping," McQuaid said, "Miss Velma had one of her intermittent flashes of lucidity." He looked at me. "She's taking some sort of herbal pills MaeBelle gives her — ginkaboo, or something like that. It seems to be helping."

"Ginkgo," I said. "Ginkgo biloba. It increases the flow of blood to the brain."

"Yeah, whatever. Anyway, she heard Joyce and me talking about Jerry Jeff's death. She put two and two together, and realized that Edna had a powerful motive to kill him. But when she started to tell us about it, Edna came into the room. Miss Velma got a vacant look and began babbling about her will and Bunny and a bunch of other stuff."

"But Edna wasn't fooled," I said, finishing out the story for Charlie. "She knew precisely what Miss Velma was talking about. So she came looking for me to make sure that *I* didn't find it."

"Speaking of Bunny," Ruby said, "did you hear what's happening to her?"

We hadn't, so Ruby filled us in. The Manor's director was now its *former* director. Liz McKenzie, the board president, had made a couple of phone calls to San

Antonio, then held a stormy session with Opal Hogge, and followed that with an emergency board meeting. Apparently, Harmon Lund had made one of his phony promises to Opal, agreeing to rewrite his will and leave a substantial sum of money to the Manor in return for preferential treatment. When Angie walked in and found Opal shaking Miss Velma, the administrator was trying to get her to reveal the whereabouts of Lund's will.

"So Opal is out of a job," Ruby finished. "The board fired her. What's more, they are conferring with the county attorney to see whether she should be charged with a crime. Which means, I suppose, that she'll never get another job in a nursing home."

"Not necessarily," Charlie said, in his best legal tone. "I seriously doubt that a charge will stick, given the tenuous nature of the evidence. The most the board can do is withhold a recommendation, and if a potential employer asks why, offer a discreet word of warning. And I do mean discreet. Anything else could open the Manor to a lawsuit."

"But what about justice?" Ruby demanded. "You don't mean to tell me that the law is powerless to keep people from abusing other people!"

"Justice is a big, sick bird," Charlie said.

Ruby looked confused.

"An ill eagle," I explained. "Old law school joke."

"Justice can't keep people from doing bad things," Charlie said. "That's what cops are for." He paused significantly, glancing at McQuaid. "Did you tell her? How'd she take it?"

"Tell me what?" I asked. "Take what?"

McQuaid stirred uncomfortably. "Well, I —"

"You better tell her," Charlie cautioned, "before she reads it in the newspaper."

"Reads *what* in the newspaper?" I asked.

McQuaid sucked in his breath, twitched his mouth, and finally said, "I'm replacing Bubba. As chief of police."

"Like hell!" I exclaimed.

"Only temporarily," McQuaid soothed. "Until the Council finds another sucker. I mean, until they hire somebody."

"But you *can't!*" I said. "You're disabled. You're handicapped. You're —"

"Just what the Council was looking for," Charlie said with a grin. "Let Kerrville have its woman chief of police. Pecan Springs has found itself a chief in a wheelchair."

There was a long silence while I contemplated this news. "How long?" I asked finally.

McQuaid shrugged. "Not very. I told them they'd better get a move on. I've got a honeymoon coming up." He grinned at me. "Who's pushing the bride down the aisle?"

"Forget that," I returned. "Who gets to steer the groom?"

Charlie chuckled. "And just how are you two mobility-impaired lovers going to manage your honeymoon?" He eyed my traction rig humorously. "Are you taking *that* with you?"

"Oh, Lord," I groaned. "I don't even want to think about it."

"That's okay," Ruby said comfortingly. "You don't have to worry about a single thing, China. I'll handle all the details. We'll have the wedding in the garden behind the shop, so there won't be any doors to maneuver your wheelchairs through. We can invite a lot more people that way, too. And afterward, we'll have the reception at —"

"No!" McQuaid and I roared, in concert.

"I'm just trying to make it fun for you," Ruby said. "You don't need to get excited."

"Fun!" McQuaid said, in an irritable tone. "It sounds like we're going to have to run away and get married, just to avoid the crowd."

Charlie looked from one to the other of us with an amused quirk of his eyebrow. "Run, huh? Now, *that* I want to see."

Resources, References, and Recipes

Until a decade or so ago, the chile pepper belonged to the Southwest, and that's where you had to go to find them. These days, however, you can buy many kinds of peppers, in many forms, all over the country. *The Chile Pepper Book*, by Carolyn Dille and Susan Belsinger, lists twenty-three different varieties, all widely available. The most common — Anaheim (mild), jalapeño (very hot), serrano (very hot), and habanero (fiery) — may be found fresh or dried in your supermarket produce section. If you prefer mail-order shopping, Penzeys, Ltd., (P.O. Box 933, Muskego, WI 53150) will send you a catalog that lists a dozen or so different dried peppers (whole, crushed, and ground), with information about each. If you plan to grow your own, an excellent seed source is Shepherd's Garden Seeds, 30 Irene St., Torrington, CT 06790. They carry peppers you've never heard of, described in mouthwatering (or eye-tearing) prose, with growing and harvesting tips and recipes, even. *The Pepper Garden*, by Dave DeWitt and Paul Bosland, is a first-rate guide to growing peppers, with chapters on drying, roasting, pickling, smoking, and freezing your crop, and a couple of dozen seed sources. They also tell you how to tie a *ristra* (a string of chiles), how to grind chile powder, and how to fend off the pests who prefer your peppers. If you would rather cultivate the inner chile, you can subscribe to *Chile Pepper* magazine (1-800-959-5468). There you will find hot articles, reviews of hot books, lists of hot shops all over the country, and ads for products with names like Viper Venom, Maddern'n Hell Sauce, Habanero Hurricane, and Raging Passion. And if you're thinking of getting into chiles in a big way, it's *Fiery Foods* magazine that you want (P.O. Box 4980, Albuquerque, NM 87196). With all these resources, a true chilehead is always cool.

But hot is healthy as well as tasty. Capsaicin, the chemical that makes you sweat, can also reduce joint pain and the pain of shingles and sore gums. If you have a cold, eating peppers clears your nasal passages and relieves the pain and pressure of clogged sinuses. Peppers have no fat, lots of fiber, and plenty of vitamin C and beta-carotene, not to mention quercetin, a phytochemical that has been shown to reduce the risk of some cancers.

Now, as to chili. There are plenty of great chili books out there. My personal favorites include Bill Bridges's *The Great Chili Book*; *The Chili Cookbook*, by Norman Kolpas, and Jenny Kellner's *The All-American Chili Book: The Official Cookbook of the International Chili Society*. But in case you can't wait to start cookin', here are three recipes that may be of special interest to readers of *Chile Death*. The first recipe is named for the slow, lazy river that flows through the LBJ ranch near Johnson City, Texas, and is said to have been a favorite of Lyndon and Ladybird. (Pedernales, in Texan, is pronounced *Purd*-nal-is.) The second chili recipe is heretical, because it comes from Oklahoma and contains peanuts — the less said about it the better. The third is . . . well, you'll see.

Pedernales Chili

4 lb ground lean beef
1 large onion, chopped
2 cloves garlic, minced
1 tsp ground oregano
1 tsp ground cumin
3 tbsp chili powder
2 #2 cans tomatoes
2 cups hot water
salt to taste

Brown ground beef in heavy iron skillet. Add onion and garlic and cook 45 minutes. Add remaining ingredients and simmer one hour. When cool, skim fat. Better on the second day, when the flavors have mellowed. Serves eight.

Ruby's Aunt Harriet's Peanut Chili, Oklahoma Style

1/2 cup peanut oil
2 cups onion, chopped
5–6 cloves garlic, minced
2 lb ground beef
1 15 oz. can stewed tomatoes
1/2 cup strong black coffee
2/3 cup chopped roasted peanuts
1/2 small can tomato paste
2–4 tbsp chili powder
1 tbsp salt
1 tbsp ground cumin
2/3 cup whole roasted peanuts
1/4 cup chopped cilantro
1/4 cup chopped green onions

Heat peanut oil in large pot, add onion and garlic and sauté until tender. Add ground beef and brown. Stir in tomatoes, coffee, chopped peanuts, tomato paste, chili powder, salt, and cumin. Simmer until thick (30 minutes, more or less). Stir in whole peanuts. At the table, pass cilantro and green onions to go on top, and extra peanut butter, in case anybody's interested. Serves four.

Pokey Clendennen's Mountain Oyster Chili (Adapted from a recipe in Bill Bridges's *The Great American Chili Book*)

2 lb calf fries,* washed, skinned, and diced
butter or margarine
1 large onion, chopped
4 cloves garlic, minced
1 tbsp ground cumin
2 tbsp chili powder, to taste
1 15 oz. can stewed tomatoes
1 tsp salt
flour for thickening

In an iron skillet, cook the fries in butter or margarine for a couple of minutes. Add onion, garlic, and cumin and continue cooking until browned. Stir in chili powder and salt. Add stewed tomatoes, cover, and cook gently, stirring occasionally, for about two hours. If necessary, add water. About ten minutes before you're ready to serve, thicken with a flour and water paste. Serves four.

*Calf fries are the, um, ancillary appendage to a young steer's sexual apparatus. If you suspect your guests of being squeamish, don't tell them what's in this dish. The less they know, the better they'll like it.

You will notice that none of the three previous recipes call for beans. For those of you who *must* mix beans with chiles, here is an acceptable way to do it:

Chile Bean Salad

1 15 oz. can pinto beans
1 15 oz. can kidney beans
1 15 oz. can garbanzo beans
1 cup chopped celery
1/2 cup chopped onion
1/3 cup chopped green bell pepper
1/3 cup chopped red bell pepper
1/3 cup chopped yellow bell pepper
1/4 cup coarsely chopped cilantro
2 Anaheim or poblano chiles, roasted,
    peeled, seeded, and coarsely chopped

Rinse and drain beans. Combine in a bowl with the rest of the ingredients. To dress, marinate for six hours in this dressing:

2 tbsp olive oil
1/4 cup red wine vinegar
2 cloves garlic, minced
1 tsp chili powder, or to taste
1 tbsp minced fresh oregano
    (1 tsp dried)
1/2 tsp ground cumin